SATAN'S SLUT

'God, no!' exclaimed the Reverend Andrew Wyatt. 'Susan, stop. This has gone far enough.'

'Don't you like me?' she asked, her voice suddenly weak. Her huge eyes grew wider still; her lower lip pouted, trembling. He hastened to reassure her, stammering out his words in a meaningless jumble.

'Then fuck me,' she cut in, her tone changing back to the open, dirty confidence she had shown before.

'Oh my god! No!'

'Oh, come on, Father Andrew. You know you'd like to. Don't you think we notice the way you look at us?' Susan laughed, and skipped away, up the aisle, to the chancel. Andrew watched in horror, still unable to speak as she bent down across the altar. She looked back, her face full of casual insolence as she took hold of her surplice and twitched it casually up over her bare legs and bottom.

'Father, forgive me,' he mumbled, and reached down for the hem of his cassock.

SATAN'S SLUT

Aishling Morgan

This book is a work of fiction.
In real life, make sure you practise safe sex.

First published in 2002 by
Nexus
Thames Wharf Studios
Rainville Road
London W6 9HA

www.nexus-books.co.uk

Typeset by TW Typesetting, Plymouth, Devon

Printed and bound by
Mackays of Chatham plc, Chatham, Kent

ISBN 0 352 33720 6

Dedicated to the
Unusual Suspects

Prologue

The Reverend Andrew Wyatt let out his breath as he pushed the door of the church shut. Beneath his cassock his cock felt uncomfortably stiff, yet the trial was over, and he had resisted temptation. True, he had deliberately walked into the vestry when the choirgirls could not possibly have been expected to have finished changing. The images of nubile bottoms and pert breasts encased in white and pastel cotton still burned in his head.

Yet he had not touched. It would have been so easy to place a fatherly hand on a bare shoulder, or even to pat a panty-clad bottom in gentle admonition for supposed tardiness, but he had not. That thought held, defying his terrible guilt, as he turned back towards the body of the church.

He heard the click of metal on stone and looked up. A girl had emerged from the vestry door, Susan, small, blonde, sixteen, and the cause of his most agonising sexual frustration. She smiled, insolent, knowing, the face she always put on to taunt him and tempt him. He muttered a prayer as she stepped towards him, swinging her slender hips.

'Locking us in, Father?' she said. 'I am flattered.'

'Did you wish to speak with me, my child?' he managed in response.

'Don't call me that,' she answered. 'I ain't no child, and you know it. See?'

Her hands went up, cupping her breasts to stretch the thin material of her surplice taut across them. Her nipples

1

showed, tiny bumps under white cotton, and he realised that they were bare underneath the garment.

'It is simply a turn of phrase,' he managed, swallowing hard.

'I'm naked underneath, you know,' she went on, ignoring him. 'Not just knickers: naked.'

'I . . . really, Susan, I . . .' he stammered, with the blood rushing to both his face and his cock.

'Fancy a feel?' she asked. 'Tits and bum if you like. For free. Normally I charge, but you're kind of cute.'

'Charge?' he demanded, horror-struck. 'Susan! How . . . I mean, your parents!'

'Don't be so stuffy!' she answered. 'Loads of girls make a bit of extra for a grope or a bit of cocksucking. But I don't want to talk about that: I want to talk about you. I bet you've got a lovely big one, and I bet you're stiff. D'you know, if you're a very good boy I might even let you fuck me.'

'God, no!' he said, his heart hammering. 'Susan, stop. This has gone far enough.'

'Don't you like me?' she asked, her voice suddenly weak.

Her huge eyes grew wider still; her lower lip pouted, trembling. He hastened to reassure her, stammering out his words in a meaningless jumble.

'Then fuck me,' she cut in, her tone changing back to the open, dirty confidence she had shown before.

'Oh my god! No!'

'Oh, come on, Father Andrew. You know you'd like to. Don't you think we notice the way you look at us?'

'I do nothing of the sort!'

She merely laughed, coming close, to look up into his face as her hand closed on his cock. He gasped, pulling hastily away.

'Oh, you are big!' she giggled. 'Come on, Father, do me – not up my fanny, that's special – up my bum. Did you know that there are more nerve endings in a girl's bumhole than her fanny? It's true. I saw it on the Net.'

The Reverend Wyatt could find nothing to say, speechless in the face of her casual obscenity. Susan laughed, and skipped away, up the aisle, to the chancel. He watched in horror, still unable to speak as she bent down across the altar. She looked back, her face full of insolence as she reached to the hem of her surplice and twitched it casually up over her bare legs and bottom. The pose left her sex lips peeping out from between her thighs, the fat apricot of her pussy pouch, with the darker spot of her anus above. She wiggled, and he felt his cock grow stiffer still.

'Father, forgive me,' he mumbled, and reached down for the hem of his cassock.

He started forward, telling himself he meant to stop her, to put an end to her obscene display. He knew it was false. As he reached the chancel he stopped behind her. Voices in his head were screaming at him to stop, to resist the utter sacrilege he was about to commit. Yet the smell of her sex was thick in his nostrils, the sight of her burning in his brain, his cock rigid beneath his cassock. He bent, gripping the hem, and lifted.

She watched as he pulled it up, eyes bright, wiggling her bottom gently to make her flesh quiver and bulge. He swallowed, still struggling to stop himself as his hand went to the fly of his pants, pulling the front down over his straining cock.

'Oh, lovely,' she sighed. 'Put it in me. You can lube me up with some of that funny grease you use to draw crosses on people.'

'Shut up, whore!' he snapped, but as he closed on her his hand was already reaching for the tin on the altar.

'No need to be nasty,' she said, 'or I might not let you. Say sorry.'

He had laid his cock into the soft crease between her buttocks as he struggled with the lid of the tin, and as she moved away he found himself babbling.

'I'm sorry, Susan, I didn't mean to call you a whore. No, stay, keep it still. Oh, you've a lovely bottom, so soft, so round. You're not a whore. You're a little darling, an absolute little darling, a little virgin darling.'

'That's better,' she said. 'And I'm glad you like my bum. Now you can fuck it.'

3

She stuck her bottom out again, against his crotch as the tin finally gave. His hand shaking violently, Andrew stuck his finger into the thick chrism oil, pulling out a wad. With everything forgotten except the beautiful young girl who was bending so willingly for him, he reached down, smearing it between her buttocks and on to the tight hole between them.

'Ow! Gently!' Susan protested as the tip of his finger popped into her anus, and up, into the hot, slimy cavity beyond.

'Sorry,' he said, but she was already moaning in pleasure.

He took his cock in his free hand, jerking at it as he fingered her bottom hole. He could see it going in, his own skin pale against the dun-coloured flesh of her anal ring, both glistening with grease. Her bottom was stuck right up, open for him, with not just her slimy anus on show, but her vulva, too, the lips swollen and puffy, the centre wet, with the taut crescent of her hymen in plain view. With the thought of buggering a virgin, his cock twitched ominously, and he realised that he was going to come in his hand unless her put it inside her.

His finger came out, sticky with oil and her natural slime. His cock replaced it, the swollen, glossy head pressed to her ring. He pushed, watching her anus go in, then spread as she relaxed, her wet flesh engulfing the head of his penis. Again he pushed, and more went in. The head of his cock forced into the little dirty hole, with grease oozing out around the stem of his penis as he jammed it deeper.

Pausing, he looked down on her, drinking in the view. She was staring at him, her pretty face framed in blonde hair, flushed pink, mouth open, eyes wide in reaction to the penis in her bottom hole. There was the raised surplice, a tumble of white cloth on her back, the shapely legs, the sweet hips, the little round bum, spread and violated anally . . .

He came, his cock erupting in her anus despite his intentions of making a proper job of buggering her. Unable to stop, he snatched at his cock shaft, jerking it frantically to put his full load up her bottom as he cried out in ecstasy and shame. She squealed as his cock was stuffed deeper into her bowels, in a pleasure that seemed to turn to annoyance as she no doubt realised he was finished.

'No!' she exclaimed. 'Father! You've wasted it!'

'I'm sorry,' he muttered. 'I'm sorry. Oh, God, what have I done?'

He pulled out, leaving her bottom hole to close with a long fart, which reverberated in the empty church. Still clutching his slimy cock, he staggered back, struggling with overwhelming shame and guilt, yet still wishing he'd made full use of the beautiful bottom he had been offered. She was looking at him, now cross.

'Well I want to come anyway!' she pouted. 'You're to feel my titties.'

'I . . .' he began, and stopped, realising in horror that he hadn't locked the door even as the latch clanged and it swung open with a groan.

The Reverend Andrew Wyatt dropped his cassock, but it was too late. In the doorway stood a lean, purple-clad figure – his bishop.

One

In Fernworthy Forest, on the eastern flank of high
Dartmoor, a young girl sat in the back seat of her new
boyfriend's car, struggling vainly against his octopus-like
fumbling and her own sexual urges. Outside it was dark
and warm. She was drunk and they were kissing. Her
passion had risen, and so had his, until she could feel the
hard lump of his growing erection against her leg. The
hand that had been mauling her breasts through her blouse
had moved to the buttons, making her realise that she was
not only to be fondled, but stripped.

'Stop it!' she hissed. 'Someone'll see!'

'Not here, baby,' he answered, continuing his fondling of
her breasts. 'Come on, boobies out.'

'No!'

He ignored her protest, holding her close to stop her
from defending herself as he struggled with the buttons of
her blouse. She tried to resist, but half-heartedly, giggling
as first one button, then another was tweaked open. With
her cleavage showing, a hot hand delved in, cupping a
breast to pop it free from the restraining material of her
bra. The other followed, leaving them lying, plump and
pale under the interior light, quivering to her breathing.
She sighed as his mouth found a nipple, resigning herself
to the undignified use of her body.

She held him to herself, wondering just how far she was
going to let him go. He had begun to rub his cock on her
leg, little, sudden jerks, and she could feel the size and

6

stiffness of it, thinking of how it would feel in her vagina. She moaned, realising that if he decided to fuck her she wasn't going to stop him and hoping he'd had the sense to bring a condom. A hand slid down her body, over her tummy to the button of her jeans. Again she moaned, closing her eyes, wanting to be touched and unable to stop him.

His fingers fumbled at her button. It came open. Her zip was drawn down. His hand burrowed into the front of her panties, down them, catching in her pubic hair, to find the damp crease of her sex. She pulled up her legs, to push down her jeans and panties, surrendering herself. Two fingers went up her vagina, making her wince, then gasp as he began to frig her, pushing in and out as he rubbed the ball of his hand on her open sex.

'Do you suck cock?' he demanded, pulling his mouth from hers.

Swallowing down a fresh pang of remorse, she nodded, opened her eyes so that she could see what she was about to be made to do, and screamed.

There was a face at the window, but no human face. Great eyes shone a brilliant green from a face as black as pitch, delicate, female, yet inhuman, the face of a demoness. Again the girl screamed. The boy jerked away, to stare in horror at the awful thing, and as they crawled back along the seat the mouth came open, to reveal sharp white teeth and the red, forked tip of a tongue.

Tom Pridough looked out from the top of Stanton Rocks, across the jumbled Devon hills with their patchwork of fields and woods, and down to the abandoned chapel below him. It stood at the side of a track, among high bracken and beech saplings. The roof was broken in places, the windows jagged rings of glass from the attention of vandals, the rear door hanging loose on one hinge. Yet the granite of the walls remained solid, and the plain concrete cross above the main door still stood. He smiled, his face setting in smug satisfaction at the thought of being able to worship in his own way, in his own premises, and of being able to lead others in that way.

As he glanced up again, to the distant haze that marked the position of Exeter, his smile changed to a frown. The site was good in that it had been designed as a place of worship, and also had the great advantage of being affordable. On the other hand it was a long way from the city and would need a great deal of renovation before he could make use of it. All that aside, the scenery around the chapel showed too much of the beauty and grandeur of nature to sit well with his own particular brand of Christianity.

Assuring himself that his abilities as a preacher would overcome any romantic or High Church inclinations his congregation might have, he set off down the rocks. Moving with the supple strength brought on from a lifetime of exercise groups and fitness regimes, he descended to the track. A few quick paces took him to the church, and he stood before the arched double door, looking at the decaying wood and peeling blue paint as he tried to imagine how it would look when restored.

Grass and a tangle of brambles had grown across the front of the door, but damage to the stalks showed that it had been opened recently. Again he frowned, annoyed by the thought that others had used the place, and of what they might have used it for. Taking hold of one door, he tugged it wide, forcing back the clogging foliage until he could step over it and inside.

Within, the bare concrete floor was littered with broken glass and slate, at least to the sides. The centre had been swept clear, although stained with bird droppings. There were also symbols, picked out in the rich purple of blackberry juice. He stared, his frown growing to a look of true anger as he realised that they formed no simple graffiti, but a careful system of runes, meaningless to him, but without doubt unchristian. Now furious, he marched down the chapel to the flat concrete altar.

His worst fears were confirmed the moment he reached it. A large pentagram had been drawn on the flat surface, hedged around with more cabbalistic symbols, daubed in the same purple juice. Five smudges of black wax stood at

8

the points of the pentagram, while its centre was marked by a disturbing stain. To one side lay a condom, the tip still bulging with fluid.

With his fists clenched in blind rage, he strode from the chapel.

Nich Mordaunt lay sprawled on a couch, his head supported by a pillow, a copy of the *Archidoxes of Magic* held in one hand. Only part of his attention was on the book, as he was also watching the other occupant of the room, Juliana. Tall, slim and black-haired, she gave an impression of elegance despite her heavy breasts and the plastic pinny that was her only garment beside a pair of loose white camiknickers. In one hand she held a small paintbrush, in the other a piece of wood in the shape of a long cone split down the middle, to which she was applying varnish with meticulous care. Several similar objects stood or lay on the newspaper spread in front of her.

'You'll have to teach me how to use them,' he remarked.

'The only real skill is in listening to the victim's responses,' she replied. 'Otherwise it's easy. I'll show you on myself if you like.'

'I'd be privileged,' Nich said, then rose as the doorbell rang.

'Post?' Juliana queried.

'Bit late,' Nich answered, walking to the window and peering down into the street.

Below him was a tall, lanky man, dressed in a black suit and a dog collar, his face set in a look of stern determination as he looked up to the window.

'Ah, Tom,' Nich called down. 'What can I do for you?'

'I wish to speak to you, Mr Mordaunt,' the man replied coldly.

'Come up, then,' Nich said, and casually tossed down his keys.

The man tried to catch the keys and missed, forcing him to scrabble on the ground for them as the grinning Nich pulled his head back in.

'Tom Pridough,' Nich announced to Juliana.

'What does he want?' she demanded.

'To save our souls, no doubt,' Nich answered.

Juliana shrugged and went back to her painting. Nich crossed to the flat door, quickly opening the latch before returning to the couch and composing himself in a deliberately idle position. He yawned, a gesture carefully timed to ensure that Pridough saw it as he came in.

There was anger in the priest's face, then shock as he glanced towards Juliana and realised how little she had on. She took no notice whatever, not even troubling to acknowledge him. Closing the door, he came to face Nich, folding his hands behind his back. Nich gave him a questioning look.

'You have gone too far this time, Mr Mordaunt,' Pridough accused.

'I have?' Nich answered, deliberately putting a hopeful inflection into his voice.

'You know full well what I'm talking about,' he went on. 'You have desecrated the old chapel at Stanton Rocks with some Satanic ritual. Don't deny it.'

'The chapel? At Stanton Rocks?' Nich queried. 'You mean that derelict eyesore with a cross picked out in concrete? How could one possibly desecrate it? The stone circle, yes, Grim's Men, in among the pines, but not the chapel.'

'So you admit it?' Pridough demanded.

'Not at all,' Nich replied. 'I merely point out that a building used by an obscure local sect for a few decades at most can hardly be considered sacred. Therefore, to have held a ritual supporting an opposing creed of the same religion can hardly be considered desecration. Moreover –'

'I know it was you, Mordaunt,' Pridough interrupted him. 'Who else would it be? A pentagram had been drawn, and symbols. Black candles had been burned. It was a Black Mass, wasn't it? In a chapel, Mordaunt, a consecrated place!'

'If I remember rightly,' Nich yawned, 'the Black Mass ritual is at its most powerful when performed in a consecrated building, so this abandoned chapel would seem an excellent choice for a venue. It was, however, not my choice, nor my ritual. The Black Mass, Tom, is a Satanist ritual. I am a pagan. Despite what you Christians like to think, there is little or no overlap between the two belief systems, save in so far as Christianity has adapted and demonised an aspect of the Horned God.'

'Be quiet!' Pridough snapped. 'Look, Mordaunt, I know it was you, and I'm warning you. One more prank like that, and I'll come down on you like a ton of bricks!'

'How, exactly?' Nich enquired. 'Not the police, surely? I doubt they'd be interested, and they'd need some proof, anyway. Or do you intend to have me beaten up perhaps? I've heard of muscular Christianity, but isn't that taking it a bit far? You can't go around behaving like Matthew Hopkins these days.'

'Enough!' Pridough broke in. 'Just don't, that's all! I've had quite enough of your childish opinions and blasphemous articles.'

He went quiet, closing his eyes and muttering a prayer under his breath. His face was red, and Nich allowed himself a quiet smile as he waited for the onslaught to continue. At last Pridough opened his eyes, just as Juliana lifted two of the wooden objects from the table, holding them together to make a long cone, which she inspected critically. Pridough's eyes flickered towards her.

'It's a cunt wedge,' she supplied. Pridough's face went scarlet. 'What you do,' she went on, 'is push the narrow end up –'

'I do not wish to know!' he snapped. 'Disgusting! You are evil, truly evil.'

'Only evil?' Nich asked. 'Come, come, Tom. You can do better than that. Couldn't you manage "spawn of Beelzebub"? I've always wanted to be called that.'

Pridough turned on his heel, his face dark with blushes as he walked quickly to the door. Juliana's laughter joined Nich's as the priest's footsteps faded down the stairs.

'He's always so angry,' Juliana remarked, 'but then Christians so often are. I suppose it's because they don't allow themselves to have any decent sex.'

11

'Very likely,' Nich agreed. 'Still, a Black Mass, eh? I wonder who it was. Mark you, I don't suppose Pridough would know a Black Mass if we sacrificed him at one. It was probably just some kids mucking about. Or maybe my efforts to promote alternative religion are bearing unexpected fruit. Anyway, I've got to see this chapel. Coming?'

Juliana nodded assent as she pushed the lid back on to her tin of varnish.

Lilith placed the box of Doggie Bix on the edge of the bath.

'Go on, get down,' she ordered.

Diana obeyed, falling immediately into a kneeling position on the black and white tiles of the bathroom floor, nude. The position made the best of her small, compact body, accentuating the size of her breasts as they hung beneath her chest, also the roundness of her bottom. Each large, dark nipple was pierced with a silver ring, matching the ones that Lilith herself had put through the girl's inner labia. A pink flush marked the olive skin of her bottom, evidence of a recently completed spanking. She looked up, her big brown eyes wide with expectation, her snub nose turned up, giving her pretty face a piglike quality.

For a while Lilith stood still, admiring Diana's naked body, before reaching down for the hem of her own simple black dress and peeling it up over her head. Beneath she was nude, her slender body pale in the fluorescent light. Long legs rose to slender hips, with the V between her thighs quite hairless, to show the trim lips of her sex. Her stomach was flat, her belly no more than a low, oval bulge, tight enough for the outlines of her muscles to show. High, pert breasts peaked in upturned nipples. Her neck was long, her face a delicate oval framed in jet-black hair, her eyes steel-grey.

'Do you like what you see?' she demanded. Diana nodded vigorously. 'Do you adore me? Do you worship me?'

Again Diana nodded her assent. 'Say it, little slut.'

'I adore you, Mistress,' Diana answered. 'I love you. I worship you. I want only to be your slave, to use as you please, to beat, to fuck, to degrade –'

12

'Enough,' Lilith snapped. 'You really are a little slut, aren't you?'

'Yes, Mistress.'

'You need some sort of mark, really. To show you're mine.'

'A tattoo, Mistress? Gladly.'

'No. I was thinking of branding that fat arse.'

'No, Karen, please. I just couldn't take it!'

'Not Karen, little one, Lilith. Karen Brown is dead, as if she never existed.'

'Sorry . . . Lilith, Mistress Lilith.'

'No brand mark, then? A pity, it would look great, with my slave mark burned into the flesh of one big fat bum cheek. You're sure you couldn't take it?'

'I couldn't, really.'

'Well we'll have to have you tattooed, then, and big time, to make up for denying me. Maybe your whole bum.'

Diana answered with a whimper, which Lilith took for assent.

'Good, girl. Now get on your belly and you can have your treat.'

Diana got down, her plump breasts squashing out on the tiles of the floor, her legs coming apart, to spread her buttocks, her whole body showing wanton surrender.

'That's good,' Lilith continued. 'You grovelling slut. You've no self-respect at all, have you?'

Diana shook her head. Her mouth had come open, and her breathing had picked up to an urgent rhythm. Lilith laughed to see her friend's excitement, and reached out for the Doggie Bix. Diana watched as one of the big, bone-shaped biscuits was withdrawn from the packet and held up for her inspection. Lilith gave her a smile, full of amusement and contempt. For all her excitement, Diana looked thoroughly sorry for herself.

Lilith sniffed the biscuit, grimacing as she caught the scent of dog, and threw it down, close to Diana's face. Immediately the girl gobbled it up, mouthing at it with her full lips, taking it in and chewing on it, with her face screwed up in disgust at the taste. Lilith laughed out loud.

Finishing the biscuit, Diana swallowed and looked up, her huge eyes now moist, her mouth open, with a few crumbs showing on the surface of her pouted, trembling lower lip. Lilith sat on the edge of the toilet, spreading her thighs as she beckoned to Diana. The girl crawled forward, eyes raised to Lilith's face.

'Lick me,' Lilith ordered.

'Say it,' Diana answered. 'Say the nasty word.'

'Lick me,' Lilith repeated. 'Lick my cunt.'

Diana's eyes moved down to the pink flesh of Lilith's shaved pussy. Her tongue came out, flicking at her lips as she shuffled forward, to bury her face between Lilith's thighs. Lilith sighed, closing her eyes in bliss as Diana's tongue found her clitoris. She let it happen, her pleasure rising, until she knew that if she didn't stop it she would come.

'Enough!' she snapped, pulling at the dark mane of Diana's hair.

Diana looked up, her eyes wider than ever, her mouth ringed with the white juice of Lilith's sex. Her expression showed surprise, and a little fear. Again Lilith laughed, relaxing, tensing the muscles of her belly, and releasing the contents of her bladder full into Diana's face.

Screaming in shock, Diana struggled to pull back. Lilith held her, filling her open mouth with urine and spraying it across her screwed-up face, laughing as she watched the pee splash over the girl's pretty features and trickle down the sodden rat-tails of her hair. Jerking Diana further back, she directed the stream lower, across the girl's neck, then over her breasts, to spatter the plump, olive-coloured globes with piddle until the yellow fluid ran in a torrent down the deep cleavage and dripped from the dark nipples and their rings.

Still laughing, Lilith finished off, holding the dripping, pee-soaked girl firmly by the hair until the last trickle had run out. Only then did she tighten her grip, and pull Diana firmly in to her sex, once more closing her eyes as her thoroughly humiliated slave began to lick. As the orgasm rose up, she thought of Diana's face with her mouth full of Doggie Bix, screwed up in disgust, yet still eating the filthy things. She groaned, gritting her teeth as her thighs clamped around Diana's head, starting to come as she thought of the tastes that would be filling her slave's mouth: dog biscuit, pee and pussy. Lilith screamed in ecstasy, wrenching and twisting at Diana's hair as the orgasm tore through her.

At length it faded, leaving her with a sense of rude contentment. Diana had begun to masturbate, and as Lilith let go of her hair she went back on her haunches, thighs spread to show off the wet pink centre of her sex. Her hair was still dripping piddle, the skin of her breasts and belly wet with it, while there was a big smudge of Lilith's pussy cream around her mouth.

'That's right, frig your dirty fat cunt, you slut,' Lilith taunted and Diana groaned, slipping three fingers into her vagina.

'Please, more,' she gasped, snatching out the juice-wet fingers to rub yet harder at her sex.

Lilith reached out a foot, put it to Diana's belly, and pushed. Diana sat down, her bottom splashing in the puddle of pee on the ground. Her thighs came yet further apart, revealing the darker dimple of her anus and the full width of her sex. Her breasts were trembling to the rhythm of her masturbation, her bottom cheeks and thighs clenching.

'Please,' she begged, 'please.'

'Shut up and rub your cunt,' Lilith snapped, and spat, full on Diana's belly.

Diana snatched at the spittle, smearing it on to her sex.

'That's right, you filthy little bitch,' Lilith continued, 'that's all you're fit for, to rub your dirty cunt in my spit. Look at you, Diana, with your dirt hole showing and your fat cunt spread out. You look like a fucking pig on heat, Diana, you worthless little slut, you little piece of shit! Shit!'

Lilith repeated the last word at the sound of the doorbell. Diana ignored it. She was on her back, kicking like an upturned beetle, her feet splashing in the piss on the

15

floor. Lilith stuck out a foot, pushing her big toe up Diana's vagina even as the open pink hole contracted in orgasm, and fucking her with it. Diana went into spasm, writhing and squirming on the pee-soaked floor, her head shaking from side to side, her mouth wide open in helpless ecstasy. Lilith watched, waiting until Diana's climax had run its course before speaking again.

'Is that a client?' she finally demanded.

'Mr Arlidge for his three o'clock,' Diana puffed. 'Oh, that was so nice, Kar – Lilith. Thank you.'

Diana rolled over, climbing unsteadily to her knees. Rising, Lilith kicked Diana's bottom, pushing her sprawling in the pee once more.

'Tell him to wait,' she ordered.

'I can't, look at me!' Diana protested.

'Just do it, you little slut,' Lilith snapped back. 'Who cares if you've been pissed on?'

Diana gave a grateful smile in response to the order and scampered to the window, still dripping. Standing on the bath, she opened the top half of the frosted window and cautiously stuck out her head. Lilith had stepped into the shower, and didn't hear the exchange, but after a brief wash Diana told her that Mr Arlidge was going to wait. She accepted this with a nod and took up a towel, snapping her fingers at the shower to indicate that Diana should get in, before reaching one long arm in to twist the control to cold. Diana gave her a sulky look but got in as Lilith left the bathroom.

In her bedroom, Lilith began to dry herself, unhurriedly. After a while the noise of the shower stopped.

'An intelligent girl would have cleaned up the piss on the floor before taking her shower,' she called out.

'Whoops!' Diana answered, in the little-girl voice she often used after an orgasm.

'Just get on with it,' Lilith sighed. 'Which one is Arlidge, anyway?'

'Little man, balding on top. Likes it tied on the frame.'

'Oh, him. Prat.'

'You should know him. He comes every month.'

'I can't tell one from another. Hey, what are you using to wipe up?'

'My blouse.'

Lilith didn't answer, contenting herself with a nod for her maid's choice. Without haste, she powdered herself, rolling up on the bed to get at the crevices of her sex and anal region and treating herself to a brief stroke of the sensitive skin before rising. From her cupboard she chose tight rubber shorts, set with studs, and a top to match, then paused, trying to remember if Mr Arlidge liked to lick her boots. Fairly sure he didn't, she selected black suede thigh boots. Her cap and a spiked collar finished the outfit, which she threw on the bed.

She began to make up, an elaborate combination of purples, black and blood red. Beyond, in the flat, she was vaguely aware that Diana was taking a second shower, drying, dressing and answering the door to Mr Arlidge. The man showed no irritation at all at having been made to wait so long. When she finally emerged from the bedroom it was to find him seated meekly in the main room with his hands folded in his lap. Beside him was a brown-paper parcel. Diana was by the door, in a loose purple dress and short black boots.

'The Specimen has paid, Mistress,' Diana announced.

Lilith gave Diana a grateful smile. She had completely forgotten about the man's slave name, let alone what it was. Walking across the room, she ignored him completely, making a show of extracting a cigarette from a packet on the window ledge. He was fumbling for a lighter, but she ignored that too, using her own, and drawing deeply on the smoke before finally turning to him.

'Specimen is about right,' she said, looking down on him with a contempt that was in no way fake. 'You really are a revolting little piece of work, aren't you?'

'Yes, Mistress,' he stammered.

She raised one booted foot, resting the toe on his thigh. He stayed still, trembling slightly, but making no move, even when she ground her heel into his leg, other than to wince. She gave a snort of contempt, took the cigarette

17

from her mouth and flicked the ash over his front. Still he failed to react.

'Spineless worm,' she snapped. 'Right, Specimen, into the room. I think you know which one. You're going on the frame.'

'I . . . I have a present for you, Mistress,' he stammered.

'Chocolates, I suppose?' she sighed. 'Or flowers. You men are so unoriginal, and so fucking mean.'

'No, Mistress,' he said quickly, 'nothing like that. A sjambok, a real one, from South Africa.'

'A sjambok?' Lilith queried, not at all sure what it was.

'The finest quality,' he went on, reaching for the parcel. 'Not rubber, but rhinoceros hide, a genuine original.'

'It's not very well wrapped,' Lilith commented, stubbing her cigarette out and taking the parcel. 'Hmm, let's see.'

She pulled open the brown paper, revealing a heavy, flexible whip, three foot in length. It was plaited from the thickest leather she had ever seen, and beautifully made. She hefted it, struggling not to smile at the glorious feel of the thing.

'Cheap tat from a tourist shop, I'll bet,' she remarked.

'No, Mistress,' he said quickly, 'the real thing, hand-made by a craftsman. I paid –'

'Shut up,' she interrupted him. 'I'm going to test it on you. Now get in there.'

He moved as soon as her foot was lifted, scurrying across to the door of her dungeon and holding it open for her. Lilith walked in, not troubling to acknowledge him. The frame stood on the far wall, an open rectangle of dark wood, supported by struts of black-painted iron. It was just one of several articles of bondage furniture, which also included a whipping stool, a squat cage, a pillory, a padded table and a great upright cross bound in black leather. Mr Arlidge went directly to the frame, raising his hands to the cuffs that hung from the upper corners.

'Strip, you idiot!' Lilith snapped.

'I . . . I would prefer Mistress to disrobe me,' he managed.

'What?' she demanded. 'Do you think I want to touch your revolting body? You can count yourself fucking lucky

I even condescend to let you show it to me. I wouldn't let you, if it wasn't for the extra pain I can inflict on that repulsive arse. Now strip!'

Mr Arlidge hastened to obey. Lilith ignored him, instead admiring herself in the full-length mirror that occupied most of one wall. It was impossible not to smile at her reflection. Even hanging from her hand, the sjambok looked lethal, although it failed to match her outfit.

'I would have preferred black,' she remarked, 'perhaps with one strand in purple.'

'I'm not sure they come in black, Mistress,' Arlidge replied as he struggled with a shoe.

She didn't trouble to reply, but turned to watch as he finished stripping, all the while with one corner of her mouth turned up in a knowing sneer. Once he was nude, he stepped into the frame, positioning his wrists and ankles against the cuffs at each corner. With a deliberate sigh, Lilith stepped forward, fastening his limbs into place one by one while she struggled to remember what his personal tastes were.

He liked to be abused verbally as well as physically, she was sure of that, but not why. Only when she was on the last cuff did she remember. As he had once explained, Arlidge was the child of an unsuccessful marriage. His mother had hated men, his father especially. She had done her best to impress on him that his sex was not only inferior, but inherently unfaithful, immoral and violent. As a result he believed that all woman were disgusted by sexual attention from men, from simply looking upwards. Even to secretly admire a well-formed bottom or an ample pair of breasts filled him with guilt, and as he was beaten he liked to be berated for his supposed crimes against womanhood.

'I suppose you've been up to your revolting little tricks again?' she demanded as she tucked the final strap into place.

'Yes, Mistress Lilith,' he answered.

'Spit it out then.'

'I've been revolting, Mistress, truly revolting. I've been ogling women in the street, and –'

'Ogling what?' Lilith interrupted.

'Women, Mistress. Women's bodies . . .' he stammered, his voice cutting off in a scream as Lilith lashed the sjambok down across his buttocks.

The blow set him jerking to and fro in his restraints, gasping and whimpering, quite unable to speak. There was also a severe welt where it had landed, thick and dark red, although she had put far less than her full strength into the stroke. Lilith looked at the implement with new respect, grinning to herself before returning to her task.

'So you've been looking at women again, have you?' she said. 'And no doubt wanking your filthy little cock over them as well.'

'Yes, Mistress.'

'Disgusting! You're a pervert, Arlidge, a dirty little wanker.'

She struck again, harder than before. Again he screamed and writhed, his very real pain providing her a pleasure she seldom got with clients, not sexual, but pure, vicious joy in hurting him. As soon as he had regained control of his body she laid in another stroke, and began to speak as Arlidge screamed.

'Do it in the bushes, do you?' she said. 'With your filthy, ugly little cock in your hand while you watch. Don't you?'

Arlidge managed to shake his head. Lilith struck again, harder still, across the tops of his thighs. He screamed, all control gone, thrashing dementedly in his pain. For an instant he was hanging by his wrists in the frame, but managed to steady himself. Lilith grinned, lifting the sjambok as he looked back with real fear showing in his eyes.

'We know what you men are like, you know,' she went on. 'You realise that, don't you? Dirty little perverts. You can't even speak to us without your eyes going to our tits, can you? And the way you turn when we walk past, to watch our arses move. You disgust us, you know that too, don't you?'

This time he nodded.

'But at least most men have the decency to keep their cocks in their pants,' she continued. 'Not you, Arlidge, oh,

20

no, not you. You go in the bushes, don't you? You pull at your horrid little prick while you watch us, don't you? Watching the way our arses move in our jeans. Watching the way our tits bounce. Dirty, filthy little man. I bet you watch the girls from St David's, too, don't you? Watch them in their little school skirts. Hoping they'll bend over and give you a flash of their panties. You'd love that, wouldn't you? Imagine, a sweet little thing, seventeen, even sixteen, bending to take something out of her satchel, right down, her little skirt rising at the back, her panties visible, white cotton tight over her cheeky teenage arse, the pouch of her cunt showing between her thighs . . .'

Arlidge groaned aloud, hanging his head.

'You're a piece of filth,' Lilith told him. 'That's what you've been up to, isn't it? Trying to look up schoolgirls' skirts to see their panties. Dirty bastard! I'm going to beat you, Arlidge. I'm going to beat you so fucking hard you'll never dare inflict your filthy attention on a woman again, ever!'

She struck, and this time she didn't stop, lashing the sjambok in as fast as she could, over and over as Arlidge screamed and writhed in the frame. His full weight was on his hands, his legs jerking up and down in agony, never still as the vicious implement cut into his buttocks and thighs, again and again.

At last she stopped. Her arm ached and sweat had begun to bead on her forehead and wrist, spoiling her poise. She struggled to recover it, drawing herself up and trying to breathe as quietly as possible. Her heart was pounding, and her mind was full of a savage joy that came only when she was inflicting a serious beating on a man, a pleasure very different from the strong sexual excitement she took from punishing Diana.

Arlidge was in a sorry state. He was hanging from his wrist straps, limp, his knees having failed. His head was on his chest, with sweat running down his face, his eyes closed and his mouth slack. Behind, his buttocks and legs were a mass of welts, showing scarlet against what little remained white. His cock had risen, swelling, until it stuck out, half erect, wobbling gently to his breathing, a sight she found genuinely obscene yet also funny. Fighting back the urge to laugh at him, she called for Diana.

'You have no shame at all, do you?' she told Arlidge. 'How can you get excited when you know how much you revolt women? What gives you the right to get turned on when they hate every dirty little glance, every sneaky little peep? You fucking pervert, you piece of shit!'

'Yes, Miss Lilith?' Diana interrupted, poking her head around the door.

'The little dirtbag's getting a hard-on again,' Lilith answered. 'Toss it off.'

Diana swallowed, but walked to where Arlidge hung in his bonds, to take his cock in her hand. She began to tug at it, rolling the foreskin back to reveal the wet redness of the glans within. Diana's face set in disgust at the sight, but she carried on. Lilith watched, enjoying not the sight of Arlidge's cock, but the humiliation on Diana's face as she wanked at it.

'The dirty sod's been peeping at girls again,' Lilith went on. 'He seems to think we wear tight jeans and tops just so that he can ogle our bodies. That's all we are to you, isn't it, Arlidge, you pervert, arse and tit? That's the only way you see women, isn't it, round bums packed into tight blue jeans, big tits straining out of our little tops, round and bouncing as we walk, with the nipples showing through. Or in short skirts, so short our panties show when we bend, or if the wind blows them up. You'd love that, wouldn't you? Some decent, ordinary woman with her skirt blown up and her panties on show in the street. Or a schoolgirl, a St David's girl, with her little tartan skirt up high and her tiny little white panties on show while you wank in the bushes. In fact you'd do it yourself, wouldn't you, if only you had the guts. Think about it, Arlidge: you catch her, your hands fumble under her skirt as she writhes in your grip. Up it comes, showing her panties, her little bottom wriggling in your lap as she struggles, pushed out against the bulge of your filthy prick –'

She stopped. Arlidge had come, groaning in ecstasy as thick white fluid spurted out over Diana's hand and the mat below him. Diana kept on wanking, her face screwed up in utter revulsion as the sperm dribbled down her hand. Lilith licked her lips, briefly considering forcing Diana to lick the revolting mess up, only to reject it as too much of a treat for Arlidge.

'Undo him,' she ordered, 'and make him clean up properly. I'll be in my room.'

'Clean up?' Arlidge queried.

'Yes,' Lilith answered. 'New rule. From now on you clean up your own filth, and count yourself lucky I don't charge extra.'

'Yes, Mistress,' he answered quickly.

She left the dungeon. As always after seeing a client, she felt somewhat soiled, despite not having touched him. In her room she pulled off her boots and climbed on to the bed. Folding her legs beneath her, she let her mind clear. Outside, she could hear Diana speaking to Arlidge, instructing him on how to clean up properly, then booking another appointment. Finally came the click of the door and a moment later Diana came in.

'Did you whack him or what!' Diana exclaimed. 'He could hardly walk!'

'Good,' Lilith replied.

'Does he really do those things?' Diana asked. 'What you were saying, about the schoolgirls.'

'No,' Lilith answered. 'He stares at girls, but don't they all? He wouldn't have the guts. I don't think he's even a flasher, for all that he likes to fantasise about it. He's too much of a coward. What's the time?'

'Twenty to three. You're seeing Hughes at five.'

'I'm going to change, then. We can go down to Craft Candles and see if our black church candles are ready yet.'

Two

Nich drew his Triumph to a halt beneath the looming grey mass of Stanton Rocks. Juliana dismounted, walking over towards the chapel as Nich pushed the bike on to its stand.

'How ugly,' Juliana remarked.

'Typical Low Church architecture,' Nich answered. 'It'll have been built by some nineteenth-century sect. I'd guess Exeter Brethren. They make a virtue of austerity. Pridough would fit right in with them.'

Juliana had reached the door, and forced it open, her nose wrinkling as the hot, stale air washed over her. Nich followed, glancing up to the damaged roof before turning his attention to the symbols on the floor.

'Lilith, Belial, Moloch,' he remarked. 'Not kids, then, unless they were exceptionally well educated. Maybe Pridough was right.'

'There's a pentagram here,' Juliana remarked. 'Wax, more symbols, and a used condom. Someone's been fucking on the altar.'

'Wonderful!' Nich said. 'That explains Pridough's fury! It wasn't a Black Mass, though, not a proper one. There'd be more stuff. I'd say there were three or four people, a simple ceremony, then a fucking as the climax. I must find out who did it!'

'Shall we fuck? On the altar?' Juliana asked.

'Absolutely!' Nich responded after a moment's hesitation.

Juliana, as always, had asked the question as casually as if she had been suggesting a shopping expedition, an

24

attitude that Nich appreciated yet still found strange. Yet one look was enough to assure him that he wanted to do it, and that the possibility of being observed would not be enough to put him off. She was in leather trousers, tight on her long legs and slender hips, and showing off the curve of her bottom as she bent to inspect the altar. Her jacket was also leather, and open, revealing a slice of her plain black top, which was straining across her breasts, to exaggerate their large size and rounded shape. Suede boots, also black, and the dark cascade of her hair added to the image, with black nail polish giving a final touch. Pridough, he knew, would have been outraged merely by her appearance, let alone by what she was suggesting.

'Shall I go nude?' she asked.

'No, keep your jacket on, your boots, too. The image of a girl in a leather jacket and boots but nothing else would offend Pridough far more than total nudity.'

Juliana smiled. Shrugging off her jacket, she began to strip. Nich watched, his cock stiffening in his trousers. Her top followed her jacket, pulled up over a lacy black bra that struggled to cope with the big breasts it supported. She tugged the bra up, casually exposing her breasts, and pulled everything off over her head.

Nich grinned and squeezed the bulge in his trousers, adjusting his rapidly growing erection. Juliana returned his smile and put her hands to the button of her trousers. It came open. Her thumbs hooked into the waistband and they came down, her panties with them, sliding to the level of her ankles. She bent to pull at a boot, revealing the rear view of her vulva and the dark, hairy crease between pert white buttocks. Nich caught the scent of her sex and blew his breath out.

As she finished stripping he took a quick glance from the door. Assured that nobody was about, he freed his cock, pulling it from his fly. He was already close to erection and, as Juliana straightened up, stark naked, he gave himself the last few tugs to make it ready. She looked back, her eyes bright with anticipation and mischief as she slipped her feet back into her boots, then put on the leather jacket once more. With one elongated nail she flicked the old condom from the altar top and jumped up, sitting her bottom down on the pentagram with her thighs wide to show off her ready sex and holding her arms wide for Nich.

'Thank you, no,' Nich said. 'Last time it took a fortnight for the scratches to heal. Besides, this is the temple of a patriarchal God: you should be in a position of sub-mission.'

Juliana pouted, but jumped down from the altar, turning to show off her bottom. Her legs came apart, wide, as she bent down, displaying her sex from the rear, the hole of her vagina already moist. Nich stepped forward, holding his cock at the ready.

'Hands behind your back, Juliana,' he said.

She looked round, her expression sulky, but obeyed, laying her chest on the altar so that her full breasts squashed out on the concrete and crossing her wrists in the small of her back. Nich reached down for her discarded panties, using them to twist around her wrists and secure her hands.

'You know how anyone else who tried to do this to me would end up, don't you?' Juliana asked.

'I do,' Nich answered, 'and that is why I enjoy it so much.'

'Good,' Juliana answered. 'Then hurt me.'

Nich considered for one moment, then put the head of his cock to the mouth of Juliana's vagina and jammed it in as hard as he could. She gasped in pained ecstasy, even as he winced at the sudden tug to his foreskin. With his hands clenched on her hips and his nails dug into her soft flesh, he began to fuck her, slamming her body into the hard concrete of the altar. She cried out, her fingers twitching in her panties as her body jerked to the rough motion.

Thrusting harder, and harder still, Nich looked down on her. Her small white bottom was spread wide, the rose-pink dimple of her anus and the stretched mouth of her vagina moving to the motion of his cock. His erection felt huge, rock-hard and on the verge of explosion, as the sight of her, her smell and the feel of her body combined to draw him towards an orgasm he was determined to delay.

26

He slowed to steady, deep pushes. Letting go of her hips, he took her by the hair, twisting a hank of it hard into his fist to force her head back and up. She gave an appreciative sigh and he increased the pace of his fucking, slapping at the flesh of her bottom and one thigh as he rode her. Her responses became more urgent, her cries more heated, more needful. Nich slapped harder, snatching at her flesh to rake his nails on the skin. She hissed in response, pushing her bottom out to meet his thrusts. Nich jerked her head back, hard, moving yet faster in her vagina and scratching at the flesh of her buttocks, to leave long red lines on the pale cheeks. She was writhing, Nich struggling to control her, even as he felt the urge to come rise up once more, this time too strong too resist. He cried out in ecstasy, jamming his cock up her vagina to the hilt, and emptied his sperm inside her.

Juliana screamed, writhing in his grip as he came up her, and turning as he pulled out, to push out her sex. She was wild-eyed, her hair disarrayed, her face and chest and belly streaked with sweat, her breasts soiled. Nich knelt, burying his face in the warm, wet flesh of her sex, licking as his fingers burrowed up between her legs, to slide into the wet cavity of her vagina and pop the tight, hot ring of her anus. She screamed again as she was penetrated, coming a moment later, full in Nich's face as she squirmed and wriggled her sex in blended frustration and ecstasy.

Diana found her sense of mischief rising as she stepped into the candlecraft centre. It was full of tourists, some customers, more simply browsing among the displays of exotic candles, wax sculptures and candelabra. Her purple minidress was drawing plenty of attention, both approving and disapproving, especially to her breasts, which were clearly braless, with her big nipples poking boldly up.

She knew full well that if she stood in front of the light streaming in through the huge windows it would become obvious that she was not only braless beneath her dress but pantiless as well. It was more than she could resist, and as Lilith moved towards the counter she changed direction, feigning interest in a twisted candle of green wax taller than herself. Several pairs of male eyes had followed her, and she was about to bend and provide a flash of bare bottom cheeks when Lilith's hand closed on her arm.

'Stop tarting around,' Lilith hissed. 'We don't want to get thrown out.'

'Sorry,' Diana answered quickly, and followed Lilith to the counter.

A girl much her own age was behind it, with typical local looks, full curves and a riot of brown curls. She smiled as they approached. The badge on her blouse announced her as Becky.

'Hi,' Lilith said. 'We ordered some candles. Church candles, only black.'

'Oh, yes,' Becky answered. 'They're ready. They're great, really cool. With you in a minute.'

Becky disappeared into a back room, quickly returning with a large box, which she placed on the counter. Opening it, she revealed a set of large, black candles, each as thick as Diana's wrists and some two feet in length.'

'Wow,' Diana said.

'They're perfect,' Lilith agreed and bent to whisper in Diana's ear. 'If you're very good, maybe I'll even take you in the lavatory and stick one up your cunt.'

Diana felt herself shiver at the suggestion, and responded with wide, hopeful eyes. Lilith chuckled and slapped Diana's bottom, drawing a look of disapproval from a woman nearby. Becky giggled, and for a moment they shared a look.

Lilith paid, leaving Diana to wonder about the assistant's reaction. There had been a nervousness to the giggle, suggesting amusement and even anticipation rather than simply a spirit of fun. Certainly Becky seemed to have guessed that the candles were intended for more than simple decoration. Considering the possibility that Becky was into spanking, and maybe also bisexual, Diana cast her another glance, admiring her heavy breasts and full bottom. Becky was pretty, also vivacious, and Diana found herself wondering how she'd look naked, preferably bent

28

across Lilith's knee with one of the candles protruding from her vagina. The thought sent another delicious shiver through her as Lilith finished the transaction and turned to leave.

'Hey!' Diana protested. 'Where are you going?'

'Home,' Lilith answered. 'Where do you think?'

'The toilets?' Diana hissed. 'You said you were going to fuck me!'

'I was teasing you, slut.'

'Lilith!'

Lilith paused, sighed, and turned abruptly on her heel. Diana followed, led by the hand, and as she passed the counter she caught Becky's eye, and winked. The assistant responded with a look that combined shock and pleasure, raising Diana's sense of mischief higher still. As she was pulled down the length of the shop she put a deliberate wiggle into her walk, sure that Becky's eyes would be fixed on the movement of her bottom beneath her dress.

The door to the ladies' toilet was discreetly concealed behind a screen. Lilith pushed it open, to find a single other occupant, a middle-aged woman who was washing her hands. Lilith feigned an interest in her make-up as Diana waited, feeling more urgent and ruder with every moment. The woman left, and she hurried into a stall, Lilith following.

'That new assistant, Becky, was flirting with me,' Diana said quietly. 'Did you see?'

'I noticed,' Lilith replied. 'You're a slut, and so is she by the look of it. I ought to drag her in here and fuck you side by side, with the candles up your fat, sticky cunts. Now get up on the pan.'

Diana hastened to obey, kneeling up on the lavatory seat and sticking her bottom out into a round ball. An instant later her dress had been tugged up and she was bare, her bottom spread for Lilith, with the scent of her sex suddenly strong in the air.

'Look at you, you're dripping,' Lilith said, 'and I bet that Becky is, too. If I had her in here I'd make you lick each other's cunt. That's right, Diana, your cunts, your fat,

29

girlie cunts. I'd make you open each other for the candles before I fucked you, and not just your cunts, your arseholes too. How would you like to lick Becky's arsehole?'

'Yes, please,' Diana moaned. 'Fuck me, Lilith. Fuck my dirty cunt.'

'I'm going to –' Lilith replied, and broke off at the sound of the door opening.

Diana was left shivering on the lavatory, her head spinning with the crude words Lilith was using to turn her on and thoughts of being made to do rude things with the shop assistant. Leaning on to the cistern, she cocked her bottom up, opening herself completely and looking back to watch as Lilith quietly withdrew one of the huge candles from the box. It looked enormous, far too big for her hole, yet she knew that was where it was going, and was determined to take it. She also knew that Lilith would hold her, and ignore anything short of serious pain.

Outside the cubicle she could hear the woman who'd come in, running a tap, just feet away, with only the lavatory door to prevent her getting a view of the obscene position Diana was in. As Lilith took her firmly around the waist Diana wondered if the woman was Becky, come to see what was going on.

'Cunt time, Diana,' Lilith whispered.

Diana shut her eyes, concentrating everything on her sex as the tip of the candle was put to her hole. Lilith pushed and Diana's mouth came open as her vagina started to fill, the sensitive mouth stretching, gaping. She let out a low moan, unable to hold it back as her flesh strained to accommodate the candle. Lilith eased it back in response and Diana felt her vagina start to close, itself a blissful sensation, only to be filled once more, deeper still, hurting, until the tears were threatening to start in her eyes. Again she moaned, and again Lilith relented, only this time Diana's vagina stayed wide, an open, aching hole, urgently needing to be filled. Lilith pushed once more, deeper, stretching the ring of Diana's vagina, wider than before, and wider still. Suddenly it was in her, and the thick shaft

30

was sliding up her hole, until she felt a new, different pressure and realised that it had been pushed right up to her cervix.

She pulled her head up, breathing hard, with her mouth wide and spittle running from her lower lip. Twisting her head, she looked back, eager to see the candle sticking out behind her. A good foot of it showed, protruding from beyond the full white curve of one bare bottom cheek, a sight deliciously obscene, and one that made her thoughts turn back to Becky. The tap had been turned off, and there was silence, but she could imagine the girl listening, wondering what they were up to.

Behind Diana, Lilith put her finger to her lips. Diana nodded weakly and bent down again, pushing her bottom out fully. The fucking started, Lilith taking the candle and easing it slowly in and out of Diana's hole. Diana responded, slipping a hand back between her thighs, to touch the fat candle shaft as it was pushed into her hole, then her clitoris. She began to masturbate, concentrating on the straining feeling in her vagina and thinking of what Lilith had threatened to make her do.

Becky would knock on the door, timidly, asking if they were all right. Lilith would be as aggressive as ever, pulling the door open to drag the shop girl in by the hair. Becky would be stripped, nude, and made to kneel on the lavatory, her protests answered with slaps to her big, fleshy bottom. Once Becky had been smacked into submission, it would be Diana's turn to be taken by the hair, forced down to her knees, her face pushed in between Becky's bottom cheeks. Her mouth would be full of plump, hairy pussy flesh, her nose pressed to the damp hole of Becky's anus. She'd be made to lick, pussy first, then Becky's bumhole. Lilith would be gloating over her, watching her tongue work in the tight brown ring of the shop girl's anus.

The candle would be put up, just as it was for real, jammed up her pussy, her cunt, deep in, fucking her as she licked and slobbered at Becky's bottom crease. She'd be moaning in her ecstasy, unable to restrain herself as she tongued the dirty little hole. Lilith would be laughing, and the door would be open, exposing her in her degradation, to several other women. They'd watch, horrified, unable to believe she could sink so low, to let herself be fucked in a lavatory, fucked up her gaping cunt with her mouth full of the taste of bum.

Diana came, her teeth clenched tight to stop herself screaming, her clitoris burning under her fingers, her sex strained to what felt like the limit. Lilith kept on moving the candle, in and out, in a rhythmic fucking motion that finally destroyed the last of Diana's self-control. She cried out, for Lilith, then for Becky, her voice trailing off in an odd bubbling sound as the pleasure finally broke. Lilith stopped, pulling the candle slowly from Diana's vagina.

'Lovely, thank you, darling, thank you,' she gasped. 'Oh my poor pussy!'

'Shh!' Lilith urged.'

Diana put her hand to her mouth, giggling as the blood rushed to her cheeks. They shared a glance, guilty but full of mischief as Lilith wiped the thick candle with a piece of loo paper. Jerking her head, she indicated the door. They waited, but there was no sound, and when Lilith finally pushed open the door there was nobody there.

They washed and left and, as they walked back down the length of the shop, Diana found Becky looking right at her, eyes wide in surprise and maybe envy. Diana winked, and stuck out her tongue, leaving the assistant to stare after her with unmistakable longing.

Walking back through the streets of Exeter, Diana found herself so elated that it was hard to resist the urge to skip. Twice she had come to orgasm, both times in deliciously rude circumstances, while there seemed to be every chance of making Becky a new playmate. The thought filled her with exuberant delight, and as they reached the low wall of a car showroom she jumped to the top, balancing herself with her arms in sheer playfulness. Lilith smiled up at her.

At the end she jumped down, laughing, and twirled to make her dress rise and show her legs and a hint of bare bottom. Her reflection showed in the display window of an estate agent, and she twirled again, faster, giggling as she realised just how much of her bottom the action showed off. Lilith laughed and gave her a gentle pat of admonition, then nodded suddenly to the window.

'Look,' she said, 'it's the chapel. It's for sale.'

Diana stopped herself spinning and followed Lilith's gaze, finding the familiar building in one of the photographs. It was the ruined chapel they had been in the night before, advertised at forty thousand pounds. She giggled. There, to the flickering light of candles and the scent of hot wax and incense, she had been held down on the old altar by Lilith, while a client fucked her, in a mock rape. The client, Mr Hughes, had thought it was Diana's first time for money, and that she'd hated it. In fact, Lilith had arranged the whole thing, including the details of a Satanic ritual that came more from the way Hughes wanted to visualise Lilith than from her own beliefs. It had worked beautifully, with Hughes so fascinated that he had been prepared to pay more or less what Lilith asked. He was a creep, and scared her, but with Lilith to hold her it had been bearable. He had left satisfied, entirely unaware that he had been tricked, with Diana lying spread-eagled and supposedly broken on the altar, while Lilith re-counted the five hundred pounds he had paid for the privilege.

She laughed at the memory.

Tom Pridough cast a disapproving look at the two girls outside Dawson and Unwin's estate agency. Everything about them jarred with his ideas of how life should be lived. The shorter of the two particularly offended him, with a loose purple dress doing very little to conceal a figure that in his view she should have been ashamed of. Far from any such reaction, she seemed to take a positively childish delight in her body, an attitude her friend evidently encouraged.

He walked past, ignoring them and fighting down the embarrassment their close presence caused him. Within the estate agents' the feeling faded, yet of the two assistants he pointedly chose the one at the further desk, who was older, and male.

'Mr Pridough, good afternoon,' the man greeted him, half rising from his chair. 'Have you made a decision?'

'Yes, I have come to make an offer on the chapel.'

'Excellent,' the man answered. 'I'm convinced you'll find it a sensible choice.'

'I'm offering thirty-two thousand pounds,' Pridough interrupted. The man's expression changed to disappointment, briefly, before returning to the bland smile he had worn before.

'Thirty-two?' he said. 'Well, I can try, of course, but I do feel that forty is a not unreasonable demand. True, it is in need of repairs.'

'It's derelict,' Pridough said. 'Forty thousand pounds is a ridiculous price to be asking. In my estimation five or six thousand would be fair.'

'But Mr Pridough, it is not actually the building, as such that is valuable. As I explained, the offer represents a rare opportunity to create a character home within the boundaries of the National Park.'

'I know all that,' Pridough said, interrupting for the third time. 'Although I find the modern greed for money deplorable, I am not blind to reality. Nevertheless, I can only offer thirty-two thousand pounds. Will you accept that?'

'I'll have to get back to you on that one,' the man answered. 'It's a council property, as you know, and they are in no great hurry to sell.'

'Doesn't it stand for anything that I intend to put it to its proper purpose?' Pridough demanded, his anger rising in the face of the man's offhand manner. 'It is a chapel, a place of worship.'

'I fear that cuts very little ice with the council,' the man answered, his eyes flicking to a couple in expensive clothes who were talking to his female colleague.

'Let me know as soon as possible,' Pridough said, and rose.

He left, feeling angry at the estate agent's lack of respect for his calling, also ineffectual. Outside, the two girls were still there, looking at the houses in the windows. For a moment his frustration gave way to a feeling of superiority. However little he could afford, it seemed certain that they would be unlikely ever to aspire to owning so much as their own tiny, squalid flats.

Lilith bit her finger as she stared into the window of Dawson and Unwin, then made an impatient gesture to stop Diana talking. She had made the suggestion of buying the old chapel as a joke, but the more she thought about it the more sensible it seemed.

In her flat noise was a constant problem. Despite her best efforts to soundproof the dungeon and to use gags whenever possible, the neighbours were starting to give her odd looks and whisper behind her back. Inevitably it would become public knowledge that she was running a brothel, knowledge that would bring with it a whole host of difficulties.

The chapel, on the other hand, was half a mile from the nearest building and stood among thick pinewoods and rocky outcrops, all of which was protected from development. Her clients would be able to scream themselves hoarse and nobody would hear. There was an acre of land, too, and with some judicious hedge planting it might even be possible to add outdoor games to the services she offered. It was perfect, while, with her operation bringing in over a thousand pounds even in a bad week, the price seemed easily accessible.

Again she bit her finger, still indecisive, then suddenly determined. Pulling Diana behind her, she strode into the estate agency.

Nich stood among the twelve great grey monoliths of granite that made up the stone circle of Grim's Men. Juliana had climbed one of the stones, scrambling up to sit cross-legged on the summit, her face set in a serene smile. Nich returned the look and glanced around, trying to imagine stunted oaks in place of the regular pines that surrounded the site, with the run passage stretching between them up to the moor.

The chapel had filled him with antagonism and distaste for its builders and everything they stood for: patriarchy, obedience and sexual repression. Sex with Juliana had been a deliberate act of sacrilege, also mockery, and as he had fucked her he had imagined all those who had worshipped there watching, their faces set in outrage.

The circle filled him with very different emotions. Awe for the long-dead people who had built it, sorrow for the passing of their religion, determination to see it revived as the faith of the land. Had he not already drained himself into Juliana, he would happily have done so now, on the soft grass at the centre of the circle. It would have been different, though, an act of worship as much as pleasure, and far from sacrilegious.

'Tell me again how it worked, the Samhain ritual,' he asked. Juliana laughed for his enthusiasm.

'There would be a feast,' she said, 'on the last night of the old year, with honey, nuts, fruit, fresh-killed meat and all the good things of the autumn, muscar as well, which you call fly agaric. At midnight a girl would be chosen, the prettiest among those still virgin. She'd be led here, naked, and the mothers and crones would sit around the outside of the stones, guarding her. Meanwhile, the men would walk up to a row that used to run above the Teign. With the first glimpse of the sun a horn would sound and they would run, racing here. The strongest, the most agile, would reach the virgin first, to take her on the ground, to impregnate her and so ensure the rebirth of the Horned God from the womb of the Mother.'

'Wonderful,' Nich answered her. 'Compare that to what they did in their chapel, their dour worship, their blind abasement to a foreign God! We must do it, this year, we must!'

'We'd need a virgin,' Juliana answered him.

Lilith frowned as she considered the pieces of paper spread out on the table. Her plan to buy the chapel had come to grief on the fact that her income was entirely unofficial and undeclared. Therefore she was unable to get a mortgage,

36

while she had no property on which to secure a loan. Between Diana and her they had somewhat over twenty-three thousand pounds, spread between a dozen building society accounts. It was more than she had realised, while Mr Hughes's five hundred added yet more, but it was still not enough. She had also learned that an offer had already been made on the property, if not accepted.

'Shit!' she swore, breaking the lead of her pencil on a full stop to her calculations. 'We need another seventeen thou.'

'We could make a lower offer,' Diana suggested.

'Maybe,' Lilith answered. 'What's the time?'

'Quarter to. Hughes will be here soon. I'd better make myself scarce.'

'Do that. I'll call you if I need you.'

Diana made a face, to which Lilith responded with a sympathetic shrug and a pointed tap on her page of calculations. They kissed and Diana made for the door, leaving Lilith to tidy up the papers and wonder what Hughes wanted the appointment for. Unlike the majority of her clients, he was dominant rather than submissive, and his fantasies were sufficiently brutal and abusive to make her feel uneasy about catering for them. That didn't stop her taking his money, and she consoled herself with the thought that as long as he was paying her he was unlikely to be inflicting himself on genuinely unwilling partners.

He was also hard to cater for. For one thing, he would use any woman only once, and 'use' was the right word. As he expressed it himself, any woman he had fucked was soiled goods, and as such of no further use to him. He also refused to go with experienced professionals, but enjoyed being the first to pay a girl, as he got off on the idea of spoiling her, of making her a whore. Lilith had played on his needs, twice tricking him into thinking he was being provided with inexperienced girls who needed to be made drunk and even then cajoled into surrender.

The first time, she had called up a friend who was working in Taunton, whose poor efforts at feigning fear and revulsion had seemed transparent, although Hughes had not noticed. The second time she had used Diana, adding the Satanic details as a distraction, while telling Hughes that the ritual would terrify his victim. Hughes had loved the idea, and happily paid the first price she demanded. He had rung first thing in the morning, to thank her and ask to discuss further business.

With her papers safely locked away she made quick work of changing, choosing a sports bra, a plain blouse and leather trousers. The outfit gave her an extra sense of security, something she felt she needed with Hughes, a fact that in turn made her resentful. Few men made her feel threatened. Hughes was an exception. His physical appearance was bad enough: six foot and more of hard, compact muscle, a heavy square jaw and small eyes of a peculiarly pale blue. In character he was worse, assured, in a way that very few men were in her presence, let alone clients, also crude, aggressive, sadistic and openly lustful, traits for which he showed not the slightest compunction. The only compensation was that, at least so far, he had treated her as an equal. With unusual self-awareness she realised that this was probably because he found his own character traits mirrored in her.

By the time the doorbell rang she felt ready for him, or at least as ready as she ever would be. She waited deliberately until the bell sounded a second time, then pressed the intercom to let him in. He greeted her politely as he stepped through the door, closing it behind him. Lilith's nose twitched at the powerful smell, aftershave over a masculine musk, a scent that always reminded her of the ape house at Paignton zoo.

'Mr Hughes,' Lilith responded, aware that her normal attitude towards men was going to seem horribly false and achieve nothing.

'Dave, please,' he said. 'I think after last night we can afford to be on first-name terms. She was a nice piece of skirt, though, wasn't she? Almost a shame to have to turn her into a whore.'

He laughed. Lilith said nothing, but motioned him into the main room. Not wishing to allow him to emphasise his greater height, she lowered herself into one of the leather chairs, crossing her legs.

'So, Dave, how may I help?' she asked.

'Can't you guess?' he answered. 'I want another cute piece of skirt. Like the last, only better.'

'Better?' Lilith queried. 'Well, I can try, certainly, but you'll have to let me know what you like. Diana's pretty enough, surely? Do you prefer blondes? A slimmer girl perhaps? Or –'

'No, no, no,' he interrupted. 'You've got the wrong idea. Diana was cute. You did a great job getting her. I don't want cuter. I want harder. I want to fuck a virgin and leave her a whore.'

Lilith swallowed, momentarily unable to answer as she thought of the moment she'd lost her own virginity, a fumbling, drunken encounter in the back seat of a car, yet still a precious moment. What Hughes was suggesting was appalling.

'Great, eh?' he went on. 'I want it in the chapel, too. I love all that weird stuff, fucking great, and, like you said, it scares the shit out of the little cuties. I want my virgin, Lilith. I want to put her on that altar and I want to stick my prick up and feel her cunt split. I want to hear her scream. I want her on the street the next day, offering blow jobs for a tenner.'

'That's not going to be easy,' Lilith managed.

'I didn't say it was going to be easy. That's why I'm coming to you. You're the fucking expert. Get it, fucking expert – "fucking" expert!'

Lilith forced a weak smile. A voice inside her head was screaming at her to tell him to fuck off, to kick out at him, to pin him to the floor and ram one of the church candles into his anus.

She realised that she was going to have to refuse him. It was too much, even if she was able somehow to fake it: just knowing that he believed it to be real would be more than she could handle.

'Five grand,' he said.

'Five grand?' she repeated. 'Five thousand pounds?'

'That's what I said, lady. And for that I want it good. I want it fucking perfect. It's got to be a doll, a real poppet:

blonde, small, tight waist, big tits, nice meaty arse. She's got to look good on her back, right, 'cause that's the way I'm going to fuck her, so I can see her hole split.'

Lilith found herself nodding dumbly. She was unable to find words, and struggling to hold her poise. Her resolve had gone, broken by the amount of money on offer, and she was already trying to work out how she could give him what he wanted. Not that she would follow his instructions. That would be too much, even for five thousand pounds, but she was sure the encounter could be faked.

Hughes opened his mouth in a characteristic grin and adjusted his cock in his trousers. Lilith swallowed once more, praying he wasn't going to demand sex.

'Makes me horny just thinking about it,' he drawled. 'I can't fucking wait.'

'It might take some time,' Lilith said quickly.

'You know what, girl,' he went on, squeezing his crotch again. 'I really fucking need it.'

'I don't know anyone suitable offhand,' Lilith said, trying urgently to keep the conversation on business. 'I mean, I don't get to meet many virgins.'

'I'll bet you don't,' he said. 'You know, if you weren't a whore I'd fuck you right now.'

Lilith shrugged and smiled, even as a wave of gratitude for her experience and reputation swept through her.

'Yeah,' he went one, 'I'd have you on the carpet, with that cute little arse up in the air. You're a great looker. You know that, don't you? Shame you had to go and spoil yourself.'

Again Lilith shrugged. Hughes paused, now openly squeezing his cock as his eyes lingered on her body.

'Reckon I could manage a blow job, whore or no whore. Fancy it? You're horny too, ain't you?'

'I don't actually suck,' she answered.

'You suck,' he replied. 'All girls suck, if there's enough money on the table. All girls fuck, too. It's just down to the money. Always is with women. That's the rub, you see. Underneath, you're all whores, and it takes a man like me to show you that.'

'I don't, really,' Lilith said. 'I do domination mainly, and –'

She stopped, realising that she'd been about to admit to Diana's helping her. Opposite her, Hughes had taken a snakeskin wallet from the inside pocket of his jacket. He opened it and pulled a fifty-pound note from a bundle and tossed it casually on to the table. Lilith sat still, forcing herself to meet his eyes. He tossed down a second note, and a third.

'You could have full sex for that,' she said, 'with any of the girls you wanted.'

'I don't want any girl,' he answered. 'I want you. I want you to suck my prick, lady, and you're going to.'

He placed a fourth note on the pile. Lilith tried to meet his eyes again and found she couldn't. He was offering two hundred pounds to suck his cock, something she'd once have done for five. Steeling herself, she thought of the twenty thousand in their accounts. Somehow it didn't seem real. The notes on the table did. Hughes put down a fifth note.

'Two hundred and fifty!' she said. 'You're joking, aren't you?'

Hughes shook his head. 'The fancy whores up London charge two grand a night.'

'Two thousand a night?'

'That's what I said.'

'I don't care. I'm not doing it.'

He placed a sixth note on the pile. Lilith swallowed. Diana would already have been sucking. So would most of the other girls she knew. She thought of Becky, the shop girl Diana had been flirting with. It was impossible to imagine her resisting. She herself was stronger, she knew it, stronger than any of them.

She put her hand in front of her face, showing a distress that was only partly acting. Peeping at Hughes's open wallet, she realised that the sheaf of notes within seemed no less thick than it had been when he had first opened it. The realisation made her feel weak, but she shook her head. Immediately, without the slightest hesitation, Hughes threw a seventh note down on the pile.

Lilith glanced at the money, wondering if he would actually let her keep it. The answer had to be yes. He valued her skill as a procuress – her *supposed* skill, anyway – and he wanted his virgin.

'I made a whore of a girl in Chelsea once,' he said. 'Posh piece she was. Cost me three grand. Would you suck for three grand?'

Lilith felt her determination dissolve, swept away on a tide of money. She could feel the tears starting in her eyes, but she knew it was more than she could resist.

'Three thousand?' she said weakly. 'OK, I'll suck you for three thousand.'

'So you do suck?' he said.

'Yes,' she admitted in a whisper.

'Speak up,' he demanded. 'I didn't catch that.'

'Yes, I suck,' she answered.

'You're no poker player, are you?' he laughed. 'I ain't offering three thousand. I'm offering three hundred and fifty. No, three hundred.'

He reached out, taking back one of the notes. Lilith stayed silent, open-mouthed, her mind boiling with anger, self-pity, resentment. Tears had started rolling down her cheeks in full view, her poise broken.

'You bastard!' she sobbed.

'Now, now,' he chided. 'No need for names. Now, if you want your three hundred you better get on your knees. It ain't staying there long.'

As he spoke he pulled at his fly, drawing it down. His hand went in, to pull out his cock, still fully erect, and Lilith realised that tormenting her had given him the same sexual excitement as talking about what he wanted to do to a virgin. He pointed at his cock, and clicked his fingers.

With tears streaming down her face, Lilith got to her knees. She felt numb, broken, her will gone. Hardly aware of what she was doing, she crawled over, fumbling with the buttons of her blouse as she went.

'Nice,' Hughes drawled. 'Tits out, eh? Know when you're beaten, don't you?'

Lilith didn't respond, hanging her head in abject misery as she pulled her sports bra high to expose her breasts.

'Nice,' he repeated. 'Not too big, but nice. Perky.'

Lilith shuffled forward, wiping a tear from her face as she reached him. His knees came fully apart and she crawled between them, reaching out to take hold of the hard shaft of his cock. He lay back, folding his hands behind his head. She went down, her mouth coming open of its own accord, to take in his thick, pale shaft. He gave a groan of pleasure as her lips and tongue touched the meat of his cock, and she was sucking, drawing her head up and down on his erect penis in a manner all too familiar despite not having taken a cock in her mouth for nearly two years.

She was crying as she sucked, slow, heavy tears rolling down her cheeks to fall on the grey-blue material of his suit. His cock felt oily, and the thick, male taste was unusually strong, the smell too. He watched her suck, his mouth twisted into a cruel leer, the same expression he had worn as he'd pushed his cock into Diana's body the night before. Feeling utterly beaten, and utterly used, she began to concentrate on making him come, using all the skill she had learned in the back alleys of Bristol. Hughes gave a satisfied grunt.

'You're one great cocksucker, lady,' he said suddenly. 'You should do this for a living. Oh, yeah, I forgot, you do.'

Lilith shook her head in a miserable and futile attempt at denial, spattering tears from her face.

'Hey, watch the suit,' he snarled. 'Fucking baby. You make like you're so fucking hard, then you're blubbering just because you've had to take a cock in your mouth. You make me laugh. Now suck my helmet, and wank me in your mouth while you do it. I like that.'

Lilith obeyed, lifting her head to take the bulbous tip of his cock between her lips, to kiss and mouth at it as she jerked his shaft. He groaned again, but with a new urgency. Sticking out her tongue, she began to lick at the underside of his foreskin, while still mouthing at his knob.

'Oh baby, you are fucking good,' Hughes sighed. 'Cocksucking little whore. I'm coming, I'm going to come in your mouth, you hot bitch . . .'

He grunted, and snatched at her hair, catching it and forcing her head abruptly down, to push the head of his cock into her windpipe. Lilith felt herself start to gag, even as her head was jerked back again, and down. Lilith struggled against the pain, all control gone as Hughes fucked her head with furious urgency, faster and faster. It stopped, suddenly. Her head was jerked back one last time. His cock flew from her mouth, even as the sperm erupted from the tip, splashing over her nose and into one eye. Lilith cried out in shock and disgust, Hughes grabbing his cock, to jerk at the shaft as he held her tightly by the hair, finishing off his sperm in her face.

Lilith took it, her face screwed up in disgust as spurt after spurt spattered across her face. Some went into her mouth, before she shut it, more over her lips and chin. When at last she was sure he had finished, she opened her one good eye, only to see him squeezing out a final blob from the end of his cock. He was grinning, and as he wiped the heavy bead of spunk on to the tip of her nose he gave a cluck of laughter.

'You want to fucking see yourself!' he said. 'What a fucking sight!'

He let go of her hair, only to take hold of her open blouse, pulling her in so that he could use it to wipe the saliva and sperm from his cock. One he'd cleaned himself he paused to feel one of her breasts, squeezing it and tweaking the nipple, which to Lilith's embarrassment was hard. He gave a knowing chuckle. She sat back, hastily gathering up the fifty-pound notes from the table and stuffing them into her trouser pocket.

'I told you, didn't I?' he said. 'Money's power, and don't forget it.'

Unable to deny what he was saying, Lilith began to rearrange her clothes, only then realising that her bra was spattered with come, while there was a good-sized blob on one breast, the one he hadn't touched. She stopped, and

44

shrugged off her soiled blouse instead, then her bra. Hughes had put his cock away and sat up, folding his hands in his lap.

'It ought to be a posh bird, really,' he said, musing. 'Some fancy piece. Into riding and that. No, that won't do. You split yourselves, don't you, if you ride too much? I've got to see that cherry burst.'

'I don't know if I can do it at all, really,' Lilith answered.

'Five grand, baby,' he said. 'Get what you can, right. It's got to be cute, like I said. No dogs, no fat birds, no titless wonders. Blonde's best, and something with a bit of class, yeah?'

'I'll try,' Lilith answered, silently promising herself that she'd cheat him if it was the last thing she did.

'I'm off, then,' Hughes announced. 'I'll ring in a week, yeah?'

He stood, only to reach down and take hold of her face, tilting her head back so that she was forced to look into his eyes.

'You play straight by me, I play straight by you,' he said. 'None of your whore's tricks. Understand?'

A sudden knot of fear tightened in Lilith's stomach. She nodded.

'Good girl,' he said and slapped her cheek, realising too late that he had put his fingers in the sperm.

'Dirty fucking whore!' he swore, and wiped the mess in her hair. 'Right, I'm gone. A week, yeah?'

Lilith rose as he walked to the door, saying nothing, but closing it behind him and slipping the catch into place, only to realise that it was a pointless gesture. She unfastened it, and walked unsteadily into the bathroom to clean up. Peering one-eyed into the mirror, she could see why Hughes had found her comical. She was plastered with come. Blobs hung from her nose and chin, while a great wad was rolling slowly down one cheek from her soiled eye, leaving a gluey trail marked black and purple with her make-up. Her skin was streaked with tear marks too, her make-up utterly ruined. Somehow she'd got lipstick on her nose, which was mingling with the piece of come that now hung from the tip. There was also come in her hair, in damp, pearl-white beads along with the slimy mark where he had wiped his hand.

She began to clean up, all the while uncomfortably aware of her erect nipples and the urgent feeling in her sex, but determined not to masturbate over what had happened. As she was finishing, Diana returned.

'He's gone,' Lilith said.

'I know,' Diana replied. 'I was watching from the café down the road. What did he want?'

'I'll explain. The bastard made me suck him off.'

'No! What, he forced you?'

'No, he paid. Three hundred.'

'Three hundred! Wow! I wish someone would give me three hundred for a blow job! Are you all right?'

Diana had come into the bathroom and was looking in concern at Lilith, who managed a weak smile.

'What happened?' Diana demanded.

'He spunked in my face,' Lilith explained.

'Don't they just *love* to do that! That or down your throat. Bastards! I'll get you a drink. Vodka?'

'No. I want air, fresh air. Let's drive up and look at the chapel.'

Nich drew in a grateful breath as Juliana rolled off his face. The atmosphere at Grim's Men had got to her, as it had to him, filling her with a nostalgic lust. She had demanded another orgasm, and taken it mounted nude on his face, stroking her body in the warm August sunlight that filtered down through the pines as he licked at her sex.

'Thank you, Nich,' she breathed as she moved up from her position. 'You are not ready yourself?'

'Later, thanks,' he answered as the scent of pine needles and musty earth replaced that of her pussy. 'I'm sure I heard a car just as you were coming.'

'Tourists. What of it?'

'It might be Pridough. I'd love to feed his suspicions.'

Juliana laughed, stretching herself with her head back, so that the black curtain of her hair hung halfway down her naked bottom. Nich wiped his mouth, admiring her body with a sense of pride that came from her choosing to be with him.

'Do you think he'd like to see me naked?' she asked. 'Think how it would craze his mind, wanting me desperately and hating himself for his own lust. There's nobody less able to handle their sexual feelings than a fervent Christian.'

'Don't!' Nich laughed. 'He'd just call the police, and I don't suppose he has any sexual feelings.'

'Oh, he does,' Juliana answered. 'They all do, deep down. It fills them full of guilt and self-loathing, and the more they deny themselves the worse it gets. You'll find that's why Pridough is always so angry.'

'No doubt,' Nich answered.

Juliana had moved to where she had piled her clothes on top of one of the standing stones, and was dressing, brushing the pine needles and bits of grass from her legs as she pulled on her socks. Nich got up and walked to the edge of the circular clearing to peer down between the rows of pines. The looming bulk of Stanton Rocks was visible, but not the chapel. The sound of a voice came to him, indistinct.

'Someone's there,' he said. 'Come on.'

'With you in a second,' Juliana answered.

Nich turned, to find her struggling into her trousers. Grinning, and filled with a pleasant sense of mischief, he began to move slowly down through the pines. Again he heard a voice, female, and caught a glimpse of brilliant red, then the glint of light on glass. He stopped, and turned, to jump as he found Juliana immediately behind him, doing up her blouse.

'Don't do that!' he hissed. 'I didn't realise you were there!'

'Sorry,' she answered. 'Is it him?'

'No, or not alone, anyway. There's a woman, and a red car. His is white.'

Juliana nodded and they moved forward, less carefully now, stopping once more as they reached the edge of the pines. Two young women stood by the chapel, looking up at the broken roof. One was small and olive-skinned, wearing a short purple dress that emphasised her waist; the other was taller and slender, in black leather trousers and a black silk blouse.

'The Satanists?' Juliana queried.

'Who else?'

Nich sat back in the settle chair he had occupied at the Black Dog. He was in his element, explaining his philosophy of religion to an attentive female audience. They had introduced themselves to the girls outside the chapel. There had been a few minutes of wariness, before the taller girl, Lilith, had admitted to holding the ritual. Nich had immediately latched on to her name, complimenting her on it and asking if it was her birth name. Lilith had admitted it was not, explaining how she had chosen it from rabbinical literature as representing a femininity that would not submit to the dominance of males. In response he had explained the Mesopotamian origins and demonic associations of the name, as both Lilith and her friend, Diana, listened in fascination. His suggestion of a drink at the Black Dog had been readily accepted.

'So what ritual did you hold?' he asked, returning his mug of beer to the table.

'A Black Mass,' Lilith answered.

'Wonderful,' Nich replied. 'Who is your priest, if you don't mind my asking?'

'I acted as priestess,' Lilith said. 'There were only three of us.'

'Then it wasn't technically a Black Mass,' Nich pointed out. 'You see, the Black Mass is an inversion of the Christian Mass, yet still a Christian rite. Christianity is inherently patriarchal. God, the Devil, the angels, are all male, and so are the priests. The same is therefore true for Satanism.'

'There are female priests,' Lilith objected. 'There's that TV programme –'

'Only recently,' Nich cut in, 'and then only because Christianity is losing its force, dying even, a process to the

48

assistance of which I have devoted my life. Indeed, I've written a good many letters in support of the appointment of female priests.'

'Hang on,' Diana said. 'If a Black Mass is supposed to be the opposite of an ordinary Mass, then doesn't having a female priest make sense?'

'An interesting point,' Nich admitted. 'Still, the Black Mass is now an established rite. You can't just make up a Satanic ritual and call it that. A male must officiate, and it has to be a defrocked priest. Other details can vary, but that's essential.'

'Couldn't you be the priest?' Diana asked.

'Absolutely not,' Nich answered. 'I could help, but nothing more. I'm a pagan, and not just that, I set myself in deliberate antagonism to all that is Christian. In fact, the very concept of the Black Mass has no meaning save in the context of Christianity. Certainly it is not a pagan ritual, still less an ancient one.'

'Didn't witches hold them?' Lilith queried.

'They were accused of doing so, yes,' Nich admitted, 'but there's no evidence that the Black Mass or any such ritual was ever practised by witches. Not true witches, anyway. It seems to have been an invention of eighteenth-century sensation seekers such as the Hellfire Club, and there is no record of the actual term until the late nineteenth century. The sort of Satanic coven popularly associated with the rite is entirely a twentieth-century phenomenon. Not that that makes it any less valid.'

'What are the details, then?' Diana asked.

'As I said,' Nich went on, 'the idea is to invert each of the ritual elements of the Christian Mass, or pervert them, you could say, so as to be as blasphemous as possible and thus please Satan. So the sign of the cross is made upside down, urine is used in place of wine, semen for chrism oil, even excrement for communion wafers. In some cases the belly of a naked woman is used as the altar.'

'We did that, more or less,' Lilith said. Diana giggled.

'Tell us,' Juliana asked. 'Don't mind what you say. Nich and I fucked on the altar earlier, with me bent across it in my jacket and boots.'

'Wow!' Diana responded. 'Cool! I got it on the altar, with Lilith holding me while this guy Hughes fucked me. He's a real pig. He made –'

'He wanted her to pretend she was unwilling,' Lilith cut in quickly. 'Like she says, he's a real pig.'

'I'm surprised you allow him to take part,' Nich observed. 'These things are normally very intimate. It's part of the attraction.'

'It's complicated,' Lilith said. 'Go on explaining.'

'Your position was more traditional than ours,' Nich went on, 'and true to the Black Mass, which often includes copulation, even buggery. The host, the wafers, may then be touched to the girl's soiled vagina or anus before being distributed to the congregation. There's another version, with the priest touching the wafers to his own anus. You did it the first way, I take it?'

'Well, no,' Diana admitted. 'We didn't have a congregation.'

'What did you do?'

'We dedicated my fucking to Satan,' Diana said. 'Lilith drew the symbols and the pentagram, from a book we've got. Lilith did the dedication and I danced for Hughes, a striptease, ending up bare on the altar. Hughes fucked me.'

'You just said he thought you were unwilling,' Juliana countered.

'Sort of, yeah,' Diana said hurriedly.

'He paid,' Lilith admitted with a sigh. 'He wanted to think she didn't like it but couldn't resist the money. Then when it came to the actual sex she pretended to change her mind so that I had to hold her down. She made out that she was scared as well. Like we said, he's a pig.'

'Cruel,' Juliana agreed. 'Still, you seem to have enjoyed it.'

'I did,' Diana agreed, 'on more than one level. I liked the ritual sex and it felt good to trick him.'

'You like sex that way, when you despise the person doing it?' Juliana asked.

Diana nodded, blushing. Juliana reached out to stroke her hair.

'I understand,' she said quietly, then smiled at Lilith's warning glance.

'It sounds a great ritual,' Nich cut in quickly. 'Not a Black Mass, technically, but fine. If only Pridough knew the full details!'

'Pridough?' Diana queried.

'Tom Pridough, the priest,' Nich said.

'Who's he?'

'A nondenominational Christian priest,' Nich answered. 'He came up here for some reason and found the remains of your ritual. He immediately accused me. I'm his pet hate.'

'Why?'

'I write articles on pagan belief and help to organise festivals.'

'Like the one a few weeks ago, what was it? The Lammas festival.'

'One of mine,' Nich answered. 'I do all sorts of things to help promote the old religions. Pridough hates me for it. He's a real zealot, cold, aggressive, prudish, totally certain of his own righteousness. Just about everything offends him. A typical Christian extremist. He objects to my beliefs. In fact they drive him berserk. He's called me a heathen, a pagan, a hedonist, a pervert, all sorts, in print and to my face. I don't think he even understands why I don't take offence at the terms. He genuinely seems to feel that his particular brand of Christian bigotry is some sort of objective ideal, and that anyone deviating from it must therefore be filled with shame. Idiot.'

'And he was up at the chapel? What does he look like?'

'Tall, spare, stringy, like someone who's spent a lifetime taking cold showers and long walks, which he has. Brown hair, receding hairline. He wears a black suit and a dog collar.'

'We saw him going into a branch of Dawson and Unwin,' Lilith said. 'That's the estate agent who's selling the chapel. It must be him who made the other offer.'

'Selling the chapel? Offer?' Nich demanded.

'The borough council owns the chapel,' Lilith explained. 'They're selling it. I want to buy it, but I haven't enough

51

money to make an offer. It looks like this Pridough bloke has done.'

'How much are they asking?' Nich asked.

'Forty thou, for the building, which has limited planning permission, and about an acre of land behind it.'

'And you want it for rituals? To convert to a house?'

'Both,' Lilith answered uncertainly.

'We want to turn it into a brothel, an SM brothel,' Diana put in. 'I don't think they mind, Lilith.'

'We don't!' Nich assured her as Juliana's mouth twitched up into a wicked smile. 'We don't mind at all. An SM brothel, run by Satanists, instead of his chapel! Pridough would be furious! He'd be spitting teeth with rage!'

'He'd inform the police,' Diana pointed out.

Tom Pridough lay in bed, staring into the darkness above him. He was praying as sleep closed in on him, asking his God to spare him the dreams that came almost every night. Even as he mumbled the final words he knew that they would not be answered, and cursed himself for his lack of faith.

There would be women, he knew, girls, plump, voluptuous, with heavy breasts and buttocks, fat girls, like the Catholic succubi, lewd, sexual girls. They would cluster around him, touching him, tormenting him, laughing at his attempts to resist as soft, eager fingers groped for his cock.

He fought back from the edge of sleep, realising that it had begun to happen even as he struggled against it. Again he tried to pray, pleading to his God to be spared the test, to be allowed just one night undisturbed. Behind the prayer a voice was telling him that he was being stupid, that all he needed to do was masturbate and he would banish the dreams. His cock felt badly in need of his touch, yet he kept his hands folded on his chest, forcing himself not to do it, despite the certain consequences.

As his tiredness overcame him his thoughts slipped further from rationality. The bed seemed wider, softer, more luxurious. It was light, too, a yellow light, flickering, from a great iron candelabrum set with black candles. A girl stood beneath it, naked, smiling through full red lips. She cupped her breasts, holding up the fat globes of golden flesh in invitation. He shook his head, telling her to leave him alone, to get back to her hell, only to realise that that was exactly where he was.

The girl smiled at his new awareness. She came forward, placing her hands on the bed, one knee, and the other, to crawl towards him. He groaned, trying to pull away, only to realise that he was tied in place, his wrists spread wide above his head, his ankles bound to the bed posts at the far end. She came on, her huge eyes staring into his, her mouth wide, a plump tongue visible between her lips. Beneath her chest her heavy breasts swung to her motion, the nipples fat with blood, distended to huge teats. Beyond, he could see her belly, also hanging down, round and fecund, ready for impregnation. Plump thighs rose behind, parted as she crawled, to raise her huge bottom high and spread the cheeks, filling the air with the thick, female scent of her sex.

He tried to cry out, but no sound came, only her laughter as she watched him writhe in his bonds. Her hand was reaching out to take his cock, to squeeze it, to tug at it, as her face set in an expression of demented glee. She was revelling in the sight of his erection, tugging and stroking, until he felt it would burst. Her fat breasts folded around it, squeezing, rubbing, enveloping him in soft, plump female flesh, engulfing him, his erection sucked up into the wetness of her vaginal flesh, a sensation impossible to resist . . .

Pridough awoke with a gasp. His body was wet with sweat, his breathing hard. In his hand he held his still erect cock, while his belly, pyjamas and sheets were wet and slimy with sperm. It had happened again, and as he kicked the soiled covers to one side a great wave of misery and guilt swept over him.

'We've got to do it,' Diana said. 'In the chapel, before it's sold. Just think how much some of the clients would pay to attend a genuine Black Mass.'

'A lot,' Lilith agreed. 'We'd have to run it like that guy Colin used to run his spanking parties back in Bristol. We could charge two hundred, maybe even three hundred, and guarantee a beating in the price, and maybe a blow job for the less submissive ones.'

'We'd have to hire other girls.'

'Only two or three.'

'I bet Juliana would go for it.'

'You watch out for that Juliana, slut. I know exactly what you're thinking.'

'So?' Diana pouted. 'Can't I have my playmates?'

'So long as I stay in charge, yes,' Lilith answered.

'And you're not sure you could with her, are you?' Diana responded.

'You are asking for trouble, Diana,' Lilith warned. 'Don't push your luck. After that bastard Hughes, I could really take it out on you.'

'Promises, promises.'

Lilith didn't answer, returning her full attention to the narrow lane and tall hedges revealed in the beams of their headlights. Diana was right. They had stayed in the Black Dog until closing time and, while she had held back on the drink, both Diana and Juliana had not. Their attraction to one another had become more obvious as glass followed glass and, despite her jealousy, she found it all too easy to understand. She herself was strong, something about which she had no false modesty. Brought up in care, sucking men off on the streets of Bristol at sixteen, a professional dominatrix at twenty, she had never once given in to the easy comfort of drugs, or allowed herself to be used by pimps. Diana had always appreciated that, enjoying her protection as much as her sexual dominance.

Juliana was stronger, carrying herself with a natural self-assurance that needed no enhancement. It was impossible to imagine her fleeing when the pressure mounted, as Lilith had done, from Bristol to Exeter. It was also impossible to imagine her giving in to Hughes, no matter how much money he put on the table. Juliana would have laughed in his face, and Lilith found herself wishing the other woman had been there. With the thought came a new understanding of how Diana felt.

The road widened, passing under the A30. Lilith slowed as they reached the lights at the outskirts of Exeter.

'So what are you going to do about Hughes?' Diana asked.

'I know what I'd like to do,' Lilith answered. 'I don't know. He's scary, but I can't trick a girl into it, not a real virgin. I just couldn't. I want to cheat him, too, and let him know, but I'm not sure I dare.'

'Don't. It's not safe. Cheat him, but let him think he's done it.'

'How do we cheat him? You know he actually wants to see the girl's hymen tear?'

'Ouch! What a pig!'

'I'm not sure it works like that, anyway. Wouldn't the cock push it in first? All I remember is a sharp pain, and Darren fucking Westcott saying he couldn't when I asked him to stop.'

'If he can't see, he can't see. What matters is that he feels it, and that she makes a big fuss, like I did. That's what he gets off on. So we get one of the girls down from Bristol and give her a fake hymen.'

'How?'

'There's a way. I read about it in some book on girls in London in Victorian times. It can't be that hard, with a bit of practice. I mean, how many blokes know what a girl's hymen looks like anyway? He's not a gynaecologist, is he?'

'I wouldn't think so. I'm not even sure what he expects is realistic. He seems to think there'll be loads of blood. There wasn't with me.'

'Nor me. It didn't even hurt much. I used to look, though: all I had was a little ring of flesh around my pussy hole. We could make one with some of that artificial skin stuff, I'm sure we could. There'll be pictures on the Net, any money.'

Three

Nich lay back on his bed, naked, and idly watching Juliana as she patted talc on to herself. They had returned from the moor in high spirits, such high spirits in fact that he had neglected the very necessary process of tying and gagging her before they made love. The result was deep scratches on his back, shoulders and chest, while he bore several bite marks as evidence of her wild ecstasy.

He winced as he moved on to his side. The sight of Juliana's naked body was making his cock stir, but he knew from experience that after one taste of blood she was unlikely to accept being put in bondage for some time. Fucking her would be a dangerous and painful operation. He watched, indecisive, as she quite casually lifted a leg on to a chair, displaying both pussy and anus without the slightest trace of self-consciousness. His cock began to swell further at the invitation implicit in the display of her sex. She dabbed her powder puff on to the underside of her pussy and between her bottom cheeks, pausing for a moment to tickle her bottom hole with one sharp talon. With a trace of regret Nich turned his mind back to the matter of the chapel and the Satanists.

'If they're going to do it properly they'll need a defrocked priest,' he remarked.

'Wouldn't it be better to steer them away from Satanism towards paganism?' Juliana queried.

'Yes,' Nich admitted, 'and in due course I will. First, I wish to give Pridough a little demonstration of action and reaction. Paganism is growing nicely, so nicely that it doesn't really attract enough attention. Look at the Lammas festival. Over two thousand people. Pridough draws about fifty on a good day.'

'So why bother?'

'For mischief,' Nich answered, grinning.

He rolled out of the bed, stretched and patted Juliana's bottom as she bent to pull on her knickers. Seating himself at his computer, he brought his database up on to the screen. The product of years of research, it listed every significant religious event in the UK he had been able to find out about. Juliana came to lean on his shoulder.

'Besides,' Nich went on. 'I don't want Pridough running his wretched little sect at that chapel. It's too close to Grim's Men. I suspect that if the altar is thoroughly desecrated he'll go elsewhere.'

'Maybe,' Juliana admitted. 'So you're going to dig out a defrocked priest.'

'I am,' Nich stated.

'Defrocked is one thing,' Juliana said doubtfully, 'defrocked and willing to officiate at a Black Mass is another. I don't suppose they're that common.'

'Common enough,' Nich responded. 'Remember, the priest only has to be Christian, the denomination is immaterial. There'll be embezzlers, lechers, all sorts. A lecher would be best, naturally, and probably easiest. You may have to seduce him, of course.'

'My pleasure,' Juliana answered, digging her nails into the flesh of his shoulder.

Nich tapped at the keyboard, trying to ignore the warm touch of Juliana's body. She had begun to knead his flesh, and her breasts were pressed to his back, making it hard to concentrate. He persevered, calling up the examples of priests dismissed from their offices and adding them to a new file. These he pruned a little, cutting out those obviously inappropriate, before ranking them in order of what he regarded as quality. One stood out.

'Reverend Andrew Wyatt,' Juliana said, reading from the top of the list, 'ex-rector of All Saints' Church, South

Harling, Wiltshire. Obscene act, query buggery, with a choirgirl . . . What do you mean "query buggery"?'

'They never actually say buggery,' Nich replied. 'Anal sex being considered too rude to mention as such by your average newspaper, but it's what is most often implied by the term "obscene act". It might just mean that he got her to suck his cock, but they normally manage to slip the word "oral" in. No, I reckon buggery, unless it was something really kinky, in which case all the better. Not only that, but he was only kicked out last May. He's way ahead of the competition.'

'Fair enough, but who's to say he isn't still a Christian at heart? They can be terribly cold, you know.'

'Not this one,' Nich answered. 'He actually did it on the altar. That's got to have been on purpose, and suggests Satanic leanings. Anyone who just wanted sex would have had the sense to take the girl somewhere quiet, where he wouldn't get caught.'

'True,' Juliana admitted. 'So how do we find him?'

Lilith watched as Diana put the gallery they had been creating on screen. Twenty pictures showed, each a close-up of a girl's vagina with the hymen still intact. Most had been downloaded from medical websites, others from sites offering advice on sexual matters. A few were intended as pornographic, designed to stimulate the lust of those obsessed with female virginity. It was hard to tell one sort from another, but each hymen was different. Some blocked almost the entire vagina, plugs of rich pink or scarlet tissue with no more than a small, taut hole situated towards the bottom. More showed a ring or crescent-shaped piece of flesh with an ample opening at the centre, while a few barely constricted the girl's passages at all.

'I reckon we can get away with it,' Diana stated. 'Twenty virgin pussies, and no two the same.'

'You're right,' Lilith agreed, nodding.

As Diana had stated, the sheer variety suggested that Hughes was highly unlikely to spot a deception, yet Lilith was sure she knew what he expected and had already decided which type of hymen to fake. Hughes, she remembered, had used a particularly ugly phrase. 'I've got to see that cherry burst,' he had said. He wanted blood, and it was plain that only the most ample, most fleshy hymen would serve his purposes. These did look something like cherries, with swollen masses of bright red flesh poking out from between the girl's inner labia. It was easy to imagine one bursting as a cock was forced past it and up the girl's vagina. Whether that was what actually happened when a real virgin with that type of hymen was first penetrated didn't matter. It was what Hughes expected that mattered. There had to be blood, and there would be, plenty of blood. All she needed to do was make a convincing fake. That was going to take practice.

Tom Pridough walked swiftly, his back straight, his expression one of superiority, of disapproval for all he saw around him. Inside, he burned, his outward calm a lie to the awful feelings of guilt and shame at his erotic nightmares and their result. It was not the first time, and the experience only ever stiffened his resolve to maintain the life of self-denial he felt was correct, and also to impose it on others.

It had been the same since adolescence, when his gawky frame and acne-pocked face had ensured him a place as the least attractive of the males in the tiny teenage social world of his home village. As with the boys, the appeal of the girls had varied, from some almost as sexually flagrant as the succubi of his dreams, to others emaciated or stocky, as lacking in appeal as he was himself. Yet the girls had been a tightly knit group, so tightly knit that it had been a social impossibility to be seen with any of those boys whom the most popular of the group considered unattractive. Pridough's reaction had been resentment and despair, from which he had turned to religion. Now, with the true cause of his misogyny and chastity pushed firmly to the back of his mind and replaced by self-righteous certainty, only the dreams remained.

His rapid pace took him quickly to the offices of Dawson and Unwin, which he entered, only to discover that the council had not yet responded to his offer. Ignoring the assistant's advice that it would be better to wait a week or so, he insisted that a phone call be made on the spot. Twenty minutes later, he left, having discovered that, while no decision could be made until the relevant committee had met at some indeterminate time in the future, his offer was almost certainly inadequate.

Lilith gave the aerosol of Fluid Skin a final squirt and sat back. In front of her, Diana lay on her back, spread out on the leather-topped table they used for medical fantasies, strapped into stirrups and with her hands cuffed above her head. The pose left her vagina spread wide, and it was puffy with arousal, the flesh moist and wet. The sexual response had made it hard to apply the fake skin, with Diana's vaginal skin needing repeated attention with cotton wool. Lilith had persevered, and her friend's vagina was now plugged by a not unconvincing hymen, the centre of which was a glossy red mass, much the size and shape of a cherry. In appearance it was, if anything, too perfect, and all that remained was to see that it burst convincingly.

'Now I get fucked?' Diana asked hopefully.

'You do,' Lilith answered. 'How does it feel?'

'Weird,' Diana answered. 'My whole pussy feels really odd, tense, and I can feel the blood bag. Go on, fuck me.'

'Patience,' Lilith teased, 'there's no rush. After all, you're not going anywhere.'

'Don't tease, please.'

Lilith just laughed, and walked across to the cupboard in which the smaller implements were kept. Diana watched, trembling slightly, to make her big breasts shiver, a sight too tempting to ignore. Lilith chose a pair of nipple clamps from their selection, twin, rubber-tipped crocodile clips joined by a chain. Taking them from their hook, she held them up to Diana, whose face was set into an expression of mixed resignation and desire. In response, Lilith's mouth twitched up into a cruel smile.

Diana closed her eyes as Lilith approached, her chest rising to meet what was to be done to her. Lilith moved

60

closer, taking one plump breast in hand and shaking it, to make the flesh quiver, jelly-like. Diana sighed, and Lilith took hold of the big, brown nipple, squeezing it, then pulling it up by the ring as she applied pressure to the clip. The jaws came wide, Lilith now grinning in sheer glee as she slid them around the bud of Diana's nipple and slowly released the pressure. Diana groaned, rolling her head to one side.

Still grinning, Lilith put the second clip to Diana's other breast, setting it firmly into place. Diana's breathing had quickened, and she was sticking her breasts up, eager for more sensation. For a moment Lilith watched, enjoying her girlfriend's response with an openly sadistic relish that owed as much to power as to sex.

An image of Hughes rose in her mind, unexpectedly, along with the memory of how he had treated her. For a moment there was guilt, and the suspicion that she was no better, only for the emotion to be thrust aside. Hughes had made her cry, Diana was squirming with pleasure.

She returned to the cupboard, her self-doubt gone as she reached in to choose a dildo. There were several. A single one was set aside for those few clients who could afford what she charged to bugger them, along with a large packet of condoms beside it. Two others, both large, one black, were intended purely for the humiliation of clients, who could be made to suck them, and otherwise parody homosexual acts. Of the others, most were reserved for fucking Diana, either privately or in front of clients, with one for the rare occasions when she wanted Diana to return the favour.

After a moment's hesitation, she chose the one most similar in size to Hughes's cock, the second smallest of Diana's range, the very smallest being intended for her anus. Satisfied with her choice, she stuck the dildo in Diana's mouth.

'Suck on that, slut,' she instructed, and began to strip.

Diana watched, sucking on the dildo, her eyes wide with anticipation. Lilith peeled off her jeans and panties, making sure Diana was given a good display of her body, before strapping on her harness. Retrieving the dildo, she pushed it into the holding ring, to leave it sticking out in front of her.

'Cunt time, slut,' she announced, stepping to between Diana's open thighs.

Despite her resentment of the fact, it was impossible to deny the sense of power that went with having a cock to use. Having Diana tied made it stronger still, while the sight of the bulging red mass in her friend's vagina added a new and cruel dimension. It might have been fake, but it was still evocative, of helplessness, of surrender, bringing her a still deeper understanding of Hughes's lust. Grinning, she put the bulbous head of the dildo to the mouth of Diana's vagina. Diana moaned, lifting her hips to the gentle pressure.

'Here goes,' Lilith announced. 'Let's see how your cherry pops.'

Lilith pushed, immediately feeling the resistance of the false hymen. Looking down, she saw the carefully constructed blood bag push in up Diana's hole. Diana gasped, gritting her teeth.

'Ow!' she squealed. 'That hurts! Lilith, it's pulling my skin!'

'Sorry,' Lilith answered, and pushed the dildo firmly up Diana's hole.

A taut, scarlet bulge appeared at the mouth of Diana's vagina, grew and burst. Diana screamed as the blood spattered over Lilith's belly and her own thighs, her teeth gritted in real pain, her back arched. Lilith began to fuck, watching the blood spurt from the now gaping hole as Diana subsided, whimpering on to the table.

'That hurt!' she gasped. 'That really hurt.'

'Shall I stop?' Lilith asked.

'No, darling. Fuck me. Fuck me well. Pretend it's real. I can feel it. I can feel it trickling out of my pussy, out of my cunt hole. Oh, Lilith!'

Lilith took hold of Diana's thighs, holding on tightly as she pushed the dildo in and out. Looking down, she could see the spattered blood on Diana's thighs and the tuck of her bottom, also her own flesh. She could feel it, too, wet and slippery around the dildo, making Diana's penetration even easier. Her own sex felt ready as well, both from the pleasure of what she was doing and the feel of the dildo base bumping against her. She was going to have to come as soon as she had finished with Diana.

Whipping out the blood-streaked dildo, Lilith spared a glance for Diana's gaping vagina, with the torn remnants of the hymen around the hole. In addition to the red-spattered skin of bottom and thighs, Diana's anus was caked with blood, mixed with the white pussy juice. Reaching out, Lilith caught hold of Diana's nipple clamps, tweaking one open, then the other, as Diana cried out at the sudden pain.

'That hurt!' Diana sighed. 'Ow, that hurt so much. Now talk to me, and make me come.'

'What do you want, slut?' Lilith demanded, putting the dildo head to Diana's clitoris. 'To hear how your cherry's been burst, to hear how you look, what?'

'Everything,' Diana gasped. 'What you've done to me, the state I'm in, that I'm helpless, that you could fuck me up my bottom . . .'

'You're a slut, Diana,' Lilith responded, 'You should see yourself. You're a mess, a real fucking mess. Your cherry's gone, and the blood's running down out of your gaping cunt. There's pussy juice, too, loads of it, running out, down between your fat cheeks, all over your arsehole. Maybe I should bugger you. You're greasy enough. I could fuck your dirty arsehole while I watched the mess dribble out of your sodden little cunt, you dirty, filthy, fucking little slut!'

Diana screamed, her mouth, her whole body tensing, her arms and legs tight against her bonds, her vagina closing with a loud fart. Lilith kept on, rubbing on Diana's clitoris until the jerks and shudders of orgasm at last died down, to leave Diana inert on the table.

Lilith wasted no time, in desperate need of her own climax. She pulled the harness free with trembling fingers, mounted the table and stuck her bare bottom firmly in

Diana's face, pussy to mouth. Diana began to lick, Lilith rubbing, using Diana's nose to get friction to her pussy hole and anus. It felt glorious, squirming her naked bottom in the face of a girl she'd just fucked; tied, humiliated, tortured and fucked. Wrenching her top up, she freed her breasts, squeezing them as she felt her orgasm start, squirming harder, to smear pussy juice over Diana's face. She came, with Diana's nose in the mouth of her pussy, her anus rubbing on the girl's forehead, in a long moment of pure ecstasy focused on her rude delight in her friend's submission.

Diana sat down, wincing slightly as she settled.

'Sore?' Lilith asked.

'Sore,' Diana agreed. 'Imagine waxing the inside of your pussy. That's what it's like.'

'Ouch!'

'Ouch is the word.'

'I'll kiss you better, later.'

'A lot later. What do you reckon, anyway?'

'It looked good, too messy if anything, but I think that's what Hughes expects. Your reaction was good, too.'

'No problem there. That was all real.'

'So the actual fucking is fine. The problem is going to be afterwards. The blood is too fluid and doesn't dry like real blood. It doesn't look right afterwards, either.'

'You reckon Hughes would notice?'

'Maybe. It's the way the false skin pulls off that's the problem. I reckon we'll have to do it as a ritual. That way it's dark, and we can probably get him pissed, too. If we work it out right he needn't see the aftermath. Risky, but five thou is five thou.'

'What we do is make it a full-scale Black Mass, with the girl getting deflowered as the climax. Hughes has got an ego like nothing else, so I reckon he'll go for it.'

'Probably, yes.'

'Sure he will. He was telling me last time how he likes to fuck girls in front of other men who're not going to get it. That's the way to do it, make him feel superior. Then, once he's done it, all we have to do is distract him and get her away quickly. She can make a lot of fuss, pretending she's in real pain.'

'He'll love that.'

'It's got to work.'

Lilith blew her breath out. The plan sounded feasible, but it was impossible to rid herself of the underlying sense of danger. She wasn't sure what Hughes might do if he discovered that he'd been cheated, but she was absolutely convinced that his threats had been genuine. Yet the money being offered was simply too much to be ignored.

'I've been thinking,' Diana went on, 'about who should do it. The girls aren't right. They just look too knowing. There's always a risk he might know them, too. We need someone fresher, someone who might actually be a virgin.'

'Easier said than done.'

'I don't know. What about Becky at Craft Candles? She was really flirting, and I'm sure she was outside the door while you were fucking me in the loos.'

'I don't know. There's a big gap between flirting and getting fucked by a bastard likes Hughes. Anyway, I wouldn't feel right about it.'

'She's a big girl. She can always refuse.'

'I don't know . . .'

'Get real, Karen! I mean, Lilith. You let him fuck me, and it turned you on, so no bullshit. At least we can see if she's up for it.'

'Oh yes? You just want to get her out of her panties, don't you?'

'Sure I do,' Diana admitted. 'And you don't?'

'She's cute, yeah.'

'You'd like to do us side by side, wouldn't you? Bent over with our hands tied up behind our backs.'

'Don't start, Diana, or your pussy's going to be even sorer.'

'OK. But, seriously, if both of us try it might freak her out. I think I should try to chat her up, to see how it goes. You can join in later.'

'You are in serious trouble, Diana. Go on, then, and I'll leave the flat clear for you, but stock up on cold cream.'

* * *

'*Crockford's Directory of Clergymen*,' Nick stated, throwing a heavy book down on the table. 'I was meaning to get a new one, anyway.'

Juliana nodded absently in response before returning to work on her wedges. They were near completion, smooth and glossy with varnish. The thought of using them sent a pleasant shiver of anticipation up the length of her spine. She glanced at Nich, thinking of the purposeful, precise manner in which he handled her, perhaps less cruel than he might have been, but totally lacking in the inhibitions that could so easily spoil her enjoyment. He was looking at the book, one black-painted fingernail to his mouth, his olive-green eyes set in concentration.

'Here we are,' he said. 'Wyatt, Andrew. Born nineteen forty-nine, Portsmouth. Educated . . . blah, blah, blah . . . theology at Keble College, curacy in south London, another curacy, living of South Harling nineteen seventy-seven . . . blah, blah, blah . . . hobbies include angling, not much use, and numismatism, better. Defrocked for buggering choirgirls. Not that it actually says that, but the implication is there.'

'My bet is that he'll be in Portsmouth,' Juliana stated. 'Broken men tend to return to their origins.'

'Who's to say he's broken?' Nich questioned. 'You may be right, I suppose, but Portsmouth is a big place. We'd be better off visiting South Harling first, and seeing what we can pick up at the rectory.'

'They won't tell you anything,' Juliana stated. 'They probably won't even know.'

'Have you anything better to do?' Nich replied.

Diana stood in the car park of Craft Candles, wondering how she should approach Becky. It was over an hour until the shop closed, and there was the normal straggle of tourists pushing in and out of the glass doors. Becky was visible through them, smiling as she accepted a customer's money. Diana admired what she could see, the sweet, open face, the brown curls, the full expanse of her chest. There was no question that Becky had a quality of fresh beauty

– innocence, even. It was hard to conceive of a girl so vivacious being a virgin, yet Hughes was older, and arrogant. Then there would be the hymen for supposed proof.

Thinking of how openly Becky had flirted, she decided on a straightforward, honest approach, in the hope that Becky could handle it and on the grounds that, if she couldn't, then the whole project was probably a nonstarter, anyway. She felt a trace of guilt as she made for the doors, but it died quickly. She had let Hughes have her, and she felt fine, the way Hughes had been tricked compensating for his behaviour. Besides that, Becky would know what was going on, and be well paid, assuming she went for it.

Becky looked up as Diana came in, smiling warmly. Diana smiled back, walking to the counter without hesitation. Two minutes later Becky had accepted Diana's offer of a coffee after work, showing a nervous excitement that suggested the expectation of more than just talk.

Diana spent the next hour browsing in the shop, until at last the staff began to usher the customers towards the exits. By then she had bought a set of spiral candles, two packets of cinnamon-and-orange incense sticks, and the prospect of seducing Becky had become more desirable than ever. Judging that if Becky had heard what had happened in the shop lavatory it was pointless to dissemble, she decided on a bold approach.

As Becky emerged from the staff door, Diana waved, and greeted her with a kiss and a pat on the seat of her well-fleshed bottom. Becky reacted with a smile and Diana decided to jump right in.

'You were listening to my girlfriend and me playing in the loo yesterday, weren't you?' Diana teased.

'No . . . well, yes,' Becky managed, blushing. 'I'm sorry, I –'

'Don't be,' Diana cut in. 'It was good. It made it special.'

'It did?'

'Sure. Do you want you know what we were doing?'

Becky nodded, swallowing. She was blushing furiously, but made no attempt to pull away as Diana took her arm, just increasing her pace and glancing back towards the shop.

'Well,' Diana said, 'first Lilith, that's my girlfriend, made me kneel up on the loo and stick my bum out. I had no knickers on under my dress. You noticed that, didn't you?'

'Yes,' Becky admitted, blushing more furiously than ever. Diana laughed, and continued.

'So Lilith pulled up my dress and I was all bare underneath. She was talking dirty to me as well, saying you and me had been flirting, and that you ought to be dragged in so we could be fucked side by side.'

'With . . . with your candles?'

'Yes.'

'Oh my god. That's so rude! I thought you'd gone for a kiss and cuddle, but . . . Oh my!'

'It was great,' Diana went on, 'and when you came in she put the candle up my pussy, and fucked me, and made me frig off. It was a great orgasm. Did you hear me call out your name when I came?'

'My name?'

'Sure, silly. I was fantasising over you.'

Becky said nothing. Her face and neck were flushed dark with blood, her lower lip was trembling, but she made no move to pull away.

'Wouldn't you like to have joined in?' Diana asked.

Becky nodded, and swallowed. Diana took a handful of bottom and squeezed, feeling the plump, soft meat in Becky's jeans.

'Not here!' Becky hissed. 'Someone might see.'

'Not here, is it?' Diana giggled. 'Where, then? Where can I feel your gorgeous bottom up, and snog you, and kiss your lovely boobs, and lick you to heaven . . .?'

'Diana! Don't. That's, that's too –'

'Rude? It's not as rude as what I was thinking of doing to you while Lilith was fucking me in the loo.'

'You do that, really? I've never –'

'Never had a girl, or never ever?'

'Never had a girl. Boys, sure, and well, you know . . .'

'Tell me!'

'You know, messed about with friends, for our boyfriends.'

'You have? More, I want more!'

'That's it, just touching and stuff.'

'I want the dirty details. Tell me! Everything!'

'I . . . my boyfriend, my ex now, he had this mate, and they used to make me and the mate's girlfriend . . . well, you know . . .'

'No I don't, but I want to.'

Becky hesitated, glancing back along the road.

'Nobody will hear,' Diana assured her.

'You're really dirty,' Becky replied.

'I know,' Diana answered. 'Now come on, tell me, or I'll smack your bottom for you, right over the bonnet of this car.'

Becky giggled, and Diana realised that she'd struck a nerve. With a jolt of pure mischief she planted a firm smack on Becky's bottom, glancing back as she did it. There was a group of people behind them, well out of earshot, but not out of sight. Becky squeaked, putting her hand to her smacked cheek.

'Tell!' Diana demanded.

'OK, I'll tell,' Becky answered. 'We were drunk, and it was just because the boys made us . . .'

'Yeah, sure.'

'It was! Well, at first. Anyway, they made us do striptease, not all the way, down to our panties, and touch each other up. I . . . I kissed her tits.'

'Nice. Do you know what I'd have done?'

'No?'

'I'd have taken the girl into another room, locked the door and had her while the boys listened outside.'

Becky giggled. They had reached a café, and Diana went inside, fighting down the urge to suggest going straight back to her flat for sex. Becky was less experienced than she had imagined, which made the prospect of seducing her all the more appealing.

* * *

For hours Tom Pridough had walked the streets of Exeter. Since leaving the estate agent's, his desire to buy the ruined chapel had expanded to become an obsession. To make it reality he needed eight thousand pounds, and after that the funds to restore it. It was a sum well beyond his reach, the thirty-two thousand he had offered representing all that he could scrape together. The idea of borrowing was abhorrent to him, yet again and again he returned to it as the only feasible option, with his congregation too fragile to be relied on for more than tiny sums.

As he turned the problem over in his mind, he repeatedly assured himself that it was a test of his faith, and that in the long term he would, by virtue of that very faith, succeed. A nagging voice in the back of his head kept telling him that this was nonsensical, yet he ignored it, pushing it back into the same recess as his erotic dreams.

His steps took him in a wide circle, so that at length he passed the window of Dawson and Unwin. He walked quickly past, only to stop fifty yards further on in sudden embarrassment. Two young girls were walking ahead of him, one of them oddly familiar. They were close, touching as often as not, and laughing, with a carefree manner that filled him first with envy, then disapproval.

He walked on, slowly, telling himself that it was because passing them on the narrow pavement would be distasteful, and that it had nothing to do with the shape of their bodies beneath their clothes, especially not their bottoms. One, the smaller, was bad enough, in a short black dress that clung to her ample curves and looked as if it would rise at the slightest puff of wind. If it did, or if she bent, he was sure that he would see not panties, which would have been bad enough, but a bare bottom. The other, taller, girl was worse, less indecent, but with a figure that might well have belonged to one of the succubi of his nocturnal struggles. Just the movement of her ample bottom within the tight confines of her black jeans was enough to set his heart fluttering and stiffen his cock. Finally he could stand it no more, and turned down a side road, angry at the girls, the estate agents, the council, but, most of all, with himself.

Becky could feel herself shaking. She was struggling to be cool, to allow her arousal to overcome her insecurity and guilt. Not that it was difficult, when all she had to do was let Diana have her way. Already Becky's top had been pulled up, and Diana was nuzzling at the big, white cups of her bra, nipping at the erect nipples beneath the material.

From the moment Diana had collected her from work all she had needed to do was stop herself from resisting. Diana had done the rest, making no secret of what she intended, until now, back at the girl's flat, she found herself being handled with as much confidence and fervour as any boy had ever shown.

No sooner had they entered the flat than she had been led to the sofa, sat firmly down, folded into Diana's arms and kissed. Her mouth had come open under the pressure of Diana's lips, and their tongues had met before she really knew what she was doing. Diana had then climbed on top and begun to feel Becky's breasts, before pulling up the top.

'Your boobs are lovely,' Diana sighed. 'Come on, out they come.'

Immediately Becky's cups were lifted and her breasts flopped out, into Diana's hands. They began to kiss again, as Diana's fingers explored the full globes of Becky's chest, stroking the nipples.

'Gorgeous,' Diana went on, breaking away. 'I bet they're even bigger than mine!'

As she spoke she pulled the front of her dress wide open, exposing big breasts in a lacy black bra. She was smiling, her eyes bright as she took hold of the undersides and flipped the cups high, letting her breasts loll out. Becky swallowed, wondering if she'd be expected to suck them, only to have the question answered for her as Diana swayed forward. Becky's face was smothered in warm breast flesh. Diana wiggled, to make the fat balls of girl flesh slap Becky's cheeks, then cupped one, offering the nipple.

71

'Suck me, go on,' she urged. 'Come on, right in your mouth.'

Becky obeyed, taking in the large, dark nipple. She was trembling as she began to suck, desperately aroused, yet still wondering what she was doing having sex with another woman, and with no watching men to make the act acceptable.

'Put your hands up my dress. Pull down my panties,' Diana urged.

For a moment Becky hesitated, before her hands went around Diana's thighs, and up, lifting the light dress, to find the full swell of a big, undoubtedly feminine bottom. She took hold of the cheeks, squeezing them through the thin cotton panties, thinking how like her own bottom they felt, and how unlike a man's.

'Pull them down!' Diana urged.

Becky responded, clutching at the seat of Diana's panties to tug them off the chubby bottom cheeks and down. Diana sighed, pressing her breasts yet more firmly into Becky's face and wiggling her out-thrust bottom. Becky put her hands to Diana's bare flesh, feeling the full, smooth cheeks, her fingers brushing the deep cleft. She began to feel her inhibitions fading beneath her arousal and Diana's open, playful attitude.

'Lovely, oh yes, squeeze them,' Diana sighed. 'That's nice. Now smack it, spank me.'

Diana cuddled in, sticking her bottom further up and wiggling it in Becky's hands. Becky patted one big cheek, gently, then more firmly as Diana responded with a sigh. Thinking of Diana's threat to give her a public spanking, Becky began to smack harder.

'Lovely,' Diana breathed, 'come on, harder. Come on, Becky darling, put me over your knee and do it properly. Spank me, spank me like the dirty little tart I am.'

Without waiting for a response, Diana moved, turning to lay her body across Becky's lap and stick up her bottom. Becky responded gingerly, lifting the back of Diana's dress to exposed the fat olive-skinned globe beneath. Diana's panties were well down, showing everything, while her

72

bottom was lifted and open, showing a hint of fur between the lush cheeks. Becky began to smack, still unsure of herself, but unable to do anything other than respond to Diana's open lust.

As she was spanked, Diana's bottom came higher, the cheeks parting to show off her crease, the dark dimple of her anus and the pouted rear of her pussy. Becky continued to smack, increasingly firmly, delighting in doing what she had so often imagined being done to her, and yet had always feared to ask for. Only once had it been done, and that on her jeans, an older cousin giving her a half-dozen swats with a rolled-up newspaper. Becky had been misbehaving, and she had never been sure that it was even sexual. With Diana there was no doubt at all. She smacked harder, wondering if she could cajole Diana into taking her revenge.

'That's right, punish me,' Diana moaned. 'Really smack it, Becky, darling. Don't I look rude, Becky, don't I, with my boobies hanging out and my bum all bare?'

'Very rude,' Becky admitted.

'Tell me, call me nasty names,' Diana demanded. 'Tell me how naughty I am. What a bad girl I am.'

'You are bad,' Becky said, 'very bad. Bad girls need to be spanked, don't they? And I'm bad too, aren't I?'

'Yes,' Diana answered. 'I'm being selfish, aren't I? Come on, darling, time we had those jeans down. Your knickers, too.'

As she spoke she rolled off Becky's lap, to kneel on the floor. Her arms came out, welcoming Becky, who responded. They hugged as Becky sank to the floor, kneeling together, kissing, their bare breasts touching. The embrace lasted only seconds, before Diana's hands went down to the button of Becky's jeans. Becky was unresisting, allowing the button to be popped, her zip drawn down. They kissed again, as Diana's thumbs went into the waistband of Becky's jeans, pushing, catching her panties, and taking the whole lot down, to expose both bottom and pussy.

Becky shut her eyes, surrendering herself to what she had wanted so badly, for so long. She felt Diana's hands move to her bottom, cupping her cheeks, pulling them wide, so that the cool air touched her anus. She gave an involuntary groan, hugging Diana closer as sharp nails raked the skin of her bottom. Her panties were down, her bottom bare, at the mercy of another girl, a situation she had imagined so often, without ever daring to make it reality. Now it was. And, as Diana began to smack, she simply melted, giving in utterly, with her bottom stuck out to the slaps.

'Who wants her bottom spanked, then?' Diana teased.

'Me, I do,' Becky answered.

'Naughty, rude girl,' Diana whispered. 'Do you like dirty words, Becky? Do you like to be told how bad you are, and what you're showing?'

'Try me,' Becky answered.

'I do,' Diana answered. 'It's my favourite thing. I'll talk about us both, then, and you can play with your pussy while I spank you, yeah?'

Becky nodded. She was lost in a haze of pleasure, the spanking too soft to hurt, and providing more of a sense of comfort than of punishment. She slid her hand down between their bodies, to find the plump swell of her sex. She was wet, her sex lips coming apart to the pressure of her fingers. Diana gave a harder smack and Becky started to masturbate.

'I can feel you rubbing, you dirty bitch,' Diana breathed. 'You've got to come like this, darling, with your bottom smacked and your fingers on your pussy.'

Becky sighed, hugging Diana. The slaps were getting firmer, starting to sting, and she could feel her bottom quivering to them. Again she thought of what she was doing, how rude it was to be masturbating while another girl cuddled her, and how soothing, how right it felt that she was being spanked as it happened.

'Imagine how we look, Becky, darling,' Diana whispered, 'with our boobies out and our bums all bare. My bum's stuck out too, bare, bare because my panties are down, because you pulled them down, just like I pulled yours down, to get at me, to spank me. Oh, you do have a lovely bum, Becky. I've got to finger you, come on, cuddle close.'

Becky obeyed, shocked by the sudden urgency in Diana's voice but too far gone to protest. They came together, thighs apart, Diana's hand slipping down to cup Becky's bottom. They began to kiss again, as Becky felt the sharp nails of Diana's fingers between her cheeks, touching not her pussy, as she had expected, but her anus. Her muffled squeak of shock was cut off by the insertion of Diana's tongue into her mouth, and a moment later her bottom had been penetrated, the little damp ring forced open around the tip of a finger. Other fingers found her pussy, two of them, all three pushing up as Diana returned to slapping at Becky's bottom.

Now feeling thoroughly dirty, Becky let it happen. Her head was swimming with guilt at the thought of a finger being put up her bottom, but it felt nice, far too nice to stop. Hiding her confusion in passion, she responded to Diana's kisses, masturbating herself as her spare hand went lower, to find a plump cheek and deliver a firm swat. Diana responded by cocking her leg over Becky's to press her sex to the denim.

As Diana began to rub, Becky felt the first twinges of her orgasm. Her muscles began to pulse, closing on Diana's fingers, which pushed deeper in response. The smacks got harder, the lewd rubbing motion on her leg firmer. They cuddled tight, smacking and stroking, rubbing their breasts together, everything forgotten but their mutual pleasure. Becky's climax rose up like a bubble in her head, growing, expanding. The last vestige of her restraint snapped and she began to thrust her bottom out on to the intruding fingers, eager to get them deeper in both vagina and anal passage.

Diana broke the kiss, pulling herself tight into Becky as she began to babble out lewd words, and all the while smacking and fingering and rubbing herself with frantic energy.

'That's right, you dirty bitch, smack me, hurt me. I'm so sore, that really hurts. I hope it hurts you, too, you bitch, with my fingers up your hot, fat cunt, up your dirty arsehole. Oh, you're so slimy and wet, and dirty and hot, and I'm going to suck my fingers and taste your cunt and taste your bumhole, and kiss you and make you taste it too, and –'

Her words ended in a scream, her whole body going tense in Becky's arms. Becky was coming too, writhing on the fingers in her body, soaking up Diana's torrent of dirty words and thinking how utterly lewd she was being as the orgasm lasted and lasted. It was stronger than anything she had experienced before, either with boys or under her own fingers, frantic and dirty, completely abandoned. As she finally began to go limp in the arms of the girl she had allowed to seduce her so easily, she was thanking herself over and over for giving in.

Diana pushed the dungeon door open. Becky's mouth went wide as she saw the interior, her eyes flicking over the bondage furniture, the whips and tawses hanging from the wall, the stand of canes, and all the other tools of Lilith's work.

After sex they had washed and she had changed, chatting happily all the while and wondering how best to take Becky to the next stage of her seduction. As before, she had decided that it was best to be bold.

'Wow,' Becky managed, reaching out to touch the leather top of the whipping stool. 'You do get up to some heavy stuff!'

'We don't use it much ourselves,' Diana admitted. 'Lilith likes to do me in more ordinary surroundings. This is really for clients.'

'Clients?'

'Men, Becky. Lilith and I do professional domination.'

'You mean you're . . .'

'Prostitutes?'

'I wasn't going to say that. Sorry.'

Becky went quiet, pretending an interest in the bondage stool. Diana waited for a reaction, until Becky finally spoke again.

'Don't you . . . you know, feel bad about it?'

'Feel bad? No way. Why should I?'

'Well, you know . . .'

'For being a prostitute?'

'Sorry, Diana, I didn't mean –'

'Relax. Let me explain. Lilith and I were in a home together, in Bristol. It was horrible, and I don't want to go into that. Let's just say that the best we could have hoped for when we left was a job in a shop or a factory, on peanuts wages, and with some git telling us what to do. That's what we were groomed for. It's all they thought we were good for. The alternative was ending up on the streets, and on drugs.

'Lilith wouldn't let it happen. We did some pretty sordid stuff, at first, but she never lost control. She found that a lot of the men wanted to be abused by her, what with her looking so tough and everything. That got her into domination, which was two or three times the money for less work and no risk. There was too much hassle in Bristol, so we moved here and set this up. Lilith acts as the mistress and I'm her maid. Now we don't have to answer to anybody, and there's money in the bank.'

'Isn't it risky?'

'Not really. We only take on submissive men, well, almost only. They're really polite, a bit pathetic even. We don't fuck either, or suck, not normally. Mostly it's just whipping.'

'Oh, right.'

Becky went quiet, walking into the room, to touch the equipment with a look on her face that bordered on awe. Diana waited patiently, for acceptance or rejection, hoping that it would be the former.

'Lilith and you are lovers?' Becky asked suddenly.

'Yes,' Diana admitted.

'Won't she be jealous? I mean, if she finds out what we did?'

'Jealous? Lilith? No way! Sure, she'll want to join in.'

'Join in?'

'Yeah, of course. You don't mind, do you?'

'Mind? I . . . I don't know, Diana. Three girls together, and you're so casual about it! You blow my mind!'

'It's great. What's the problem?'

'I don't know. Nothing, really. It's . . . I always wanted . . . to be like you, to be able to just have fun and not get all the crappy fallout. Like the time I was telling you about, with my boyfriend and the other couple. We split up, right, and the next thing I know he's telling everyone that I'm a slut!'

'I know. Men. I used to get the same. The only difference is that I am a slut, and proud of it. That way they can't get to you.'

'I wish I could be that confident.'

'All you need to do is go with your feelings. You like being spanked, don't you?'

Becky nodded. She had gone to the display of punishment implements, and was touching them with trembling fingers.

'Then enjoy it,' Diana said.

'Easy for you to say,' Becky answered. 'I get embarrassed asking, and it freaks some men out. I'd like to be led into it, or just punished.'

'I understand,' Diana went on. 'It's not always easy.'

'You did it just right,' Becky said as she reached for a heavy leather strap, 'the way you never really gave me a chance to back out, but never really pushed, either.'

'Thank you,' Diana said. 'It's called a tawse. They used to be used in Scottish schools, for real.'

'Ouch!' Becky answered.

'It's nice,' Diana assured her. 'Once your bum's warm, anyway. Try it.'

'I'm not sure . . .' Becky began, and stopped, biting her lip. With a sudden, slightly embarrassed motion, she unhooked the tawse and threw it to Diana.

'Good girl,' Diana said. 'Now stick that lovely bum out.'

Becky put her hands on her knees, sticking her bottom out to make a plump ball in the black denim of her jeans. Diana stepped close, hefting the tawse, to bring it down gently across Becky's bottom.

'Harder?' she asked. Becky nodded.

Again Diana brought the tawse down, this time with a firm smack to make Becky's bottom quiver. Becky gave a little squeak, but kept her bottom out.

'It's better on the bare,' Diana said. 'Pop them down.'

'You're going to have me, aren't you?' Becky said softly as she pulled open the button of her jeans.

Diana said nothing, but watched as Becky pushed down her jeans and panties with trembling fingers, exposing the meaty cheeks of her bottom. Bare-bottomed, Becky looked back again, her large brown eyes now wide and showing expectation and a trace of fear. Diana put a hand out, to give Becky's big, naked bottom a reassuring pat.

'You're lovely, Becky,' Diana said. 'Yes, I could have you again. Maybe I will, but what I'd really like is to be done *with* you, together.'

'Together?'

'Yes, by Lilith. She'll be back soon.'

'I don't know, Diana. I'm not sure I'm ready.'

'Oh, you will be, darling, because by then your lovely cheeky bottom is going to be all warm and glowing. Now keep it pushed out, there's a good girl. Lean on this table if you like.'

Becky moved, leaning her forearms on the surface of the medical table before sticking her bottom out again. Her back was dipped in to make the best of her cheeks, enhancing their size and rounded shape, also making them part to show a hint of her pussy. It was a target far too good to resist, and Diana smacked the tawse down on it, full across both cheeks. Becky squeaked and jumped as her bottom quivered to the smack, but held her position.

'You know how to pose, don't you?' Diana said.

'Another boyfriend,' Becky answered. 'He was really into jeans. He liked me to bend over like this, and slide my jeans and panties down over my bum, again and again, while he wanked.'

'I don't blame him,' Diana answered, and smacked the tawse down again. 'Do you know what you're leaning on?'

Becky shook her head, looking up, only to jerk as the tawse hit her again.

'It's a medical table,' Diana explained, continuing to beat Becky gently. 'There are stirrups to go with it, and straps at the top. Lilith puts me on it when I'm really bad, or in a really dirty mood. Once I'm in the straps I can't do anything, nothing at all, only take what I'm given. Sometimes she gags me, so that I can't even cry out, or adjusts the stirrups to roll my legs right up high, so that she can smack me, and fuck me, and stick things up my bottom.'

Becky listened, her body quivering to each smack of the tawse. Her cheeks were reddening, the skin flushed, with darker areas where the tip of the tawse's triple tail had caught her. Her squeaks were getting louder, and more pained, while her breathing had slowly become more laboured. Yet she held her position, rocking slightly to the smacks, but always keeping her bottom well pushed out.

'You do look good,' Diana went on. 'I'm going to kiss you better when I'm done with you, right on your bum, and maybe rub some cream in. Or maybe I'll make you lick my pussy, kneeling, with your bare bum stuck out behind, all red and rosy. I bet you'd like that, wouldn't you?'

Becky nodded, then cried out as her body jerked to a harder smack. Diana laughed, grinning to herself at Becky's response. Twice more she swung the tawse in, watching Becky's bottom flesh jump and quiver to the blows. She could smell Becky's sex, and her own felt urgent, while, for all the role she was taking, her bottom was badly in need of smacking.

'Right, my girl, time you had your boobies out,' she declared. 'Come on.'

She moved forward, sliding her hands under Becky's chest to hold the heavy, dangling breasts. Becky's nipples were hard, pushing out the material of her bra and top. Diana paused to stroke them, moving her fingers as she did it, to inch Becky's top up. Becky's breasts were soon hanging in her bra, tempting Diana to make them swing and feel their weight in her hands. Becky was trembling, completely surrendered, and gave no resistance to the casual fondling of her body, even when Diana caught up

80

the bra cups and flopped out the big breasts, bare, into her hands.

'Gorgeous,' Diana declared. 'Oh, I could just drown in these, right in my face.'

She ducked down, under Becky, to smother her face in plump breast flesh, then to take a nipple in her mouth, sucking at it. Becky responded with a low moan, as Diana pulled up her dress, to her neck, and freed her own breasts. She played with them as she suckled Becky, until her nipples were stiff and urgent, while the desire to be dealt with was becoming unbearable.

'Wait,' she ordered, rising.

Becky looked round, watching as Diana peeled the dress off and hung it over the whipping stool, the bra following. In just panties and shoes she went into the main room, quickly tapping out a text message on her mobile. Returning to the dungeon, she found Becky as she had left her, big red bum stuck high, boobs swinging gently beneath her chest.

'Hands behind your back,' Diana ordered, and smacked Becky's bottom.

'What are you going to do?' Becky asked. 'Tie me?'

'Never you mind,' Diana answered. 'Just do as you're told.'

Becky made a face, but crossed her wrists behind her back. Diana took a pair of cuffs from the rack, quickly fastening one to each of Becky's wrists and linking them with their clips.

'Now come with me,' she said, taking Becky by the strap of her bra.

Diana returned to the main room, Becky following with an awkward hobble, her jeans and panties falling lower as she went. Diana giggled at the sight, positioning Becky by the sofa and pushing her down, into a kneeling position. The pose left Becky even more exposed, her big bottom wide, to show off the brown dimple of her anus and the chubby lips of her pussy. The sight made her want to lick, to make the spanked girl come, but she resisted, instead climbing on to the sofa beside Becky, in the same rude pose. Reaching back, she pushed her own panties well down.

'What are you doing?' Becky asked. 'I thought you were punishing me.'

'Oh, you'll get your punishment, don't worry,' Diana answered. 'Just keep your bum up and think dirty thoughts. You look great from behind, you know, so rude, with that fat pussy and your sweet little lips. Even your bumhole is pretty, ever so neat and tight. I'd like to lick it.'

'Diana! That's dirty.'

'I know. I loved the way you squeaked when I put my finger in. You're virgin, aren't you?'

'No, I said –'

'I mean up your bum.'

'Of course I am!'

'I'm not. A boy I met when I was still in the home had me. He got me drunk, and put butter up my bum, then stuck his cock in. They love it, men, up girls' bums, the dirty bastards. They love it because our bumholes are nice and tight, but mostly they love it because it's dirty, and they love to be dirty with us, to fuck us up our bottoms, and make us suck their dirty cocks, and spunk in our faces.'

'Diana! I thought, you . . . you preferred girls. I thought you were a lesbian.'

'I'm a slut, Becky, and so are you, at heart. Feel the heat in your smacked bum. Think how it would feel to be spanked, then fucked up your bottom by the man who'd punished you. Oh, sod Lilith! I can't wait for her. Let's frig each other off while we talk dirty, like this, and imagine we've been beaten and we're going to be buggered.'

'Lilith's coming? How long?'

'Just do it, Becky. I'll finger your bumhole again, while you rub off. Then you can get the tawse, and beat me, and shove a dildo up my bum, and bugger me while I come.'

'Diana, I don't!'

'Sorry, Becky, I'm sorry, I'm just so horny. Just beat me, then, for being such a dirty slut.'

Becky made to reply, but stopped at the sound of a key being turned in the lock. She tried to rise, but Diana grabbed her, only to roll sideways in a tangle of bare limbs and disarranged clothing as Lilith stepped into the room.

'Don't waste time, do you?' Lilith stated coolly as Becky struggled ineffectually to cover herself.

'I was rather hoping you'd spank us both,' Diana said sweetly.

'What has she done to you?' Lilith asked Becky, ignoring Diana completely. 'The tawse, right?'

'Look, I'm sorry,' Becky managed.

'Don't be,' Lilith said.

'I told you,' Diana cut in. 'She's cool. The worst she'll do is make a proper job of spanking our bums.'

'Is that what you want?' Lilith asked.

'I . . . I really don't know,' Becky stammered. 'I'm not sure I can handle this.'

'I'll go, if you like,' Lilith offered. 'I'd rather play with you. You've got to be warm at least.'

'Do it, Becky,' Diana urged. 'Come on, bums up, let's get our spankings.'

Becky hesitated. Her cheeks were red, her embarrassment and uncertainty obvious. She bit her lip, and for a moment Diana thought it had gone too far, only for Becky to roll around, back into her kneeling position, with her bare bum raised to Lilith.

'Do it, then,' she panted. 'Just do it.'

Lilith responded with a heavy swat to the offered cheeks, even as Diana also scrambled back into the rude position. Becky was shaking, and had her face buried in a cushion, red with shame, yet she kept her bottom up. Lilith came close, standing right behind them, and began to spank, one bottom, then the other, slapping at the quivering cheeks with her fingertips.

Diana closed her eyes, revelling in the sensation of being spanked, of her exposure, with every intimate detail on show to her mistress, of the feel of Becky's flesh next to hers and the knowledge of the girl's excitement and shame. The smacks tingled and stung, bringing her arousal slowly up, until once more thoughts of the dirty possibilities offered by the situation had begun to run through her mind.

'Harder, darling,' she sighed. 'Get the tawse. Beat me.'

'Shut up, slut,' Lilith answered.

'Please,' Diana whined, 'pretty please. Or take me in the bathroom and let Becky watch while you –'

'Shut up!' Lilith repeated. 'Right.'

The spanking stopped. Diana looked back as Lilith's hands took a firm grip on her panties. They were tugged down, and off. Her mouth was already open, and Becky watched, wide-eyed, as the tiny scrap of cotton was packed in.

'She usually needs gagging,' Lilith remarked. 'Do you need gagging, Becky?'

'Don't speak,' Becky sighed. 'Just do me.'

Lilith chuckled, Diana turning to watch as Becky was rapidly divested of her lower garments, pulled off to leave her bare from her breasts to her feet. She opened up obligingly, and the panties were stuffed in her mouth, leaving them looking at each other with their faces flushed and bits of panty cotton hanging out from between their lips.

The spanking started again, slow and rhythmic, with the slapping noise ringing out around the room as Lilith beat them. Diana stayed down, letting her arousal build up and fighting down the urge for more, harder sex. She watched Becky, who had buried her face in the sofa again, admiring the way the girl's big breasts swung and jumped to the rhythm of the slaps, and how well she took it. The spanking stopped, eventually, with a finger slid into the wet cavity of Diana's vagina. There was a damp, smacking noise as Becky was given the same treatment.

'Soaking, as I suspected,' Lilith stated. 'Becky's as bad. Right, time I used something a bit more effective, and I don't see why you should have your hands free, Diana, when Becky's tied. In fact, I don't see why you should be free at all.'

Lilith chuckled and walked quickly to the dungeon. Diana braced herself, wondering if she was going to be caned, or even beaten with a whip, scared, as always, despite the anticipation, but determined to be brave in front of Becky. Lilith quickly returned, one hand full of black leather straps, the other holding a coil of rope and the tawse.

'Right, Diana,' she announced, 'as you're so keen on the tawse, you can have it, and more. Hands behind your back, close up together.'

Diana hastened to do as she was told, putting herself into the same awkward position as Becky, so close that their hips and shoulders pressed together. Lilith came behind her, to lock the cuffs in place. Rope was threaded through the rings, tied off, passed down beneath her belly, and Becky's. She stayed still, her trembling growing slowly stronger as they were lashed together, first around their waists, then their thighs, to leave them helpless, tied into their lewd kneeling position with their bottoms completely vulnerable to Lilith. Diana could hear her own breathing, deep and hard, also Becky's, the breathing of helpless girls waiting for punishment. She was to be beaten, in tight bondage, an experience that never stopped being strong, yet one that she knew would be stronger still for Becky.

It began, the tawse smacking down on Diana's bottom, hard enough to make her jerk in her bonds. The next caught Becky, and Diana heard the smack and felt the shiver run through her playmate's body. Another hit her own bottom, and another, harder, and more, smack after smack, to leave her wiggling in her bonds, quite out of control, her eyes wide with pain, chewing in desperation on her panties. Only when she emitted a loud fart did it stop. She buried her face in the sofa, sudden shame mixing with the burning pain of her bottom. Lilith laughed.

'That evens you up, more or less,' Lilith said. 'And do try not to be so vulgar, Diana. We have a guest.'

Unable to respond, Diana felt a fresh stab of frustration at her helplessness and the awkwardness of her position. The tawsing started again, smack after smack, Becky's bottom, then hers, until their flesh was damp and hot, while the urgency in her sex had risen to a desperate need. Her hot bottom had become the focus of her body, with the twin entrances at its centre eager to be filled, her anus as much as her pussy.

85

The smacks went on, Diana ever more desperate for her fucking, wanting to call out for it, but knowing that to do so would only prolong her torment. Her whole bottom was throbbing, her anus wet with sweat, her pussy dribbling juice. Lilith could see, she knew, but kept on, slapping the tawse on to quivering bottom flesh until Diana felt she would burst.

It stopped, finally, and Diana watched as Lilith walked casually back into the dungeon. Becky was trembling and breathing hard, eyes shut, her face flushed. Diana also shut her eyes, surrendered to her helpless state. Her body felt intensely sensitive, aware of the stinging tawse cuts, of the dull ache of the spanking, of the taste and texture of the panties in her mouth. Her mind was full of thoughts of how she was, tied and beaten, showing everything – and, best of all, with Becky beside her.

Diana became aware of Lilith's return only when something cold and slimy touched between the cheeks of her bottom. She stuck it up, eager for penetration, and purred deep in her throat as a creamy finger penetrated her anus. It went deep in, Lilith moving it about as Diana wiggled her bottom in pure joy.

'Little slut,' Lilith said gently.

The finger came out, leaving her anus feeling juicy and weak, adding to the awful helplessness of her bondage. There was a wet, squashy sound and Becky gave a little cry of shock, making it clear that she, too, had had a finger used to grease her bottom hole.

'Beads,' Lilith said simply, and a moment later Diana felt the smooth, cold surface of one of the stainless-steel balls touch her anus.

Her ring opened, taking the ball, and a second, pushed past the well-lubricated muscle, a third, and a fourth, until she could feel their weight in her rectum and had begun to pant in her gag. The weak, helpless feeling was growing, and as the fifth and sixth balls were squeezed up her bottom she was wriggling her toes in desperation. A great bubble of shame was growing in her head as well, despite the knowledge that the awful, bloated feeling in her rectal chamber was caused by the steel balls.

With the seventh and last of the anal balls inside, Lilith let go of the string, to leave it trailing down over Diana's pussy. With her buttocks well parted and the string protruding from her anus, she knew just how obscene she would look, a thought she held until Becky gave another of her little shocked noises. Immediately, Diana found herself wanting to grin. She remembered how much fuss Becky had made over having a finger in her bottom hole, and imagining the awful humiliation the girl would be suffering as the steel balls were fed up the same tight little hole. Sure enough, Becky's body jerked with each insertion, and by the time all seven had been fed up her bottom, her breathing had become a laboured, nasal panting. Diana watched, delighting in Becky's reaction and sight of the pretty face twitching with emotion.

Leaving both girls' bottoms packed with the steel balls and with the strings hanging ready from their holes, Lilith stood back. Diana watched as well as she could, all the while holding her bumhole tight against the pressure in her rectum. A buzzing noise started, and she tensed in expectation, only to see Becky's face go suddenly slack in obvious ecstasy. Lilith chuckled, and patted Diana's smarting bottom. Becky's eyes came open, round and moist, to stare briefly at Diana before once more closing. Diana wiggled her bottom, desperate for her share of attention.

'Guests first, slut,' Lilith said. 'Don't worry, I'll get to you, just as soon as Becky's nicely off.'

Diana watched Becky's face. Her own rear felt urgent, both for penetration and the lavatory, and she could imagine the feelings going through Becky's head, the ecstasy blending with the awful helplessness. Lilith had taken hold of the string in Becky's anus, and was keeping it tense as she worked the vibrator over the soft, wet pussy. Little shivers were going through Becky's body, like tiny orgasms. She had abandoned herself completely, chewing on her knickers and panting through her nose, which was running mucus. A moan escaped her, from deep in her throat. The muscles of her thighs went tight against Diana's flesh. There was a sticky pop as the first of the balls was drawn from her anus, and she was coming. Her control fled, and she was sniffling and grunting in piglike ecstasy. Diana watched it all, and listened to the wanton, abandoned noises and the wet, squashing sounds from behind, until at last Becky went slack in her bonds.

Immediately Diana braced, knowing it was her turn and wondering if she would make such a rude show of herself. She felt the string go tense in her bumhole. The vibrator touched her flesh, slid deep up her vagina, and all thoughts of trying to hold on to her dignity were pushed aside. Lilith pulled, and the steel ball went tight in Diana's rectum. She felt her ring stretch, opening, the helplessness and shame growing until she wanted to scream. The ball popped clear of her hole, to leave her snivelling and shaking. Lilith began to fuck, pushing the vibrator in and out, to leave Diana writhing and squirming in her bonds, utterly unable to cope with the sensations in her vagina and anus. The second steel ball met her ring, plugging it, to leave both holes straining wide for an instant, then abruptly empty as ball and vibrator left her together. She was panting, struggling to breathe, like Becky, with mucus running from her nose; and, like Becky, she was too far gone to care. The third ball was pulled from her anus, the vibrator put to her pussy, between the lips, then to her clitoris.

The touch of hard, buzzing plastic sent Diana straight over the edge. Her muscles contracted, a shock taking ecstasy to the level of pain, her vagina squeezed tight, expelling air with a rude, wet, bubbling sound, and she was coming. The fourth ball pulled free as her climax hit her, tugged past her pulsing anus. The fifth came out, and the last two, quickly, bringing the awful fantasy of losing control of her bowels to a peak that joined with her physical orgasm, in a blinding, burning ecstasy that grew and burst, grew and burst once more, before it finally died to leave her shaking and limp, exhausted, sore and wet, but completely grateful.

'There we are,' Lilith's voice sounded from behind Diana. 'All done. Wasn't that what you needed?'

Diana nodded as Becky gave a mew of agreement, then collapsed slowly into her bonds, her mouth set in a happy smile. What they'd done together turned over in her mind, a happy melange of faces, breasts, bottoms and pussies, all tumbling together in a blissful memory. It had been good, among the best, and she was absolutely certain of one thing – Becky was far too sweet to be given to Hughes.

Four

Lilith sat at the kitchen table, amid a jumble of coffee cups, bowls, plates, cereal packets and papers. Across from her, Diana and Becky sat side by side, looking at the estate agents' presentation of the chapel at Stanton Rocks. Both girls were animated, happily discussing the possibilities offered by the place, while Lilith made only the occasional comment. She was happy, tired, yet still replete with the night's pleasures, and with a satisfying sense of ownership drawn from the two girls' submission.

They had slept together, the three of them cuddled up in her bed, talking and touching until the early hours of the morning. Becky had been eager, her inhibitions pushed aside by Lilith's casual use of her body while in bondage. She had even tried to accept the enjoyment of her anus, something she had been brought up to believe was impossibly taboo. They had told her about the ritual in the chapel, and their intentions of holding a Black Mass, although not the full extent of the involvement of Hughes. Becky had been more than enthusiastic, and in the morning had returned to the subject immediately, until Diana had brought out the presentation and their calculations.

With no appointment until the early afternoon, there was no hurry to do anything, and they had not even bothered to dress, simply pulling on tops and panties against the slight chill of the late-summer morning.

'It's great!' Becky was saying. 'I wish I could help. I can do candles and stuff for the Black Mass, anyway. You'll let me come, won't you?'

'Sure,' Lilith promised, thinking of Hughes, with the awful picture of Becky spread out on the altar and him advancing with his erection in his hand.

'We get loads of breakages and seconds at the centre,' Becky went on enthusiastically. 'It's not worth remaking them, so they just get chucked. I can get as many as we need, and some moulds. There's a set of men and women making love. That would look great, yeah?'

'Sure, let's do it,' Diana answered. 'Get black, and purple if you can –'

She stopped talking at the sound of the doorbell.

'Probably a parcel,' Lilith said, rising. 'I'll get it.'

She walked to the door, buzzed the intercom and opened the flat door a crack, peering out, only to find Hughes himself coming up the stairs. He had seen her.

'Mr Hughes,' she said. 'Er . . . Hi.'

'Hi, doll,' Hughes replied, pushing inside.

'We're not really up,' Lilith began, trying to steer him away from the kitchen.

'Don't mind me, I've seen it all before,' he answered, glancing around the main room, where the rope and cuffs still lay on the table. 'You start early.'

'That was last night,' Lilith managed. 'We –'

'Punter or a cunt party?' Hughes asked, turning into the kitchen.

'Hi,' Diana said nervously.

'Who's the poppet?' Hughes asked, nodding to Becky.

'Becky, a friend, not –' Lilith responded, and stopped, realising what she'd been about to say.

'Not a tart?' Hughes asked.

Lilith shrugged. Hughes gave Becky a leering grin, the implication of which Lilith recognised all too well. Becky responded with her happy, guileless smile.

'Pleased to meet you, Becky,' Hughes said. 'Dave Hughes.'

He extended his hand as his eyes roved down over her braless breasts to where her bare legs and the front of her

91

panties showed under her top. Becky blushed, shaking his hand before quickly pulling her chair in to cover herself. Hughes chuckled, pulled out the remaining chair and sat down.

'So what's this?' he demanded, picking up the presentation. 'That chapel we did the business in?'

'Yes,' Lilith answered, eager for any conversation that didn't involve Becky.

'You buying?' Hughes asked, looking up.

'No,' Lilith admitted.

'Why not?' he queried. 'It'd be a great place for your business. Miles from anywhere.'

'Not enough money,' Becky put in gaily. Hughes turned to Lilith.

'I can't raise forty thousand,' Lilith admitted. 'You see –'

'I know,' Hughes interrupted. 'In your line of business it's not easy to raise money. I know that, but I'm insulted. Why didn't you come to me?'

'You?' Lilith asked.

'Me, yeah,' Hughes said. 'I'm the money man, you know that. It's my business.'

'You're a loan shark?' Diana put in.

'Please, doll,' Hughes replied. 'I loan money to people who need it, people who can't get it any other way. Like you. Now look, you're earning, I can see that. All the gear you've got, your car. How many tricks do you turn a week?'

'Five or six,' Lilith admitted.

'Five or six? Fuck me!' Hughes answered. 'What does that earn?'

'That's my business,' Lilith answered.

'Hey, this is me you're talking to,' Hughes responded. 'I'm trying to help here.'

'A thousand, give or take,' Lilith admitted.

'A grand a week?' Hughes said. 'Jesus, talk about easy money!'

Lilith shrugged.

'Look,' Hughes went on, 'you need forty grand, right?'

92

'Seventeen,' Lilith said.

'Seventeen? Right, so you've been saving up. Sensible girl. So you can pay, maybe five, six hundred a week. Better still, now I've turned your little girlfriend here into a whore for you, you can earn double, maybe more. I know a good investment when I see one. So, I'll loan you twenty, to leave a bit for doing the place up, which you've got to admit it needs. You do your stuff, pay me a grand a week, for six months . . .'

'Twenty-six thousand, on twenty?' Diana demanded. 'That's . . . what, thirty per cent interest, sixty per cent per annum.'

'OK, I'm being generous,' Hughes said, spreading his hands. 'Normally I charge a straight hundred per cent, unless you get behind. You won't, you don't need to. So how about it?'

'Take it,' Becky urged, her voice filled with innocent excitement.

Lilith paused, biting her lip. What Hughes said made sense, and opened a path to the sort of security she craved, with her own property, away from prying eyes. Her distrust and dislike of Hughes was stronger, and there was the horrible thought that, once in debt to him, she would never be able to break away. Yet still it was tempting. Hughes spoke again before she had reached a decision.

'All right,' he said, 'you reckon I'm pricey. Here's another offer. You put up twenty, I put up twenty. We go into partnership. You do the whoring, I take half, and I'll have one of my lads up with you to make sure you don't get any shit from your punters. How's that?'

'No way,' Lilith answered immediately. 'That makes you my pimp. I won't, ever!'

'Touchy, touchy!' Hughes responded. 'Raw nerve on that one, eh, baby? Got smacked around a bit, did you?'

'Twenty pays back twenty,' Diana said suddenly, 'and you can fuck me whenever you want, until the money's paid back.'

Lilith looked around in surprise. Diana was pale, and clutching her coffee cup so tightly that her knuckles showed white. Lilith tried to make eye contact, but Diana stared fixedly at Hughes.

'I don't fuck whores, I only make them,' Hughes answered. 'Still . . .' He turned to Lilith. 'You don't fuck the punters, do you?'

'No,' she said firmly.

'All right, then. I want twenty-four back from my twenty, in your own time, and I get to fuck you, exclusively.'

'No way,' Lilith answered. 'I don't fuck.'

'You said you don't suck,' Hughes answered. 'How long was it before you had my cock in your mouth?'

'She doesn't,' Diana put in. 'Not ever. Have me. I'll be just for you, pussywise.'

'Thanks, doll, but I want the main bitch,' Hughes answered. 'Come on, baby, you know it makes sense.'

Lilith glanced around the table. Diana was tense, Becky open-mouthed with wonder, Hughes relaxed, amused. She thought of how she'd been tricked into sucking his cock, how in the end she had been unable to resist his money. It had broken her pride, and she knew that to accept his cock inside her vagina would be far worse, yet she was unsure whether, at the end, she would be able to resist. Hughes had turned to Becky, and began to speak again.

'The girl hasn't been born who won't put out for money. Sure, some are cheap, some aren't, but they all do it in the end. I mean, what do you think marriage is? I'll tell you. It's a deal for sex. The guy gets his cock seen to, girl gets security and cash for doing fuck all. That's what women want. It's nature, it is.'

'I . . . I'm sure you're wrong,' Becky answered.

'I'm right,' Hughes said, and turned back to Lilith. 'You'll fuck. You know you'll fuck. The deal stays on the table until noon. Meanwhile, there's what I came over here for. A word, babe.'

He stood, and beckoned to Lilith. She followed him out of the room, and into the dungeon, where he shut the padded door firmly behind them.

'So, is poppet in there my virgin?' he asked.

'No . . . I mean, I'm not sure,' Lilith said, frantically trying to think of a way out of the situation and failing. 'I thought you said a week.'

'I was passing, thought I'd see how you were doing. Maybe get a blow job. I like it in the morning, sets me up for the day. So is she?'

'Look, Mr Hughes . . . Dave. She's just a friend. I'm not sure she's up for it at all.'

'Are you pissing me around?' Hughes answered, his tone immediately threatening. 'She's a girl, she fucks. If I'm her first, all the better.'

'I'm not even sure if she's a virgin or not,' Lilith persisted. 'Look, you can't just rape her!'

'Who said anything about rape?' Hughes asked. 'There's money on the table here, girl, five grand. Offer her two, her legs'll be apart so fast she'll split her cunt before I get there.'

'I don't know,' Lilith managed. 'I was looking for someone . . . someone different, someone –'

'She'll do nicely,' he interrupted. 'Look, I'll fuck her anyway. Five grand to pop her, like I said, if she's virgin. What d'you reckon she'd go for if she ain't?'

'I really don't know if she'll –' Lilith began, only to stop as Hughes took her hard by one wrist.

'Hey, no crap, we agreed,' he said. 'Get her up the chapel with the candles and shit if it makes it easier for her. Get her pissed, too. You've got three days. Let me know when it's fixed.'

Lilith nodded.

Nich pulled the motorbike to a halt between two parked cars outside the Blue Boar Inn at South Harling. Juliana climbed off the back, stretching herself in the pale sunlight and slapping at her leather-clad thighs. Nich kicked the stand into place and got off himself, turning to look up to where the steeple of All Saints' Church rose above the trees.

There was a sleepy air to South Harling, and it was hard to imagine the events that had led to Andrew Wyatt's downfall taking place in such an apparently quiet and respectable environment. Yet the church was there, recognisable from the photographs he had found in papers, with the rectory beside it.

'Deep currents below a quiet surface,' Juliana remarked, echoing Nich's thoughts.

'Often the way,' he agreed. 'Many a Satanic cult has started from simple boredom. "The Devil finds work for idle hands", as they say.'

'Talking of hands,' Juliana asked, 'aren't you worried that the black nail varnish and symbolic rings will freak this new guy out? Not to mention the earrings and eye shadow.'

'Very possibly,' Nich admitted. 'With luck he'll tell us what we need to know simply in order to get rid of us. I shall also ask him if he's Wyatt. In the circumstances that should really throw him.'

Juliana shrugged, waiting as Nich took pictures of both church and rectory, examining the results in the window of his camera before putting it away. He made for the rectory, Juliana following. It was old, possibly as old as the church itself, pale stone stained green with algae in the shade of thick-boled yews, dark wood and diamond-paned glass. Nich approached with the same mixture of antagonism and envy the trappings of the older Christian sects always gave him. In another world, he felt, he himself might have lived in such a building, or one grander still, presiding over the pagan ceremonies he loved.

Channelling his anger to resolve, he made his way to the front door, ignoring the modern bell in favour of the great iron knocker at its centre. A moment of silence followed, before the door swung open, revealing a thin, pale-faced young man in a black suit and priestly collar. His eyes showed momentary surprise at Nich's appearance, but the glance was directed at his motorbike leathers and not at his jewellery or make-up.

'Good afternoon,' Nich enquired, using his best Queen's English in the hope of keeping the priest off balance. 'Am I addressing the Reverend Andrew Wyatt?'

'No,' the priest answered hastily. 'Are you a reporter?'

'Absolutely not,' Nich answered. 'Would you be the Reverend Wyatt's curate, then?'

'No, no, not at all,' the priest said quickly. 'Mr Wyatt has, er ... left us. I am the new incumbent, Peter Grimsdale. Sorry, you are ...?'

'Interesting,' Nich stated, 'that a Christian priest should have a name relating to one of the pre-Celtic manifestations of the Horned God. I refer, of course, to Grim. But I digress. Nich Mordaunt, my girlfriend, Juliana. We are students of religion.'

'Ah, theology students?' Grimsdale said hopefully.

'No,' Nich answered. 'Our primary interest is in the resurgence of paganism, although the Christian religions do interest us, Catholicism, Anglicanism, Methodism, Satanism ...'

'Satanism?' Grimsdale responded.

'Nich,' Juliana said.

'I'm sorry,' Nich said quickly. 'An enthusiasm of mine. The subtleties of the various dogmas alone are fascinating. Anyway, we were hoping to speak to the Reverend Wyatt.'

'As I say, Mr Wyatt has left us, er ... permanently.'

'Oh, what a pity. He had several very interesting ideas on the subject of sanctity. You don't know where I might contact him, do you?'

'I do, yet I fear that I have been given specific instructions not to pass his address on. It was, um ... all rather difficult, you see.'

'You hint at scandal?'

'I'd rather not speak about it, thank you. Now if you would excuse me ...'

'Very well,' Nich answered, and gave a sweeping bow.

They walked away, silent until well out of earshot of the rectory.

'You gave in pretty easily,' Juliana remarked, 'and you might have got further had you been a little less bombastic.'

'I enjoy bombast,' Nich answered, 'especially for Christian priests. It unsettles them, which is in itself a worthwhile thing.'

'Sure,' Juliana agreed, 'but we didn't get the address.'

'No,' Nich admitted, 'we didn't. However, note his honesty in admitting that he has the address in question. Note, also, what was visible beyond him.'

'His living room, furniture, a bookcase.'

'Books, exactly. Various pieces of Christian mummery, but also books on angling and coins. Not Grimsdale's books, Wyatt's books. If some of Wyatt's property is still there, the address will doubtless be with it.'

'You're going to break in?'

'I am.'

Lilith knelt, her top pulled high over her breasts, her mouth wide around Hughes's erect cock. A small wad of notes had been pushed into the back of her panties, payment she had not had the will to refuse.

Becky had gone home and, after a long talk with Diana, they had decided to accept Hughes's offer of money. That alone had been enough to make Lilith feel weak and insecure, yet the possibilities offered by the chance to own the chapel were simply too great to be resisted. Hughes had returned at noon, demanding an answer. They had agreed to his terms, and he had demanded his cock be sucked to seal the bargain. Lilith had refused, but the money had come out. Before long she had been back on her knees, with the feel of the notes in the waistband of her panties a poignant reminder of how he had manipulated her.

She cried as she sucked, slow, heavy tears running down her cheeks to mingle with the wet from her mouth. Despite her misery, she kept her bottom stuck out and her breasts bare, an odd professional pride driving her to do her best at the degrading task. Hughes was rock-hard in her mouth, and pushing his cock in, a sign she knew from experience meant he would soon be coming. She sucked harder, determined to get it over with, even though she had been told to swallow his sperm.

'Come on, doll face, deep throat,' Hughes gasped suddenly. 'I'm going to spunk in you, any moment.'

Lilith moved, stretching out her neck to take more of his cock in her mouth. The head was already nudging between her tonsils, making her want to gag, while the thick, male taste of his cock was strong in her mouth. He moaned and took hold of her head with both hands.

'Let me fuck your head,' he demanded, suiting action to words as he jammed his penis yet deeper into her throat.

His cock pulled back, then in, the bulbous head squeezing deeper into Lilith's throat. She shook her head, trying to pull away, unable to breathe as her gullet filled with cock flesh. Hughes groaned, pulled back, jabbed again, deeper still, and Lilith was gagging on cock, her throat going into spasm as a thick wad of salty sperm was ejaculated down her windpipe.

'Swallow it, swallow my load, you fucking bitch!' Hughes grated.

With her head clutched hard in his hands and his cock wedged so far down her throat that she was completely unable to breathe, Hughes emptied his cock into her. Lilith was choking, and trying to pull away, her throat full of slimy sperm, her stomach twitching in rebellion at the rough treatment.

At last Hughes pulled back, leaving Lilith gasping for air, her mouth wide, with tendrils of mingled sperm and saliva hanging from her lips. For a moment she thought she had control of herself, only for her stomach to clench tight as Hughes wiped his cock into her hair.

Lilith's cheeks blew out, her mouth filling with her breakfast as she ran for the lavatory.

'There is perhaps nowhere quite so easy to break into as a rectory,' Nich stated. 'It is empty at regular times, these stated on a large board close to the property. Even should the incumbent have a wife, and I suspect Grimsdale does not, then she is sure to be religiously inclined and therefore in attendance at her husband's service.'

'I suppose so,' Juliana admitted. 'So we wait for evensong and break in then?'

'Yes,' Nich answered. 'I do, anyway. You can attend the service and text me on progress.'

'I can't,' Juliana answered. 'Not possibly, not a Christian service. I'd rather do the breaking in.'

'Well I certainly can't,' Nich said. 'OK, listen outside. You can enter the church, can't you?'

'Yes.'

'Then we'll go in this afternoon and see if Grimsdale has posted an order of service. I'd like to see the altar Wyatt so thoroughly desecrated as well.'

'So would I,' Juliana answered.

Nich finished the pint he had been drinking, raising the glass to his mouth and draining what remained. Juliana followed suit, and went into the pub to pay for their meals and drinks. Nich waited, eyeing the church spire where it was visible through the trees, in pleasant anticipation of what he was about to do.

Juliana returned, and they set off back through South Harling. Having reached the churchyard, Nich stopped to read the announcement board, noting the time of even-song, and hurried after Juliana, joining her in the nave of the church. She was staring thoughtfully up at the beams, apparently lost in thought. Nich also paused, taking in the hushed atmosphere and still air, admiration for the beauty and atmosphere of the building warring with envy for its keepers.

The interior was typical, a tall space with coloured light lancing in through stained-glass windows showing scenes from the Bible. Inscriptions to long-dead local dignitaries decorated both walls and floor, along with the memorials of wars, while a green baize noticeboard provided more prosaic information. The pews were dark wood, some carved, some plain, all worn glossy with time and the touch of innumerable hands. Beyond them, two steps led up to the choir, with the pulpit to one side. Further still was the chancel, with the square block of the altar at its centre, an altar over which a young girl had been buggered just months before.

Nich found himself smiling at the thought, and trying to imagine the sheer sacrilege that such an act would represent to a religion that regarded chastity as a virtue. Wyatt, surely, had to have turned against his own church to have done such a thing, a rebellion that strongly implied taking the path of Satanism.

100

'There's a key in the door,' Juliana stated. 'Lock it.'

'Lock it? What about Grimsdale?'

'What about him? It's years since I've done this. I must. Will you join me?'

'You're right,' Nich stated. 'I will.'

Juliana reached out her hand. He took it, his heart hammering in his chest despite his determination to remain calm. Side by side they walked between the rows of pews, Nich thinking of all the couples who must have taken the same walk before. Each had gone to be united in Christian marriage, a ceremony that made sex permissible, within, and only within, those boundaries imposed by the church. With a sudden urge to mischief he bounded forward, leaping on to the steps to turn and face Juliana as if he were the priest, half bent, one arm out, crooked, a finger extended to beckon.

Juliana came close, knelt, not in the traditional position for prayer, but with her bottom stuck out to make a glossy ball of tight black leather. Nich spoke.

'Bare yourself, girl! How dare you remain covered in the House of God!'

'Your pardon, Father,' Juliana said meekly, and abruptly pulled her top and bra high, baring her heavy breasts to the soft red light striking down from one of the stained-glass windows. Her leather trousers and her panties followed, pushed quickly down to leave her bare bottom stuck out down the length of the church.

'A most suitable posture,' Nich remarked, changing his pose to one typical of Tom Pridough, erect with his hands clasped behind his back and an expression of unctuous self-satisfaction on his face.

Juliana giggled. Looking up at him with the light reflecting from her vivid green eyes, she cupped her breasts, running her thumbs over her nipples. Her mouth came open, her tongue lolling out.

'Wanton slut,' Nich went on. 'So, where was I? Oh, yes. Dearly beloved, we are gathered here today so that this woman, this wanton slut Juliana, may indulge her most base lusts with this man, Nich Mordaunt, here, in the

101

church of All Saints, and thus commit an act of sacrilege in honour of their own pagan gods, and in keeping with the tradition established by the Satanic Father Andrew Wyatt, lately rector of this parish.'

He paused, coughed, adjusted his cock in his trousers, then continued.

'Do any here have objection to this congress, other than wishing to fuck Juliana themselves, which is entirely understandable and may be done at leisure in the vestry after the service?'

No answer came from the empty church, only the echoes of Nich's own voice. Looking into the high, empty space, with the dust motes dancing in the coloured light, Nich let the contrast between what they were doing and the atmosphere of sombre piety sink in before speaking again.

'No?' he demanded, looking around the vacant pews. 'Splendid, splendid. So, let's get on with the fucking, shall we? I mean the er . . . wedding, of course.'

Juliana was still stroking her breasts, and had parted her knees, putting herself in a pose yet more blatantly sexual. Nich swallowed hard and adjusted his cock again, finding it a hard bar in his trousers, almost fully erect.

'Yes, my dear,' he said, 'I'm sure they all have a very nice view of your vulva. 'So, now, do you, Juliana, maidservant of the god Txcalin, wish to commit sacrilege, here, upon the very altar of Yahweh?'

'I do,' Juliana answered.

'And do you, Nich Mordaunt, Hierarch of Pagan Gods, Bane of Lah, wish to indulge this woman in her lust?'

He jumped down from the steps, falling quickly to one knee, head bowed, one arm lowered, one back to allow him to fondle Juliana's bottom.

'I do,' he stated, allowed one long fingernail to brush the pouch of Juliana's sex and leaped back into his priestly pose.

'You do? Excellent! Then you may fuck the bride!'

Springing back to the nave, he caught Juliana up, lifting her in his arms and walking, bent-kneed, towards the altar. Juliana laughed as she was carried, clinging on to him, with

102

her breasts wobbling to the motion of his gait. As he reached the altar Nich put her down and performed a mocking genuflection to the cross.

Juliana got quickly into position, bent across the altar, legs wide, her jeans and panties stretched taut between her upper thighs. Her pert bottom was raised and parted, the lips of her sex prominent and puffy with blood, her hole glistening wet. Nich smacked his lips in anticipation, focusing on the magnificence of her rear view as he lowered his zip and freed his cock into his hand.

Coming close to her, he pushed the head of his erection to the wet flesh of her sex, rubbing over her clitoris until she began to moan. Taking her hips, he adjusted her pose a little, until her hole was at the right height. His cock found the mouth of her vagina immediately, sliding up her juicy passage until his balls met her flesh. He began to fuck her, kneading her buttocks with his thumbs as he pushed, to spread her anus and show off the junction of cock and pussy hole. Juliana began to purr, catlike, and to clutch at the altar cloth with her fingers.

Nich began to push harder, in both physical and spiritual ecstasy, revelling in his act as he raised his eyes to the face of Jesus picked out in the great stained-glass window above him. His own eyes met the cold, dead glass of the deity's face and he laughed, jamming himself deeper still into Juliana's sex, to make her cry out and clutch yet harder at the table.

The cross crashed over, landing on a brass chalice with a clatter of metal. Juliana screamed, her body bucking against Nich's crotch, her hands tearing at the altar. Nich slowed, cautious of the frenzied state into which she could so easily be driven. Her cries turned to sighs, then once more the low, catlike purring she so often made when there was a penis inside her.

'You are exquisite, Juliana,' Nich sighed, 'and think, the same altar across which Wyatt buggered his choirgirl, probably in the very same pose.'

'Not quite,' Juliana answered. 'Do it, Nich, put it up my bum.'

103

Nich didn't answer, but pulled his cock out of her hole. It was wet and sticky, the head slimy with thick, white fluid. Grinning in manic glee, he took hold of the base of his cock, lifting it to smear Juliana's anus with her own juices. She gave a contented sigh, and dipped her bottom into a more convenient angle for penetration. Nich continued to grease her, using his cock as a brush, to pull out her pussy juice and spread it over her anus, each time pressing a little harder. Juliana accepted the treatment passively, purring gently and moving her bottom up and down to rub herself on his cock. Soon the little hole was starting to open to the pressure of his cock, accepting half the head, so that he could feel the taut muscle open around it, reluctantly accepting penetration.

'Not like that,' Juliana said suddenly. 'Let me get ready. Watch me.'

Nich took a step back, stroking at the slippery shaft of his erection as he watched. Juliana's anus began to pout, the tiny, wrinkled ring blooming to reveal a centre of wet, pink meat as the flesh between her buttocks bulged out.

'Now do it,' she sighed.

Again Nich stepped close, pressing his cock to the wet, squashy flesh of Juliana's anus. He felt her ring open, easily now, and as the head of his cock popped inside her she moaned, her buttocks going tense and her fingers tightening on the altar cloth. Nich began to push, slowly, as Juliana pushed back, to slowly engulf his penis in hot, moist rectal flesh. Only when the full length was inside her did she tense her buttocks, squeezing herself on his cock to make him groan in pleasure.

He began to bugger her, rocking slowly back and forth and watching her anal ring pull in and out on his shaft. It felt glorious up her bottom, soft and wet and slimy, a sensation so delicious that he knew he would come within seconds if he increased his pace. She was breathless, her fingers locked in the altar cloth, scratching at the surface beneath, her bottom moving to the rhythm of his pushes. He took her hips, admiring the sleek roundness of her neat buttocks, trim, pretty female flesh, in delicious, obscene contrast to the cock protruding from the central hole.

Suddenly it was too much for him. Unable to hold back, he jammed himself hard up her bottom. Juliana grunted, the breath knocked from her body as he slammed into her buttocks. He gripped hard, sinking his nails into the soft flesh of her hips, thrusting harder and deeper, his balls slapping against her empty pussy, his cock rock-hard in the squashy wetness of her back passage.

As he rammed himself in and out of her bottom her reaction became stronger, an urgent squirming, changing to a desperate bucking motion as he felt himself start to come. His head went up, his teeth met, his eyes locked to those of the glass Jesus and he came, crying out in debauched ecstasy as his sperm erupted up Juliana's bottom.

Her ring had tightened as he had come, as if to pull his cock deeper into her body. She held, squeezing out his come as his cock spasmed inside her. Nich gasped at the sensation, holding himself tight up her bottom with his head thrown back and his teeth clenched.

Suddenly Juliana moved, relaxing her sphincter and twisting at the same moment. Nich clutched for the altar, weak-kneed from his orgasm, steadying himself as his cock pulled from her bottom hole. For an instant he glimpsed the gaping red hole into her body, and then Juliana had swung round, kneeling at his feet, her mouth going wide, to close on his erection.

Juliana began to masturbate, sucking lovingly on his dirty cock as she rubbed at her sex, her throat moving as she swallowed down his come and her own taste, over and over. Her eyes were closed, her face set in blissful ecstasy, her body trembling to the urgent motions of her fingers. Nich looked down, his mouth spreading into a broad grin at the sight of the beautiful girl, naked from thighs to neck, her breasts quivering as she masturbated and sucked on a penis that had just been up her own bottom. As if in answer to his obscene thought, Juliana went suddenly tense, her muscles locking, her mouth pressing around his cock, one finger alone moving as she hit her orgasm. She finished that way, cock in her mouth, dead still, but for one

105

fingernail held gently to her clitoris, holding her climax on and on, until at last it finished and she subsided slowly down on to her haunches.

'Beautiful, glorious,' Juliana breathed. 'Thank you, Nich.'

'My pleasure,' Nich responded.

'Photograph me,' Juliana said. 'Spare nothing.'

'Nothing whatever,' Nich promised.

She got back into position, spreading herself across the altar with her bottom lifted to show off her buggered anus. Nich pulled out the camera, to take first a shot of the whole scene, then a close-up, showing Juliana's bottom in its full glory, with his sperm still oozing from the central hole.

'Excellent!' he said happily.

Juliana rose, and for a moment they paused, grinning at one another in childish delight at their obscene act. Taking tissues from a pocket in her leathers, Juliana passed one to Nich and wiped her bottom before pulling her knickers back up, then her trousers. Nich put his cock away and began to tidy the altar, straightening the cloth, setting up the cross once more and placing the various sacramental objects as near as he could to their original places. Now decent, Juliana watched him with a trace of amusement.

'You're very considerate,' she said. 'My lot would have wrecked the altar, and very likely set light to the church.'

'Such acts soothe the soul,' Nich admitted, rubbing at a slight dent in the chalice on which the cross had fallen, 'yet they also tend to be counterproductive. Religions are always at their strongest in the face of open antagonism.'

'Won't that be exactly what we're doing with the Black Mass?'

'Maybe, to an extent. I trust the benefit will exceed the cost. Remember also that the Black Mass is a Christian ritual, and, if anything, leads to the discredit of the church.'

Juliana simply made a face. Putting her hands behind her back to adjust her bra strap. Nich was about to continue, but stopped at the sound of a door being opened.

A moment later Grimsdale himself emerged from the vestry door. He cast them a suspicious look, and seemed to sniff the air.

'We were admiring your church,' Nich stated blandly.

'Yes,' Grimsdale answered, his tone cold.

'Yes,' Nich assured him. 'We were wondering if it was one of those built on a site of pagan worship, like Knowlton Henge.'

'Knowlton Church?'

'Knowlton Church to you, perhaps. Knowlton Henge to me. Pray at least allow my beliefs the courtesy of precedence.'

'As you say, yet at the time Knowlton Church was built Christianity had been firmly established in this country for centuries. It is twelfth-century.'

'I am aware of its date of construction, but that in no way alters my case. Knowlton Henge is a classic example of forced Christianisation in medieval England. Consider the altar block, which is quite clearly adapted from an original pagan altar like that at Stonehenge itself.'

'Perhaps so, yet as I say, by that date Knowlton would have been a purely Christian community.'

'Nonsense! Typical Christian propaganda. Pagan belief continued –'

'Excuse me,' Juliana interrupted. 'I've just realised I left my purse in the pub.'

Juliana walked from the church, unlocking the door as quietly as possible. Nich and the priest took no notice whatever, still arguing as she left. Outside she broke into a run, leaving the churchyard and doubling back to the rectory. A window stood fractionally ajar, at her head height. She reached up to open it, only to have second thoughts and try the door. It opened, and a moment later she was leafing through the large black notebook beside Grimsdale's phone. As Nich had predicted, Wyatt was listed, and to her own satisfaction the address was in Portsmouth.

A squat pad stood on the telephone table. She quickly wrote down the address, tore off several sheets to hide the

107

evidence of her crime and left. Of Nich there was no sign, nor of the priest. Returning to the churchyard, she waited, reading inscriptions, until he finally emerged.

'Christians!' he spat. 'I have perhaps sown the seeds of doubt in his head, but the sheer arrogance! Imagine denying that the building of Knowlton Church was a deliberate attempt to subvert local worship.'

'Knowlton was a fort,' Juliana stated, 'with no more religious significance than the army camp near Okehampton. The block you said was an altar was for standing on to make speeches.'

'Oh,' Nich answered, crestfallen. 'I wish you wouldn't tell me these things. So why build the church there, then?'

'I don't know. Perhaps the Christians *thought* it was a sacred pagan site. It hadn't been used for years.'

'Ah, yes, that would explain it, and adds an amusing irony at their expense. You weren't carrying a purse, were you?'

'No. Wyatt lives at Number One Greenwood House, Chalmers Close, Portsmouth.'

'Good girl! Greenwood House, eh? Doubtless a deliberate choice. Christians often associate Satan with the greenwood. Wyatt is our man, have no doubt of it.'

Tom Pridough stood outside the offices of the Exeter and West Building Society. He was struggling to fight down his anger, his fists clenched, his eyes closed, praying to himself in an effort to contain his feelings. For the third time that day he had been refused the loan he needed. Each time the story had been the same. Smooth, well-dressed young men and women, people he would normally have despised for their worldliness, had informed him that he had no credit record, that he had no proof of regular income, that he was unable to provide sufficient security. Finally, he had managed to secure an offer of six thousand pounds, two thousand short of what he needed.

Cursing the modern world, which he saw as the source of his frustrations, and the financial aspects of it in particular, he strode away. A few streets later he paused at the door of Dawson and Unwin, taking a moment to adjust his hair. The male assistant was at his desk, and Pridough went straight to him.

'I have been to a great deal of trouble, but I am able to make a new offer,' he announced. 'Thirty-eight thousand pounds.'

'For the chapel?'

'Naturally for the chapel.'

'Then I'm afraid you're too late, Mr Pridough. An offer was made earlier today, at the full asking price. It's been accepted, provisionally at least. Still, possibly you can make a better offer?'

Pridough stood, too numb to reply as the information sank slowly in.

'I must think,' he said finally. 'A moment.'

He turned to the wall map of southeast Devon staring at the familiar place names along the Exe valley. He struggled to contain his anger, at the social system that denied a man of his worth preferment, at the world's overwhelming failure to respect him and, underneath, at his own futility.

At length he brought his feelings under control, and began to wonder if it would be feasible to make a higher offer and attempt to secure the extra money from his congregation. The answer was almost certainly no, yet at the least it might delay the sale. He was still attempting to decide when two young women entered the shop, girls he was sure he'd seen before, one tall and slim, the other what he could not stop himself from thinking of as voluptuous.

The tall girl moved to the male assistant's desk.

'We want to buy a property,' she said. 'We can put a deposit down.'

'Which property is this?' the man asked.

'The old chapel out at Stanton Rocks,' the girl answered. 'We came in for the brochure yesterday. We've decided to buy.'

'Very popular, all of a sudden, that chapel,' the man said. 'You're the third today, but, as I was just telling this gentleman, an offer's already been made and provisionally accepted, at the full asking price.'

'Damn,' the girl swore. 'I was really counting on getting it. What if I made a higher offer? I can go to forty-one thousand.'

'I can certainly pass your offer on,' the man said, 'but I should warn you that the other client is offering an immediate cash payment. Once that's paid, he will have the right to occupy the property, full ownership subject to ratification by the council, which is a formality.'

'Oh, but we wanted to make a cash offer, too. Well, we can. Damn. Look, Diana, we'll have to get Hughes over here.'

'Possibly there's some mistake here,' the man put in. 'Did you say Hughes, David Hughes?'

'Yes, Dave Hughes. He's backing us.'

'Then you have no need to make a higher offer. It's Mr Hughes's offer that's been accepted.'

Diana hastened to keep up as Lilith jumped up the steps to Hughes's house. It was big, a detached Edwardian villa, three storeys high and set on a shallow hillside overlooking the city. Hughes's black 7-series BMW stood in the driveway. Lilith kicked a tyre as she passed, jabbing her finger on to the bell as soon as she reached the front door. Hughes himself opened it, and Lilith pushed past him into the house. Diana followed, to find herself in a hallway with Lilith standing facing Hughes, her face dark with anger.

'What are you doing, Hughes, you bastard?' Lilith demanded. 'You've bought the fucking chapel from under us, haven't you?'

'Hey, hey, just you cool down, doll,' Hughes answered.

'I'm not your fucking doll!' Lilith yelled.

'Just shut it, right?' Hughes retorted, suddenly angry. 'In here.'

He grabbed Lilith by the arm, tugging her towards a door. She tried to pull free, but his grip held as she was pulled into another room. Diana followed, determined to try to help her friend, but with no idea of what she could do. The room was a living room, with a huge three-piece suite at its centre. Two bulky men occupied the single chairs, both looking up in surprise. Hughes jerked Lilith hard towards the sofa, sending her sprawling, off balance, but quickly recovering herself.

'Sit down!' Hughes ordered.

'Fuck yourself!' Lilith spat back. 'I want to know what the fuck you think you're playing at, Hughes. Well? Well? You little shit!'

'Sit down and shut up!' Hughes ordered. 'What the fuck is this? You come into my house, shouting and screaming . . .'

'I've every right to shout and scream!' Lilith retorted. 'What do you think you're doing, buying my chapel like that? You're a bastard Hughes! I know your game, you arsehole! You want to set yourself up as my fucking pimp, don't you? Don't you, you piece of shit!'

'Jesus, but you've got a fucking mouth on you!' Hughes answered her. 'You want to watch yourself, doll. I don't take that sort of language, not from anyone.'

Lilith went quiet. Her face was red, her breathing deep, still facing Hughes with clenched fists.

'You want to learn some respect, girlie,' Hughes said. 'I'm not one of your limp-dick punters. This is the one I was telling you about, boys, the one who gets her kicks taking a whip to men's arses.'

'Needs a dose of her own medicine then, seems so,' one laughed.

'You could just be right there, John,' Hughes said. 'You could just be right.'

'Just piss off,' Lilith snapped, but the expression on her face had turned from anger to worry. Hughes laughed.

'Touchy on that one, ain't she?' he stated. 'Right, boys, we'll do it, then. Get her over the sofa, pull her pants down, and give her what she needs.'

'Just . . . just, fuck off!' Lilith snapped, backing hastily away. 'You can't do this . . . you can't!'

'Watch us,' Hughes answered.

'Just drop it!' Diana tried. 'Or –'

'Or what?' Hughes asked, and grabbed her, pulling her in. 'Yeah, what?'

111

'Let go of me, fuck off!' Diana swore.

Hughes caught Diana's arms, twisting them behind her back. The two men had cornered Lilith, who was looking at them, wild-eyed with fear. One man reached out and Lilith kicked him, only for the other to dart in and grab her around the waist.

'No!' Diana spat. 'You can't! You mustn't!'

'Oh, shut up,' Hughes yawned, 'and stop struggling or you get a smack.'

Diana stopped, to watch in futile anger as Lilith was dragged out into the middle of the room, her desperate struggles and furious protests ignored by the big men. Still she struggled, kicking and cursing as the two men took her to the sofa and threw her over the back of it, leaving her bottom the highest part of her body. She tried to rise, but was grabbed again before she could do it. They held her arms, keeping her head well down as they grappled with her trousers, all the while avoiding her furiously kicking legs. She cursed, kicked and thrashed, trying to bite, to scratch, threatening them with everything she could think of. It did no good. Her jeans were unbuttoned, and hauled down, revealing white panties with a pattern of pink flowers, a sight that drew laughter from Hughes and his men.

The panties were already halfway down off Lilith's bottom, revealing the neat V of her crease. A moment later they were all the way down, one of the men snatching them off her bum to the sound of her scream of fury. Hughes laughed to see her bare, and stepped forward, pushing Diana down into a chair.

'Hold her legs, boys,' he ordered.

The men obeyed, catching hold of Lilith's still kicking legs to force them down and open, leaving her lowered clothes stretched taut between her thighs. Her vulva came on show, the shaved lips pink between her thighs, also her anus, the little dun-brown muscle winking lewdly to the ragged tune of her breathing.

'Nice cunt, doll,' Hughes observed. 'Nice to see you shave, too, but you need to learn to wipe properly.'

'Fuck off!' Lilith swore.

'Temper, temper,' Hughes answered her. 'Now, what was I going to do? Oh, yes, I was going to teach you some manners, wasn't I? And what it feels like for your nancy-boy punters.'

He stepped close, extending his palm flat, to press it to Lilith's upturned bottom and squash out the flesh of her cheeks.

'Don't!' Diana yelled. 'Do me. I'll suck you, all three of you. I'll do anything, just leave her alone!'

'I already told you once, you little whore,' Hughes snarled. 'Shut up! Right, here goes. Spankies time, babe.'

He began to spank Lilith, not hard at all, but with rhythmic pats delivered with the palm of his hand, just hard enough to set her bottom cheeks bouncing and quivering. As he spanked he began to chant.

'Pat-a-cake, pat-a-cake, baker's man, bake me a cake as fast as you can. Prick it and pat it and mark it with B, and pop it in the oven for baby and me ... No, we can do better than that, can't we doll? Pat-a-cake, pat-a-cake, dirty tart, we've pulled down your pants and that's just for a start ... No, no, got it ... Pat-a-cake, pat-a-cake, dirty whore, your cunt's wet and dripping, you're begging for more! She is and all – fucking look at it!'

Diana looked, unable not to. Sure enough, there was already a trace of moisture at the mouth of Lilith's pussy. Hughes went on spanking, laughing as Lilith's buttocks turned slowly red and her pussy blossomed into readiness. He'd stopped chanting, only to suddenly begin once more.

'Smack-a-bum, smack-a-bum, filthy slut, your cunt's getting wider, you can't keep it shut. We'd fuck it, you know that, your dirt box as well, but your arsehole's all shitty, we don't like the smell!'

All three men laughed. Lilith burst into tears. Hughes gave her a final salvo of hard smacks and stopped, nodding to the men. They let go immediately and she slumped on to the sofa, still crying, and not bothering to pull up her clothes. Diana ran over, putting her arm around Lilith and pulling at the flowery panties in an effort to cover her friend's bare sex.

'Now, maybe we can talk a bit of sense,' Hughes said calmly. 'Go on, pull your knicks up, and stop blubbering like that, you fucking baby.'

Lilith stood up, her face a mask of misery, streaked with tears as she struggled back into her panties and jeans.

'She belts seven kinds of hell out of her punters,' Hughes told his cronies, 'and look at the fuss she makes over a little spanking, not even what I'd call a spanking, really.'

'Bastard!' Lilith managed weakly.

'Watch it, doll, or you'll get more, and next time I might not be so playful,' Hughes warned.

Lilith sat down, still snivelling as she accepted a tissue from Diana, to wipe her tears and then the mucus that had begun to run from her nose.

'Right,' Hughes said. 'Like you say, I've bought the chapel, but I'm not trying to fuck you over or anything, and if you call me a pimp again you're going to find out I'm not always so easy going. Now this is the deal. I'm paying forty grand. That's your loan. That way you can spend your twenty doing it up. You pay me five hundred a month, that's the interest. See, no need to get your knickers in a twist, was there?'

'What about the capital?' Diana asked.

'Don't worry about that, doll,' Hughes answered. 'You only need to pay the interest.'

'But that means –' Diana began and stopped, realising the futility of trying to make Hughes behave fairly.

'I've got the paperwork all sorted,' he went on, 'above board and fully legal. All you've got to do is sign.'

'Can we think about it?' Diana asked.

'No, you can't think about it. Sign.'

'I'm not going to sign,' Lilith said softly. 'Forget it.'

'No?' Hughes retorted. 'Now that's a pity, because I'd hoped we'd be in business together. It looks like I'll just have to do my duty as a concerned and responsible citizen.

'What do you mean?' Diana demanded.

'What's the catchphrase?' Hughes went on. ' "Rat on a rat"? Or is that drug dealers? Anyway, there's one for fiddling the social, and I dare say there's another for not paying your taxes . . .'

'Yes, and what about what you just did to me?' Lilith demanded.

'We didn't do anything, did we boys?' Hughes responded, looking to his two men with an expression of injured innocence. 'You won't have any bruises, and who do you think they'll believe? They'll think you're trying to get back at me for shopping you, that's all. You'd just dig yourself further in it, you silly tart, wouldn't you?'

'You can't do this,' Lilith managed.

'Can't I?' Hughes answered, and sat back.

For a moment Diana considered trying to run for it, only to realise that one of Hughes's men had moved to the door.

'I'll sign,' Lilith said suddenly.

'Good girl,' Hughes answered her. 'I knew you'd see sense. I'm just sorry I had to smack it into you. Now, the papers.'

He moved to a cabinet, extracting a number of papers, which he spread out on the table before taking a pen from his inside pocket. Lilith signed, her hand shaking as she put her name to each of the places indicated. Diana and one of Hughes's men added their own signatures as witnesses.

'Great,' Hughes said as Diana pushed the last of the documents back towards him.

'All done,' Hughes said. 'You can make your first payment next week. John or Daniel'll be round to collect it, and I dare say they wouldn't say no to a free blow job for their trouble.'

'No way,' Lilith answered.

'Fair enough,' Hughes said, 'but you'll find we all get along much better if you're nice. Oh, and when you need fucking, come over.'

'Never!' Lilith spat.

'Oh, you'll come to me soon enough,' he answered. 'Don't forget, I've seen how wet you get for me. And if you don't I'll just have to put some money down, won't I?'

The block of flats was far different from the secluded hideaway Nich had imagined. It stood in a short dead end, one of five squat blocks of red brick, each fringed with a grassy area that also appeared to serve as an impromptu rubbish dump. To judge from the names of the other blocks, 'Greenwood' referred not to the location but to some forgotten Labour politician.

'I see he still has a preference for the cul-de-sac,' Nich remarked in a vain attempt to break his sudden disappointment.

'Very funny,' Juliana replied. 'Number One would be a bottom flat, I suppose. Probably bottom left.'

Nich shrugged, walking to beneath one of the grimy windows, where an abandoned washing machine allowed him to climb up and peer within. Nobody was visible, only the flickering screen of a television set among furnishings that were obviously second-hand and had been cheap to start with. A single armchair stood at the centre of the room, surrounded by beer cans, crushed and empty, wine and cider bottles, also the containers of takeaway meals. A chipboard table and an ancient chest of drawers were the only other pieces of furniture, both covered with the same sorry debris. The carpet was threadbare, and laid over ancient linoleum, while the walls had been painted a dull grey-green, with the paint cracked and bubbled with damp.

'What's it like?' Juliana asked.

'Squalid,' Nich replied.

'Any evidence of Satanism?'

'None.'

Nich came down. The state to which Wyatt appeared to have been reduced filled him with further disappointment, also melancholy. The priest seemed to be a broken man, sunk into spiritless squalor and very likely alcoholism. It was far different from the images he had been building up in his mind, of defiance, of laughter in the face of the world's disapproval. He had hoped, even, that Wyatt might have managed to set up a small Satanic cult, a possibility that now seemed very remote indeed.

Juliana had taken his place at the window, and was frowning as she inspected the interior of the flat. Nich looked around, to find a man approaching. He was sandy-haired, balding, of medium build, while his face was full of aggression and fear. It was clearly Wyatt, for all that his appearance showed the same degradation as his flat. In his hand he carried a plastic bag, from the top of which three bottle necks protruded.

'Our man, I think,' Nich remarked.

Juliana looked round, jumping down to the grass as Wyatt approached. The expression on his face hardened to wary antagonism. Nich attempted an ingratiating smile, then bowed politely as Wyatt reached them.

'Andrew Wyatt, I presume?' he stated.

'What do you want? Go away,' Wyatt responded.

'We wish you to preside at a Satanic ritual,' Nich continued.

'No you don't, you vultures,' Wyatt answered.

'We do, I assure you,' Nich insisted, somewhat taken aback by the response.

'Just leave me alone!' he whined. 'You've had everything from me, my career, my home, my friends. Isn't that enough?'

'I'm sorry?' Nich queried.

'Damn reporters!' Wyatt snarled, coming here with your tricks and smooth voices.'

'We are not reporters, Mr Wyatt,' Juliana interrupted him. 'Far from it.'

'Ha!' Wyatt snorted. 'Why is it that I don't believe you?'

'We are not reporters,' Nich insisted. 'Do we look like reporters?'

'No,' Wyatt admitted. 'Nor did the woman who came offering to represent me at my hearing. I'll not fall for that again.'

'Nevertheless,' Nich went on, 'we are not reporters. Here.'

Nich stepped forward, activating the camera to show the image of Juliana bent across the altar. As Wyatt leaned close, Nich caught the stale, alcohol-laden scent of his breath. Wyatt stared, first at the image, then at Juliana, and back. Nick changed the image, to the close-up of Juliana's bottom, with a trail of sperm running from her glistening bottom hole down over her sex. Wyatt swallowed hard.

'All Souls Saints', South Harling,' Nich said. 'Your altar. The same altar over which you committed the same exquisite sacrilege.'

'You are Satanists,' Wyatt said, stepping hastily backwards.

'Yes,' Nich answered. 'At least, we represent a Satanic cult, intent on holding a true Black Mass. For this, as you doubtless know, we need a defrocked priest. You are that priest.'

'I'm no priest, not any more,' Wyatt responded. 'Just leave me alone!'

He made for the door.

'We wish to speak, Mr Wyatt,' Nich insisted.

'Well I don't,' he answered, fumbling his key into the lock. 'I've had enough trouble as it is.'

'Mr Wyatt,' Juliana said. 'We want to speak to you, and we are going to. You say you have had enough trouble, and we sympathise, believe me. On the other hand, if you do not let us in I intend to photocopy the front pages of certain newspapers and plaster them on every wall in this estate.'

Wyatt looked immediately horror-struck. He quickly pushed open the door, making no effort to stop them following, nor as he entered the internal door to his flat. Inside, he walked into the squalid sitting room, pulling one of the bottles of cider he had been carrying free from his bag the moment he had sat down.

'Thank you,' Nich said, settling himself against a wall. 'You will not regret your decision.'

'What makes you so sure?' Wyatt demanded.

'Well,' Nich stated, 'as a devotee of Lucifer –'

'Hold on,' Wyatt cut in. 'What is this? You think I'm a Satanist too?'

'Yes, aren't you?' Nich answered.

'No.'

'You must be.'

'Why?'

'You must at least have Satanic leanings!' Nich asserted. 'You buggered a young girl on your own altar! Are you telling me that was not a deliberate act of sacrilege?'

'She made me do it,' Wyatt answered, now with a whining note in his voice.

'Made you?' Juliana queried.

'Made me,' Wyatt insisted. 'Yes I know she's only sixteen and I'm over fifty, that I'm a man and a figure of authority at that – at least I *was*. I've heard it all before. She made me, and I don't care if you won't believe me. It's the truth.'

Nich and Juliana exchanged glances.

'We might believe you,' Juliana said. 'We are at least prepared to listen.'

For a moment Wyatt appeared to consider, then spoke, in a gush of words.

'No one would believe me!' he whined, running a hand back through his straggling hair. 'She flaunted herself at me, for months. I resisted and, believe me, it took willpower. She's so pretty, so innocent, a little unsullied flower, with the mind of a demented whore. For months she teased me and I held off. Then there was that day. I couldn't take it any more. She was bare under her surplice. She bent over the altar, and lifted her surplice, asking me to commit that unspeakable act! I did it, what she asked. We got caught, and she blamed it on me, said I'd seduced her, practically made out I'd raped her. And they believed her, every word, and the more they believed the more she said – awful things, things I'd never even dreamed of, things I could never do!'

'Like . . .?' Nich asked, wondering what a clergyman who had buggered a sixteen-year-old choirgirl over his own altar might consider unthinkable.

Wyatt didn't answer. He was staring at the wall, and twisting the top of his cider bottle in his hands. Nich waited, and suddenly the priest began to speak again.

'I tell you,' he said, shaking his head. 'If you want someone for your satanic rites, ask Susan Blake. You never saw a girl so innocent, so sweet, but underneath she's a child of hell.'

'Susan Blake? Your choirgirl?' Nich asked.

Wyatt nodded, twisting harder at the bottle neck. The top came loose, and he twisted it off, then upended the bottle over his mouth, pouring cider down his throat until he was forced to stop for breath. Nich waited, deeply disappointed in Wyatt's attitude, yet still hopeful.

'Very well,' Juliana said softly as Wyatt lowered the bottle, 'so Susan tempted you. Yet you gave in. You did it. At the least you might have taken her somewhere that was not sacred to your God.'

Wyatt shook his head miserably.

'You see,' Juliana went on, 'you do have Satanic leanings, even if you do not recognise them in yourself. Was it not delightful, knowing the sacrilege of the act? It was for me.'

Again Wyatt shook his head, hunching himself further into his chair.

'It's the truth, isn't it?' Juliana said firmly. 'Be true to yourself, join us. We have much to offer.'

'What?' Wyatt grunted.

'What can we offer you?' Nich stated. 'A great deal. You'll be paid for a start, a tithe.'

Wyatt answered with a grunt.

'The restoration of your pride?' Juliana suggested.

'Pride?' he answered. 'Oh I had pride. I thought they'd make me a bishop. They might have, one day, if only . . .'

'You shall have pride again, as our priest,' Juliana urged.

'And girls,' Nich added. 'We Satanists revel in the sexual act. Anal sex we find particularly satisfying.'

'You will drink rich red wines,' Juliana put in, 'at the expense of the cult.'

Wyatt took another swallow of cider, saying nothing, and glancing around as if seeking escape.

'Surely what we offer is better than this,' Nich said, indicating the squalid flat with a sweep of his hand.

Wyatt didn't answer, merely shaking his head miserably as he sank down further into the chair.

'Let me do this,' Juliana said.

'Very well,' Nich answered. 'I'll wait in the passage.'

He stepped from the room, half closing the door and squatting down to listen as Juliana addressed Wyatt.

'You,' Juliana said, 'are a Satanist.'

'No, never, nothing of the sort,' Wyatt babbled.

'Your acts say otherwise,' Juliana retorted.

'No. I told you. She made me. She flaunted herself.'

'Face facts, Wyatt,' Juliana said quietly. 'No man commits sodomy without the need. You were erect, weren't you? How else to enter a girl's anus? The images were there, weren't they? In your head. Little Susan, bare and willing, bent for you, open, ready, that dirty, secret little entrance offered to you.'

'No!' Wyatt exclaimed. 'It wasn't like that!'

'No?' Juliana queried. 'You lust, don't you? You want. You have needs. The need for naked, female flesh. The need to sheath your bloated cock in the hot flesh up Susan's bottom.'

'No! It's not true! Shut up! She devil! You're as bad as her!'

'Very probably worse,' Juliana replied. 'Like Susan, I enjoy my bottom used. Did she show you, as she readied herself? Did she?'

Wyatt took a sudden swallow from his bottle, spilling cider down his front.

'She did, didn't she?' Juliana laughed. 'She greased herself, didn't she, until her bottom hole was as soft and easy as a mouth. What did she do it with, in a church? Nich used the juice from my sex. Was that what you did?'

'Chrism oil, she used the chrism oil,' Wyatt sobbed.

'Oil of anointment?' Juliana laughed. 'And you buggered her with it? Wonderful! I'd have liked to do that myself. I love to show myself as I make my anus ready. I might even be available, anally, to a man, to a proud, strong priest of Satan, but not to a stinking, whining drunkard!'

Wyatt was shaking hard, his jaw slack and trembling. Again he put the cider bottle to his mouth, but more went down his front than past his lips.

121

'Think on it,' Juliana declared. 'Your choice. Here, squalor, self-pity, defeat. As our priest, pride, money, the adulation of young girls, all the wages of sin, of what you are, Andrew Wyatt, of your rightful inheritance as a Satanist! And me, Andrew, eager, pliable, ready to do as I'm told, any rude thing your imagination can conjure up.'

'I don't believe you,' he answered. 'You're lying.'

'I am?' Juliana queried.

There was silence, then a muffled grunt and the sound of a zip being pulled down. Nich quickly put his eye to the crack in the door, to watch in surprise as Juliana burrowed her hand into the fly of Wyatt's trousers, to pull out a thick, dark-skinned cock. A moment later she was on her knees, sucking on it as Wyatt watched with no less astonishment than Nich.

She was urgent, sucking hard, her black hair bobbing to the motion of her head, her eyes closed in concentration. At first the effort seemed futile, but Wyatt started to harden, his cock growing, until Juliana was sucking on a thick, dirty-brown column of flesh. She put her hand to it, masturbating him into her mouth as he watched, slack-jawed in drunken lust and wonder, only to go abruptly tense, and Nich realised that he had come in Juliana's mouth.

Juliana rose, leaving Wyatt's erection shiny with her saliva and still dribbling sperm from the tip. Standing over him, she stuck out her tongue, displaying the pool of sperm in her mouth, then swallowing, her face showing only a momentary flicker of disgust.

'So I was lying, was I?' she said.

Wyatt just stared, making no effort to put his cock away.

'Tidy yourself up,' Juliana ordered. 'Bath, change, pack. We'll wait outside.'

Wyatt nodded dumbly, and Nich stepped quickly back as Juliana made for the door.

'That was impressive,' Nich said as they stepped out into the suddenly brilliant afternoon sunlight.

'It was easy enough,' Juliana said. 'He's pathetic. His will is so weak I have no doubt he'll do as he's told, but I don't think he'll make much of a priest.'

'I don't know,' Nich responded. 'He's debauched, drunken, soured, a fallen man in every way. Who better to act as priest for the fallen angel?'

Juliana shrugged.

Five

Diana looked up at the chapel. Now the atmosphere had changed. The sense of naughtiness at enjoying sexual acts in what had been a public place for all its remoteness was gone, replaced by a pleasantly proprietorial feeling marred only by Hughes.

With the purchase complete, they had gathered to inspect their property. Hughes himself was leaning on his car, full of smug satisfaction. Since trapping Diana and Lilith into the deal, he had been both friendly and helpful, with little of the malice he had shown before. What he had done was keep up the pressure to be given Becky as his virgin. Torn between guilt and greed, Diana and Lilith had maintained the pretence that she was one, while avoiding the issue as much as possible.

Diana glanced to where Becky and Lilith were standing together, feeling a fresh pang of guilt at the sight of her friend's fresh, pretty face. Becky was full of innocent enthusiasm for the project, and had already hinted that she might be prepared to try her hand at domination, while she was more than keen to play her part in the Black Mass. She remained blissfully unaware of exactly what part that was likely to be. The roar of an engine cut into Diana's thoughts, and a moment later a motorbike emerged from the trees, pulling up in a spray of gravel behind Hughes's car.

'Some of your friends?' Hughes demanded.

'Nich and Juliana, our experts,' Diana answered.

Hughes stood as Nich dismounted and removed his helmet. As usual, his red hair was pulled back into a short ponytail, while he wore a trace of black eyeliner and eight pointed earrings of red enamel in gunmetal. Hughes's face immediately showed his distaste. Juliana had paused to put the bike on its stand, and as she too removed her helmet his expression changed once more.

'Nice,' he remarked. 'Like Lilith but with tits.'

Juliana ignored the remark, shaking her hair out to let it fall in a cascade of jet black. Hughes nodded, stepping forward with his hand outstretched to her.

'Dave Hughes,' he announced, 'the man with the money. Juliana, eh? Pretty name, unusual too. You're into this Satanist stuff big time, yeah?'

'To an extent, yes,' Nich answered him. 'Certainly, you may rely on us.'

Diana walked quickly over, eager to diffuse a situation that was obviously becoming tense.

'Nich knows everything there is to know about Satanic rituals,' she said to Hughes, 'and pagan stuff, too. He's amazing, Juliana too.'

'That I can see,' Hughes answered.

'They organised this great festival, at Lammas,' Diana went on. 'It was great. How do you know all that stuff?'

'Guesswork, mostly,' Nich admitted. 'Some was ancient in origin, but, to be honest, most of it, like most modern paganism, is made up. Not that that makes it any less valid, any more than the elaborations of any religious festivals. For Samhain, though, I intend to replicate the original ritual, on the details of which Juliana has done a great deal of research. Have you seen the Grim's Men stone circle, up in the woods?'

'No,' Diana admitted.

'I'll take you later,' he went on, now indifferent to Hughes. 'It's one of the finest examples of a Bronze Age ring on the moor.'

'I'd love to see it,' Diana answered. 'So what do you reckon to the chapel?'

They walked towards the building, Lilith and Becky coming to greet them, with Hughes walking behind, still

125

doing his best to ingratiate himself with Juliana. They gathered in front of the door.

'There's a lot of work to be done,' Hughes said. 'The roof for starters.'

'There's a builder in our road –' Lilith began.

'Don't worry your pretty head about that stuff, babe,' Hughes interrupted. 'Leave all that to Dave. I've got contacts. You just sign the cheques.'

'I'd rather do it my own way,' Lilith answered.

'Don't be stupid,' Hughes said. 'You'll just get ripped off. Trust me.'

Lilith threw Diana a look of disbelief, but said nothing.

'The roof first, then,' Hughes went on, 'and we'll want to keep any busybodies out and all. We need a big hedge, right round the land. What's that fast-growing stuff?'

'Leylandii,' Diana supplied.

'That's the one. Right around it, nice and high.'

'People will still be able to see from up on the rocks,' Diana pointed out.

'Yeah well . . .' Hughes answered. 'Not much we can do about that, is there? Maybe another hedge to cut off the bottom bit.'

'Hang on,' Lilith cut in. 'Who said we'll be doing anything outside, anyway? I'm not sure I want to risk attracting attention.'

'You've got to use the outside,' Hughes insisted. 'I've been looking on the Net, right, and there's all sorts of stuff you can do, stuff the punters'll travel miles for and pay top wedge. There's pony stuff, where you put the punter in a load of straps, like a horse, and train him and stuff. Weird, sure, but the money looks good.'

'I'm not –' Lilith began.

'For fuck's sake, girl,' Hughes cut in. 'Wake up and smell the roses! There's a fucking fortune to be made here. I tell you, you're lucky you've got me around. You do pony stuff, right, and you can have them do the gardening in the nude, like in that film, *Personal Services*. Then I saw a picture of this bloke who liked being hung from a tree by his feet . . .'

Hughes trailed off. Nich and Juliana had walked a little way to the side as they had been speaking, and were looking out across the valley.

'Hey,' Hughes said quietly. 'She's fucking gorgeous, that one, tits like footballs and the tightest little arse you ever saw. She's not one of your lot, is she? She's not a whore?'

'No,' Lilith sighed, 'she's not.'

'Soon fucking will be,' Hughes grated. 'She's got me horny just looking at her. So, while we're up here, how about a little inauguration ceremony, then? I'll fuck you over the altar. With a bit of luck I can at least persuade little Julie to get her tits out.'

'I said I wouldn't do that,' Lilith answered.

'Not still playing that old record, are you?' Hughes demanded.

'I doubt you'll want to,' Lilith answered.

'Oh, I want to, babe,' Hughes said. 'Don't put yourself down. Whore you may be, but you're so far up yourself it gives me a kick, like the way you cry when you suck cock, beautiful.'

'Talking of sucking cock,' Lilith responded, 'would you ever let a man suck yours?'

'Eh? What are you talking about?' Hughes demanded. 'What, you asking if I'm some sort of faggot?'

'I just wondered if you could handle having your cock in a man's mouth,' Lilith went on. 'Sort of, anyway.'

Diana stiffened as she realised what Lilith was going to do. She put a hand to her mouth to suppress a giggle as Lilith coolly undid her jeans. Two swift motions laid her bare from the tops of her thighs to just below her neck, and left Hughes staring slack-mouthed.

From immediately below her neck to her crotch, Lilith's body was a mass of colour. Despite having seen it done, it took Diana's eyes an instant to adjust to the patterns of the hideous face they formed. Black, crimson and scarlet mixed with minor tones and shades. At the level of her collarbone, two short horns sprang from a wide and hairless forehead. Thick eyebrows and heavy lids rose in arcs over the bulbous, bloodshot eyes that had been formed from her pert breasts, with each nipple a piercing black pupil in an iris of glaring orange-brown. Between them rose a twisted nose, long and hawklike, with her belly button cunningly worked to form a nostril. A wide philtrum stretched down over the lower slope of her belly, to her pubic mound, where a thick, dark upper lip rose above the screaming mouth that had been created from her vulva.

'Meet Satan,' Lilith stated.

'Superb, exquisite, the artist is a genius!' Nich declared, settling into what had become his preferred seat at the Black Dog. 'And you, also, Lilith are a genius for arriving at the concept.'

'It was really just to put Hughes off,' Lilith answered, 'and it was as much Diana's idea as mine.'

'A fine one in either case,' Nich responded, 'and efficacious to say the least. Even so, I felt his language excessive.'

'I was sure it would work,' Lilith went on. 'I mean he hates gays, and, with this thing he's got about purity and virginity, it had to. By the way, the tattooist, Phil, wants to come along to the Mass.'

'The more the merrier!' Nich said. 'So long as they are of the right mindset. With the equinox approaching, we must discuss the details.'

'You decide,' Lilith answered. 'I just need it to be showy, and dirty, to justify the ticket price.'

'Which is?'

'Two hundred, basic, which has got to include watching the deflowering plus either a blow job or a whipping. Most of them want to be whipped, some want both, which is fifty extra. You don't mind dishing out a whipping, do you, Juliana?'

'My pleasure,' Juliana answered.

'You know how to do it, yeah?'

'Certainly I do.'

'Give her a heavy cat-o'-nine-tails,' Nich suggested.

'That's what we'll be using, anyway,' Lilith said.

'I don't mind helping with that,' Becky put in.

Lilith went suddenly quiet, glanced at Diana and took a sudden swallow of her drink. Diana made a face.

'Thank you, Becky,' Lilith said. 'We'll take you up on that – some of the time, anyway. We really had a different part set up for you, a more important one.'

'Yeah?' Becky responded, clearly flattered.

'Yeah,' Lilith replied. 'The thing is, like, you know how the big climax is a girl losing her virginity on the altar.'

'Yeah, sure.'

'Well, er . . . we want you to do it, yeah?'

'Me? But I'm not a virgin, Lilith.'

'I know. That's the thing, you see . . .'

'We're not really very big on virgins,' Diana put in, 'let alone virgins who don't mind losing it in a Black Mass.'

'We . . . we can fake it, you see,' Lilith went on. 'With this stuff called Fluid Skin and theatrical blood. We've been practising.'

'And you're so cute, and you look like you *might* be a virgin,' Diana babbled, then suddenly slowed as Becky turned to look at her. 'We just thought . . . Please, Becky. There's two thousand pounds in it for you.'

'And Hughes gets to have me?' Becky said softly.

Diana made a face. Lilith shrugged.

'Do it,' Juliana suggested, 'if only for the joy of cheating Hughes. I will, if you won't.'

'I don't think he's going to believe that you're a virgin,' Nich pointed out. 'Do it, Becky, it would be a glorious climax to the ritual, compounding deceit with the most magnificent sexual excess!'

'I – I don't know,' Becky stammered. 'Let me – let me think about it.'

'Of course, darling,' Diana answered her. 'You take your time.'

'We really ought to go through the finances,' Lilith said quickly. 'Diana?'

'It seems to work out,' Diana responded. 'Twelve guys have paid up, and I reckon on three more at the full price. Phil's paying fifty, just to watch from the back, and we could maybe get a few more like that. So I reckon three thou minimum. Hughes wants his half, but will take that off what he offered in the first place.'

She gave an uneasy glance towards Becky, who was staring into her drink, and paid no attention.

'That leaves us maybe five thou up on the night,' Diana continued. 'Becky takes two, if she's going to be a sweetie.'

Again, Becky said nothing, but drained her drink suddenly.

'So we get three thou between us,' Diana continued.

'I don't need anything,' Juliana put in.

'A little wouldn't go amiss in my case,' Nich added, 'and we'll have to pay Wyatt his tithe.'

'I've been meaning to talk to you about that, Nich,' Lilith said. 'The guy's just a pisshead. If anything he ought to be paying.'

'No, no,' Nich responded, 'a real defrocked priest is essential. Otherwise it's not a genuine Black Mass at all. Just as in the ordinary Mass the call of Yahweh is voiced through an ordained minister who, by virtue of his ordination, is authorised by a Christian church to speak in the name of that church, and can therefore undergo transubstantiation to become as one with Jesus, so in the Black Mass the call of Satan must be voiced by a minister specifically rejected by that same church, a fallen priest achieving transubstantiation with Satan rather than Jesus. This reflects the fall of Lucifer from grace.'

'Does that really matter?' Lilith queried. 'You seem to know a lot more about it than he does.'

'I do,' Nich admitted, 'but that's not the point. However, I realise that to you the actual theological position may seem oversubtle, pedantic, even. Perhaps more importantly, from your point of view, if we're charging fifty for members of the Lower Congregation, I should be able to provide enough worshippers to make up for his tithe, easily.'

'Fair enough,' Lilith said, 'so long as having him pays. Lower Congregation, that's a good one. We need that stuff, jargon. So the guys paying full price are the Upper Congregation?'

130

'Higher Congregation perhaps,' Nich answered. 'Maybe we should seat them or something, to make them feel special.'

'You haven't quite got your head round submission, have you, Nich?' Lilith answered. 'Sure, they'll want plenty of attention, believe me, they crave it, but in a submissive role. They should be naked, and kneeling, perhaps with their hands tied, while some will want their own special fetishes, like being in a rubber hood, or a nappy.'

'Wonderful,' Nich responded. 'I must take a photograph and send it to Tom Pridough.'

'You were right to say I haven't got my head round submission,' Nich stated. 'I, personally, would have to be paid a considerable sum to spend a Sunday afternoon of hard manual labour. Yes, I appreciate that there can be pleasure in pain, the bite of the whip, perhaps, or the tension of a caress withheld. But digging holes, scraping pigeon shit off a church floor, and paying for the privilege! I confess that it is beyond my understanding.'

'You're confusing submission with masochism,' Diana answered. 'The more degrading it is, the more they like it, so long as they get Lilith's attention.'

Nich shook his head. Below them, beneath the bulk of Stanton Rocks, which he, Diana, Becky and Juliana had climbed, the old chapel had become a hive of activity. A fence now marked the boundary of the land, from the track down to the tumbling stream at the bottom of the slope. Several men were visible, digging at intervals to plant young leylandii from a pile that had been delivered the previous day. Fifty were already in place. Nearer, other men laboured in and around the actual chapel, clearing undergrowth, scrubbing at the walls and floor, one even working a power drill run from a small generator beside Lilith's car.

Most were conventionally dressed, in work clothes or less practical suits, although a few had chosen to express their pet fetishes and dress in rubber or leather. Among them strode Lilith, clad in head-to-toe black leather, high boots, trousers that laced at the side to reveal diamonds of soft white flesh, a top that rose to her chin – completely concealing her tattoo – gloves and a whip. Occasionally she would bark out an order, or crack her whip across a man's buttocks, more or less regardless of how well they were actually working.

'Of course we'll have to invert the cross,' Nich remarked, 'and we need a name for the cult.'

'You must choose,' Becky said. 'You know so much about it all.'

'It's not really my area at all,' Nich said. 'Ancient pagan belief is my speciality, and there I defer to Juliana. The truth is that the whole background to Christianity is alien to our culture, and our climate.'

'Our climate?' Diana queried.

'Yes,' Nich explained. 'Our climate is northern and temperate, also maritime, which means that we get strongly marked seasons and very variable weather. Thus the most crucial factors to any ancient culture living here are sure to be the annual cycle of nature, and the quality of harvest. In consequence, Celtic and pre-Celtic festivals follow the cycle of nature, birth, growth, harvest and death. Christianity, by contrast, derives from the Middle East, with a more even climate, and thus their festivals relate largely to events in Jewish history. True, they have tended to appropriate the original pagan festivals, with harvest festivals and so forth, but that alone I consider proof of the alien nature of the Christian God. Take Samhain, the festival of the last harvest, which the Christians have never really managed to take over, instead making it a time of evil doings in the form of Hallowe'en.'

'But the pagan Samhain is all about nuts and flowers and sheaves of corn and stuff, isn't it?' Diana said. 'I'd have thought you'd be into something a bit more gutsy.'

'Nuts and flowers?' Nich laughed. 'Hardly. You're thinking of the sort of bloodless modern interpretation favoured by Wiccans and so forth. It's valid, in its way, but hardly authentic. No, the original Samhain ritual would put your average Wiccan in shock.'

'Tell us, then,' Becky demanded.

132

'The ritual,' Nich explained in his most didactic manner, 'is commonly supposed to be Celtic in origin, but this is not the case. Just as the Christians so often adapted Celtic rituals to their own ends, so the Celts took over the rituals of their predecessors. The word "Samhain", and its various forms derive from Celtic, yes, but the festival to mark the last harvest and therefore the death and rebirth of the year is older by far.

'We can tell how ancient the ritual is, because only the two primary deities are involved: the Mother, representing the female principle and the earth, and the Horned God, representing the male principle and the sun. Essentially, the ritual reflects the actions of the deities. The goddess is immortal, the God is not, in the conventional sense, but is born, flourishes and dies in a perpetual cycle that reflects the seasons. The God, in his last act before death, must plant the seed that will lie in the womb of winter. Thus, each Samhain, a maiden, representing the Goddess, must accept the sperm of a man, representing the God.'

'The man then being sacrificed?' Diana queried.

'Maybe,' Nich answered.

'Not normally,' Juliana put in. 'There were one or two cults, but very few societies can afford to sacrifice a young male every year. You forget how small communities were.'

'Oh,' Diana answered. 'I was hoping we could sacrifice Dave Hughes.'

'Tempting,' Nich responded, 'but I think not. The authorities, I fear, would regard it as murder, and it would undoubtedly do harm to the pagan cause.'

'I thought it was supposed to be the girl who was sacrificed,' Becky said.

'A Christian slander,' Nich answered. 'Female sacrifice was never a part of the Samhain ritual, or any other. It would be in direct contradiction to the primary mythos of the cycle. Besides that, as Juliana says, small social groups can't afford to sacrifice fertile members, let alone females.'

'Why females any less than males?' Diana asked.

'Simply because,' Nich answered, 'one male may fertilise a great many females in a short period, but females can produce children only once every nine months, saving occasional twins. In theory, quite a large society could function with only a single male.'

'Kept in a cage,' Diana suggested, 'and brought out only when needed. What an excellent idea!'

'The idea has been explored in a number of novels,' Nich put in. 'Remember I promised to show you Grim's Men, the stone circle? That was a site for the original Samhain ritual. Come up now.'

'Great,' Becky responded immediately.

'I'd better not,' Diana answered. 'Lilith gets pissed off if I wander off while I'm supposed to be working.'

'She seems to be coping very well,' Nich said.

'I really ought to go and help,' Diana insisted.

'I'll see you later, then,' Becky said.

Diana nodded, jumping down to a lower rock and taking a careful hold of the iron handrail that led to the summit. Nich followed, and then Becky, Juliana jumping carelessly down to the lower level.

'As I was saying,' Nich continued as they made their way down among the lower rocks towards the thick pines of the forestry plantation, 'each year a virgin girl would be chosen, at a feast. That in itself was a fine ceremony, and one that has modern echoes – in the choice of May Queens and Lammas Queens, even in beauty contests in rather a squalid fashion. She would then be led up here, by the older women, the mothers and crones. That would be at midnight, a procession in the light of torches, the virgin naked but for the flowers in her hair. They would go to the circle, which she alone was allowed to enter. There she would wait, representing the Mother herself. Imagine her feelings: devotion, pride, religious ecstasy. She'd be –'

'High on muscar and drunk on mead,' Juliana cut in, 'very horny and barely aware of her surroundings. It would be about a couple of hours before dawn by the time they got up here, and the older women would have made sure she stayed aroused, suckling her, licking her. In the circle she'd just lie there playing with herself.'

'Wow!' Becky said.

'The men would be ready,' Juliana went on, 'strung out along a stone row to the west. They'd have been working themselves into a frenzy, and could see the torchlight through the trees in the distance. This was an oak wood then, like Wistman's Wood on the high moor. At dawn, the priest of the Horned God would sound a horn. The men would run for the circle. The strongest, the most virile would reach the girl first . . .'

'And rape her,' Becky breathed.

'Hardly,' Juliana answered. 'She'd be more aroused than he was.'

'But she'd have no choice about it,' Becky insisted, 'or who did it.'

'You're thinking in modern terms,' Juliana replied. 'You still see sex as the man fucking you, taking something from you. They didn't think like that. To be the virgin at Samhain was the highest possible honour, and in fact the only reason girls kept their virginities. Yes, a girl might hope a particular man would reach her first but, girls being girls, it was probably the most virile anyway. It took brains as well, for the men, and courage. They had to pace themselves, to appear to be making the most of the feast yet not overdo it, and there was nothing to stop them waylaying each other in the woods.'

'And you're going to do this?' Becky demanded.

'We intend to try,' Nich said. 'Fully liberated pagan virgins are not easy to come by. In fact, they're more or less a contradiction in terms.'

'Fake it. Lilith knows how.'

'That would be out of the question.'

'You didn't seem worried about me faking it?'

'Naturally not. Satan is the Great Deceiver, so to provide a fake virgin would seem appropriate. Not so for the Horned God. It would be a gross sacrilege.'

'You're going to do it, then?' Juliana asked Becky.

'Yes,' Becky sighed. 'I want to help Lilith, and I don't mind, really. Not that I fancy Dave Hughes – well, I do, I suppose. I don't know why, but I always seem to be drawn to real bastards.'

135

'Many women are,' Nich stated. 'The shrinks say it represents a primitive urge for physical protection.'

'Something like that,' Becky admitted, 'maybe. Anyway, I'm going to do it.'

They had reached the circle, and Nich made a quick gesture with his hand as he stepped between two of the monoliths.

'Warding off evil spirits?' Becky asked.

'No,' Nich replied, 'it's just that a man shouldn't really come in here, except on Samhain, and then only the one who represents the God.'

'Hundreds of men must have been here since it was last used.'

'True, but to me it is still a sacred place. Think, this circle was used for something like two thousand years, maybe more. That means that two thousand girls have lost their virginity where you're standing. Their emotions still linger, in the air, in the stones. Can't you feel it?'

'I can,' Becky answered. 'You're right, that's powerful.'

'So I show at least a modicum of respect,' Nich said. 'A genuflection to the Mother.'

Becky did not answer. She had closed her eyes. She stood, silent and motionless, her expression serene.

'I wish I'd been one of them,' she said suddenly. 'That would have been so fine.'

Nich stood by the door of the chapel, his slim body entirely concealed beneath the black robe and yet blacker dog collar he had chosen to denote his role as Wyatt's assistant. He was grinning, and making no effort to hide the fact, as car after car drew up to park beside the track. The chapel was going to be crowded, something he doubted it had ever been when used for its intended purpose. Most of these were pagans, and others drawn in by his reputation and previous successes, the rumour of what he planned having spread within hours of his announcement. Most carried bottles, or packs of beer, some candles. In addition there were the fifteen men who had paid full price for a place in the Higher Congregation, all Lilith's clients or the clients of her contacts. These were easily picked out, older men, whose guilty, sheepish behaviour stood them in sharp contrast to the cheerful and extrovert pagans.

Greeting both types impartially, either with a nod or a word to those he knew, Nich watched the chapel fill, until the newcomers had died to a trickle. He then went within, walking up the nave with his sense of achievement growing with every step. Candles burned on all sides, black, purple and scarlet, arranged with deliberate lack of symmetry, in front of the windows and in numerous candelabra. Incense hung heavy in the air, with scented smoke rising from chafing dishes on every windowsill.

Lilith, Diana and Juliana were acting as ushers, guiding the ever-growing congregation to their places. The pagans sat on benches at the rear, talking cheerfully, many already drinking. The submissive men knelt on the bare concrete floor, coats thrown off to reveal near-naked bodies, most in collars, several hooded or masked. One enormously fat man was in an outsize nappy and a gas mask.

Beyond the area defined as the nave a pulpit had been set up, to one side of the altar, now clean and covered with a black cloth. On it stood a heavy cross of black iron, inverted from the traditional Christian symbol and set with candles. To one side sat a plate loaded with communion wafers, and a large brass chalice stood to the other side. Beyond that were drapes, again black, hiding the sanctum, into which Nich pushed. Three people looked up, Hughes in his black robe, chatting volubly to Becky, who was still in her ordinary clothes and fiddling with the full glass of vodka in her hand. The third was Wyatt, sitting well away from the others with a bottle of strong red wine clasped in trembling fingers.

'An excellent congregation!' Nich declared. 'Is everyone ready?'

'Ready enough,' Hughes answered casually. 'I've just been setting my little poppet here at ease.'

He tousled Becky's hair and her mouth twitched briefly into a nervous smile.

'Father?' Nich asked, turning to Wyatt.

'I'll never be ready, not for this,' Wyatt answered, taking a pull from his bottle.

'Bear up!' Nich answered. 'You're sure to be a success. Already your deeds are notorious in Satanic circles. Your name is spoken with awe!'

'That's what I'm worried about,' Wyatt said. 'What if the press get hold of this?'

'Nothing,' Nich stated. 'As you say yourself, they have taken everything. We plan nothing illegal. Come, man, show some defiance! Laugh in the faces of your persecutors!'

Wyatt took another swig from his bottle. For a moment the look on his face hardened, only to return to sullen resignation.

'Don't overdo it with the wine,' Nich advised. 'Drunk is fine, desirable even, but you have to deliver the service properly. You won't forget your lines?'

'As if I could!' Wyatt answered. 'How can you be so depraved and feel no guilt?'

'Guilt?' Nich answered. 'There is no guilt, not in this. I glory in what you call depravity, sexual depravity. In other matters, you might be surprised by the rigidity of the moral code I impose upon myself.'

Wyatt answered with a snort of disbelief.

'Regardless,' Nich went on, 'we expect your best, and we are on in a few minutes. David, you should come out as I do. Father Andrew, wait until I announce you, then take over as I relinquish my place at the pulpit.'

'Sure, sure,' Hughes answered, rising. Wyatt nodded weakly.

Nich peered around the side of a drape. Lilith had come up to the front and was standing with her back half turned to him. The black silk of her robe concealed her body as completely as it did his own. Yet from where it touched the roundness of a breast and one slender haunch it was plain that she was naked underneath. Many of the Higher Congregation were already staring fixedly at her, with lust, dumb adoration and less readable emotions.

Diana was at the back, peering out of the half-closed door into the gathering twilight. She beckoned, urgently,

138

and a woman hurried in, joining the pagans at the back. Diana shut the door and nodded towards Lilith. Nich felt a sudden tightness in his stomach, the familiar surge of excitement. Stepping back into the sanctum, he beckoned to Hughes.

'With you,' Hughes said, then turned to Becky. 'You'll be all right, doll. You get the best.'

Nich stepped out, walking boldly to the pulpit and raising his hands for silence. The buzz of conversation died down slowly, and he waited for quiet before speaking.

'Tonight, it is with immense delectation that I join in presenting to you an authentic Black Mass. For many, perhaps all, it will be your first such occasion, if not your last. Yet, even for those who have dedicated their lives to the worship of the Dark Lord, this will be no ordinary communion. Tonight, as a climax to the evening, you will witness the ritual deflowering of a beautiful virgin.

'Therefore, I ask your brief indulgence, that you may appreciate the true quality of your experience. First, allow me to introduce the Chapter of our nascent cult. I, tonight, serve as acolyte to our President, without whom our gathering would have no meaning. Defrocked for the sodomy of one Susan Blake, a choirgirl of just sixteen years, I give you Andrew Wyatt.'

Nich made a sweeping gesture. For a moment nothing happened, then Wyatt emerged from the sanctum, his bottle still clutched in one hand. A murmur passed through the congregation, then sudden clapping, cheers and voices raised in support of Wyatt's act. Nich watched, to see the drink-dulled expression of the priest change, flicker to life with a sudden smile. Nich smiled himself, and raised his hands for silence.

'Beneath Father Wyatt,' he continued, 'and all but as essential, we have Lilith, our representative of the dark delights of womanhood, of carnal pleasure and carnal pain, deep in lechery and skilled in the lewd vices. Beside her we have her assistants, Juliana and Diana, no less venal, and ready to provide both chastisement and succour, at the needs of the High Congregation.'

As he spoke Lilith stepped forward from the shadows, with Diana and Juliana behind her. Raising her arms, she threw open her robe, to reveal her body, naked but for black leather thigh boots, with the Satanic face glaring out at the congregation in manic glee. There were gasps, and several of the submissives fell to their knees, grovelling on the floor. She stepped forward, taking her whip from Diana, to strike one man's raised buttocks and push another over with the toe of her boot. Ignoring the rest, she turned back.

'Magnificent,' Nich stated. 'Scarcely less worthy is David Hughes, the man chosen to deflower our virgin. Seeped in the sins of avarice and lust, a man to whom usury is a way of life, who delights in the corruption and debauchery of girls, leading them to the pleasures of their flesh. Who better to plunge his erect penis into a virgin orifice, and thus honour our Lord?'

Nich turned to indicate Hughes, who scowled back.

'One more remains,' Nich went on, 'our virgin herself, who for the present remains hidden. A further word, however, before the celebration of the Antieucharist. As you know, we gather here this evening to give honour to Lord Satan, and to indulge our lusts. First, we should understand something of what we do. In Christian society, Satan is sadly misrepresented as inherently negative, as the reverse of all to which we should aspire. This is not true. One need merely observe the facts. Satan is often blamed for the bad things of this world, for war, for disease, for poverty, all such things. I say he has been made a convenient scapegoat, no more. But do I, as the Christians do, ask you to accept this on faith alone? No! The truth of my assertion is demonstrably accurate. Look at our culture, forged in Christian belief. Across the ages, how many have suffered death, often horrible death, in the name of Satan? Few if any. In the name of Yahweh? Uncounted millions. Yahweh is a God of war and hate and rage, of the Inquisitions, of the Cathar massacres, of Pope Urban the Eighth, who drained the blood of three children that he might attempt to maintain his own sodden vitality.

140

So should we shun the obverse of these horrors? No, we should worship!'

He paused, looking out over the faces of the congregation, Lilith's slaves largely passive or staring at the girls, his own pagans attentive and thoughtful.

'And nowadays?' he continued. 'What is it the Christians teach us? It is the hushed voice, the averted glance, the slow dirge, dour misogyny, the denial of sexual pleasure, to be obedient. And the teachings of our own Lord, of Satan? The cry raised in passion, the bold stare, the vibrant song, the love of woman, the ecstasy of orgasm, to be human, to be an individual. I reject the sombre, creeping patriarchy of Yahweh, and I ask you to do the same, joining with me this evening in celebration of the Satanic virtues, and one in particular.

'At the time of the Reformation many hierarchies of demons were developed. These included an example in which a specific demon is linked with each of the seven supposedly deadly sins, of our virtues, those traits that give humanity the drive to achieve, that give life. Each is an aspect of our Lord. As Satan he is linked with passion, as Mammon with avarice, as Lucifer with pride, as Beelzebub with gluttony, Leviathan with envy, Belphegor with sloth and Asmodeus with lechery. Sin is pleasure. In sin we rejoice. And thus we give thanks to the Lord of Sin, our Lord Satan, tonight, in his aspect of Asmodeus, patron of our cult. Let it begin!'

The fluttering sensation in his stomach had gone, leaving only a touch of apprehension for Wyatt's ability as he stepped down from the pulpit. Wyatt was swaying slightly, but made the pulpit, to stare out over the heads of the congregation. His eyes were wild, unfocused, his face scarlet in the candlelight. He said nothing, and for a moment Nich had a vision of him collapsing in a drunken stupor, before he spoke.

'I am with the damned,' he said, almost inaudibly, his eyes dropping to the man in the nappy and gas mask.

He fell silent again, his eyes closed, then spoke, his voice now loud and almost steady.

'Brothers of the Cult of Satan Asmodeus,' he announced, 'we are gathered here today in the sight not of that God to whom I once dedicated my life, but of his Satanic Majesty, Lucifer, Beelzebub, once Son of the Morning, now Lord of Darkness, the snake, the deceiver, high devil of the Lah religions, ape of Yahweh, demonic aspect of the Horned God. As he fell, so I am fallen. As he defies his former master, so do I.

'You who have come here, I ask you to celebrate with me the Unholy Communion, whereby we remember our Lord's fall and partake together in his body and blood. Brethren, Our Lord's Prayer.'

Wyatt began to chant, Nich leading in response and others quickly joining in.

> Our Lord, who art in hell,
> Acclaimed be thy Name.
> Thy kingdom come.
> Thy will be done on earth
> As it is in hell.
> Give us this night our venal sin.
> And indulge us our trespasses,
> As we indulge those who trespass with us.
> Lead us deeper into temptation;
> And unto the joys of evil:
> For thine is the kingdom,
> And the power,
> and the glory,
> For ever, and ever.
> Amen.

Wyatt finished, the chapel ringing to the congregation's final amen. He paused. Nich took up the chalice from the altar and nodded to Diana.

'Brethren,' Wyatt announced. 'The preparation of the gifts.'

Nich bowed to Wyatt and fell to one knee, holding out the chalice. Diana stepped forward, to throw aside her robe and reveal her naked body beneath. She stopped, spreading her knees and sticking out her belly, to open the damp pink flower of her vulva. Nich pushed the chalice between her thighs and she let go, her pee tinkling into the chalice in full view of the congregation.

Golden fluid swirled in the polished brass of the cup, the rich scent filling the air, both sharp and hormonal, an intensely feminine musk that set Nich's nose wrinkling. Diana stayed still, holding her sex lips open until the gush died, leaving the big chalice more than half full. Nich lifted it, feeling the warmth from Diana's body through the bowl. Bowing once more, to Diana, then to Wyatt, he returned the chalice to the altar.

'Brethren,' Wyatt intoned. 'The desecration of the host.'

Again Nich bowed to him. Lilith went to the altar and turned, throwing herself across it even as she flicked up her robe, leaving her trim buttocks naked, with her head to the inverted cross. Raising herself on tiptoe, she pulled in her back, to thrust her bottom high and spread her cheeks, with the lips of her sex and the dimple of her anus showing blatantly behind her.

Nich stepped around her, standing so as not to obscure the view of her bottom as he took up the plate of wafers. She smiled as he leaned close, and gave her head the tiniest jerk behind her.

'They've never seen my bum bare, not one of them,' she whispered. 'What are they doing?'

Nich looked back, to find the slaves at the front of the congregation staring at Lilith's bottom as if hypnotised. Their expression varied, from outright lust, through guilty desire, to an awed yearning unlike anything he had seen before. Several had begun to masturbate, others knelt with their arms limp and their mouths wide, as if too shocked to react.

'Staring,' Nich whispered back, 'as if at a Goddess.'

'Touch me,' Lilith said quietly, 'they'll hate it.'

Nich nodded and quickly stood. With deliberate intimacy he pushed down on Lilith's back, to leave her bottom yet more openly flaunted. With her slim buttocks wide, her anus was on plain view, stretched out, dry and clean, with traces of talc caught in the tiny creases and the central hole. On sudden impulse he put a finger to her vagina, sliding it up the moist hole, and back, to daub her own juice on to her anus. Lilith shivered, faintly, and a susurration swept through the slaves, of shock and envy. Struggling not to grin, Nich pushed at the tight hole of Lilith's anus, watching as the now slimy ring gave to the pressure. With the slaves staring in wordless outrage, he fingered her bottom, until her anus had become wet and juicy. She gasped as he pulled her finger free, but made no protest.

Well pleased with himself, Nich took a wafer, touching it to the now moist dimple of Lilith's anus. With each he did the same, until each was ready, when he returned the plate to the altar.

'I didn't mean touch me quite like that,' Lilith whispered as she rose.

'I'm sorry,' Nich answered. 'It was more than I could resist.'

Lilith gave him an unreadable look and stepped to the side, once more taking up her place. Nich nodded to Wyatt.

'Brethren,' Wyatt announced. 'The Rite of Satanic Communion. All those who are entitled to receive the desacrament, come forward.'

Many of the submissives began to crawl forward, their eyes turned up to Lilith; others hesitated, most following, two staying back. Slowly, jostling each other for position, they formed a line. Lilith strode forward, shaking out her whip as she stepped over one who had prostrated himself completely.

'Faces in the dirt!' she ordered. 'Arses high!'

They moved, quickly, several catching blows from her whip anyway.

'Mouths wide! Tongues out!' she snapped.

Immediately a row of tongues were extended, the men open-mouthed, like so many eager dogs. Nich restrained a snigger at the sight. Lilith laughed aloud. Rewarding one with a last kick to his bottom, she came back to the altar.

Nich took up the chalice and passed it to Wyatt, who raised it high above his head and began to speak.

'Brethren, when we eat this bread, and drink this cup, we proclaim Lord Satan, our master. As the bread, I give you this, touched on the anus of your Mistress, which you yourself are not worthy to touch. And as the blood, I give you the urine of a whore, as fitting libation.'

Wyatt walked solemnly to the end of the line of kneeling men, Nich following with the plate of wafers. The first in line was one of the younger submissives, a man who normally might have been passed in the street without a glance, now naked but for his leather collar, from which a lead hung to the ground. Wyatt bent to him, placing the wafer on his outstretched tongue, and began to speak:

> Hear us, Lord Satan, we humbly pray,
> and grant that, by your unholy power,
> we receiving these gifts of your dedication,
> this tainted bread and this whore's urine,
> do, according to your aspect as Asmodeus,
> Demon of Lust, our patron master,
> in celebration of his lust and of his passion,
> may be partakers of his most priapic body
> and most lecherous spirit;
> take, eat, drink.

The man waited, and swallowed at Wyatt's order. His face twitched briefly into what seemed to Nich a blend of ecstasy and self-disgust, and once more he opened his mouth as Wyatt offered the chalice. Swallowing, and again making his peculiar face, the man mumbled his response and Wyatt moved on to the next man.

With each of the kneeling men the ceremony was repeated. Wyatt maintained a solemn expression throughout, and Nich's opinion of the priest's abilities rose further. With each man fed, Wyatt came to the altar and addressed himself to the inverted cross, mumbling something Nich could not hear as he made a sign across his front, before returning to the pulpit.

Lilith, Juliana and Diana had begun to move the slaves back, applying their whips to buttocks and backs, and their booted feet to those who simply grovelled to the ground. Some went easily, others seemed desperate for attention, crawling behind the girls and even clinging to their boots.

'Patience, brethren, your moment will come,' Nich announced.

None of the men paid any attention. Juliana reached down, gripping a man's collar to drag him back to where he was supposed to be. Others crawled after her, and Lilith followed suit, pulling one hard by his collar and another by his hair. Diana was left, smacking her whip on the back of the fat man in a nappy, who seemed not to notice. Juliana walked over, bringing her whip down in a hard arc. The man's nappy snapped at one side, then the other, too, as he was driven back, to fall with a squashy sound to the floor. At that he seemed satisfied, and stayed meekly with the other slaves. Wyatt cleared his throat.

'Brethren,' he announced. 'I now exhort you to further the work of Lord Satan. When you go forth from this place, display your lust, which is good in the sight of our Lord. Have no shame, nor yet guilt, but pleasure alone. Enjoy, in particular, those lusts held by the Christians to be immoral, the sensations of the mouth and of the anus, the joys of sensual pain and of the warm fluids of the body.

'To this end, and in honour of our Lord, Brother David will now perform the ritual of defloweration, dedicating the broken virginity of our Sister Rebecca to our Lord Satan Asmodeus.'

As he finished Diana and Juliana drew open the drapes of the sanctum. Beyond was darkness, then a figure appeared. Becky stepped into the light. Her hair was entwined with autumn flowers, her body clad in a robe of white silk, loose but touching in places to hint at the full contours beneath, a picture of innocent beauty made disturbing by the uncertainty and fear on her face. Again a murmur went up, this time from the entire audience. Nich, despite knowing that she was acting for the benefit of Hughes, felt a sudden tremor of unease.

146

Becky stepped forward, walking as if in a trance. Juliana and Lilith took hold of her, guiding her to the front of the altar. They bent, gripped her robe and raised it, revealing her naked body, the long, shapely legs, her full hips, soft, sleek belly and heavy breasts, with the nipples hard in arousal. The robe was pulled off, over her head. She was lifted, unresisting, to sit on the altar. As Juliana took up the cross, Lilith pushed Becky slowly back, until she was laid out with only her legs hanging down at the front. Carefully, Juliana positioned the cross, so that the strongest of its many shadows fell across Becky's breasts and belly.

Hughes stepped close, his hand on the crotch of his robe, squeezing his cock beneath. Juliana took hold of one of Becky's legs, Lilith the other, spreading her open to Hughes, and to the congregation. She gave no more than a meek whimper, although her chest was rising and falling to heavy breaths, urgent, almost panicked. Even in the dim, flickering candlelight her false hymen was plain to see, a dark red bulge below and between the neat inner lips of her sex. Nich glanced at Hughes, to find no hint of suspicion, only a powerful, even feral, lust. Behind them the congregation had pressed close, and were staring, now silent, at the open mouth of Becky's sex.

Nich nodded to Diana, who knelt down, her mouth wide. Hughes pulled up his robe, revealing an already growing cock, which he fed into her mouth. Diana sucked, holding his balls as she mouthed on him, then the shaft of his cock as it quickly grew stiff. Every eye was on Diana's face and Hughes's erection, except Becky's. She lay limp and passive, ready for her fucking, legs as wide as they would go, the dark bulge of her hymen glistening in candlelight.

Diana pulled back, Hughes's now fully erect cock springing up from her mouth. He took it in his hand, favoured the audience with a leer and turned to Becky, stepping between her open thighs. She looked up, her mouth wide, her lower lips trembling, her eyes wide and moist. Hughes grinned back and touched his cock to her

147

sex, pressing the bulbous head to the ragged hole beneath her hymen. Becky mumbled something, shutting her eyes. Hughes looked down, his eyes fixed to where his cock touched her virgin hole, and pushed, suddenly, hard, his mouth setting into a determined line. Becky gasped, her muscles tensing, her fingers closing on the altar cloth. Hughes pushed harder still. Becky gave a squeak of pain, then screamed as blood burst out across her thighs and Hughes's belly. Hughes gasped in ecstasy, his cock sliding up her, to the hilt, and pulling back, red with blood. He began to fuck her, looking down at the red smears where their bodies met, Becky gasping and panting, showing pain and distress that slowly faded to rapture.

'How does that feel?' Hughes rasped. 'Look at yourself, you little whore. Just popped, with a hundred dirty bastards staring up your cunt, and you're already loving it! What a dirty, fucking slut you are!'

Becky just moaned. Her eyes were closed, her legs rolled up high and wide, her sex completely spread and completely surrendered. Beneath her, the blood had run down along the crease of her bottom, and was dripping on to the floor with each push of Hughes's cock into her vagina. He had her by the thighs, ramming himself into her, harder and harder, until her breasts were jumping to the motion, with tremor after tremor running through her flesh.

'Look at her, you bastards!' he yelled. 'Look at the little whore on my prick! I've burst the little bitch's cherry and there's blood all over my balls, and it feels fucking great! Look at her tits shake. Look at the way she's rolled her fat legs up. She was a fucking virgin five minutes ago and now she's a fucking whore, a filthy fucking whore!'

He finished with a grunt. His teeth gritted. His fingers sank into the soft flesh of her legs. Twice he pushed, jamming his cock into her as hard as he could, then suddenly whipping it free, to jerk hard at his shaft. A spray of sperm erupted across the soft, chubby mound of Becky's belly, and higher, spattering one breast.

'That's fucked you,' he puffed. 'Now take your money, whore.'

He reached in under his robe, to pull out a handful of five pound notes from an inner pocket. Spreading them like a fan, he held them up to Becky's face, then put them down on her sperm-slick belly. Becky made no effort to move, lying limp on the altar, her thighs spread wide. Nich moved quickly in even as Hughes stepped away. He inserted a finger into the wet cavity of Becky's vagina, then drew it out dark, and sticky with fluid. Putting his soiled finger to the smooth flesh between her breasts, he carefully marked out a symbol, that of Asmodeus. She looked down, her eyes bleary with pleasure, saw the symbol and moaned as she lay back once more.

'You are dedicated,' Nich said softly. 'Show your pleasure.'

Becky responded, bracing her feet on the altar top as her hands came on to her body. Her fingers found her sex, briefly touching the tattered remains of her hymen before moving to her clitoris. Nich stayed in place, shielding her sex from too direct a view, as she began to masturbate in an open, lewd display. Her spare hand went to one big breast, holding it, her thumb moving over the stiff nipple.

Her body began to shiver, dislodging some of Hughes's notes, which fell to the altar top. Becky took no notice, rubbing harder, snatching at herself, clutching her breast. She began to pant, short, sudden breaths, and Nich saw the muscles of her stomach tighten, go slack and tighten again as she came, with her head thrown back and her mouth wide in a wordless cry of ecstasy.

Nich waited until the last shivers of her orgasm had gone through her, then leaned down and helped her to rise. She came with him, unsteady as she found her feet, and allowed him to lead her into the sanctum. She sat down in one of the chairs, Nich staying beside her with his arm around her shoulder until she finally spoke.

'I'm OK,' she said. 'I just need some tissues and stuff. I'll be fine in a minute.'

'Don't play it too cool,' Nich warned. 'I suspect Hughes would like to think you're crying your eyes out right at this moment.

'You're right,' she said. 'See where he is, could you?'

'Sure,' Nich answered, and poked his head out through the drapes.

In the body of the chapel, the service was beginning to degenerate into an orgy. Directly in front of the altar Diana was stark naked, even her boots gone, and licking Lilith, mouth to mouth with the Satanic face, held by the hair as the men looked on in envy. Juliana was already among the slaves, ordering them into groups according to their needs and using her whip to make sure they did as she said. Beyond, the pagans had thinned out, but, among those remaining, several couples were kissing or pulled close together as they watched. Wyatt was propped against the wall, the poise he had shown during the service gone, cursing incoherently, as he struggled to open a new bottle. For a moment he could not see Hughes, then he found him, near the back, looming over one of the pagan girls as they talked. Nich pulled back.

'He's occupied,' he told Becky. 'It's getting heavy out there.'

'Go,' Becky said. 'I'll see you later.'

Diana had her eyes shut, licking lovingly at Lilith's pussy, lost to everything but the pain of the hand twisted in her hair, the feel of her lover's body against her face, her own overall arousal. That so many men were watching didn't matter, and the fact that Lilith had stripped her in front of them only made it nicer. With the sexual tension that had been building up for the whole evening finally allowed to show, her craving for submissive sex was at its highest, her desire first for her own humiliation and then Lilith's pleasure.

Lilith came, with a low moan as her hand locked harder in Diana's hair. Diana kept licking, flicking her tongue on her mistress's clitoris in a constant, even rhythm, until at last her head was snatched back. She sat down, panting for the air she had denied herself with her face full of flesh, and looked up, to find herself staring into the distorted, Satanic face above her. A delicious shiver went through her, and she knelt forward once more, to kiss Lilith gently, as if kissing the demon.

'I need to come, darling,' she breathed, looking up once more to Lilith's face. 'Piss on me, or let me lick your bumhole while I frig off.'

'Later, my dirty little slut,' Lilith answered. 'Best keep that high for your cocksucking.'

'Men's cocks? Oh shit,' Diana answered. 'Come on, take me in the back. Make them suck each other off. That would be funny.'

'Uh, uh,' Lilith answered. 'Now I want to see you with your mouth around a big fat prick within a minute. Move, slut.'

'Yes, Mistress,' Diana answered. 'Is that an order?'

'It's an order,' Lilith answered. 'Crawl to them, now, and get sucking, and be dirty.'

Lilith tousled Diana's hair and reached for where her whip lay on the altar. Diana began to crawl along the ground, her humiliation burning in her head. Lilith had ordered her, that was what mattered, not what the men wanted, but the order, to suck and be dirty. It had to be done, and it didn't matter how she felt, so long as she made all eight of the men signed up for sucking come. It was a filthy thought, and she held it as she crawled on her hands and knees to where Juliana had marshalled the four who had paid only for a suck into a line beside a chair.

'I'm here,' she said as she reached them and knelt up to find her head at the level of the men's crotches, faced with two bulging leather pouches and two bare sets of male genitals.

'Good,' Juliana answered. 'Now you men, one at a time, no pushing in, no cocks slipping up places they shouldn't go. I'll have an eye on you and, if any one of you wants hot wax on their balls, then just disobey me.'

The men nodded, not one answering her back. She responded with a cold look and went to join Lilith, who had her eleven men lined up for whipping. Diana swallowed hard, and looked up at the first man in the queue with a nervous smile. He was a regular, one who liked school games. When he came he liked to play out a scene, with Diana as a schoolgirl, caught letting him feel her breasts. Lilith would cane them together, in their uniforms with their pants pulled down, after which Diana would suck his cock. Now he was naked.

'Hi,' Diana managed. 'Sit down.'

He sat, spreading his thighs so that his cock and balls hung down between them. Diana moved around, side on to the queue, suddenly conscious of the weight of her breasts as she leaned forward. Her head came down, her mouth open, to take in the fat, soft flesh of his cock and balls all at once, the way he liked it. She closed her eyes, trying to ignore the dirty, male taste of what was in her mouth, sucking and rolling his balls over her tongue, until he began to stiffen and she could transfer her attention to his penis alone. His stubby, thick cock was soon hard, stretching her mouth wide and slowly wider, until she was agape, and at last the pleasure of sucking on a cock began to overcome her revulsion. Eager to get him off, she began to tickle his balls.

'Yeah, nice,' he gasped. 'Do my arsehole.'

Diana opened her eyes and looked up, trying to express her disgust in her look. He took no notice whatever, and with a fresh stab of humiliation she allowed a finger to stretch lower, extending one long nail to tickle at the slippery hole of his anus. He sighed, called her a good girl and took a gentle hold of her head. Diana let him, remembering how he liked to fuck her head with her hair in a ponytail when she was in school uniform, and watch as he did it. The thought held: she in her diminutive outfit, the red tartan skirt up, her panties down at the back to show off her freshly caned bottom, her blouse wide and her bra up, her breasts swinging free as she sucked cock, as she was doing now, only in the dancing red light of a Satanic ritual . . .

He came, stiffening an instant before his sperm erupted into her mouth. Ready, Diana caught it and swallowed, grimacing at the slimy texture in her throat, but keeping his cock in and draining him before at last pulling back.

'Next!' he said as Diana rocked back on her haunches.

Beside her, the second man in the queue was already erect, and had obviously been masturbating over the sight of her sucking on the first. Without bothering with the chair, he took a grip of Diana's hair and plunged his cock deep into her mouth. For a second she tried to resist, but gave in, sucking. He was bigger, and tasted of salt and sweat and man. He was urgent too, and rough, controlling her head and staring down at the junction between his cock and her lips. Diana struggled to get into the rhythm of the sucking, and to stop him jamming his cock into her throat, which was making her gag with every push. He took no notice, and she began to slap at his leg, scared that she'd be sick on his cock, even as he came, right down her throat, to leave her coughing and spluttering on the floor. The come rushed up, into her mouth. She tried to spit, only to start coughing again, the sperm spraying from her mouth, over his legs and hers, also on to her breasts and belly. He just laughed.

Diana swallowed hard, trying to get her breath back and also to get hold of her feelings. Her head was spinning, her senses filled with the smell and taste of sex. She felt soiled, abused, also in need of more, but with Lilith standing over her, or at least watching. Busy dishing out whippings, Lilith was paying no attention whatever. With a resigned sigh she looked up.

The next man was already sitting down, his leather pouch pulled aside to expose heavy, dark genitals. He was another regular, one of the oldest and politest, always grateful for her attention. Diana crawled in between his open legs. He had a big foreskin, thick and rubbery, which he liked played with. She leaned in to kiss his cock. Using her lips, she peeled his foreskin down, wincing at the taste of stale urine as the knob within entered her mouth. For a moment she sucked on it, before taking the whole thing into her mouth She began to suck, as the last man's sperm seeped slowly down her breasts, wet and slimy on her bare skin. She did it slowly, relaxing to the pleasure of being allowed to suck while knowing that he wouldn't make her gag on his cock, try to spunk in her eyes, piss in her mouth or any of the other nasty tricks she had had played on her.

He gave a moan of satisfaction and began to stroke her hair, soothing her as she sucked, something she always liked, something that made the dirty act easier to accept. She closed her eyes, now feeling comforted and deliciously dirty, even wondering if she shouldn't do something rude to make the others jealous, put his cock between her tits, even kiss his anus.

'I've saved this for you, Diana,' he sighed and came full in her mouth.

Diana's eyes came wide in shock, sperm bursting from around her lips as it filled her mouth. There seemed to be an impossible quantity of it, pumping into her mouth as he held her head gently but firmly in place Her throat tightened in reaction. She jerked away, only just in time to stop herself being sick, his sperm splashing out from her mouth, to fall in a thick clot on to her already filthy breasts.

She sat back, unable to speak, with a great curtain of sperm hanging from her lower lip. It was in her throat, so much she couldn't breathe, and suddenly she was choking, struggling for air, swallowing hard, only for her gorge to rise in protest. Her mouth filled with a mixture of sperm and sick, and she swallowed desperately, bent double to the ground, her eyes closed tight in pain and nausea.

'You all right, love?' a voice sounded from beyond the haze in her head.

Diana shook her head frantically, unable to do more as she fought to stop herself being sick. Fresh humiliation was welling up in her head, stronger than she could remember, and she cursed herself at the sudden desire to be taken by the hips and fucked while she knelt puking on the floor. A moment later she had been, firm hands gripping her an instant before her vagina filled to the pressure of a man's cock.

She gasped, trying to turn and see who it was even as fresh sperm burst from her lips and out of her nose, bringing the tears to her eyes and rendering her incapable

154

of protest or resistance. The man kept on, humping away happily at her bottom, indifferent to her distress as he used her. She could barely take it, bent to the thrusts of his cock, her mouth agape, sperm and mucus bubbling from her nose, barely able to see, hearing only the wet slapping noise of his cock in her hole and the cries of the whipped slaves in the background.

She was swallowing, desperate to speak, even as her body rocked to the motion of the cock inside her. Again her gorge rose. Salty, slimy fluid welled up from her throat, but she fought it down, opening her mouth to speak only to have it filled by the bloated erection of another man. Her eyes went wide, to find herself staring at the hair-covered belly of the man in her mouth an instant before her face was pulled into the wall of blubbery flesh. She began to flail with her fists, frantically, desperate for breath, for even a moment's respite. One ignored her, the other laughing at her struggles and jamming his cock yet further down her throat. Choking on cock, her body utterly out of her control, Diana gave in to panic, her limbs thrashing wildly, her hair flying, her breasts jiggling and bouncing beneath her. Her breath was gone, her nose full of sperm, her gullet blocked with penis, the shoves into her rear jamming what little air remained from her lungs, the fat belly slapping over and over in her face. Her vision went red, her senses started to slip away, even as the cock in her mouth erupted, filling it with sperm, to burst out around her lips and explode over the fat man's balls and legs.

The cocks left her body, suddenly. Diana collapsed, sperm running from her mouth and nose, her ears buzzing, her head ringing with sound, her vision blurred. Vaguely she was aware of the concrete floor beneath her and the wet feel of the sperm that coated her breasts and neck to mingle with her own sweat. Voices penetrated, slowly, female and sharp, Lilith, then Juliana.

'Let me have this one. I'd warned him,' Juliana was saying.

Diana rolled to her side, weak with reaction to the way she'd been used. She could see shapes, vaguely, moving colours, red, orange and rich flesh pink in front of shadows that themselves seemed to move.

'All yours, make it hard,' Lilith's voice came through, and Diana shook her head.

Her vision cleared, slowly, to find Juliana standing with one hand locked tight in Mr Arlidge's leather collar. His face was purple, his eyes bulging and, as Juliana twisted, his mouth came open. Lilith sank down beside Diana, cradling her. Diana collapsed exhausted into her lover's arms.

'Careful, Juliana,' Lilith said, 'you don't actually need to strangle him.'

'No?' Juliana queried. 'Fair enough.'

She let go, shoving Arlidge to the floor. He collapsed, gasping.

'What did I say?' Juliana demanded. 'What did I say?'

'Wax,' Arlidge panted. 'You . . . you said you'd wax our balls if we misbehaved. I have, I've been revolting, Mistress, truly revolting. I deserve the wax.'

'You threatened him?' Lilith queried. 'Not a good idea.'

'I didn't expect the pig to *want* it!' Juliana spat. 'Well, maybe I did. I'm going to do it, anyway. You four. Hold him out. Now!'

She had pointed as she spoke to the four nearest men, those who had already come in Diana's mouth. They hesitated, shuffling their feet.

'Do it, or you get the same, you little pricks!' Juliana yelled. 'No, not you, on second thoughts, you're too old. You two, and you, the fat bastard who went last, and count yourself lucky you aren't getting it, too.'

The fat man came forward, and Diana saw that he had already been whipped, his buttocks marked with the dark, irregular blemishes of a cat-o'-nine-tails. He sank down, taking one of Arlidge's wrists. Others were crowding in, and Juliana snapped her fingers at one. He knelt, reluctantly, along with the others, each taking a limb to spread Arlidge out on the floor.

'I deserve the wax, Mistress,' he repeated, looking up at Juliana where she stood over him.

A shadow fell across Diana and she turned to find Nich above her, holding out one of the thick black church candles. Juliana took it, smiling as she admired the flame, then sinking into a squat between Arlidge's open thighs. His cock was still hard, and moist with Diana's juice, which glistening in the candlelight. Juliana took it, very gently, between finger and thumb, and began to masturbate him as she moved the big candle slowly closer. Arlidge was looking up, his face twitching between fear and expectation. Juliana spat on his balls, her phlegm quickly trickling down below them.

'Is this punishment enough?' Juliana asked sweetly. 'To give you pleasure?'

'Pain, Mistress, real pain,' Arlidge sobbed. 'Do it, Mistress, for the revolting things I've done.'

'No,' Juliana answered. 'I deny you.'

Arlidge's face went slack, then began to twitch, emotion chasing emotion across it as Juliana calmly blew the candle out, lowered it, and stabbed suddenly forward, forcing the thick shaft hard into Arlidge's wet anus. Arlidge screamed, his whole body bucking in agonised response, his limbs pulling from the other men's grip, even as sperm erupted from his erect cock, in a high arc, to catch his face and land in a long, sticky line down his body.

'More appropriate, I think,' Juliana said as she rose to her feet.

Lilith laughed, somebody clapped, then another, applauding Juliana. Arlidge lay still, the candle remaining wedged in his anus, not even troubling to wipe the sperm from his face. Those who had watched began to disperse, several following Juliana as she walked away. Lilith helped Diana up, and into the chair. Only three men had stayed close, clustering around Lilith and Diana. All three were naked, and all three had been whipped.

'What do you want?' Lilith demanded.

'We've still got our blow jobs to come,' one explained.

Becky stood up, her curiosity finally overcoming her caution. Her vagina was sore, and her head was a jumble of emotions from the way Hughes had treated her. He had thought he'd taken her virginity, and he'd called her a whore as he did it, even making a symbolic payment to ensure that everyone knew. It was hard to take in, even to understand, with the bad feelings that came with the word in sharp contrast to those she held for Lilith and Diana.

To accept money for sex was something she had always been taught was wrong. Hughes obviously thought so, and delighted in making girls do it, and in their tearful, shamed reaction. But she didn't feel ashamed of herself. She felt naughty, excited, somehow special.

Stepping to the gap in the drapes, she peered out. The chapel was a lurid sea of colour. Bodies, most naked or near naked, moved in the shifting yellows, oranges and reds of the candlelight. The floor was a mess, littered with bottles and bits of clothing. Lilith was seated to one side, with Diana on her lap, cuddling while a man beside them stroked his erection. Across from them, Juliana had a circle of men around her, on their knees, some licking and kissing at her boots, others pushing to get close. More were near, apparently waiting their turn. Of Hughes there was no sign.

On sudden impulse she stepped out, determined not to seem weak or repressed in front of the other girls. She had put her jeans back on, but not her top, and as several males turned to look at her she felt a surge of embarrassment for her bare breasts. She bit it down, trying her best to seem confident as she walked to where Juliana was marshalling her slaves.

'I'll take some, if you like,' she called.

'Do,' Juliana answered, adding something that was lost in the sudden babble of male voices, pleading with her for punishment and humiliation.

'Behave!' Juliana snapped as men began to cluster around Becky. 'Get down! Ignore them, Becky. What do you want to do?'

'I . . . I could spank some,' Becky volunteered.

Again there was an immediate cacophony of voices.

'Shut up!' Juliana shouted. 'Right, you haven't had much, and you, and you. Get in a line – and you saw what happened to Arlidge, so mind your manners.'

'May we toss while she spanks us, Mistress?' a man asked, his voice filled with desperate urgency.'

'Becky?' Juliana queried.

Becky nodded and took the man by the hand.

Nich sat back, placing his hands behind his head as he surveyed the results of his work with absolute satisfaction. With the candlelight flickering on bare skin and black robes, with every person there either indulging in sex or watching, it was a scene that might have come from the sort of lurid hell he had always imagined to haunt the nightmares of Christians.

Lilith had a masked man standing, his hands on his head as she simultaneously whipped him and jerked at the stubby erection that protruded from a bush of coarse grey pubes. Diana was on her knees, between the open thighs of a man in nothing but a spiked collar, her head bobbing up and down on his erect cock, her face and breasts slimy with sperm. Juliana was riding another man, perched on his back with a lighted candle in one hand, so that she could drip hot wax on to his already whipped buttocks as she rubbed her naked sex on his spine. Others clustered around her. Even Becky seemed to have abandoned herself, seated on a bench with the fat man who had been in the nappy bent over her knee, his buttocks turning quickly red as she spanked him. As he was beaten he jerked at a small penis with frantic energy, while two other men awaited their turn. Hughes was nowhere to be seen, but Wyatt was, propped in a corner, a bottle clutched in his hand, his face slack, his mouth twitching in a stupefied smile. Filled with benevolence, Nich promised himself he would persuade Diana or Becky to give Wyatt a treat before the evening was through.

Most of the pagans were simply watching, in couples or small groups, some shocked, more amused, a few clearly aroused. Others had joined in more heartily, and several copulating figures could be seen among the shadows to the back of the room. One pretty girl was sucking her partner's cock with no more shame than that shown by Diana or Lilith.

Nich watched, admiring the serenity in her face and the way her cheeks moved as she fed the thick shaft in and out of her mouth. The man was looking around as he was sucked, obviously thoroughly pleased with himself. For a moment he caught Nich's eye, and smiled in thanks. Nich responded with a nod of approval, and continued to watch as the man began to show off, masturbating into his girlfriend's mouth. Suddenly the girl's expression changed, briefly to surprise, then bliss. She sucked him in deep, then brought her head up, smiling, with a long streamer of sperm hanging from her lower lip.

Nich turned his attention elsewhere, to Diana, who was sucking yet another man as she stroked the erection of one more. She was in the same kneeling position, but now with her knees well apart and her bottom stuck out, with the big olive-skinned cheeks parted in a tempting display of her sex. His cock twitched in response.

Diana sucked hard at the cock in her mouth, all the time tugging awkwardly at the one in her hand. She still felt dizzy, rather detached from what she was doing, but after her cuddle from Lilith she was once more eager for sex. Lilith had held her until she had recovered physically, stroking her back and bottom and whispering soothing things to her. The three men had been made to wait, until Lilith was satisfied, when Diana had been gently told to suck their cocks for them.

With the delicious feeling of having to do something dirty under her mistress's orders, she had obeyed, first taking a man in her mouth as she sat on Lilith's lap, then going back to her knees. The man had come in her face, and been replaced also immediately, with the last of them demanding his cock be nursed until it was his turn.

She now needed her own orgasm, and was intent on masturbating just as soon as the two men had come. Her sense of humiliation was burning in her head, and focused on the way Arlidge had mounted her unexpectedly, had caught her unawares and just fucked her from the rear. She had her bottom stuck out, half hoping that some other man would have the guts to take her, half dreading exactly that.

The man she was sucking grunted. Diana sucked hard and his sperm exploded into her mouth. Quickly she swallowed, gulping at each spasm before releasing him and quickly taking in the last man. His cock was thick, and a good length, a pleasure to suck on, and at the feel of it in her mouth she realised that she was going to have to masturbate then and there. She took her breasts in her hands, stroking them, rubbing the sperm on them into her skin, tugging gently on the nipple rings, teasing herself until she could no longer keep her hands away from her pussy. They went down, to the warm, wet opening of her sex. She pushed her bottom right out, inviting entry as she sucked on the fat erection in her mouth.

'Take this,' the man grunted.

He snatched at his cock, pulling it free to jerk at the shaft. Diana opened her mouth wide, hoping he'd spunk in it. He came, thick white come bursting from the tip of his penis, up into her hair, across her forehead and down over her nose in a thick, slimy trail. The next spurt caught her in the mouth and she quickly sucked him back in, draining the rest of his sperm down her throat as she rubbed hard at her clitoris, trying to reach climax while her mouth was still full of penis.

She nearly made it, only for him to pull out as the first tremor of orgasm hit her. Her mouth stayed open, gaping for cock. He just left her, slumping to one of the benches. Diana stayed down, still rubbing at herself, on the edge of orgasm, but desperate for one final dirty act to tip her over. She saw Nich coming towards her, with Wyatt behind him. The priest was staggering drunk, but Nick was squeezing what looked like a well aroused cock through his robe.

Diana gaped wide, in hope. Nich smiled down at her, pulling his robe up. As soon as his cock came on view she took it in, sucking with frantic urgency. Her orgasm started to rise again. She began to buck her bottom up and down to the rhythm of her masturbation, holding back only to let Nich get fully erect in her mouth. He soon was, and the satisfaction of having her mouth full of male meat once more joined her ecstasy. She let herself go, bouncing frantically on her thighs, her breasts swinging, her bottom jiggling wildly behind her.

Nich stopped, pulling back. Diana gave a squeal of frustration, gaping for him. He moved round, and her annoyance turned to gleeful bliss as he took her by the hips, to slide his cock up into her gaping vagina. He began to fuck her, his front slapping hard on her bare buttocks, and she was lost, rubbing frantically, mouth wide, in absolute ecstasy, as in front of her Wyatt began to lift his robe.

She gaped, nodding frantically as he exposed himself, his large, flaccid penis inches from her mouth. He came close, taking it in his hand. She kissed it, mouthing on the wrinkled flesh. Her orgasm rose in her head. She took him in, desperate to suck and fuck as she came, sucking, bucking on Nich's cock. It was all perfect, dirty, filthy, lewd, her utter humiliation with a hundred men and women looking on, and Wyatt's cock erupted, not sperm, but urine, full down her throat.

Diana's whole body went into spasm. Urine exploded from her nose and around Wyatt's cock as her throat closed in rejection. Her head jerked back, a great burst of piddle gushing from her mouth and down his balls even as the stream sprayed high, full into her face, closing her eyes and splashing out around her head. She screamed, in full orgasm, Nich hammering into her from behind as the stream of Wyatt's piss fell lower, into her mouth again, over her neck and then her breasts. The cock in her vagina went rigid and at the very peak of her orgasm she knew that she'd been filled with sperm.

She collapsed, sinking down in total satisfaction. Nich's cock slipped from her hole, which closed with a loud fart at the final contraction of her orgasm. Her breasts squashed out on the concrete, slippery with sperm and urine. Her hair was dripping, her skin slick, utterly soiled and utterly content as Wyatt drained out the last of his piss over her back and buttocks.

Six

Lilith stood at the centre of the chapel, looking around. It had changed almost out of recognition. Rather than the rotting beams and broken roof there was a smooth ceiling, now plain white, but due to be painted with some suitably Satanic motif. The windows had been repaired, in red glass bullseyes that threw the interior into a jumble of tones from orange and scarlet to the deepest crimsons. Benches had been installed, and carved chairs for the Chapter. At the far end screens rose to hide the sanctum, and also the spiral staircase that led up to the roof space, which when finished would be an airy, open-plan flat for herself and Diana. Even the smell had changed, from damp and pigeon droppings to sawdust and fresh paint.

'Nice work,' a voice sounded from behind her, and Lilith turned to find Hughes standing in the open doorway. He stepped inside.

'Expensive work,' Lilith answered.

'What do you expect, when you need everything done yesterday?' Hughes rejoined.

He began to inspect the room, with his hands in his pockets and the same calm, proprietorial air that always annoyed her so much. Since the Black Mass he had been less demanding, yet his presence still made her intensely defensive and ill at ease. It was also impossible to forget the way he'd tricked her and the spanking he'd given her, or to forgive. She said nothing, watching him, until the clatter of heels sounded on the staircase and Diana appeared from the sanctum.

'Hi, doll,' Hughes said, leering at her.

Diana returned a nervous smile and joined Lilith. Hughes continued his inspection, walking to the altar and smiling at he looked at the place where he had supposedly deflowered Becky.

'Just about ready,' he said suddenly. 'So when's the next one?'

'Nich wants to do something on Hallowe'en,' Lilith answered. 'Not like last time. A shorter Mass, then some pagan thing.'

'Whatever, so long as it's dirty and we make plenty of money,' Hughes replied. 'I've been thinking about it. We could make a lot more, you know.'

'I don't know,' Lilith said. 'Most of my clients I see once every two or three months. There's only so much they'll pay.'

'Get more clients, then,' Hughes answered, 'and remember, you'll be able to do all that new stuff once you're in here. I was talking about the Mass, anyway. What you need is to have a basic price, then they pay more for what they want, right? That's the way to do it. Get them horny, and they'll pay through the nose. Say a hundred to join in the Mass, with the piss and stuff. Fifty for a whipping, fifty to be jerked off, a hundred for a blow job, two hundred to fuck one of your tarts, and five hundred for the head tart. That way we can maybe get something out of the weird lot Nich brings and all. There were more blokes than girls.'

'I've told you,' Lilith answered him. 'I don't fuck, not for money. Anyway, my clients don't want to fuck me: they want to worship me. Until the Mass they hadn't even seen me naked, none of them.'

'They don't want to fuck you?' Hughes echoed. 'Don't make me laugh, doll. If men fancy you, they want to fuck you. Take it from me. If they don't ask, it's because they haven't got the guts, bunch of ponces. Did you see that old fart in the nappy? What a fucking pervo!'

'That's Mr Ackland,' Lilith answered him. 'He's one of my best clients.'

'Ackland!' Hughes exclaimed. 'I was sure I knew his face, only of course normally he's in a suit, not an overgrown nappy. He deals in brown-field sites, for industrial estates and that.'

'That's right,' Lilith admitted.

'Oh he'd fuck you,' Hughes went on. 'Believe me, he'd fuck your little arse until you were begging him to stop.'

'No,' Lilith said. 'All he wants is his nappy fantasy. He's never asked for anything else.'

'From you, maybe, because it's not on offer. The guy's married, with about six kids, and his wife's a dog. Show him your cunt and he'd fuck it.'

'He wouldn't,' Lilith insisted.

Hughes answered with a snort of contempt.

'Anyway,' Lilith went on, 'we can offer different things for different prices all right. It just gets a bit complicated to keep track of it all. With Becky and Diana we should manage.'

'What about that Juliana?'

'She won't take money. She wouldn't even take her share from last time.'

'Oh yeah?' Hughes asked, his interest suddenly quickening.

'We don't want too many, anyway,' Lilith said quickly.

'Right,' Hughes agreed. 'And another thing, next time, make sure we get some pictures. We'll put some of those miniature cameras in. That way, if we have any problems with any of them, we pull out a picture of them in the communion line, or having their cock sucked. That'll shut them up. Better still, we can charge a security payment, say a hundred a month, more for the rich buggers, to ensure our discretion. Show them the photos and they'll pay up smartish.'

'That's blackmail!' Diana objected.

'More like extortion,' Hughes replied. 'Safe, too. Guys who'll take a visit from my boys to make them pay their interest will cough up sweet if they think their bare arse is going to get an airing in the papers. And there's no way they'll go to the police. The knack is not to get greedy. Never ask more than they can afford. That way they don't get panicky.'

'I won't do it,' Lilith answered. 'My clients trust me and I return that trust.'

'Bollocks! You treat them like shit. Trust! You've got no respect for them, any more than they've got respect for themselves!'

'There's still trust, professional trust. Anyway, I'd lose the lot if I tried that. Word gets around quickly nowadays. There's this site on the Net, where men compare notes on girls they've visited. Anyone can log in.'

'That doesn't matter,' Hughes insisted. 'We only need to do it once and they're caught. Sure, some may have the guts to tell us to fuck ourselves. I doubt it, not your lot.'

'I don't care,' Lilith said. 'I won't do it.'

'I don't know why you're being so fucking precious,' Hughes snapped. 'You're already a whore, so what's the odds? Not that I give a fuck. If you won't do it I can easily find someone who will.'

'Not in my chapel,' Lilith said.

'*Your* chapel?' Hughes said. 'No, doll, *my* chapel. If you look in your contract – and by the way, some free advice, always read a contract before signing it – you'll see you're a tenant, paying rent.'

'No, we –' Lilith began in outrage.

'Save it!' Hughes cut her off.

'We still have ordinary tenants' rights,' Diana said. 'No matter what it says in your contract!'

'What, when you're running a brothel on my property?' Hughes responded. 'I don't think so, doll. Anyway, there's no call for unpleasantness. You just do as you're told and we'll be fine. All right?'

Tom Pridough sat at his desk, carefully drafting out the words of the sermon he intended to preach on the coming Sunday. He had chosen one of his favourite themes, avarice, which he intended to illustrate by criticising the demand for extravagant worldly goods, and in particular property. That would allow him to comment on the chapel he had so narrowly lost, and how wrong it was that Christian groups were not given the priority they deserved in such matters. Looking at the passage he had just written, he began to read it aloud.

'How is it, that land may be purchased by compulsory notice for the building of a road or railway, for any construction to serve the material needs of the population, and yet not for their spiritual needs?'

He mulled over his question, wondering how to answer it in a way that projected the righteous anger he felt and not the self-pity he knew was the root cause of that anger. Before he had decided, the doorbell rang, and he put the unfinished sermon down with as much relief as regret.

The caller proved to be one of his congregation, Jeffery Sands, and from the expression on his face it was immediately obvious that he was ill at ease. Ushering Sands in, Pridough smiled inwardly, looking forward to the feeling of superiority that listening to the troubles of his flock always gave him.

'I have done something terrible, Reverend. I need to talk,' Sands blurted out as soon as the door had closed.

'It is always a pleasure to provide guidance to one of my flock, Jeffery,' Pridough answered him. 'But do sit down. Perhaps I can offer you a cup of tea?'

No. No, thank you,' Sands answered, following Pridough into the kitchen. 'Oh, dear.'

'What seems to be the matter then?' Pridough asked.

Sands sat down, resting his forehead in one hand. Pridough waited, wondering if Sands had finally left his domineering and aggressive wife, or worse.

'I have done something terrible, Reverend,' Sand repeated. 'For some months I've been paying a woman . . . not for sex, to whip me. I . . . I don't even really know why. I just crave it.'

'I am very sorry to hear that,' Pridough said earnestly. 'We all must strive –'

'That's not all,' Sands interrupted. 'Oh God, what have I done?'

He went quiet, pulling at his hair.

'Do go on,' Pridough urged.

'The woman,' Sands went on, 'is called Lilith. She offered the chance to be whipped in front of other people, which she knew I needed. I took it, I had to . . .'

'We never have to,' Pridough said gently. 'To resist temptation is not easy, never easy, yet –'

'Shut up, I haven't finished!' Sands broke in. 'Sorry, Reverend, sorry. Forgive me. This whipping, it was to be at a ceremony. I didn't know it was Satanic, Reverend, I didn't!'

'A Satanic ritual? A Black Mass.'

'Yes, they called it that, a Black Mass.'

'A Black Mass?' Pridough echoed. 'Where? When?'

'Two weeks ago, at an old chapel they've bought out towards the moor, at Stanton Rocks.'

'The chapel at Stanton Rocks!'

'Yes. It was awful. Blasphemous, utterly blasphemous. They made a mockery of the Eucharist, Reverend, with a girl's urine for wine and the wafers touched . . . touched between the buttocks of Lilith!'

'And you received this?'

'No, Reverend. I held back, but I watched. I didn't have the willpower to leave, not with all of them watching. When the Communion was done a girl was placed on the altar. A man had sex with her. She was a virgin, they said. He gave her money for her virginity. Then I was whipped, and allowed a lewd act to be done to me. Can I be forgiven, Reverend? Is it possible?'

'And who did this?' Pridough demanded, ignoring his question. 'This woman Lilith?'

'Her, and others. There was a priest, a defrocked priest they said he was, and a thin man with red hair, who seemed to have organised it all.'

'Mordaunt, Nich Mordaunt?'

'I don't know. He never used his name. He just seemed to assume we would know who he was.'

'I do,' Pridough answered. 'I know very well.'

Nich sat sipping his beer in the alcove of the Black Dog they had made their own. Juliana was beside him, on one high-backed settle, Lilith, Diana and Becky together on the other, Wyatt and Hughes across from them in chairs. Since the Mass their roles had changed. Lilith and Diana now seemed in thrall to Hughes, and a great deal less enthusiastic. Becky had retained her enthusiasm, and gained in confidence. Where she had remained quiet before, she now happily put in suggestions. Wyatt had also grown in confidence and, like Becky, seemed keen to take an active part. Hughes was as brash as ever, opinionated, loud and pushy, giving way only in the religious details, in which he had no serious interest.

'So it's Hallowe'en, Lilith tells me,' Hughes said. 'We want a big one this time, Nich, real dirty.'

'That you may rely on,' Nich answered.

'Hallowe'en, a good night,' Wyatt said. 'That should bring us in a fine congregation. Do you think we should include some death symbolism?'

'It's only you Christians who regard the festival as sinister,' Nich cut in. 'To me it's Samhain, the festival of last harvest. We should celebrate fecundity, ripeness.'

'Nonsense,' Wyatt answered him, 'even the Celts regarded Samhain as a time of death.'

'Only in a metaphorical sense,' Nich insisted. 'Death and rebirth. The death of the Horned God, which is essential to his rebirth as the New Year. A death motif would be inappropriate. Better we do something involving fertility, impregnation.'

'Like maybe have one of the girls fucked by all the men?' Hughes put in. 'All the men who pay, anyway. You'll be up for that, won't you, doll?'

He reached out to tousle Diana's hair. She returned a sulky look and Hughes favoured Nich with a shrug.

'Well at least you'll admit that it's a time at which the boundary between our world and the next is thin,' Wyatt went on. 'Not a good night to go out alone, that surely we can agree on.'

'Rubbish!' Nick laughed. 'Another misinterpretation. This derives from interaction between the Celts and their predecessors, the folk who built the circles. The Celts, who were twice their size and far more aggressive, quickly drove them off the better land, up on to the moors. They also found them uncanny, unnaturally quick, almost inhuman, so they became associated with magic. Hence the Celts took up pre-Celtic festivals, blending them with their own, much as the Christians later absorbed the Celtic festivals, although with less cynical motives. Last Harvest, the Celtic Samhain, was the major pre-Celtic festival, the crucial link between the old year and the new. It involved the males racing for the honour of taking the virginity of a girl representing the Mother. Only one succeeded, the most virile, so the others would have been running over this countryside, drunk, lustful, high on fly agaric and ripe for mischief. Hardly surprising the Celts thought it was a bad night to be out alone, the women especially!'

'How can you possibly know all that?' Wyatt scoffed. 'It's pure speculation!'

'I don't imagine it's something they teach at Keble,' Juliana said, 'but it's essentially true.'

'How did you know I was at Keble?' Hughes demanded.

'She knows a great deal,' Nich said.

'More likely you've been reading my entry in *Crockford's*,' Wyatt answered them.

'Now there you have us!' Nich laughed. 'Anyway, it is this pre-Celtic festival I wish to re-create, after the Mass, with all the males invited to race for the Grim's Men circle, and the first there to deflower our ritual virgin.'

'That should draw the bastards in,' Hughes said. 'Every randy fucker in Exeter will want to be there. Nice one, Nich. What d'you reckon? Fifty? Or do we set it lower and go for the big crowd?'

'It should be free,' Nich objected.

'I don't know about that,' Wyatt said. 'Being able to afford to attend could well be regarded as an element of virility, in modern terms.'

'Dead right,' Hughes agreed.

'Regardless,' Nich said, 'we can't do it without a willing virgin.'

'Too late, mate,' Hughes said, throwing a glance at Becky. 'The man got there first.'

'Susan Blake,' Wyatt said.

'Susan Blake, your choirgirl?' Nich queried. 'What about her?'

'She's a virgin,' Wyatt said. 'Or she was last May.'

'You're certain?' Nich demanded.

'I saw,' Wyatt assured him. 'She's also a greedy, calculating little bitch. Offer her enough and she'll do it.'

'And a genuine virgin,' Nich said thoughtfully. 'It has to be worth a try. We'll go up tomorrow, shall we, Juliana? I take it you have her address, Andrew?'

'She lives in South Harling, Kiln Lane,' Wyatt said, 'but go alone: she'll see you as a threat, Juliana, not a comfort.'

'Fair enough,' Nich said. 'Any other advice?'

'Let her lead you,' Wyatt said. 'She loves to tease, to enjoy her power over men.'

'And this girl's a virgin?' Diana queried.

'She was in May,' Wyatt insisted. 'Her hymen was intact, I swear to it.'

'It has to be worth a try,' Nich repeated. 'Let's hope. The other thing we need is a worthwhile climax to the Mass. I thought maybe we could summon an egregore.'

'An egregore? What's an egregore,' Lilith demanded.

'An egregore,' Nich explained, 'is a person possessed by a summoned spirit, whose body has been borrowed, to put it simply. The person then takes on the behaviour of that spirit.'

'Sounds good,' Diana answered.

'Sounds heavy,' Becky put in.

'Dramatic, certainly,' Nich went on.

'It's got to be something the slaves can get off on,' Lilith pointed out.

'Oh, it will be, I assure you,' Nich said, grinning at her. 'A popular choice is the summoning of the egregore of your namesake, she who represents the dark side of femininity in rabbinical literature. The Babylonians saw her as a demoness, yet many of her supposed faults would be seen today as virtues – a refusal to take the passive role to men, sexual aggression. In any case, the prime attribute of Lilith is a strong, independent sexuality, and that is what is expressed in the egregore.'

172

'What, and this is for real?' Becky queried.

'It is very real,' Nich assured her. 'Anyone who doubts need only see the extraordinary transformation that occurs. I have seen a normally mild, even timid, woman display a lust bestial in its purity, without the slightest trace of inhibition. It is magnificent. Be warned, however, Lilith is anything but passive. Scratches, even bites are normal, while Lilith egregores are noted for an understanding of erotic pain.'

'And it would be me who got possessed, yes?' Lilith asked.

'It would be right to allow you first choice,' Nich answered.

'You seriously mean I'd be possessed by her spirit, don't you?' Lilith questioned him.

'Absolutely,' Nich answered. 'It is real, have no doubt.'

'If you don't want to, I will,' Juliana said.

'No,' Lilith said quickly. 'I want to. It's scary, but I want to.'

'What a load of bollocks!' Hughes broke in. 'Don't get me wrong, I think it's a great idea for the punters. It's crap, though, isn't it? Come on, Nich, mate, you're not stupid, we both know that. You're like me, aren't you? You just do it to get in the girls' knickers.'

'Absolutely not!' Nich retorted.

'Yeah, sure, don't make me laugh!' Hughes went on. 'Like this egregore crap. You know how it works. I'll tell you how it works. The thing with girls, right, is they don't like to admit they enjoy sex. It's not their fault, mind, it's the way they're brought up. So, right, they want it, but they want an excuse. Like being a whore. They get paid, and they can fuck, without having to admit they like it. Sure, then they get fucked up about being whores, but that's girls all over, isn't it? Contradictory, never know their own fucking minds. So it's the same with this egregore crap, right? You do your ritual bit, you summon a spirit that is known for fucking everything in sight and, bang, your prissy little piece can be a right tart for an hour and blame it all on the spirit.'

'This is absolutely not the case,' Nich said hotly. 'I shall prove it to you!'

'Yeah, sure!' Hughes sneered. 'Come on, mate. I'm not one of your gullible prats. Sure you can make a girl do stuff like she was possessed. You may even be able to make her *believe* she's possessed. It's still bollocks, though, and you know it.'

'Not an egregorial summoning, no,' Nich answered, 'a true corporeal manifestation.'

'What, like, summon the devil?' Hughes laughed.

'No,' Nich answered, 'that would be foolish. I think, however, that I can contain some lesser being.'

'This I've got to see!' Hughes said. 'This I've got to fucking see!'

'You will,' Nich assured him.

Nich stopped outside the pub in South Harling. The village was as before, quiet, sleepy, and if anything prettier still, with the rich greens of late summer replaced by the gold and red of autumn. Dismounting, he spent a moment enjoying the atmosphere, and contrasting it with the events that had happened there. He smiled happily, taking the map with which Wyatt had provided him from his pocket. Susan Blake lived at 24 Kiln Lane, which was almost directly opposite the pub. Nich set off down it, admiring the cottages. Outside one there was a girl sitting on the wall, petite, freckled, with her blonde hair caught up in bunches. She wore a blue dress, knee-length, with long white socks showing beneath and smart black shoes. Nich gave her a polite smile and walked past, keeping his eye on the house numbers. Most had none. When he did find one it was 32. Walking back, he counted the houses, to discover that 24 was the one outside which the girl was sitting.

'Excuse me,' he asked. 'Do you happen to know if this is the Blakes' house? I'm looking for Susan Blake.'

'Sure,' the girl answered, 'who are you?'

'My name's Nich,' Nich answered.

'I'm Susan. What's up?'

Nich paused, wondering how to introduce the subject of having her virginity taken at a Satanic ritual to such a seemingly innocent girl. From Wyatt's account she was anything but, yet it was hard to reconcile her appearance with her supposed behaviour. He paused, wondering if her depravity was simply a figment of Wyatt's imagination.

'You fancy me, don't you?' she said suddenly.

'I . . . er . . .' Nich managed.

'How'd you like to feel my tits, then?' she asked.

'I beg your pardon?' Nich answered, taken aback.

'Straight up,' the girl said. 'Two quid for a grope, a fiver and I'll get them out.'

'That's, er . . . very nice of you,' Nich managed. 'Look, er . . . might we have a word?'

'What about?'

'More or less what you've just suggested,' he replied, glancing quickly up and down the lane. 'Over a drink, perhaps, at the Blue Boar.'

'They won't serve me.'

'Coke or something, I meant.'

She shrugged and jumped down from the wall. With her standing, he realised that she barely reached his shoulder. Coupled with the blue dress and her bunches, it made her seem disconcertingly young.

'You're sixteen, yes?' he asked.

'Seventeen,' she said. 'A couple of weeks ago. Don't worry, mister, I'm legal.'

'You seem very certain of my intentions,' Nich stated.

'What else would you want?' she answered. 'How come you're looking for me?'

'It's a long story,' Nich said cautiously. 'Let's just say a mutual friend recommended you.'

'What? Some bloke been bragging and now you fancy your share?'

'No . . . Not at all,' Nich said quickly, but she had ceased to pay attention, running forward to where his bike stood at the roadside.

'Nice,' she said, stroking the black paint of Nich's Triumph.

'It's mine,' Nich told her.

'Cool!' she exclaimed.

'It has style, I like to think,' Nich responded.

'Take me for a ride,' she demanded.

'Should we? What about your parents?'

'Dad's at work. Mum's gone in to Warminster to shop. Take me to the Pitt Arms at Deverill. They serve me there.'

'Well, all right,' Nich said uncertainly.

Juliana peered carefully from the window of the flat, expecting to discover Tom Pridough standing below. Instead there was the more solid form of Dave Hughes, suited and holding a bottle of Moët et Chandon. Intrigued, and amused, she threw open the window. Hughes looked up at the sound.

'Hi, doll,' Hughes announced, waving the bottle.

Juliana nodded and reached back for the keys, tossing them down. Hughes caught them one-handed and was already sliding the door key into place as Juliana shut the window. Opening the inner door, she made herself comfortable on the couch, adopting a careless posture that made the best of one slender hip and the fullness of her breasts beneath her top. Hughes appeared in the doorway.

'You've come for sex, I take it?' Juliana asked.

'Don't mess about, do you?' said Hughes. 'Well, yeah, since you're going to be straight. What with Nich up in Wiltshire, I thought you and I might get better acquainted.'

'Fine,' Juliana answered, 'stick the bottle in the freezer, then. We'll have it after we've fucked.'

'No need,' Hughes answered. 'It's come straight out of the chiller cabinet at my place.'

'The glasses are in the second cupboard along, the higher ones, then,' Juliana went on. 'Would you like me to act innocent, pretend I'm shy or something?'

'No, none of that stuff,' Hughes said, sounding suddenly disappointed. 'I don't like it fake, doll. I like it real.'

'Oh, right,' Juliana responded. 'Would you like to torture me, then? Or be tortured? You could rape me if you like. I'll put up a proper fight.'

'No, no, no, you don't get it at all, do you?' he said. 'I don't want it like that. I want to seduce you, to turn you on, to watch as you surrender to me.'

176

'How very old-fashioned,' Juliana answered him. 'I just do what I please, so I'm afraid I don't really have anything to surrender.'

'Oh, you do,' Hughes answered. 'You do, girl.'

'I do?' Juliana queried.

Hughes didn't answer, grimacing as he twisted at the top of the champagne bottle. The cork came free, a gush of froth bubbling up over his hand. Juliana watched as he poured, and took the offered glass.

'Tell me, then,' she demanded.

'What you have to surrender, doll,' Hughes said, sitting down, 'is your dignity.'

'What, do you want to spank me over your knee, or put me in nappies?' Juliana laughed.

'No, babe. I want to make you a whore.'

'Oh, yes, they told me about your little fantasy. So you actually want to pay me for what I'd give willingly?'

'No, doll, I want to find something you won't do willingly and see how much it takes to make you put out.'

'Right, I get it. There's a problem, though, if I'm up for anything.'

'You reckon you're up for anything? You don't know you're born, girl. How old are you, twenty-two, twenty-three?'

'Older than you think.'

'Hey, one thing you're not is old enough to want to hide it. So how much to fuck you up your tight little arse? And I don't mean from behind: I mean up your dirt box.'

'Go ahead. I love anal sex. Nich did me over the altar in the church in Wiltshire, where Andrew Wyatt used to preach, the same way Susan Blake was buggered.'

'All right, so you're a dirty bitch. What if I put it up your arse, then make you suck me?'

'If you like. I do that for Nich, too.'

'You really are dirty, aren't you? So what if I was to piss right in that pretty face?'

'Let me take my clothes off first.'

'No, fully clothed, in here.'

'That's not fair on Nich. We'd wreck the couch, and the carpet.'

'Fully clothed, on the couch. I piss on you, in your mouth and all. I fuck you in your wet clothes, cunt and arsehole, and finish off in your mouth.'

'In the bathroom fine, not here.'

'Here. One hundred quid.'

'Don't be stupid, the couch cost over nine hundred.'

'A grand.'

'I'm not up for it, Mr Hughes, no matter how much you offer. Look, you're a big man, for all that you're a complete arsehole.'

'What did you call me?'

'A complete arsehole. I mean, surely you're aware of that?'

'You've got one fuck of a mouth on you, girl, you know that?'

'I'm only telling the truth. There's no need to get offended. You are an arsehole, but you've got a good body, plenty of power. You've got a nice cock, too. I like them thick – it makes me feel stretched. Come on, you're angry now. Why not slap me about a bit and drag me into the bathroom? Piss all over me and rape me on the bathroom floor, up my bumhole. Force me to suck your dirty cock and spunk up in my face, right in my eyes. Just leave me like that, blinded and sopping with piss, with my bumhole aching and my mouth full of the taste of my own dirt. Come on, I'm waiting.'

'That sounds about what you need,' he rasped, 'but you take it here, and you take money for it, so while you're sucking on my dirty prick you can think what a whore you are. Two thousand.'

'No.'

Juliana stood to walk into the bathroom, deliberately swaying her hips. At the door she turned. Hughes was still in his seat, but looking at her. There was a conspicuous bulge in his crotch, and she smiled, raising her eyebrows.

'Get back here, bitch,' he ordered. 'Three grand.'

In answer Juliana pulled up her top, exposing her large black bra. Taking hold of the wires beneath her breasts, she flipped it up, letting them fall. Casually, she began to play with her nipples, tickling one with a long nail and ignoring Hughes as she touched herself.

'Four grand,' he said.

Juliana shook her head. Taking a breast in each hand, she bounced them, feeling their weight and texture.

'Actually,' she said, 'I think I feel more dominant. Last chance. You can get really heavy. I want my bum done, but you can do my face too, really slap me around. When you've got me on the floor and pissed all over me I'll suck you so lovingly. Fuck me, and bugger me, use me until I'm grovelling in your piss with your lovely big cock in my mouth. Come on, or the game changes, and I'll have you.'

'Twenty grand,' Hughes offered. 'Twenty fucking grand, Juliana. I bet that's more money than you see in years.'

'You'd better take me,' she answered, 'or the rules change and you miss out.'

'Fuck off. I make the rules. Twenty grand, I'm offering, just to come over here and take what you want, bitch.'

'You're not. You're lying. I know that trick. I accept twenty and you tell me it shows I'm a whore. I lose my cool and do it for peanuts.'

'Shit! You've been talking to that bitch whore Lilith, haven't you?'

'No. I just know the game. I've played it before. What are you really offering?'

'Five hundred maybe, and no crap about the upholstery. You can clean it up if you have to – in fact I'll pay fifty extra to watch you scrub up if you do it nude. If it doesn't work, tell Nich you pissed yourself.'

'Five hundred? Fair enough, I'll pay that, for you to come to the next Mass wearing a nappy.'

'You what?'

'Five hundred to come to the Mass in a nappy and take a punishment from me. Nothing hard: an over-the-knee spanking will do nicely.'

'Bollocks, girl. Don't try to twist this on me!'

'A thousand, then.'

'Cut the crap and get over here. Where would you get that sort of money anyway?'

179

Juliana shrugged and reached up to take out her earring. She threw it to Hughes, who caught it, peering suspiciously at the great dark stone.

'Paste,' he said.

'Sapphire,' she answered, 'salvaged from the Spanish galleon *Sao Joao*. I've no idea what it's worth, but it should cover your price.'

Hughes looked at the earring again. His face had gone dark, and he rose suddenly, hurling it back at her.

'You are full of shit, you know that?' he stormed as he made for the door. 'But I'll have you, you just fucking wait. I'll have you begging to be made my whore! Five hundred, the offer stays down!'

Juliana said nothing, but put her glass to her lips as he slammed the door, hiding her smile.

Nich stepped from the door of the Pitt Arms, wondering if the third pint of beer had really been sensible. Susan had expected him to drink, and he was sure that any attempt to go easy would have met with her scorn, and the destruction of his carefully built-up image. As it was, he had drunk, and so had she, bottles of Pils that had left her giggly and unsteady on her feet.

'Let's go for a ride,' she suggested, following him out.

'No, a walk,' Nich answered, nodding to where an ancient public-footpath sign showed in the hedge opposite the pub.

'Oh, yeah, want to get me in the bushes, do you?' Susan giggled. 'Well I might not want to, mister – or I might.'

Nich simply grinned back and took her arm, leading her unresisting across the road and over the style. Beyond was a field, yellow with stubble, the footpath showing as a flattened line that led towards a bank of distant trees. It had been impossible to broach the question in the pub, with crowded tables to either side of them and Susan keeping up an unbroken flow of conversation. He had admitted to knowing Wyatt, which had caused an awkward moment, saved only by his frantic assertions that the priest bore Susan no ill will. Now, with Susan's hand in his and the empty field stretching away to all sides, there was no longer an excuse for holding back. Initially, he needed to know if she was still a virgin, and his best chance seemed to be to express a personal interest.

'So you might?' he teased. 'Might what?'

'Might, you know, let you have a feel,' she answered. 'Maybe more if you get me horny. Yeah, what the fuck, I'll suck your cock for a tenner. You can't fuck me, that's all.'

'Right,' Nich answered, once more astonished by her openness. 'I can respect that. Wrong time of the month?'

'No. I've never been, and you're not going to be the first.'

'Fair enough. You seem, so er ... liberated,' Nich replied, struggling for a polite word to express what he thought. 'So how is it that you're still a virgin?'

'Oh, that. Yeah, well, Mum and Dad are into this American thing, yeah? Band of Virtue, it's called. When you join it you take a pledge, yeah, not to fuck until you get married. If I do it, they're going to buy me a car. Cool, huh?'

'Yes,' Nich said, 'but Wyatt sodomised you, at your own request, according to his story.'

'Sure, the pledge don't say nothing about taking it up the bum.'

'Still ...'

'Sure, they'd be pissed off. That's why I said old man Wyatt made me, and 'cause the papers wanted me to. Fifty grand we got for that. Well cool.'

'Fifty thousand pounds? I see.'

'Yeah. There's these doctor blokes who come round to look at the girl's fannies to check we've kept the pledge. Load of old perves if you ask me, staring up girls' fannies. They don't know if you've had it up the bum, do they? I wouldn't have split on Wyatt if we hadn't got caught. I fancied him, for real. I like dirty men. I can't stand stuffy types. I tell you straight, Mum and Dad ain't going to like you. I do, though: you're freaky. Tell you what. I'll give you a freebie. You're dirty, I can tell from how you talk. Want to put it up my bum like old man Wyatt did?'

Nich swallowed hard, trying to think of a reason to refuse her and finding none. She was beautiful, willing and completely open in her lust, also crude, mercenary and brash, not just a slut, but a brat as well.

'Well, er . . . yes,' he managed. 'You have a beautiful bottom. I'd be honoured.'

'You haven't seen it yet,' she laughed, 'not properly. I'll show, just as soon as we get in the wood.'

She ran ahead, laughing. Nich followed, chasing her across the field, to where another sign indicated that they should take a right turn. Susan ignored it, scrambling over the ancient fence that cut off the wood, but too slowly to stop Nich catching her by the arm. She pulled away, giggling, only to stop a few yards into the trees.

'Who wants to see my knickers?' she taunted. 'Dirty man!'

Nich grinned, striding forward. Still giggling, Susan reached down for the hem of her dress and quickly flipped it up, giving him a brief flash of white panties before running on into the wood. Nich came after her, Susan skipping between the trees until the field was lost from view and stopping in an open area carpeted with yellow-brown chestnut leaves.

'Shall I pull them down now?' she said. 'So you can watch my bum as I walk? I bet you'd like that.'

Not waiting for him to answer, she turned her dress up and tucked it behind its waistband, once more showing Nich the taut white seat of her panties. They were too small for her, and bulging with pert teenage bottom. Nich squeezed his crotch. Susan giggled, looking back over her shoulder. She took hold of the panties, her innocent face full of mischief. She began to push them down, exposing her bottom bit by bit, until the whole, glorious, cheeky orb was naked, pink and bare in the autumn sunlight. Nich's cock was stiffening rapidly.

'Naughty, isn't it?' she said. 'Going bare bum in the woods. I love it. I just love stripping off. I used to go bare under my surplice for old Wyatt. He loved that. He's a dirty sod, you know. He used to come in while we were changing, and we'd be in our bras and knickers. You could see how randy he got.'

'I'm not surprised,' Nich answered. 'A room full of pretty girls in nothing but knickers and bras. You'd be inhuman not to.'

'What is it with men?' she said. 'You get so into girls' knickers.'

'It's what's in them we get obsessed with,' Nich replied, 'what they hide, and what they show. I'd say you had to be quite perverse to become excited by knickers as such.'

'Yeah? There was this guy once, a businessman, paid me twenty to take off the pair I was wearing for him. Nothing else. I reckon he wanted to sniff them while he wanked.'

'Could be,' Nich admitted vaguely, his eyes still fixed on the movement of her bottom.

'No guts, these blokes,' she went on. 'That's their problem. Like, they can't ask a straight question, or they think they have to trick us into it. He was all right, him, the knicker man. Stiff, but not bad-looking. I'd have sucked him off for twenty and he could have had my knickers and all. You're not like that, are you? You're just dirty.'

'I prefer wicked,' Nich answered. 'Certainly I have no problem in making my desires known, such as that to sheaf my cock in your delightful bottom.'

'You talk funny.' Susan giggled, stopped, reached back and pulled the cheeks of her bottom apart, to show off the dark spot of her anus.

Thinking she was ready, Nich gave a quick glance around the wood and reached for his fly.

'You want to fuck it, you've got to catch me,' Susan said, pulled up her panties and ran.

Nich gave chase, quickly gaining on her, until she reached a massive chestnut, which she hid behind, laughing and dodging from side to side as he tried to catch her. Nich tried to feint and missed, attempted to rush and missed again, only for Susan to collapse in the leaf mould, laughing so hard she had tripped over a root. Nich sank down beside her, pinning her arms to the ground.

'Now,' he announced, 'I intend to bugger you.'

'Let me suck you first,' she demanded. 'I love cocksuck-ing.'

Without hesitation, Nich released his cock from his fly. Susan made a little eager noise and buried her face in his lap, taking it straight in, to suck with clumsy passion. Nich winced at the feel of her teeth on his foreskin, but let her do it, relaxing back to watch her face as she sucked. She moved up to a kneeling position, with her panty-clad bottom stuck out towards him. Nich began to stroke her buttocks through the thin cotton, admiring the way her cheeks bulged inside the panties. His cock was growing in her mouth, quickly, and she was sucking with more and more urgency, not so much to excite him, but for the pleasure of doing it. Nich wondered if she would like to be told what a slut she was, but decided against it, contenting himself with exploring her bottom. She kept sucking, until he was rock-hard and his cock was beginning to twitch, threatening the onset of orgasm.

'You had better stop, or I'll come in your mouth,' he warned.

Susan pulled her head up from his cock, paused and plunged it back, her cheeks drawing in as she sucked hard with his erection jammed to the back of her throat. Again she pulled off, smiling, her eyes bright with excitement, to roll over on to her back. Nich moved close, kissing her. She responded, opening her mouth under his as she took his cock in her hand, jerking at it in raw lust. Nich relaxed, enjoying her, until the need for orgasm once more became overwhelming.

'Time that went up your bottom, Susan,' he said as he pulled back.

Susan immediately rolled herself up, giggling as she pulled her panties up over her bottom, to give Nich a view of both her anus and her vulva. He moved into position, admiring his view. Her sex lips were pressed tight together, bulging into a little fat fig, yet she was aroused, the pink folds of her vaginal opening moist and puffy with blood.

'Want to see my cherry?' she asked happily.

Nich nodded. Susan immediately reached down to spread her vaginal lips and show the hole between, a tiny black cavity surrounded by a smooth half-circle of flesh stretching up towards her clitoris.

'Very pretty,' Nich said.

'I bet you'd just love to pop it, wouldn't you?' she said. 'Well you can't, but you can put it up my bum.'

'Open yourself,' Nich said. 'Use the juice from your pussy.'

'Oh, you dirty sod,' Susan answered.

Her finger went to the tiny, wet hole of her vagina, which was awash with fluid. Slopping it out, she put her finger quickly to her bottom hole. Nich watched, stroking his erection as she teased her anus, wetting the little brown ring, then popping the top joint inside. Susan sighed, pushing in more of her finger as her anal ring spread to take it, exposing pink, mushy flesh. His cock was straining, the head glossy with pressure.

Susan began to finger herself, sliding it in and out as her anus quickly spread wider and grew more juicy. A second finger went in, then a third, pushed deep as her back arched in pleasure. She moaned, pulling at herself to show a dark cavity between her fingers. Knowing he would come in his hand if he didn't act quickly, Nich edged forward. Susan moaned, starting to buck on her own fingers in flagrant anal masturbation. Nich took her hand, gently, pulling it free with a sticky pop and substituting the head of his cock. Most of it went in, the wet, slimy ring already receptive enough to take him. He pushed, and watched the head of his cock disappear up her bottom. Again Susan moaned, squeezing her anal ring on the head of his penis. Once more Nich pushed, still watching, to see his cock push into her bottom hole, deeper, and deeper still. She was arching her back, pushing against the ground, eager for more of his erection up her bum. It went, inch by inch, until his balls pressed between the soft cheeks of her bottom. Susan gave a long, satisfied sigh and reached for her panties, tugging them free of one leg to leave them flapping from the ankle of the other. She lifted her bottom, to tug up her dress, high over her breasts, taking her bra with it. Once more her legs came up, high and wide as she took hold of herself behind her knees. Nich pushed again, forcing the last little bit of his shaft up into her anus.

'That's nice,' she sighed. 'Your balls are all ticklish on my bum. Don't spunk yet, will you? Do me properly.'

In answer, Nich took her firmly around her thighs, pulling her body hard on to his cock. She gasped and he did it again, lowering his body on to hers as he increased his pace, using her bumhole as if he had been up her pussy. Immediately she was squealing, odd, piglike noises interspersed with a frantic panting as her face went slack and her arms came up to lock around his neck in passion. Nich continued, hammering into her until he could stand no more, unable to hold himself back from orgasm except by stopping.

'Nice,' Susan sighed. 'Oh, you dirty bugger. Again.'

Nich paused, sliding his erection slowly up and down inside her. His cock felt impossibly sensitive, squeezed in the hot, slimy cavity of her rectum, desperate for the friction that he knew would take him very quickly to orgasm. Blanking his mind, he leaned into her, kissing her mouth. Her own mouth opened immediately, Susan kissing with frantic passion as he once more increased his pace up her bottom, faster and faster, until she broke away, once more squealing piglike and bucking her body on his cock. Nich stopped, leaving Susan panting and urgent, her back arched. He was on the edge of orgasm, his mind fussy, his cock rock-hard.

'I'm going to do it again,' he managed, 'and come up you.'

'No, don't,' she moaned. 'Let me jill off while you're up my bum. Watch me do it.'

Ignoring the urge to rebel and just bugger her to his own satisfaction, Nich shook himself as he sat back up. Susan's hand went straight to her sex, her fingers covering the little pink folds as she began to masturbate. Nich took her by the ankles, holding her legs high and wide as he buggered her with long, slow strokes, pulling her stretched anus in and out as she masturbated. He knew it was too much, his cock pulsing, even as her anal ring tightened on him, squeezing his shaft, her body going into spasm, her whole rectum squeezing, sucking on his cock – and he was coming, spurting into her as he lost control and hammered himself into her body to the sound of the piping, high-pitched squeals of her own orgasm.

Nich collapsed on to Susan, kissing her and pulling her body into his. She responded, open-mouthed, her arms coming up around his neck. For a long moment they held still, as his cock slowly shrank inside her, to slip from her greasy hole without difficulty.

'Thank you,' he gasped.

Susan blew out her breath.

'Exquisite,' he went on. 'You bugger divinely.'

'I'm all sticky,' Susan answered, rolling over on to one elbow.

She adjusted her dress, to find a pocket and dig into it, producing a handful of crumpled tissues. Nich watched in fascination as she wiped her bottom, then her pussy, casually tossing the soiled tissues aside. Only when she had finished did she pass him those that remained.

'Good?' he enquired.

'Yeah, good,' she answered. 'Better than old man Wyatt. He shot his load up my bum before he even got it up properly.'

She began to rearrange her clothes, pulling up her panties and adjusting her bra. Nich put his cock away, thoroughly pleased with himself, and feeling that, even if she reacted to his proposal with an angry denial, the day had not been wasted. With her underwear straight, Susan stood, to brush the leaves and bits of moss off her dress, at the sides and back, before craning backwards in an attempt to inspect her bottom.

'Is my bum dirty?' she asked.

'Free of leaves, yes,' Nich said.

'Great,' she said. 'So what's the deal? You were after my cherry, weren't you?'

'Not as such,' Nich answered. 'Well, yes, I suppose I am, in a sense. It's hard to know how to phrase this, actually, although I must admit it seems a lot easier now. Basically, I do want to make an offer for your virginity.'

'Oh yeah, how much?' Susan demanded.

'You don't seem shocked, even surprised,' Nich said.

'What's to be shocked about?' she asked. 'That's what men want, isn't it? The first bloke to try that with me was old farmer Banter. A tenner, he offered me, cheeky git.'

'That does seem undervalued,' Nich admitted, 'if these things are to be valued at all. Obviously you didn't accept his offer.'

'He ended up paying me thirty for a suck and a feel of my tits,' Susan answered. 'That desperate, he was. So how much?'

'Well certainly more than twenty pounds,' Nich said. 'About two thousand, in fact, maybe more.'

'Two grand?' Susan queried. 'Not worth it, is it? My car's going to be one of those flash new Minis, the BMW ones, or maybe an open-top sports if something nice comes along. That's got to be worth over ten grand.'

'True,' Nich admitted. 'But you have no objection in principle, then?'

Seven

Dave Hughes lounged at his desk, idly scanning a list of his accounts, and making an occasional mark beside one or another. His man John sat opposite him, sunk into the comfortable office chair Hughes had purchased in order to make potential clients feel at ease, and hopefully secure enough to take out larger loans than they needed.

'Good month,' he remarked. 'Bang on time, most of them. The lark with the chapel's working out to be a good earner and all. What a pair of stupid tarts, eh?'

'You're not wrong, boss,' John answered.

'Three stupid tarts now,' Hughes went on, 'thanks to me. It'll be four soon and all. That weird bloke, Nich, he's talked some Wiltshire girl into it. The new one, Becky, she's a nice-looking piece, big tits, arse like a ripe peach. You know that candle place on Dawlish Road? She works there when she's not on her back.'

'Oh, *that* Becky.'

'You know her?'

'Yeah. My brother Steve went out with her for a bit. He used to take her out to the pictures and that, then fuck her over the back seat of his car. Horny bitch, he says, and he's right.'

'He's full of shit, John. She was a virgin, until I popped her.'

'Virgin? No way, Dave. They came out with me and Cheryl one time. Steve brought her back after and they stayed over. We made the girls do striptease, and feel each

189

other up and that. Becky was well up for it. Steve fucked her on the sofa later and all.'

'You sure?'

'We could hear them. Half the fucking night they was at it. Like rabbits.'

'He fucked her? No way!'

'Well if he put it up her arse I'm surprised she could walk in the morning, the way they were going at it. Four, five times, I reckon.'

'No way. I took her cherry. There was blood all over my prick. She screamed the fucking place down. This is the same girl, yeah? Becky, average height, brunette, curly, big tits, big arse, tiny waist, looks like butter wouldn't melt.'

'Yeah, Becky. Works at . . . what's it, Craft Candles.'

'And Steve fucked her? When?'

'Loads of times, like I said. They must have been together two, three weeks, before she chucked him in for that bloke who works in the big Granada on the motorway. You know him, skinny bastard with loads of tatts –'

'The fucking little bitches!' Hughes cut in.

Lilith looked out from the round window at one end of what was now a comfortable open-plan flat. The main room was large, sunny and airy, filling her with a feeling of ease spoiled only by the nagging knowledge of who actually owned it. Even with the area set aside for the bathroom and dungeon, it was larger than the old flat, while both those rooms were bigger and better fitted than before. Outside, the bulk of Stanton Rocks and the dark of the pine plantation surrounded the chapel land, providing her with a sense of stability she had never known before. Everything, in fact, was right, except for Dave Hughes.

As if summoned by her thinking his name, Hughes's black BMW appeared from among the trees. Lilith sighed, wondering what he wanted. It was never easy to predict his mood, and there was every chance he had simply come to see how the work was progressing. On the other hand, he might want money, or even have changed his mind about

190

her tattoo and be after sex. She bit her lip, knowing full well how easy it would be for him to bribe her into surrender. He simply had too much that she wanted for her to resist.

The car stopped below. Hughes emerged and slammed the door behind him. Lilith started back in shock at the rage on his face. He vanished from view; the chapel rang to the crash of the door. Lilith turned, now scared, but with nowhere to run and, before she could think what to do, Hughes appeared at the top of the stairs.

'You've had me over, haven't you, you fucking little bitch?' he roared.

'No,' Lilith answered, backing quickly away. 'I don't know what you're talking about!'

'You know full fucking well what I'm talking about, you conniving little whore. That slut, Becky, she was no fucking virgin, was she? *Was she?* What was it, you bitch, red ink, food dye?'

'I . . . I mean . . .' Lilith stammered. 'It was real. I swear it. I thought . . . we . . .'

'Don't try any of your crap on me,' Hughes snarled. 'I know, right, because my boy John's kid brother had her, didn't he? And by the sound of it so has every other cunt-happy teenage fucker in Exeter!'

'She'd never been paid, though, I swear it!' Lilith managed.

'By the sound of it she didn't need to be fucking paid!' Hughes yelled.

He snatched out, grabbing Lilith by her blouse and jerking her towards him. The material tore, spilling buttons on to the bed and leaving one tattooed breast hanging out as he pulled her close to his face. She pushed against him, striking out, only for Hughes to catch her wrist and twist it hard down to her side.

'Don't even think about it,' he rasped. 'Enough bollocks. No more Mr Nice Guy. From now on, you work for me, and your bitch-whore girlfriend, too. You do what I say, when I say. If some freak wants to shit in your mouth, you take it, right?'

191

Lilith nodded her head, her face white with fear, her jaw shaking. Hughes threw her hard down on the bed and spat, catching her full in the face. She crawled quickly away, pressing herself to the iron bedstead. Hughes leered down at her, watching his spittle trickle down one cheek. When he spoke, his voice was quiet and low.

'And you're going to earn me the money back,' he said. 'On your backs. And, on Hallowe'en, I fuck little Susan. Got that?'

Again, Lilith nodded, her eyes wide with fright, fixed on Hughes, and following him as he walked from the flat.

'I shall collect her Tuesday lunchtime, while her father's at work and her mother's shopping,' Nich explained. 'She will claim to be visiting a friend's caravan on Dawlish Warren, where indeed she will be staying. Tuesday evening we brief her, Wednesday is Samhain, and we debrief her, if you will excuse the dreadful pun.'

He lowered himself on to the floor, draping an arm around Juliana's shoulders and lifting his glass of wine to toast the others.

'And she's going for the full ritual thing, everything?' Becky demanded.

'It took a while to talk her round,' Nich admitted, 'and she wants a big slice of the take, which I must say seems fair enough. Of course that's really down to you, Lilith?'

'Don't ask me,' Lilith said miserably. 'Ask Dave Hughes.'

'Hughes?' Nich demanded. 'Why? Are you all right?'

'I'm fine,' Lilith said testily, and paused, only to speak again, her voice suddenly weary. 'No, I'm not all right. It's Hughes.'

'Hughes? This stuff with the chapel?'

'That and more,' Lilith sighed. 'I may as well tell you. He's found out Becky was fake. I don't know how. He's . . . he's set himself up as my pimp, Diana's and mine, and he wants Susan, at the Mass, and all the money. You need to negotiate, speak to him.'

'He can't do that!' Nich protested.

'What's to stop him?' Lilith demanded. 'That's not all either. He wants cameras installed, so he can film the Mass and use the pictures to extort money from my clients.'

'No way!'

Lilith nodded sadly.

'It must be said, Nich,' Juliana remarked, 'that Hughes is a good deal more like the Christian representation of Satan than your own. He has to go.'

'Very true,' Nich admitted, 'but he's not going to get away with it. Susan's agreed to the Samhain ritual. That's my business, and nothing to do with Hughes.'

'Please, Nich,' Diana put in. 'Don't make waves. Just let him do it. You don't know what people like that are like. We do.'

'No!' Nich protested. 'Let's just go and tell the greedy bastard to fuck off, all of us together. He's paying for the chapel, so what? If he wants his rent he's going to have to let us do something.'

'It doesn't work like that,' Lilith objected. He owns the building, or at least he will do after the council meeting. He made me sign a contract. It gives him just about every right you can think of and me none. Because I'm running a brothel I can't even claim my normal rights. He's got us.'

'A contract?' Nich asked. 'Are you sure it's valid?'

'He said it was. Look.'

She rolled on her bed, reaching for a drawer in the squat cabinet beside it to pull out a slim sheaf of papers. Nich took it and lay back, Juliana leaning in on his shoulder so that she also could read it.

'Agreement between, blah ... blah ... blah ...' Nich read out. 'Hmm, he doesn't leave you much room, does he? What a bastard! If you quit he takes the lot.'

'Maybe, but it's not valid at all,' Juliana pointed out. 'Hughes's offer hasn't even been formally accepted. You can't enter into an agreement over a property you don't own, except with the owner.'

'He said it was legal!' Lilith protested.

'He lied.'

'The bastard! The utter, fucking bastard!'

'So tell him to fuck himself,' Nich suggested. 'What can he do?'

'Plenty,' Lilith answered, 'and I don't want to know. I thought I'd got away from all this shit when I left Bristol. Oh, fuck!'

'You'll have to persuade Susan to go with him,' Diana said. 'Please, Nich, for our sake?'

'We're going to have to do it, Nich,' Juliana added.

Juliana lay sprawled across a heap of pillows, naked, her bottom raised high and wide, each limb tied firmly to one of the four bedposts. Nich knelt behind her, his face fixed in a grin of manic glee as he focused on the open lips of her sex and the tight dimple of her bottom hole. In one hand he held a shallow dish, open, with a blunt knife embedded in the soft yellow butter it contained. Slowly, carefully, he scooped a large pat on to the tip of the knife. Juliana looked back, her anus twitching in anticipation.

'Here goes,' Nich announced, 'one buttered bumhole.'

Juliana nodded, sticking her bottom up to splay her cheeks. Nich applied the knife, wiping the butter directly on to her bottom hole and pressing the knife to the centre in an attempt to force a little up. She responded with a soft moan and a delighted wiggle of her bottom. He sat back, watching as the pat moved in her hole, sinking suddenly lower as she relaxed her ring, rinsing again as she tightened it, to press out a trickle of now molten butter. The drop ran down over the narrow bar of flesh between anus and vagina, to mingle with the white fluid that had begun to bead in her sex.

'I'm ready,' she sighed. 'Put them up me.'

Nich nodded, reaching to put the butter dish down and take up Juliana's cunt wedges from the bedside table. She watched as he held up the polished wooden stakes, her eyes round with expectation. He traced a finger over the rounded tip, a split bulb of wood much the size of the head of his cock. Juliana nodded eagerly.

'The butter's running down into your pussy,' Nich remarked, 'but there should be enough.'

194

'Bugger me, anyway,' Juliana answered, 'deep, stretch me.'

Nich put the tip of the wedge to Juliana's buttery anus. Her ring twitched. Gently, he pushed, watching the flesh move in under the rounded end, then abruptly spread open around it. She sighed and he pushed again, her anus stretching slowly wider under the pressure, until it had become a taught pink band around the polished head of the wedge. For a moment he held it in place, enjoying the view and the pained twitching of her buttocks, then pushed again and watched the head disappear into her rectum, her anal ring closing around the neck.

'Now the bulge,' Juliana sighed.

Again Nich pushed, watching her ring spread once more, tight, and tighter still, as the thick shaft spread it out. Juliana's muscles began to twitch again, her breath turning to a ragged panting. Her bound hands started to clutch at the bedposts, her feet to wriggle. Nich eased the wedge deeper still, and for the first time she cried out, a little gasp of reaction. Nich reached to scoop up some more butter, applying it to Juliana's straining ring. As the butter ran slowly down her flesh he began to bugger her with the wedge, moving in and out, but a tiny bit deeper with every push. Her panting became more pronounced, her cries more pained, her clutching more desperate as her anus stretched wider and wider still. Nich kept on, buggering her mercilessly, until at last her anus was stretched to the full thickness of the bulge at the centre of the wedge, in a thin, taut ring of pink flesh. With a last push Nich slid the bulge in. Juliana's anus closed on the second neck, a section still at least twice as thick as any normal cock.

'It's in,' he said.

'I know,' she panted. 'That hurts so much. I feel so full. Now wedge me.'

Nich reached for the bedside table once more, picking up the smaller of the two wedges and a mallet. For a moment Juliana watched, then buried her face in her pillow as Nich pressed the tip of the small stake into the groove at the end of the one up her bottom. It fitted snugly and, as he

195

worked it into place, he saw the elastic bands on the thick wedge begin to stretch. Juliana moaned. Nich tapped the wedge with the mallet. Juliana cried out in sudden shock and the gap hole of her anus was forced wider still. Again Nich tapped, Juliana shivering in reaction and letting out a hollow groan. Ignoring the very real pain in her response, Nich continued to hammer one wedge into the other, watching her anus spread slowly wider with each blow. She had quickly begun to clutch at the bedposts again, and her breathing had become a series of urgent gasps, while the muscles of her thighs and buttocks were twitching uncontrollably.

'I'm going to split!' she panted suddenly. 'Stop it, stop it!'

He stopped. Taking hold of his cock, Nich began to masturbate himself, holding the wedges up Juliana's anus as he did it. She was making peculiar grunting noises in time to her breathing. Her muscles were jerking and twitching, while her open, buttery sex was moving in response, her vagina pulsing. With his cock ready, Nich climbed on to the bed behind her, stationing himself between her open thighs. Her clitoris showed, a tight pink bead of glossy flesh between the soft folds of her inner lips. He put his cock to it, rubbing, to make her stiffen and whimper in response. The end of the wedges met his stomach as he adjusted himself. His cock went to her hole, and up, pressing close, to jam the wedges into her protesting anus and wring a cry of pure pain from her lips.

'Fuck me, hard,' she gasped. 'Just do it. Don't mind what happens.'

Nich obeyed, taking her by the hips to shove his cock into her, fucking her with a slow, lazy motion. Her body jumped at each push, her anus straining on the wedge. She cried out, and again, an agonised moaning that grew in volume as he got faster, pumping in and out, the wedge jammed into his flesh, and hers, to bugger her mercilessly even as she was fucked. His hand went down, his long nails scratching at her sex, over the puffy lips and across her clitoris.

Juliana screamed, her body bucking crazily, in a single, agonised spasm. Nich scratched again, harder, and leaned his body on to hers, forcing the cunt wedges yet deeper into the wire-tight ring of her anus. Again Juliana screamed, a wild screech of agony as her ring gave. Nich felt the splash of warm fluid on his skin as Juliana went into a frantic, crazy bucking, writhing and screaming, in what seemed to him pure pain, although she was obviously coming. Hot, wet liquid had filled her vagina around his cock and he was pumping it, spurting and splashing around his balls, until it was simply too much for him to hold back. He came, deep inside her, holding himself tight to her body so that the wedges were kept up as far as they had gone, with Juliana cursing and spitting like a cat as he emptied himself into her body.

He held himself until his orgasm had run its course, clinging to Juliana's writhing body by main force. Even when the ecstasy in his head broke he stayed up her, lost in the feel of her insides and of the warm fluid running down over his balls. Only when she finally went limp did he pull out, easing his cock from her vagina and sitting back on his haunches. Juliana's anus had split in two places, and blood was welling from the cuts, to pool in her slowly closing vagina.

'May I watch?' Nich asked, taking a careful hold of the cunt wedges.

'If you like,' she answered, 'and pull the bulge out quickly, get it over with.'

Nich nodded, and began to ease the smaller wedge out. It came, and the instant the thicker wedge had closed Nich gave it a sharp jerk, pulling it clear of her bottom hole. She gasped in pain, her muscles twitching. Nich put the wedges down and watched as her hole closed, the muscle now flaccid, to leave a dark hole into her body. In utter fascination he stared as the two cuts healed, sealing to two tiny white scars. They in turn faded and vanished, even as her anus closed to a tight knot.

'That was beautiful,' she sighed. 'Truly beautiful. Do it again, Nich.'

'I'll take a bit to get ready,' Nich answered.

'Use a dildo in my pussy, then,' Juliana said, 'a big one, and this time really split me wide.'

'OK,' Nich agreed. 'Shall I clean you up first?'

'No,' Juliana said. 'I like it. My pussy's full of it, isn't it?'

'Fairly full,' Nich said, 'and it's all over your thighs and under your bum. You'll need buttering up again, too.'

'As you like,' Juliana answered. 'Just take it slow.'

Nich set to work, taking his time as he buttered Juliana's bottom, playing with her anus until she was once more greasy and open. The thick cunt wedge went up as before, with her reaction rising slowly as her anus was stretched, until the full mass of the main bulge was wedged into her rectum. Nich spent a moment gently buggering her, and left her with the wedge sticking obscenely from her anus as he went for the dildo. He selected the thickest of the three in her top drawer, a great black thing with a bulbous head and grotesquely exaggerated veins. He let her watch as he came behind her once more, and readied her for entry, only for the doorbell to sound even as he was pushing the fat head to her sopping vagina. Nich ignored it, but it rang again immediately, an insistent buzz showing a complete lack of patience from the visitor.

'Leave it,' Juliana said. 'They'll go away.'

'Uh, uh,' he said. 'There's only one person who rings like that, somebody whose sex education probably skipped over such things as cunt wedges, even giant dildos.'

'OK,' Juliana sighed. 'If you must.'

'I must,' Nich assured her, planting a smack on her bottom as he jumped up from the bed.

The bell rang again, still more insistently, and he hurried into the first thing that came to hand, a dressing gown of Juliana's in scarlet silk with a black octopus embroidered on the back. Collecting the keys, he thrust his head from the window, to find Tom Pridough below, as he had expected.

'Morning, Tom,' Nich called cheerfully.

'I wish to see you, Mordaunt, now,' Pridough replied.

'By all means,' Nich answered, and tossed the keys down.

He pulled back in, wondering at the source of Pridough's anger, which had been plainer even than usual.

'What does he want?' Juliana called from the bedroom.

'That we shall discover,' Nich answered, opening the inner door to greet Pridough with a sweeping bow.

'I'll speak to you now, Mordaunt, and you'll listen!' the priest demanded, pushing inside.

'With pleasure,' Nich answered. 'I always enjoy your little rants. Excuse me a moment, though. I was torturing my girlfriend, and the wedges are still in. I won't be a second.'

He walked to the bedroom, casually pulling open the door to leave the bed, and Juliana, in full view of Pridough, with her blood-smeared thighs wide, the huge dildo lying between them and the wedge protruding from her gaping anus.

'What – what have you *done* to her?' Pridough gasped.

'Used cunt wedges,' Nich said. 'It's her favourite, although the terminology is perhaps inaccurate as they're in her bottom.'

'Pervert! Foul ... unnatural ... beast ... sodomist ... Satan!' Pridough screamed.

Nich shut the door, both he and Juliana stifling their laughter. Quickly, Nich untied her, returning to the main room to find Pridough standing as before, still gaping at the door.

'You were saying?' Nich said.

Pridough made the sign of the cross, his eyes shut. He was shaking, his face a rich purple, a vein in his forehead pulsing. Nich choked back the remark he had been going to make, worried that Pridough was going to have a stroke.

'Sit down,' he said instead, 'and calm down. 'We're just playing, all right? Just sex, no big deal.'

'Sex? No big deal?' Pridough repeatedly slowly.

'Are you OK, Mr Pridough?' Juliana asked, emerging from the room, rubbing her wrists and still stark-naked.

Pridough just stared, the vein throbbing dark, his eyes following her as she walked into the bathroom. She had removed the wedge, and held both in one hand, while red smears of blood still showed on her legs and in the crease of her bottom.

'Make him a cup of tea, Nich,' she called. 'I'll be out in a minute.'

'Good idea,' Nich said. 'Tea, Tom? Or do you prefer coffee?'

He walked into the kitchen, not giving Pridough a chance to respond, and made a show of washing his hands. In the bathroom the shower started. As Nich began to make tea, Pridough finally found his voice.

'Do you have no sense of morality whatever?' he demanded weakly.

'I have very high morals,' Nich replied in an offended tone.

'High morals?' Pridough demanded. 'You claim high morals, while you torture women and hold Satanic rites? You have no understanding of what morality is, Mordaunt, none at all!'

'Certainly my moral values differ from yours,' Nich replied. 'Being Christian, I imagine you consider your personal moral choices to be in some way universal; a typically narrow-minded view, if I may say so.'

'There are certain universal moral laws, yes,' Pridough replied, 'but I did not come here to discuss your warped philosophies. I came to speak to you about the Black Mass –'

'I would question the existence of universal moral laws,' Nich interrupted, 'while the degree to which my philosophies are warped, if at all, is highly subjective. As to the Black Mass, to which Black Mass are you referring? Do you want to come?'

'You know full well what I'm talking about!' Pridough answered. 'Do you deny officiating at a Black Mass held at the Exeter Brethren chapel by Stanton Rocks?'

'Categorically,' Nich answered.

'I know you were there, Mordaunt,' Pridough insisted.

'Certainly I know what you are talking about,' Nich answered. 'I do not deny that I was there, but I did not

200

officiate. I am not entitled to, after all. As you should know, being a man of the cloth yourself, only a priest who has received formal ordination and has subsequently been defrocked may officiate at a Black Mass. But then you don't actually have descendant authority, or whatever it's called, you know, when the right to officiate at rituals has been passed down all the way from Jesus, do you? Furthermore, the chapel should properly be referred to as the chapel of Satan Asmodeus.'

'I'm not interested in the details of your perverted cult!' Pridough snapped. 'And as to my ordination, no, I will not be drawn. The Black Mass was held, and I have no doubt you organised it. Now, I will say this once, and you will listen. It will not happen again –'

'No?' Nich interrupted. 'Are you sure? I would speculate that it will. Indeed, I would be prepared to place money on the fact. We intend to hold regular services, one every month or two, on auspicious occasions. As to the organisation, yes, I think I may fairly claim to have done the main share of the work. But I cannot take all the credit. On the matter of your ordination, did you just assume your status, then? Your first point, my last, I must take issue on. You have always seemed fascinated by the details of –'

'Will you stop doing that!' Pridough snapped.

'What?' Nich asked.

'Trying to split the conversation into several different topics at once, as you very well know,' Pridough answered. 'I am serious, Mr Mordaunt!'

'Clearly so,' Nich answered, pouring the contents of the kettle into the three cups he had arranged on the kitchen work surface. 'Milk? Sugar? Or do you take lemon? A lot of people do, nowadays, you know. Juliana, do we have any lemons?'

'In the fruit basket,' Juliana answered, stepping from the bathroom, with her wet hair confined in one towel and another wrapped around her body.

'I do not want tea!' Pridough said brusquely.

'I thought you said you did,' Nich answered.

'I do not,' Pridough answered. 'I . . . Stop! Enough of your taunting! Enough of your childish, idiotic behaviour!'

201

'What's the matter?' Juliana queried, straightening up from where she had bent to pick a shoe from the floor, and in doing so provided Pridough with a full view of her bare bottom.

Pridough said nothing. His eyes were shut, his hands to his temples, his mouth moving in prayer. Nich took a sip of tea, hiding his grin.

'If another Black Mass is held,' Pridough said quietly, 'or any similar abomination, I shall be calling the police. You will be charged with gross indecency.'

'I think you may be a little rusty on your law there,' Nich cut in.

'Gross indecency,' Pridough repeated firmly, 'and I shall also bring a private prosecution for blasphemy.'

'An expensive process,' Nich commented. 'Still, be my guest, protestors, police, blasphemy prosecutions, whatever amuses you. I can think of nothing more likely to attract attention to my cause. However, if you want anything that might actually give you a chance of anyone being charged, don't get there until nine o'clock. It should have got good and dirty by then.'

Mr Arlidge hung in the straps, his naked body wet with sweat, his buttocks a mess of purple bruises. Lilith stood behind him, the sjambok in her hand, her hair disarrayed, her own body nearly as sweaty as his. He was groaning, his head hung down to his chest in exhaustion, yet his cock stood proud from beneath his belly, a straining erection induced by the beating.

'Beat me, Mistress, harder,' he whimpered. 'Punish me. I've been so dirty, so wrong . . .'

His words broke off in a scream as Lilith lashed the sjambok down across his buttocks with all her strength. She had barely heard his words. In her mind he was David Hughes, and it was with difficulty that she kept her blows to the intended target of his buttocks. Her arm ached, her leather catsuit felt tight and uncomfortable, but there was a savage pleasure in beating him, and other men, far stronger than she had been used to.

'More, Mistress, you're going to do it!' Arlidge moaned. 'Oh what a horrid little specimen I am, so dirty, so crude . . .'

Lilith laid in, thinking of Hughes, anger welling up inside her, her strokes delivered with every ounce of her strength, smacking into his flesh, her vision blurred with sweat. Arlidge was screaming, and dancing frantically in his straps, his erection waving wildly to and fro. Lilith grabbed it, wrenching. Arlidge screamed louder still, a new note of demented pain entering his voice as her nails dug into his cock, which exploded in a gush of sperm, across the floor, up Lilith's arm as she wrenched harder still and out once more on to the floor. Lilith dropped his cock, flicking the come from her arm in disgust.

'Wonderful, Mistress, wonderful,' Arlidge babbled. 'Thank you, Mistress, oh, thank you. Nobody's done that before, not ever. Oh, thank you.'

Lilith threw the sjambok at him and walked out, not bothering to reply. Diana was in the main room, reading a magazine, and got hurriedly to her feet as Lilith jerked her thumb back towards the dungeon door.

'Sands is here,' Diana said as she went to the sink. 'I told him to wait in the chapel.'

'It's not his day,' Lilith answered. 'What does he want?'

'Details about the next Mass. He insisted on talking to you,' Diana answered. 'You know what they're like.'

'Demanding little pricks,' Lilith said. 'Why do they always imagine they're so fucking important? I'll go down in a minute.'

She went to the bar they had installed in one corner, pouring herself a glass of vodka and tipping it down her throat. Despite whipping Arlidge, anger and frustration still burned in her mind, a helpless desire to revenge herself on Hughes, which she knew was futile unless she ran once more, an option she was struggling to resist. Cursing him, she poured herself another drink, added ice and a piece of lime, quickly adjusted her hair and made for the stairs. Sands was in the chapel, as Diana had said, kneeling at one of the benches, apparently in prayer.

'Yes?' Lilith demanded, walking towards him.

'Ah, Mistress Lilith,' he said, climbing quickly to his feet. 'I was wondering if you might tell me about the next event here.'

'You don't have to see me to buy tickets,' she answered, 'and they're a hundred this time, more if you want special treatment.'

'Oh I will, Mistress, I will,' he said. 'Will it be soon?'

'Hallowe'en,' Lilith answered.

'And will there be anything special? Oh that was wonderful last time, what you arranged. So clever.'

'Yes, there'll be plenty,' she assured him.

'What would that be, Mistress? I must know.'

'Right,' Lilith sighed. 'There'll be the Mass, with Communion, like before. Then there's going to be a sort of cabaret, lots of sex, with a girl as a demon. Then Hughes is going to fuck another virgin. Enough for you?'

'Oh yes, Mistress,' he answered, 'wonderful. Oh, I'm so looking forward to it.'

'I'll get a ticket,' she said.

'Oh no, Mistress,' he answered. 'I'll buy one later, if I may. Money's a little difficult, just now. Thank you, Mistress. Goodbye, Mistress.'

He hurried out. Even as the door shut behind him Lilith had forgotten him, her mind turning once more to David Hughes, with sudden inspiration.

Nich entered the Black Dog, looking around for his friends. Wyatt alone was visible, sitting at their favourite table with an open bottle of red wine in front of him. It was already half empty, and there was a distinct flush to his face. Otherwise he was immaculate, his hair neatly brushed, and in the black robe he had taken to wearing, complete with black dog collar, a choice that had raised several eyebrows in the pub. Nich nodded to him and walked to the bar, ordering beer, which he took to the table.

'Is Juliana not with you?' Wyatt queried as Nich sat down.

'She's in Exeter,' Nich answered.

'It's going well?'

'Sort of. There's a lot of interest, anyway.'

'Will the chapel be big enough?'

'No, frankly. You'd better conduct the service from the steps, and hope for decent weather.'

'Our Lord will grant it, no doubt.'

Nich raised his eyebrows as he took a swallow of beer, surprised at the devotion in Wyatt's voice.

'I note your surprise,' Wyatt said. 'Yes, over the last few weeks I have been thinking, and I have come to appreciate my position.'

'And to believe?' Nich questioned.

'I never doubted,' Wyatt answered. 'How could I, when every day I had to wrestle with the temptations sent me? When I gave in, when I fell, I thought Satan had destroyed me. Now I realise he wanted me for his own, and sent you to bring me to his ministry.'

'Yes?' Nich queried, trying to detect mockery or doubt in Wyatt's voice but finding neither.

'Yes,' Wyatt went on. 'At first I was just going along with it. It was better than that flat, anyway, and there was Juliana, of course. She is wonderful, isn't she? Then, when I stood up in the chapel, I felt different, stronger. I know now where that strength came from, but it was when you called upon me to give communion that the real transformation came. I felt a change in my body, as I used to when I took on the role of Christ in true communion, a transubstantiation. Only this was different . . .'

He trailed off, to stare thoughtfully into his wineglass.

'You felt possessed?' Nich asked. 'By the spirit of Satan?'

'Maybe,' Wyatt answered. 'I was numb for a long while, but when you came over to me to suggest we join the orgy I felt a real power, a raw lust, very different from what I felt for Susan. That was not me. Was it Satan Asmodeus? Maybe.'

'Diana would probably accept that,' Nich answered.

'That is it, exactly,' Wyatt said. 'For all the lust I tried and failed to control, I would never have urinated on a woman. It would never even have occurred to me to do so.'

205

'No?' Nich asked.

Wyatt shook his head emphatically. Nich shrugged.

'So I have come to accept my place,' Wyatt went on, 'and you have my thanks for the part you played. Juliana, too. I am a new man, reborn.'

'A sort of born-again Satanist, then?' Nich joked.

'Perhaps,' Wyatt laughed. 'Certainly my faith is strong again, albeit inverted. In fact, I have several innovations for the next Mass.'

'Go on.'

'Well, for one thing, I thought of more decoration. Goats' skulls, perhaps, and the Asmodeus symbol on our robes, in scarlet, I thought.'

'Excellent,' Nich agreed, 'but why stop at skulls? There's a version in which supplicants kiss a goat's arse to show their devotion to Satan. I can get a goat, from a Wiccan friend of mine who runs a petting farm near Moreton-hampstead. For skulls, we might use sheep's in practice. Dartmoor is littered with them, while goats' are hard to get hold of, although I have a few at home we can borrow.'

Wyatt nodded and continued. 'More importantly, in the Christian Mass it is traditional to confess before Communion, so that you go up to the altar rail pure. We might invert that, with a declaration of erotic sins before the Communion.'

'Good idea,' Nich agreed.

'More importantly still,' Wyatt went on, 'I fear I must object to your linking your pagan ritual to the Mass. I'm sorry to –'

'Don't worry,' Nich broke in. 'There's a change of plan. That's what Juliana's trying to sort out in Exeter. Susan's not going up to the circle. Hughes will deflower her on the altar. It's a real pain, actually. We'd done this great flyer, with a picture Susan mailed me, of her in a white dress. Tickets were going like wild fire. Anyway, I don't see the problem. Essentially, the evening is a celebration of the Horned God, in one aspect or another.'

'You're wrong,' Wyatt said. 'Satan, as Lucifer, is part of the Christian faith, to which I am committed, albeit in

206

inversion. It has nothing to do with modern paganism, most of which is simply made up.'

'Not at all,' Nich objected. 'Damn it, it was the Christian church that linked Satan to the old gods. And they're as real as your God, believe me, and a great deal more accessible.'

'So you do believe in God?' Wyatt queried.

'If by God you mean the Christian God, Yahweh or Lah, then yes,' Nich answered. 'Why not? However, I consider the religion alien to this country, also patriarchal and repressive, especially sexually. Belief is one thing, worship quite another. I worship the old gods of our islands, Cernunnos, Grim, Herne, particularly Sigodin-Yth, who is an aspect of the pre-Celtic Txcalin, Juliana's patron deity.'

'I tell you it's pure nonsense,' Wyatt said, 'like the rest of this modern pagan business. Take the Herne legend, for instance. I believe it to be fourteenth-century, relating to the reign of Richard the Second, while the earliest actual reference comes from Shakespeare. Hardly Celtic.'

'That's immaterial,' Nich responded. 'Herne is an aspect of the Horned God. Such deities have many names, and to seek a true or original name is an exercise in futility, as is claiming that a particular name is invalid because it was unknown to any particular culture. Gods may be named by believers, in the very nature of gods, and the name may well be regarded by the worshippers as a sacred thing in its own right. In essence a god is the product of human thought, as is the name. Real, be assured of that, but dependent on the belief of worshippers. Besides, the name Herne seems to be a pretty direct derivation from Cernunnos. If modern pagans choose to worship the Horned God as Herne, then they may. It requires considerably less in the way of mental gymnastics than some of the Christian concepts. The Trinity, for instance, or why saints don't count as minor deities.'

'Saints can only intercede; God alone can act,' Wyatt explained.

'And Satan?' Nich queried. 'He can act, surely?'

Wyatt didn't reply, taking a swallow of his wine.

'Having said that,' Nich went on, 'one can argue that essentially there are only two gods, the Horned God and the Mother, representing the male and female principles respectively. One can argue that the Christian God is simply an aspect of the Horned God, also Satan. It's a simplistic viewpoint, but I espouse it sometimes, if only to annoy the likes of Pridough.'

'Pridough?'

'Our local bible basher.'

'Yes, I remember you saying. You're quite wrong though . . .'

Wyatt stopped, turning as Lilith appeared beside him, to place a cluster of drinks on the table. Diana took her place on the settle, also Becky, Lilith squeezing in between them, and finally Susan, pressing close to Nich's side.

'OK,' Diana said. 'This is how it works. We've got twenty-three blokes signed up, at a hundred each, plus what we take on the night. Susan's OK about Hughes.'

'Yeah,' Susan said, 'as long as I get a lot of money, and I mean a lot. The guy sounds a real creep.'

'We've only got so much!' Lilith answered in exasperation. 'You know, we can't give what we don't have!'

'That's not my problem,' Susan said. 'He wants my cherry, he can fucking pay for it. We agreed ten thousand, didn't we, Nich?'

'We did, yes,' Nich stated, 'although that was before Hughes stuck his oar in. We'd already sold over a hundred tickets to the Samhain ritual, and now we're having to tell people it's off and they just get to watch. It's a mess, believe me. Juliana's trying to sort it out, but we'll be lucky if we get two thousand out of it.'

'Two thou, then,' Diana said, 'and maybe two hundred each from our clients, on average. That's six thousand six hundred.'

'You can have it all, Susan,' Lilith said, 'as long as Hughes lets you.'

'Bullshit!' Susan exclaimed. 'I want my ten thousand, and I want it up front. Where is this bloke Hughes, anyway?'

208

'He's supposed to be here,' Nich said. 'I'm surprised he's not. He generally turns up when you speak his name.'

As if on cue, Hughes appeared in the doorway. Another man was with him, whom Nich didn't recognise, short, balding, with small round glasses on an equally round head.

'That's your man,' Nich said. 'The tall one.'

Susan made a noise in her throat, either fear or anticipation, Nich was unsure which. Hughes approached, his eyes flicking over the group before settling on Susan.

'So you're my poppet?' he asked, extending his hand to Susan. 'Beautiful, fucking gorgeous. You've done good, Nich, just so long as she's the real thing.'

'I am,' Susan answered, bold even in the face of Hughes's leer.

'Yeah, well, we're going to make sure of that,' Hughes answered, jerking his head back towards the short man. 'This is a mate of mine, Dr Evans.'

Evans smiled, a leer if anything dirtier than Hughes's.

'He's going to check you over,' Hughes went on. 'He'll be coming to the Mass and all, and I want you girls to be extra nice to him, got that?'

None of them responded, Evans running his beady eyes along the settle on which they sat, at breast level.

'Get a round in, Andy,' Hughes said, sitting down and nodding to Wyatt. 'How's it going, then? All sorted?'

'Not really, no,' Nich admitted. 'Juliana's still trying to sort out the mess with the tickets and, by the way, she'll be ready for you after the service, at the price agreed.'

'I fucking knew it!' Hughes answered, then paused. 'You don't seem bothered. You know what she's talking about, don't you? I'm going to fuck her, for five hundred quid, to make her a whore.'

'Juliana does as she pleases,' Nich answered.

'Sure,' Hughes answered. 'She's just a little whore like the rest of them. And, talking of whores, I want a couple of changes this time. You three girls will be naked, except for kinky boots, right?'

'That just ruins my image!' Lilith protested.

209

'Just shut it and do as you're told,' Hughes answered. 'You go nude. The punters love it. You can have whips, all right, and dish out all the thrashings they can take. Oh, and I want you to take the communion, with the piss drinking and that. And, before you start, no bollocks, or it'll be my piss in the cup. Got me?'

Lilith gave a sulky nod, Diana and Becky instinctively pulling close to her on either side.

'Another thing,' Nich said. 'Susan's worried she's not getting enough money.'

'You've nothing to worry about, doll,' Hughes answered immediately, turning to Susan. 'When it's down to money, I'm the man. How much do you want?'

'Ten thousand,' Susan answered.

'Ten grand?' Hughes answered. 'Yeah, all right, doll.'

'Up front, cash,' Susan said.

'Fuck me,' Hughes answered. 'Where d'you get her, Nich? Off the fucking Mafia? Look, doll, even *I* don't carry that kind of cash around on me. I can have it by tomorrow, right?'

'Whatever,' Susan answered.

Nich reached down to choose a sheep's skull from the box Becky was holding. Placing it on the windowsill, he took up a candle, using another, already lit, to melt its base and glue it to the top of the skull.

'What is it, three per ledge?' he asked, glancing around the chapel.

'About that,' she answered. 'Some of them are pretty mouldy.'

'We'll put those inside,' Nich said, 'and the real goat skulls can go on the altar and the ledge above the door. It's looking good, yeah?'

'Great,' Becky answered, glancing up to the colossal motif on the ceiling, a great golden pentagram, on a background of vivid red, speared through by an inverted cross, and surrounded by symbols, with that of Asmodeus at the apex.

'Where d'you want this lot, mate?' a voice called from the door.

Nich turned to see Hughes's man John looming in the doorway, a pile of beer cases in his hands.

'Stack it in the back,' Nich answered him, 'behind the drapes. You'll find tables to set up the bar with. And remember to keep it out of sight until we get started.'

'I know mate, I've been doing this since I was a kid,' John answered as he pushed the sanctum drapes aside with his foot.

John disappeared, his voice sounding from behind the drapes a moment later.

'There's a fucking goat in here!'

'Ignore it,' Nich advised. 'It's part of the ceremony.'

'It is, is it?' John asked as he emerged. 'What? You going to have it fuck a girl or something?'

'No,' Nich answered. 'It represents an aspect of Satan.'

'Shame,' John answered. 'You'd have 'em queuing round the block. Up for it, Becky?'

'No, I am not!' she answered. 'You bastard!'

'He's probably right,' Nich said as John disappeared through the door, laughing.

Nich chuckled and reached for another sheep's skull. As he placed it on the windowsill the door was pushed open again, this time to admit Hughes, with Dr Evans behind him.

'Susan here?' Hughes demanded.

'Upstairs, getting ready,' Nich replied.

'Right, leave that to her. I want you as a witness to this.'

Nich jumped down, nodded to Becky and followed Hughes and the doctor. The smell of goat hit him as he pushed through the drapes, and he caught the last few words of some crude remark from Hughes, and the doctor's answering laugh. Upstairs, Wyatt, Lilith and Diana were seated around a table with an open bottle of red wine between them, while the sound of running water came from the bathroom.

'Is the poppet in the shower?' Hughes demanded.

Wyatt nodded.

'Time to have that darling little cherry inspected, doll,' Hughes called loudly. 'Come on out.'

211

There was no response, and Hughes pushed open the door, revealing Susan standing naked and dripping wet outside the shower. Evans leered, his eyes fixing on her bare, round bottom, then her breasts as she turned, to reach out her foot and kick the door shut. Hughes laughed.

'Give me a break, will you?' she demanded.

'We haven't got all day, doll,' he answered. 'There's already about a hundred blokes up on the rocks and that. Oh, and don't bother to dress.'

'Yeah, right,' Susan answered as the sound of the shower stopped.

'How d'you want her, Doc?' Hughes asked as he strolled into the main body of the flat. 'Spread out or what?'

'I think bending allows the clearest view of the hymen,' Evans answered. 'Yes, I think we shall have her bend.'

Hughes gave a cluck of amusement, throwing himself down on the sofa. Evans joined him. Nich glanced from the round window, where he could see the people gathering on the rocks and in clumps along the sides of the tracks. Many were clearly pagans, but more were not, both male and female. He gave a grim smile and turned back at the sound of the bathroom door opening. Susan emerged, now wrapped in a white towel, with another twisted around her head like a turban. She walked over, without hesitation, or the least sign of concern at being about to have her vulva inspected.

'We er . . . won't be needing the towel, my dear, I don't think,' Evans said.

'You are one dirty old bastard, you know that?' Susan replied, but casually dropped her towel. 'Right, you want to see my cherry, yeah?'

'Yes, my dear,' Evans said. 'Now, if you could just turn your back to Mr Hughes and myself . . .'

'From behind?' Susan queried.

'Yes, my dear, that is the normal –'

'No, it's not, you fucking old perve. I should know: I get done once a year. If you want to see my bum, just say so, right?'

She turned, setting her feet wide. Nich moved closer, unable to resist the view as she bent down, her back well

212

dipped, to rest her hands on her knees. The position left her bottom well parted, with the lips of her pussy sticking out prominently from between her legs, the hole on clear show, as was her anus.

'Like the view, Doc?' she asked. 'Shame you're not going to get it, ain't it?'

Dr Evans leaned forward, a fat pink tongue flicking out to moisten his lips as he reached one podgy hand out to Susan's sex. At the far end of the flat the two girls and Wyatt were watching, in silence. Evans's fingers found Susan's sex, gently spreading the chubby lips, to reveal the bright pink flesh of her vaginal passage, with the taut membrane of her hymen clearly visible. She held still, her emotions betrayed only by a faint trembling of her fleshy bottom. Evans moved his fingers, spreading her sex a little wider.

'Yes,' he said. '*Virgo intacta*, without question.'

'I told you so,' Susan answered him. 'Right, if you've finished groping me up and staring up my fanny, I want to see the colour of your money.'

'A virgin,' Hughes drawled as Susan straightened up, 'and what a fucking poppet. Shame about the mouth on her.'

'On me?' Susan answered him. 'You're one to talk!'

She reached for her towel, wrapping it loosely around herself.

'Out, you two,' Hughes ordered, jerking his thumb at Lilith and Diana. 'Over here, Andy.'

Diana made straight for the staircase, Lilith opening her mouth to protest but thinking better of it and following her friend. Hughes waited until they had disappeared then pulled a thick wad of fifty-pound notes from his pocket.

'Not sure I trust those two,' he explained as Wyatt joined them. 'I wouldn't put it past them to do a runner if they got the chance. Right, poppet, ten grand. Want it counted?'

'Yes,' Susan answered, reaching out.

'Uh, uh,' Hughes said. 'Not you. You get it once your cherry's split, not before.'

'How do I know you'll give it to me?' Susan demanded.

'Because I'm not holding it either,' Hughes said. 'Mr Wyatt here is.'

'Bollocks!' Susan spat. 'Give me my money, now!'

'You'll get it when you've earned it,' Hughes answered. 'Now mind your manners.'

'I will not mind my manners, you bastard!' Susan snapped. 'Give me the money, arsehole, now!'

Hughes's hand lashed out, dropping the money. Susan darted back to avoid the blow, only to have her wrist caught in his other hand. He laughed, jerking her towards him. Susan screamed as her arm was twisted into the small of her back. Hughes's knee came up on to the sofa, and an instant later she was across it, her chubby bottom stuck high, her legs wide, then wider still as his hand landed full across her naked cheeks.

'Just you mind your fucking language, you little bitch!' Hughes swore, spanking furiously at her bottom. 'Now just do as you're fucking told, will you?'

Susan said nothing, just squealing and gasping in pain and shock at the unexpected spanking. Nich had risen, wanting to intervene but catching sight of Andrew Wyatt's face. The priest was smiling. Nich contented himself with a shrug, watching Susan's bottom bounce and admiring the way her virgin sex moved to the rhythm of her spanking, until at last her angry squeals changed to a broken sobbing and Hughes dropped her.

'Well?' Hughes demanded.

Susan opened her mouth, but shut it abruptly as Hughes picked up the money and shook it pointedly under her nose.

'That's better,' he went on. 'You see, it takes a man to teach you a bit of respect, just like it's going to take a man to pop that precious cherry of yours. Now, the priest holds the money, OK?'

'Well, all right,' Susan agreed sulkily. 'I suppose.'

'That's the way, darling,' Hughes answered her. 'Now run along and get your kit on, and you know what to do, yeah?'

'It's not hard,' she answered.

'It will be, girlie, it will be,' Hughes answered and laughed at his own crude joke.

Hughes handed the money to Wyatt, who took it with every sign of reluctance. Susan walked away, her towel trailing forlornly in one hand, not troubling to cover her bare red bottom as she went back to the bathroom. Immediately Hughes drew Wyatt and Nich to one side, where he put his arms around their shoulders.

'Right,' Hughes whispered, 'this is how it is. You keep hold of that, Father, until I've fucked poppet over there. Then you give it back to me. Got it?'

'That's hardly fair,' Nich objected.

'Ten grand for a shag is hardly fair,' Hughes answered. 'Want to talk it over with John and Daniel?'

'No, er ... not at all,' Wyatt said quickly. 'I'd rather have nothing to do with it.'

'Give it to me,' Nich said. 'I'll hold it.'

Wyatt promptly handed the money over, allowing Nich to stow it in the interior of his robe. Hughes stepped back, Wyatt immediately reaching for his bottle.

'Good boy, Nich,' Hughes said. 'Now you're not stupid, are you?'

'Far from it,' Nich assured him. 'You'll give Susan something, won't you?'

'Maybe a grand,' Hughes answered. 'Right little bitch, isn't she? Full of mouth. Nice body, though. Fucking gorgeous. That's got me going, that has. I think I'll fuck your Juliana, now, as it goes. Sod waiting until afterwards. Where is she?'

'I've no idea,' Nich answered. 'She was in a funny mood this morning, and said she'd follow on in Lilith's car. She never turned up there.'

'Shit!' Hughes answered. 'Oh, well, you've got to laugh, haven't you? All that show, and then she bottles it. I've got to stick it somewhere, or I'll pop my cork. Where's that slut Diana got to?'

'Downstairs I suppose,' Nich answered. 'Probably helping Becky with the candles.'

'Right,' Hughes responded and made for the stairs, with Evans following.

215

Nich turned to Wyatt.

'Have you seen outside?' he asked. 'The congregation will be in the hundreds!'

'Then I shall do them justice,' Wyatt answered. 'I feel a new man, Nich. Here, have some wine.'

Nich allowed a glass to be poured for him. Wyatt was full of energy, utterly different from the broken man Nich had first met, even seeming taller and a great deal less frail.

'A toast!' Wyatt declared, raising his glass. 'To Lord Satan Asmodeus!'

'Satan Asmodeus,' Nich responded and took a swallow of wine.

Wyatt did likewise, then turned a guilty glance towards the stairs.

'You and I,' he said, now speaking quietly, 'may have our theological disagreements. Yet we are, I think, essentially of like mind?'

Nich nodded.

'David Hughes,' Wyatt went on, 'is not. We must ensure, Nicholas, you and I, that he does not ruin what we have created.'

'Absolutely,' Nich agreed.

'He crushes the girls' spirits,' Wyatt continued, 'which cannot be good, while his obsession with money may taint the message we are struggling to proclaim.'

'Hardly struggling,' Nich remarked, glancing from the window.

'Nevertheless,' Wyatt insisted, 'he is a bad influence, as I'm sure you'll agree. I have been speaking to Lilith and Diana, and they are in agreement. Her property contract, as you know, is invalid, so we are legally in a strong position to at least curtail his influence. Unfortunately, legality is not something with which he seems unduly troubled.'

'True,' Nich agreed, 'although he's not the only one who can play at that game.'

'No?' Wyatt questioned. 'I trust you're not thinking of trying to challenge him on his own terms. When it comes to unpleasantness, Hughes is an expert.'

'Me? No, no, not at all,' Nich assured him.

'I'm glad to hear it,' Wyatt answered. 'For now, I trust that you are with us in this matter?'

'Completely,' Nich assured him.

'Then I may safely tell you,' Wyatt said, 'that Lilith intends to have him outbid – gazumped, I believe, is the technical term. This will happen immediately before the borough council meeting, hopefully to Hughes's profound discomfort. As you know, the meeting is on Friday. I suggest you and Juliana make yourselves scarce for a while afterwards. I certainly intend to.'

'Thank you for the warning,' Nich answered. 'Now, you'd better get ready. I'm going to keep an eye on things outside – we don't want anyone pinching any regalia for souvenirs.'

Wyatt nodded his agreement as Nich made for the stairs, and descended to the sanctum. There, Diana was down on her knees in one corner, her top pulled up over her breasts and her mouth open around Hughes's cock. The goat watched them, passively chewing cud, to the same rhythm as Diana's sucking. Nich refrained from commenting, contenting himself with a private smile as he pushed through the drapes and into the main body of the chapel.

Diana had her eyes closed, her involuntary arousal mixing with hatred as she sucked on Hughes's cock. The air was thick with the smell of goat, oddly similar to the tang of male flesh and aftershave from Hughes. The animal was watching her, and its constant gaze was disconcerting, for all Nich's assurances that it was too old to be dangerous. Old or not, it was disturbingly sexual, with its overpoweringly musky scent, great coiled horns, and the huge balls that hung between its hind legs.

'Fucking stinks, that thing,' Hughes remarked suddenly. Diana pulled back.

'Shall I stop?' she said hopefully. 'You ought to save it for Susan, really.'

'Shut up and suck, you little bitch,' Hughes answered. 'I know what I ought to do, and that's spunk up in your mouth.'

217

She began to suck again, mouthing on Hughes's cock as she handled his balls, eager to make him come as quickly as possible.

'I reckon it's getting randy, as it goes,' Hughes said.

Diana peered round, from the side of one eye, to find that a red tip had emerged from the hairy sheaf of the goat's penis. She moved quickly away, pressing herself between his thighs. Hughes laughed.

'I reckon we should have your pants down, let him have his fun. He'd be up your cunt in a second, any money.'

Shaking her head in frantic denial, Diana began to suck harder, desperate to distract Hughes from what he was saying.

'That would be a laugh,' he went on. 'We'll have to do it, next time. You'd look great, tied down with your fat arse in the air and a wad of lube in your cunt. Wouldn't your punters just love that, to see you get a goat fuck, right up your greasy cunt? You'd love it and all, don't pretend you wouldn't.'

Diana shut her eyes tight, trying to resist the effect his crude words were having on her. She could feel the need in her sex, and it was impossible not to imagine herself, stripped and tied with her bottom raised for rear entry, Lilith leading the great shaggy animal behind her, between her thighs, on top of her . . .

'You'd do it, wouldn't you?' Hughes rasped suddenly. 'You would, you goat-fucking little bitch whore.'

He broke off, grunted, and whipped his cock from Diana's mouth, jerking at it frantically as he snatched her by the hair, to force her head back and her mouth open. Diana gasped in shock, shutting her eyes to the sight of the bulbous, glossy cock head inches in front of them.

'Hold still,' he grated. Hold still, you little bitch fuck! Yeah, nice!'

He finished with a groan as his cock erupted, depositing a thick wad of semen into Diana's mouth, then another, to splash on her tongue, the third catching her higher, across her nose and one eye, wet and sticky against her flesh. It stopped, and his cock head was wiped in her face, leaving a smear across one cheek. Her mouth was full of it, pooled on her tongue and trailing down over her lower lip.

'What a fucking state!' he laughed. 'Go on, swallow the lot, you slut.'

Diana swallowed, grimacing. Hughes still had her by the hair, her head well back, and as the thick, slimy fluid went down her throat, he began to scrape the rest from her face.

'Eat up,' he said, his slimy finger pressing to her lips.

Slowly Diana's mouth came open, to allow him to feed her the rest of his sperm, bit by bit, until only smears remained on her face. Then he made her suck his finger. She was close to tears, but determined not to give Hughes the satisfaction of seeing her cry. Choking back her sobs, she swallowed the filthy mixture of sperm and mascara in her mouth.

'Good girl,' Hughes said as he wiped his finger on her top. 'Now you're to see to my mate. I'll send him in.'

'Who?' Diana asked. 'Not Evans?'

'Yeah, Doc Evans, what's the problem?'

'He's just so gross!' Diana objected. 'I don't want to suck his dirty cock!'

'You suck, girl, and you like it,' Hughes answered her, 'and you can keep your tits out.'

He pushed out through the drape, and Diana heard him call to Evans. Resigned to sucking the lecherous doctor, she squatted down miserably on her haunches, wishing her sex didn't feel quite so ready, and that her nipples weren't so blatantly erect. The goat watched her, chewing and wrinkling its nose.

Evans appeared around the far edge of the drapes. He said nothing, not meeting her eyes, but glancing at the goat as he fumbled with his fly. Diana watched in disgust as he pulled his genitals free, a thick, dark cock and heavy balls tight in their sac. Pushing a wine case clear of the stack, he sat down, to leave his cock and balls protruding obscenely from his fly, with his round belly bulging out above them, the buttons of his shirt straining to reveal ovals of pasty, hairy flesh. Diana swallowed, trying to tell herself that he was no worse than many of the men she had sucked or masturbated, even allowed to fuck her. Yet there was a difference, and as she crawled forward with her heavy breasts lolling bare beneath her chest she was painfully aware of what it was. Whatever she might have done, it had been at Lilith's instigation, for years. Now it was not Lilith who had given her the order, but David Hughes.

The tears were already welling in her eyes as she opened her mouth to take in the fat doctor's cock. He took hold of it, and fed it in, gripping her firmly by the back of her neck. She closed her lips around the rubbery shaft, sucking, and grimacing at the sour taste, to squeeze the droplets from her eyes. At that she gave in to her emotions, and with tears running freely down her cheeks she began to suck. Evans took no notice whatever of the fact that she was crying, just moving his crotch to push his cock in and out of her mouth as she sucked.

Blind with tears, Diana did her best to arouse him, sucking and rubbing her tongue on the underside of his shaft. Very slowly his cock grew, swelling and stiffening in her mouth, until at last, with her jaw aching and her lips sore, she had a little fat erection to suck on.

Evans's grip had tightened, his hand locked in her hair, painfully tight as he fucked her mouth. She tried to make a tube for him with her lips, pouting them out in the hope that it would make him come. He got faster, and began to grunt, Diana filling with relief at the realisation that it was going to happen, then starting suddenly as something warm and wet touched her side. Jerking back, her eyes came wide, to find the goat next to her, its muzzle inches from her flesh, a great pale tongue stuck out inquisitively.

'Fuck off!' she squealed. 'Get away!'

'He only wants the salt from your skin,' Evans said testily, pushing at the goat.

It retreated, reluctantly, and Diana's head was pulled back on to the doctor's cock. He was less hard than he had been, and Diana cursed as she went back to sucking him. Once more he began to fuck her mouth, and also moved, to let one podgy arm down, his damp, soft fingers closing on one of her breasts, to squeeze it and flick at the nipple.

Diana sucked hard, all the while horribly aware of the goat, and sure that at any moment it would come up behind her, to mount her and rub itself off in the groove where her tight jeans covered her bottom. It was an awful thought, yet nothing to what Hughes had threatened: to have her staked out naked, and mounted by it, for everyone to see her goat-fucked.

Evans was starting to groan, but Diana was only half aware of the stubby cock being pushed in and out between her lips. In her mind she was outside, nude in front of the altar, tied and helpless, her broad bottom naked to the sky, the goat behind her, its cock hard because Becky or even Lilith had been made to suck on it.

Cursing Hughes and sucking the cock in her mouth with fresh fervour, she reached for her fly. The button came open, the zip down, and her hand was in her panties, burrowing between her full pussy lips. Her finger bumped on her rings and she found her clitoris, as the appalling fantasy ran through her head, stripped, bound, goat-fucked . . . stripped, bound, goat-fucked . . .

Evans came, full in her mouth, but she didn't stop, eagerly swallowing his sperm and sucking up more as her own orgasm hit her in a great rush of filthy thoughts, an ecstasy that left her weak and whimpering with shame and physical reaction as she slumped to the floor.

'Nothing you girls like quite so much as sucking on a cock, is there?' Evans remarked, patting her head and favouring her with a self-satisfied grin as he stood up.

Still crying, Diana ran up the stairs to attend to her make-up and change. Behind her, the object of her fantasy continued to chew the cud.

Lilith stepped from the chapel, glancing quickly down the line of cars parked alongside the track. At the far end, almost in the trees, was a silver Jaguar. With a last glance behind her, she made for it. As she approached, a fat man pulled himself from the driver's seat, to walk to the boot, extracting a bag and smiling unctuously as he saw Lilith.

'...d evening, Mistress Lilith,' he greeted her.

'...ust Lilith, for now, Mr Ackland,' she answered. 'Can I have a word?'

'Certainly,' he answered.

'Come down this way, then,' she said, taking his arm.

She drew him into the shadow of the leylandii hedge that marked the edge of the chapel property, and down the slope, out of sight of the chapel.

'Is something wrong?' Ackland asked.

'Yes, sort of,' Lilith answered. 'Look, we've got a problem, and I wanted to warn you. You know Dave Hughes, who had Becky on the altar last time?'

'Certainly, and she gave me an excellent spanking afterwards.'

'Well anyway, Hughes has put the money down for the chapel, and basically tricked us, so that he runs the show. The thing is, during the ceremony tonight, keep your gas mask on, because he's got miniature cameras rigged up to film the service.'

'Good heavens! Well, thank you for warning me.'

'No problem. We've tried to fix it so that there'll be too much glare from the candles to see much, but it's best to be on the safe side.'

'Absolutely!'

Lilith went quiet, waiting until they were fully screened by the hedge before speaking again.

'Hughes tells me you deal in land,' she said.

'That's right, redevelopment of derelict sites, mainly,' Ackland answered.

'You know about buying property and stuff, then?'

'Certainly.'

'I'd like your advice. Hughes has brought the chapel, but his offer needs to be ratified by some borough council committee meeting. It's supposed to be a formality. Is it?'

'More or less, yes. They'll just read out a list, and rubber-stamp it if nobody comes up with any objections.'

'And if somebody does?'

'It depends on the circumstances. Certainly there *would* be objections if they knew what you're up to here.'

'I want you to tell them, not what I do, just about the Black Masses, although from the number of people up here I wouldn't be surprised if they find out anyway. Nich Mordaunt and Juliana have no sense of discretion at all.'

'Very likely, but what are you driving at?'

'I want you to tell them so that Hughes's offer is rejected, then to put in an offer of your own.'

'It's possible,' Ackland said doubtfully. 'Not easy, but possible. What do you gain?'

'The chapel,' Lilith answered. 'You pay forty thousand, I pay you back. You know I'm good for it.'

'Forty thousand, for a site like this?' Ackland queried. 'It's undervalued. I could redevelop and sell at two hundred, maybe two fifty. Usually I deal in larger properties, but still . . .'

'I want the chapel, Mr Ackland. I've already put over twenty thousand pounds into it.'

'Risky, when you don't have full title.'

'I don't wish to point out the nature of our relationship, Mr Ackland.'

'You don't have to, my dear. I'm aware than an enjoyment of being nappied and spanked would not be easy to live down.'

'I wasn't going to blackmail you, Mr Ackland!'

'Of course not.'

'No, really. We have an offer, Diana and I. You turn the chapel over to us at forty thousand, payable at five hundred a week, and you get your fantasy free for the duration.'

'I get my fantasy free full stop. Whenever I like.'

'All right, starting as soon as the deal's through.'

'No, starting now,' he answered.

'OK, if we're quick,' Lilith agreed, glancing back towards the chapel.

The roof was visible, nothing more. They had reached the stream at the bottom of the chapel land, which ran in a series of pools between rounded boulders of granite. Lilith chose one that made a good seat on which to take him across her knee and sat down. He had gone to his bag,

223

open to extract a huge adult nappy from within.
gave a wry smile. At first, the grotesque sight of the
blubbery Ackland in nothing but a nappy had disgusted
her, no less than his habit of wetting it so that he could be
punished. Over time her reaction had largely been replaced
by amusement, and even some pleasure at inflicting such
intense humiliation.

'Here we are,' he announced, 'and, seeing that our
relationship is no longer on the same footing, I'd like you
to put it on rather than me.'

'Me?' Lilith echoed in outrage.

'Yes, you,' Ackland answered. 'Come, come, you are
asking a great deal of me. There should be no barriers
between us.'

'Well, no,' Lilith said hastily, 'it's just that you're into
wearing a nappy. I'm not.'

'No?' Ackland queried. 'Try it. I think you'll like it.'

'I'm a mistress,' Lilith insisted. 'Your mistress. That's
your fantasy, to have me dominate you, to humiliate you,
and to remain aloof. If I go in a nappy it'll ruin it for you,
believe me.'

'Not at all,' he insisted. 'I've always liked it both ways,
but I was aware it was not part of your service. Now I find
myself in a position to bargain.'

'Yes, but –'

'I don't want to be difficult, Lilith . . .'

'Oh, OK! Men, honestly!'

Lilith stood up, to snatch the oversized nappy from
Ackland's hand and throw him a look of disgust. He
merely grinned. Furious with herself, but aware that she
had no real choice, she began to undress. Ackland waddled
over to the rock she had been sitting on and took her place.

'Leave your top on,' he instructed as she made to peel it up.
'I like that the best, with the nappy showing under a hem.'

'What do you want to do?' she asked. 'You're not
fucking me, you know that, don't you?'

'That's fine,' he answered. 'I just want the same fantasy,
in reverse as it were. You're to wet your nappy, and I'll
spank you for it, that's all.'

'All?' Lilith echoed.

'Well, I'll want to masturbate,' he said. 'You can pose for me, crawling, with your wet nappy dropped and your bare bum showing.'

Lilith said nothing, trying to fight down her rising anger and humiliation as she stripped. With her boots, socks and trousers gone, she hesitated, her thumbs in the waistband of the blue polka-dot panties she had chosen randomly that morning, not expecting to be showing them off to a man.

'Very pretty,' Ackland commented. 'You can put them back on over the nappy.'

With a resigned sigh, Lilith pushed her panties down, and off. Ackland had his cock out, a little pink worm protruding from his fly. He was tugging at it as he watched, his eyes seeming to burn into her bare flesh as she bent to pick the nappy up. Determined not to ask for his help, she opened the thing, her fingers twitching in disgust just at the feel of the spongy material. She had seen him put them on before, so she followed the same ritual: spreading the nappy out on the ground and sitting her bottom into it, before lying back to close the sides and stick the tabs into place.

It felt odd, immediately, a strange bulging sensation around her middle, that filled her with intense humiliation as she looked down to see the puffy white material around her belly and hips. Casting him another dirty look, she pulled her spotty panties on over it, creating an image she found even more humiliating. Ackland was erect, tugging hard on his little cock, his face red, his eyes bulging with lust. Lilith wondered if she could make him come without having to undergo the far worse humiliation of wetting her nappy, and stuck out her bottom towards him, wiggling it.

'Gorgeous,' Ackland responded. 'Doesn't it feel so good?'

'Yes, really naughty,' Lilith lied.

'Just wait until you've peed in it,' he advised. 'Take your time, then let yourself go when you're ready.'

He slowed the pace of his masturbation, his eyes still glued to the back of her nappy. Lilith kept her bottom

225

..., automatically tensing her bladder. She knew she ... manage, and had a horrible suspicion that, if she ...tended otherwise, he'd just make her wait, walking around in the awful combination of nappy and panties until she was ready. Closing her eyes in her dreadful shame, she pushed. Her bladder gave, pee spurting into her nappy with a loud hissing noise, wetting her pussy and running down between her bum cheeks, to soak into the nappy. She felt it swell between her legs, bulging out behind her and growing heavy beneath as the scent of her piddle filled the air. Sobbing with humiliation, she let it all out, her nappy filling slowly, growing heavier still, until it was fat with piddle and a yellow stain had begun to spread up the front of her panties. She opened her eyes as the last of the piddle trickled out, to find Ackland staring in crazed lust, his cock jerking in his hand. The thought of having her bottom smacked by him was suddenly too much.

'Shall I help you with that?' she asked, praying he would consent to a hand job.

'Dirty little girl!' Ackland admonished. 'Don't be disgusting. Over my lap with you, now!'

'I'll suck it,' Lilith offered desperately.

Ackland shook his head, and patted his leg. In despair, she crossed to him, the bulge in her nappy wobbling behind her as she walked, an obscene feeling that set her belly fluttering. Ackland grinned. Thinking of how often she had been in the same controlling position he was, her face hot with blushes, Lilith draped herself across his lap. His hands went straight to her panties, peeling them down off the soggy seat of the nappy. With her panties well down, he put a hand to her nappy, squashing the pee-laden bulge against her bottom as the other hand went to a tab. The tab went, and Lilith shut her eyes tight, her tears starting as she struggled against the appalling humiliation.

With one tab open, Ackland began to peel her nappy down, tugging it free of her bottom, with the weight of her pee helping to drag it low. She felt the cool air on her wet bottom skin as she was exposed, and she gave in, crying freely and sniffling up the mucus that had begun to dribble from her nose. Ackland paid no attention, simply inverting the nappy around her thighs so that the soggy interior showed behind her. His hand came down on her bottom, hard enough to spatter droplets of piddle on to her back. She tensed, waiting, in an agony of frustration, shame and misery made worse by the urgent tingling in her sex.

The spanking began, hard, deliberate swats to her nude bottom, stinging on her wet skin, to make her buttocks dance and send urine spattering out behind her. She struggled to control herself, briefly, only to give in as the smacks got harder, blubbering freely, and kicking. Her knickers fell down, then came off altogether as the spanking became harder and her kicking grew more frantic, to leave the wet nappy waving wildly from one leg. His cock was pressed to her side, and rubbing as she was beaten, constantly reminding her that she'd offered to suck it, and might well end up doing it.

'You are such a baby!' Ackland crowed, obviously delighted by her reaction.

'I know, I'm sorry,' Lilith gasped miserably. 'I'm sorry!'

'Don't be,' he answered. 'What could be better than an adult baby girl who blubs when her bottom gets smacked?'

As he spoke he delivered a sudden salvo of hard spanks, to make Lilith gasp in pain and shock, her eyes flying open, her legs kicking wide. It didn't stop, either, but continued, mercilessly hard, until she was howling with pain and thrashing wildly on his lap, her legs going like pistons and her fists hammering frantically in the soft grass. Ackland laughed to see her reaction, and spanked all the harder, stopping only when his breath finally failed him.

Lilith rolled off his lap, to sit hard into the wet nappy, her bottom splashing in the pee-soaked material. She made a face of utter disgust, and rolled quickly up into a kneeling position, at which the nappy fell down, landing on the turf with a wet, squashy plop.

'Perfect. Stay there,' Ackland panted.

She looked back, finding him red-faced and puffing as he tugged at his cock with desperate energy. His piggy eyes were fixed on her bottom, and she realised he could see everything: not just her reddened, smarting cheeks, but the lips of her sex and her anus. Her head was whirling with emotions, pain and humiliation, utter shame, disgust, but arousal too, her vulva tingling, her vagina ready for entry. With a hollow groan she reached back, to rub at herself, with her smacked cheeks flaunted and the soggy nappy lying between her knees, in blatant evidence of what she'd done.

Ackland was coming, jerking frantically at his cock, with it aimed over Lilith's bare bottom, to add a final, awful touch to the feelings in her head. Bucking her bottom rudely up and down, snatching at her sex, treading her knees in her ecstasy, she too came, calling out in a burning blend of despair and rapture as it tore through her. She hit her peak with the final, terrible need for Ackland to jam his skinny cock to the hilt up her vagina and spunk inside her instead of wasting it across her buttocks and back.

She collapsed, spent, bottom still high, and open to him. He touched her, fat, hot hands gripping her legs, and a moment later his small, hot penis had been inserted into her vagina. Lilith did nothing, just sobbing into the grass as she was briefly, peremptorily, fucked, Ackland pulling out only at the last second, to spunk into her crease, over her anus and across the buttocks he had so effectively reddened.

'Glorious!' he puffed as he sat back. 'I said you'd enjoy it.'

Lilith could find no reply. She got slowly to her feet, to kick the soggy nappy away. Ackland was grinning happily as he wiped his cock with a handkerchief. Lilith stepped into the stream, using her top to wipe the tears from her face, then squatted down to wash her bottom.

'That was good,' he said. 'I look forward to many more such encounters, and you rely on me to sway the committee. I may have forgotten to mention that my brother is the chairman.'

Lilith began to splash water on to her hot bottom, smiling despite her humiliation.

* * *

Nich stood at the altar, watching the light fade slowly in the western sky. The area around the chapel was thronged with people. Stanton Rocks glittered with hundreds of candles, more marking the sides of the track, to throw the whole area into dancing orange light and black shadow, faint at the far edges, bright around the altar. Behind him the chapel doors had been thrown wide, a mouth into a red hell of candlelight and shadow, the great painted symbol clearly visible on the ceiling.

Most of the crowd were barely visible, lost in shade or with their faces turned dull orange by the light, except where eyes glittered with reflections. Only close to the altar, in the pool of brighter light that surrounded it, were they visible, the twenty-three men who made up the Higher Congregation, with some of the bolder pagans behind and the squat Dr Evans to one side.

He glanced at his watch, then back into the chapel. Lilith's face was visible, peering around the edge of a drape, and she nodded, signalling him to begin. Nich pressed a button beside the door, to make a single bass chime ring out from the loudspeakers hidden among the rocks and below the eves of the chapel. As the noise faded the crowd was left silent, save for the quiet whisper of voices from the rear. Nich raised his hands and the last murmurs faded away, leaving him for a moment in complete silence.

'Brethren!' Nich called out, his voice amplified by the speakers. 'Welcome to the second gathering of the Cult of Satan Asmodeus, an event yet more extraordinary than the first. Tonight bear witness to the Unholy Communion, to the summoning of a spirit of hell and to the ritual deflowering of a beautiful virgin. So, without further ado, pray welcome our priest, chosen of Satan, sodomist and defiler, Andrew Wyatt!'

With a quick twist to the volume control he stepped aside, allowing a clear view into the chapel. Within, Wyatt was visible, standing proud in his black robes and collar of office. Lilith stood to his side, her face deathly pale, stark naked but for boots, the Satanic face that covered her front

229

moving grotesquely as she walked. Her expression was hard, unyielding, and her sjambok trailed from one hand. At the sight several of the slaves put their faces to the ground, grovelling openly before her.

Diana followed Lilith, then Becky, both naked but for their thigh boots, and carrying whips. As they reached the chapel door they split apart, Wyatt going behind the altar, Lilith and Diana to one side, Becky to the other, joining Nich. Only then did Hughes appear, to lean in the doorway, looking out over the crowd with a mocking sneer.

Wyatt began his dedication, calling out the names of Satan with a note of defiance in his voice that had been absent before. As he spoke, his words boomed out above him, echoing and re-echoing from the rocks, loud enough to be heard throughout the congregation and well beyond. Nich paid little attention, looking off into the darkness beyond the candles, to where the shapes of trees showed ragged black against the stars of the sky. The night was still, absolutely, and he could hear the dull drone of the motorway in the far distance, but nothing more. Beside him, Wyatt began the Satanic prayer, and Nich quickly joined in, leading the responses, which the crowd took up with enthusiasm, producing a low muttering sound that spread to the very back. Nich found himself grinning wildly at the final, crashing amen, and again silence fell.

'Brethren,' Wyatt announced. 'Let us now partake of our most Unholy Communion, and that we may be unclean in our Lord's sight as we receive our desacrament, those of the Higher Congregation may now declare your venal sins, and revel in them before your brothers and sisters in Satan!'

Lilith stepped forward, among the slaves, to strike about her with the whip. They failed to move, cowering to the ground. Lilith kicked one, who gave her a pained look, but crawled forward as she swung her boot back for a second kick.

'Well?' Wyatt demanded.

'I . . . I am unclean, Father,' he said quietly.

'How so?' Wyatt demanded, as Nich pushed a microphone towards the supplicant, only to receive the whine and thud of feedback as the man spoke again.

'I have had unclean thoughts,' the man said, speaking at the ground yet with his massively amplified voice ringing out above him. I have indulged myself carnally with my wife . . .'

'Fellatio? Sodomy?' Wyatt demanded.

'Cunnilingus, Father,' the man admitted, cringing down, 'and . . . and worse, her . . . her bottom.'

'You licked your wife's anus?' Wyatt demanded.

'Yes, Father,' the man admitted, his face dark, even in the yellow candlelight.

'Splendid!' Wyatt declared. 'A fine act of depravity! Next!'

The man scurried gratefully back to his companions, who shuffled back. Lilith put out a booted foot, stopping one from crawling away, and looked around.

'Where's that rat Sands?' she called out. 'He was keen enough.'

'Not here,' Diana answered.

'You're next then, Specimen,' Lilith declared, addressing Arlidge. 'You love to crow over your dirty little habits, don't you?'

'Mistress, I –' Arlidge began, only for his protest to turn to a squeak of pain as Lilith's sjambok caught him hard across his back.

'Declare!' she spat. 'Now!'

Arlidge crawled forward, Lilith lashing his buttocks to make him hop and jerk as he came up before the altar, words already tumbling from his mouth.

'I am wicked indeed, a lewd, worthless specimen, a piece of dirt, leering at the girls I know I can never have, sweet girls, pretty girls, girls whose feet I'm not worthy to lick, girls who would kick me in the face if I tried, and rightly!'

'That's all you've done, just look?' Wyatt demanded. 'No lewd acts? No sodomy?'

'No, Father,' Arlidge answered.

'Pathetic!' Wyatt yelled. 'Sister Lilith, have our brother prove his devotion. Brother Nicholas, fetch out the goat!'

Nich hurried to comply, grinning to himself as he ran the length of the chapel. In the sanctum the goat had made itself comfortable among a litter of chewed cardboard and empty beer and wine boxes, and was asleep. Nich began to untie it, hesitated, and ran quickly up the stairs. Susan turned as he reached the top, smiling blearily and lifting the bottle of beer she had been drinking from in salute. Nich smiled and quickly hurried back down the stairs to untie the goat.

It came, reluctantly and, when Nich finally managed to pull it to the chapel door, not only Arlidge but five other men knelt before the altar, with Lilith standing over them.

'Turn the goat about,' Wyatt ordered. 'You, all five of you, must now prove your devotion, and apply your lips to the goat's arse.'

'You first, Specimen,' Lilith ordered Arlidge as Nich struggled to make the goat turn around. 'Kiss it.'

Arlidge hesitated, glancing first at her, then at the goat's bottom, and back.

'Kiss it!' Lilith screamed, snatching at his hair, to jerk his face in below the goat's tail, his suddenly open mouth pressing to its anus.

A great wave of sound ran through the audience as Arlidge's face was forced against the goat's anus, shock and laughter mixed, cries of disgust and claps of delight. Nich chuckled to himself, watching in rising glee as each slave was forced to kiss the goat's anus, while the crowd roared with amusement or gasped in shock, clapping and jeering, even calling out lewder suggestions. All five did it, and moved back, their faces working with emotion, submissive ecstasy, self-disgust, embarrassment, shame.

'It is done,' Wyatt called. 'Our brothers approach the altar impure, their sins black upon their souls, to partake of the body and blood of our Lord, Satan Asmodeus, in full transubstantiation!'

Abruptly he turned to the altar, mumbling a prayer that went unheard against the excited buzz of the congregation. When he turned back there was yet more determination in his face, coupled with a sly, lewd smile. He spoke, and his voice was deeper and richer.

'The preparation of the gifts!' he declared. 'You have an amplitude of piddle, I trust, Sister Diana?'

Diana nodded, sinking quickly into a lewd squat, her sex pushed out to the audience. Nich hurried across with the chalice, pressing it to her sex just in time to catch the gush of piddle. Even as Diana's piss splashed and gurgled into the cup, Lilith moved to the altar, kissing the cross as she spread herself out, feet planted well apart, bottom high to display the dark spot of her anus. She stayed in place, the slaves clustering behind her for a better view, until Diana's stream died to a trickle and Nich came to her. After sucking on his finger, he pushed it quickly up Lilith's bottom, to draw it out wet and sticky with fluid, which he wiped on the tight ring as it closed. Lilith gave no reaction.

Taking the wafers, he began to desecrate them, touching each to her now damp anus and returning it to the tray. Wyatt waited, watching with a look of approval. Nich handed him the chalice, bowed and stepped back. Wyatt raised the chalice, mumbling the antieucharistic prayer as he did so, but then put it to his own lips, sipping at Diana's urine. Nich quickly extended the platter, allowing Wyatt to choose a wafer and place it into his own mouth.

'Brother Nicholas?' Wyatt questioned.

'Father,' Nich responded. 'Lord Satan Asmodeus.'

He bowed, his fingers trembling as he reached for the chalice, to sip and swallow, with the sharp, hormonal tang of girl's pee strong in his throat. As he lowered the chalice he found Wyatt already holding out a wafer, which Nich took on his tongue, his mouth suddenly filling with the rich, earthy taste of Lilith's anus.

Nich bowed and stepped back, as Wyatt once more began to chant the antieucharistic prayer. The slaves were spreading out into a ragged line under the girls' whips, some already tugging at their cocks, others trying to kiss at the sleek black thigh boots or cling to elegant legs. Wyatt began to dispense the desacrament, moving among them, and all the while mumbling the prayer. As they took it they grew more urgent in their attentions to the girls, one clutching to Becky's leg and rubbing his cock against her

233

boot, fucking her leg as if he were a dog, another nuzzling his face into Diana's bottom in an effort to lick at her anus.

Lilith snarled at them, striking about herself with the sjambok, to force them back. Reluctantly they gave way, moving aside to allow her to step free, and to pull Diana clear. Becky followed, kicking the man on her leg away, but not before he had deposited a long, sticky trail of glistening sperm up one side of her boot.

'Have patience, brethren!' Wyatt called as the slaves milled behind Lilith. 'Your moment will come each of you, to slake your lust as you please on our Sisters, yet they first must receive the desacrament. Come, girls, to the altar.'

With the slaves still trailing behind them, all three girls approached the altar. Wyatt held the cup to Lilith, watched her sip at the urine and placed a wafer in his mouth.

'Kneel!' Wyatt commanded the others as Lilith stepped back, Diana and Becky quickly falling to their knees.

'Drink the wine of Lord Satan from the wellspring, Sisters!' Wyatt commanded. 'From my cock!'

Without hesitation Diana crawled forward, taking the priest's cock in her mouth. A moment later her eyes shut in bliss as yellow fluid bubbled out from around her lips. Becky was more hesitant, sitting back until Wyatt took her by the hair, to pull her forward. His cock pulled from Diana's mouth, spraying urine in both girls' faces and across their breasts, then full into Becky's mouth as she gulped it in. Her eyes screwed up tight, her cheeks bulged, urine suddenly burst from her nose and she was swallowing it down, then sucking, eager and wanton on his cock as he began to gently stroke her hair.

As Wyatt's cock began to stiffen in Becky's mouth, Nich set to work at the altar. He put the cross to one side and ducked down to bring a box out from underneath. Having broken a vial of dark red fluid into what remained of Diana's urine, he used a finger to daub a blood-red pentagram on to the scarlet altar cloth, surrounding it with the symbols for Lilith and for Asmodeus.

234

From one side Hughes watched, alternating his attention between the sight of Becky sucking cock and Nich's preparations, his expression half smile, half sneer. Nich returned a bland smile as he set a heavy bronze crucible at the centre of the pentagram and filled it with a pungent green oil that shimmered in the candlelight.

Wyatt had his eyes closed, his face set in rapture, and was clearly not about to claim his right to announce the summoning. Nich quickly glanced at his watch, shook his head and raised his hands. Slowly the crowd fell silent, until only the smacking sound of Becky's lips on the priest's penis was audible.

'Brethren!' Nich called. 'You have come and you have seen, some joining us, in lustful worship of Lord Satan Asmodeus, but also in doubt, or in disbelief. These are worthy emotions – we ask no blind abasement. Not for us the simple faith of the Christian path! Not for us humble acceptance of what we are told to believe! For us, proof of our belief, as I summon the demoness Lilith from the very flames of hell!'

As he finished he snatched a burning candle from the cross, thrusting the flame on to the glimmering surface of the oil. Fire caught, smoke wreathing up over a green flame, the air filling with the pungent scent. The smoke spread quickly, hanging heavy in the still air. Nich stepped back to the doorway of the chapel, raising his arms, to spread his robe wide across the opening, his head alone visible above the smoke.

'Chant for the demoness Lilith,' he called. 'Set your minds to hers. Think of her lust and of her beauty. Women, I call upon you to mount upon your men, those who dare, those who have spirit. Those who have none would be best to flee! Now join me in chant! *Ave Lilitu, Venite Lilitu, Ave Lilitu, Venite Lilitu . . .*'

Tom Pridough pulled himself up on to the summit of Stanton Rocks. His face was set and grim, expectant of lurid, sexual images, of nudity, even copulation. What he saw left him slack-mouthed, his torch dropping from nerveless fingers, to bounce down among the rocks, scattering candles as it fell.

The chapel stood beneath him, in a sea of candlelight, the front bright around a long, low altar, wreathed in smoke, with the unmistakable figure of Nich Mordaunt behind. His arms were raised as he cried out a chant that boomed and rang from the rocks and trees. He was robed in black, his neck circled by a black collar, the same sacrilegious vestments as two others. One stood watching calmly; the other had his robe lifted to reveal spindly legs and a blatantly erect penis, on which a plump, dark-haired girl nuzzled and sucked.

Before the altar naked men writhed on the ground beneath the whips of two other women, also naked. Several men were tugging at erections; one had a finger all too obviously inserted in his own anus; another was rutting his cock on the smaller woman's leg. Beyond, in the dimmer light, other figures jerked and writhed, shifting light showing bare flesh orange or red: a pair of trim, dark buttocks moving frantically between wide pale thighs; a plump matron, mounted high, huge breasts and long hair bouncing as one; a slim red-haired girl, naked, and straddled on a huge black man, his great belly wobbling to their fucking; two girls, clothes disarrayed, pawing and sucking at each other's naked breasts; others alone, masturbating. Most stood or sat still, answering Mordaunt's chant word for word.

'Sweet Jesus!' Pridough mumbled.

As Pridough stared, Mordaunt's chanting became suddenly more urgent, the congregation responding instantly. In the smoke a shadow had become visible, swaying, rising, growing slowly more distinct as it rose. A female figure became apparent, black, naked, stark-bald, slender, but with heavy, round breasts standing proud from her chest. She was dancing to a slow, salacious rhythm, supple and intensely sensual. Pridough gaped, fighting down his lust and envy, to replace both emotions with an all-consuming sense of self-righteous indignation.

Another man climbed up beside Pridough, in the blue uniform of the police, to exclaim in amazement at the sight below, then to babble urgent instructions into his radio. Pridough paid no attention, his teeth locked in fury at what Nich Mordaunt had achieved.

Nich stepped quickly back as the girl halted in her dance. She stood stock-still in the smoke, hands cupping her breasts, to caress the straining nipples with slow, lazy motions.

'Nice one, Nich,' Hughes drawled, 'but no cigar. Tell her to come out.'

Immediately the girl turned her head towards Hughes, and stepped from the obscurity of the smoke into the glare of light. Suddenly it was obvious that she was no painted girl, or human at all, but a black-bodied demoness. Her skin was as smooth and black as cut tar, her body sleek, her legs impossibly long, her clawed feet and hands utterly inhuman, her eyes a blazing emerald green.

Hughes's words died in his mouth. For a long moment there was absolute silence, abruptly broken as somebody screamed. Becky leaped up, to run screaming into the chapel. Others broke, pushing backwards in blind panic, Diana and Lilith dashing away into the chapel grounds, the slaves scattering. Wyatt alone stood his ground, an odd, chattering laugh issuing from his open mouth. Ignoring all others, the demoness stalked directly towards Hughes, who ran.

Nich darted for the chapel door, to push the switch beside it and release a great blast of noise, tortured screams, wailing sirens, the staccato clack and whirr of helicopter rotors. Almost immediately a real siren cut through it, then an amplified voice, ordering them to remain where they were and stay calm. Nich laughed, and grabbed for the microphone.

'Never!' he yelled, his massively amplified voice immediately crashing out around him, made more hellish still by the whine of feedback. 'Run, pig servants of Yahweh! The demoness Lilith is upon you, run in terror!'

For a moment he paused, grinning maniacally as he watched the chaos before him, before ducking into the chapel. It was empty, candles burning to all sides, the black drapes of the sanctum slightly open. He ran up the nave and pushed through the drapes, glancing quickly around. Of Becky there was no sign, but the goat was visible, or at least its haunches, sticking out from behind a stack of empty beer boxes and moving with a suspiciously rhythmic motion. Nich ignored it, dashing for the spiral staircase and up. Susan was at the top, her big eyes wide with fright, her white virginity gown clutched to her chest.

'What's happening?' she demanded. 'What's all the screaming?'

'Police,' Nich answered. 'We're being raided.'

'Shit!' Susan swore.

'Come with me, quick,' Nich ordered. 'I know a safe place.'

'I can't!' Susan protested. 'I'm too drunk. I've been drinking, I had to!'

'Trust in me,' Nich answered, and ducked down, to lift her beneath her arms.

Grunting with effort, he half pulled, half carried her down the stairs. In the sanctum the goat's haunches were still moving in urgent rhythm behind the beer cases, to the tune of bleats, groans and an odd slopping sound.

'Go to it, friend,' Nich urged, setting Susan down and delivering a violent kick to the rear door.

It burst open. He pulled her through, and quickly down into the shade of a line of the young leylandii, even as two dark figures appeared around the side of the chapel. Breathing hard, his heart hammering in his chest, he skulked slowly down the line, from bush to bush, until at last he reached the edge of the trees. The darkness was close to absolute but, as he turned to glance back towards the chapel, headlights flashed on, throwing a section of the rocks into stark white light. Nich ducked down, biting at his lip.

Several policemen were visible, moving quickly to surround the panic-struck throng of the congregation. So was Tom Pridough, waving his arms wildly and bellowing instructions, which were being completely ignored.

'Thank you, Tom,' Nich said quietly. 'Your punctuality does you credit.'

Muttering a hurried prayer to the Horned God, Nich stole on, supporting Susan's weight on his shoulder.

Juliana moved forward, slowly, thrilling to the power in her legs. The crowd melted away before her, scattering in their panic. Hughes was ahead, fumbling at the door of his car, his face twitching in raw fear. She sped up, and he ran, into the dark mouth of the lane. Her nose flared, catching scents of candle smoke and incense, of pine resin, and of Hughes. The mix of aftershave and man was unmistakable, and grew stronger, more distinct, as she padded into the blackness behind him.

The noise of the Mass breaking up faded quickly behind her as she moved deeper into the forest, using the gap of starry sky visible between the lines of trees as a guide. Hughes was ahead, his shoes crunching on the gravel of the track, trying to run, but stumbling in the darkness. Juliana followed, unhurried, almost silent, letting his emotions work, fear and panic, hope, then new fear as she deliberately snapped a pine twig. She slowed, allowing him to gain, then ran once more, until she could hear his breathing, full of urgency and dread. Again she slowed, and stopped.

Hughes ran on, gasping and staggering, calling on God and Jesus. Juliana waited, then came forward, high on the balls of her feet, along the grassy ridge at the track's centre. Ahead the trees ended, abruptly, giving way to the open night and black loom of hills across the valley. Light showed, a pool of yellow where the track met the moor road. Briefly Hughes was illuminated, glancing back, his face contorted in horror. He disappeared once more, down the road, now running fast. Juliana increased her pace, down to the pool of light, where she stopped, sure that he would look back.

She heard his cry, her mouth coming wide at the terror in his voice. She ran, fast, between the high hedges, indifferent to the lash of brambles across her face. Hughes was babbling in his fear, his shoes ringing on the tarmac, louder as she gained, and fading as once more she slowed to an easy, silent lope. A second street light appeared, well ahead, where the road rose from a wooded dip. Juliana watched it, still running, only to slow to a walk. Ahead was silence, with only the distant sounds from towards the chapel and the faint hum of the motorway as background noise.

Juliana's nostrils flared, sniffing the night air as she entered the small wood. Scent filled the air: damp leaves, cow dung, stinkhorn, aftershave. She ducked down, sniffing, moving a pace at a time, slow, then fast, rushing through a gap in the hedge, to snatch at air as a frantic scream rang out, then at cloth, and flesh beneath. The smell of fresh blood filled her senses as she launched herself on to Hughes, expecting blows and the strength of pure fear. Nothing came, his body limp beneath her, his limbs slack. She chuckled, the sound harsh in her throat. Her mouth came wide, opening around his neck, her fangs touching his flesh, pricking it, hesitating, to hold back, pressing hard enough only to leave the clear impression of a bite.

She rose, to take Hughes beneath his armpits, dragging at his unconscious body. Her feet slipped on wet soil. Yellow light gleamed on moving water. Again she pulled, and Hughes slithered down into the shallow stream. Hissing with joy, Juliana mounted his body, kneeling on his arms, his eyes flickering open to reflect the lamplight. For one instant there was recognition, and she laughed as she smothered his face under her crotch. She began to rub herself, using his nose and mouth to stimulate her vulva and anus, her clitoris bumping on his flesh. His body had begun to twitch, but no more, his legs splashing faintly in the stream as they kicked in futile, half-sane resistance.

Her pleasure rose quickly, her buttocks tightening on the hard bulge of his chin, her hands going to her breasts, to claw at the soft, heavy flesh. She let her bladder go, filling his mouth and nose with urine and laughing as she did it, piddle spraying over his face and her legs as her rubbing

240

became more urgent and more urgent still. She came, screaming out her lust in a wild cry with her sex smeared into Hughes's staring face and the blood running freely from the gouges on her breasts. Underneath her, Hughes thrashed, his limbs jerking in the water as she bucked on his face. She was smacking her sex over and over into his mouth, her piddle still spraying wildly to all sides and bubbling hot over her pulsing sex.

It finished, at last, and she climbed slowly off. Hughes erupted into a series of choking coughs, urine bursting up from his mouth and nose, his body racked with spasms, his limbs jerking in the mud and water. Casually, she pulled up his robe, to dig into his pockets, one by one, until she found what she wanted, the bundle of notes meant to pay for making her a whore. Rising, she threw them down on his chest. Hughes made no response, lying limp, his eyes staring upwards, devoid of all sanity or even awareness as Juliana padded silently away into the wood.

Nich sank to his knees in the soft grass at the centre of the Grim's Men stone circle, lowering Susan beside him. She clung to him, mumbling with urgency but no meaning to her words. Nich grinned, gently detaching her fingers from his robe. Standing, he reached under his robe, to draw Hughes's notes from an internal pocket and toss them to the ground beside her. She gave no response, and Nich dug back into the pocket, drawing out the stub of one of the thick black candles from the mass, and matches.

Carefully, he set up the candle on the tallest of the stones, melting the base to glue it firmly in place before lighting the wick. Blind to the flare of the matches, he stood blinking until his vision cleared, only then turning to the centre of the circle, and Susan.

His hair was full of bits of twig and cobwebs, his face scratched, one ankle throbbing with pain from where he had twisted it in the darkness of the woods. None of it mattered, sheer elation burning in his head to the exclusion of all else as he looked down on Susan's body. Her eyes were wide and bright, the reflected candle flame flickering

241

in each, a demonic aspect given the lie by the soft, sweet, drunken smile on her lips. He stepped to the side, his shadow falling over her upper body, the candle and stone behind him, to frame his head in a halo of light. Reaching down, he took hold of the hem of his robe, lifting it high up over his naked body, to stand bare before her.

Susan's own robe had worked up, showing her bare legs, to her thighs. As he looked down on her, toying with his penis, her knees came slowly up and open. The hem of the robe fell away, exposing the gentle swell of her belly and the plump, golden, thatched mound of her sex. She was moist, the pink flesh of her vulva glistening in the candlelight, her hymen taut and red. Again she moved, lifting herself to pull her robe up higher, above the pert bulges of her breasts, and off, moving the wreath of flowers in her golden hair. Again her thighs came wide, and she raised her head, looking at him with her dirty, drunken smile, nude and ready as his cock grew in his hand.

Nich drew in his breath, tugging harder at his rapidly stiffening cock. From behind him, muffled by the trees, came shouts, screams, curses, then the wail of a siren. He took no notice whatever, readying his cock for Susan's penetration. His eyes were fixed on her sex, and as he watched a bead of thick white fluid spilled from her vagina, to run down on to the dark spot of her anus. Nich grinned, remembering how he'd buggered her, a thought that set his cock to full, perfect erection. Susan moaned, pushing her hips out towards him. Nich took a step forward, raising his arms and looking to the sky as he called out in a blend of sexual and religious ecstasy.

'Witness this! By virtue of my cunning and of my skill I declare myself the representative of the Horned God! And thus I address myself to the body of the Mother!'

He came forward, quickly now, to kneel between Susan's spread thighs. She lifted her bottom, her cheeks tightening, then flaring, as urgent as he was. He took hold of his cock, shuffled forward the last few inches and pressed it to her vulva. She moaned, louder than before as he rubbed the tip of it briefly on her clitoris.

'Now,' she sighed. 'Do it!'

Nich moved his cock down, his face split into a demented grin as he found her hole, wet and ready, yet far too small to take his girth. He pushed, felt the constriction, the ring of virgin skin, tight against the head of his cock. Susan groaned, shutting her eyes, her arms reaching up for Nich. He laid himself down on her, taking her body firmly in his arms as hers closed around his neck. Again he pushed, feeling her hymen stretch to the head of his cock. She gasped in pain. He kissed her. Her mouth came open beneath his, his cock tightening as he started to come, pushing hard, Susan screaming to Nich's cry of blinding ecstasy, calling wordlessly on his God even as his penis erupted sperm inside her at the exact moment her hymen tore around it.

NEXUS BACKLIST

This information is correct at time of printing. For up-to-date information, please visit our website at www.nexus-books.co.uk

All books are priced at £5.99 unless another price is given.

Nexus books with a contemporary setting

ACCIDENTS WILL HAPPEN	Lucy Golden ISBN 0 352 33596 3	☐
ANGEL	Lindsay Gordon ISBN 0 352 33590 4	☐
BARE BEHIND £6.99	Penny Birch ISBN 0 352 33721 4	☐
BEAST	Wendy Swanscombe ISBN 0 352 33649 8	☐
THE BLACK FLAME	Lisette Ashton ISBN 0 352 33668 4	☐
BROUGHT TO HEEL	Arabella Knight ISBN 0 352 33508 4	☐
CAGED!	Yolanda Celbridge ISBN 0 352 33650 1	☐
CANDY IN CAPTIVITY	Arabella Knight ISBN 0 352 33495 9	☐
CAPTIVES OF THE PRIVATE HOUSE	Esme Ombreux ISBN 0 352 33619 6	☐
CHERI CHASTISED £6.99	Yolanda Celbridge ISBN 0 352 33707 9	☐
DANCE OF SUBMISSION	Lisette Ashton ISBN 0 352 33450 9	☐
DIRTY LAUNDRY £6.99	Penny Birch ISBN 0 352 33680 3	☐
DISCIPLINED SKIN	Wendy Swanscombe ISBN 0 352 33541 6	☐

THE TORTURE CHAMBER	Lisette Ashton ISBN 0 352 33530 0	☐
UNIFORM DOLL £6.99	Penny Birch ISBN 0 352 33698 6	☐
WHIP HAND £6.99	G. C. Scott ISBN 0 352 33694 3	☐
THE YOUNG WIFE	Stephanie Calvin ISBN 0 352 33502 5	☐

Nexus books with Ancient and Fantasy settings

CAPTIVE	Aishling Morgan ISBN 0 352 33585 8	☐
DEEP BLUE	Aishling Morgan ISBN 0 352 33600 5	☐
DUNGEONS OF LIDIR	Aran Ashe ISBN 0 352 33506 8	☐
INNOCENT £6.99	Aishling Morgan ISBN 0 352 33699 4	☐
MAIDEN	Aishling Morgan ISBN 0 352 33466 5	☐
NYMPHS OF DIONYSUS £4.99	Susan Tinoff ISBN 0 352 33150 X	☐
PLEASURE TOY	Aishling Morgan ISBN 0 352 33634 X	☐
SLAVE MINES OF TORMUNIL £6.99	Aran Ashe ISBN 0 352 33695 1	☐
THE SLAVE OF LIDIR	Aran Ashe ISBN 0 352 33504 1	☐
TIGER, TIGER	Aishling Morgan ISBN 0 352 33455 X	☐

Period

CONFESSION OF AN ENGLISH SLAVE	Yolanda Celbridge ISBN 0 352 33433 9	☐
THE MASTER OF CASTLELEIGH	Jacqueline Bellevois ISBN 0 352 32644 7	☐
PURITY	Aishling Morgan ISBN 0 352 33510 6	☐
VELVET SKIN	Aishling Morgan ISBN 0 352 33660 9	☐

Samplers and collections

NEW EROTICA 5	Various ISBN 0 352 33540 8	☐
EROTICON 1	Various ISBN 0 352 33593 9	☐
EROTICON 2	Various ISBN 0 352 33594 7	☐
EROTICON 3	Various ISBN 0 352 33597 1	☐
EROTICON 4	Various ISBN 0 352 33602 1	☐
THE NEXUS LETTERS	Various ISBN 0 352 33621 8	☐
SATURNALIA £7.99	ed. Paul Scott ISBN 0 352 33717 6	☐
MY SECRET GARDEN SHED £7.99	ed. Paul Scott ISBN 0 352 33725 7	☐

Nexus Classics

A new imprint dedicated to putting the finest works of erotic fiction back in print.

AMANDA IN THE PRIVATE HOUSE £6.99	Esme Ombreux ISBN 0 352 33705 2	☐
BAD PENNY	Penny Birch ISBN 0 352 33661 7	☐
BRAT £6.99	Penny Birch ISBN 0 352 33674 9	☐
DARK DELIGHTS £6.99	Maria del Rey ISBN 0 352 33667 6	☐
DARK DESIRES	Maria del Rey ISBN 0 352 33648 X	☐
DISPLAYS OF INNOCENTS £6.99	Lucy Golden ISBN 0 352 33679 X	☐
DISCIPLINE OF THE PRIVATE HOUSE £6.99	Esme Ombreux ISBN 0 352 33459 2	☐
EDEN UNVEILED	Maria del Rey ISBN 0 352 33542 4	☐

------ ✂ -----------------------------------

Please send me the books I have ticked above.

Name   ....

Address   ....

            ....

            ....

            .... Post code.................

Send to: **Cash Sales, Nexus Books, Thames Wharf Studios, Rainville Road, London W6 9HA**

US customers: for prices and details of how to order books for delivery by mail, call 1-800-343-4499.

Please enclose a cheque or postal order, made payable to **Nexus Books Ltd**, to the value of the books you have ordered plus postage and packing costs as follows:

   UK and BFPO – £1.00 for the first book, 50p for each subsequent book.

   Overseas (including Republic of Ireland) – £2.00 for the first book, £1.00 for each subsequent book.

If you would prefer to pay by VISA, ACCESS/MASTERCARD, AMEX, DINERS CLUB or SWITCH, please write your card number and expiry date here:

....

Please allow up to 28 days for delivery.

Signature ....

Our privacy policy.

We will not disclose information you supply us to any other parties. We will not disclose any information which identifies you personally to any person without your express consent.

From time to time we may send out information about Nexus books and special offers. Please tick here if you do *not* wish to receive Nexus information. ☐

------ ✂ -----------------------------------